A PLACE UNMADE

CARLA SEYLER

Black Rose Writing | Texas

ISBN: 978-1-68513-421-1
LIBRARY OF CONGRESS CONTROL NUMBER: 2024936795
PUBLISHED BY BLACK ROSE WRITING
www.blackrosewriting.com

Printed in the United States of America
Suggested Retail Price (SRP) $24.95

A Place Unmade is printed in Gentium Book Basic

*As a planet-friendly publisher, Black Rose Writing does its best to eliminate unnecessary waste to reduce paper usage and energy costs, while never compromising the reading experience. As a result, the final word count vs. page count may not meet common expectations.

For my brother, Tom, who made this book possible.

PRAISE FOR
A PLACE UNMADE

"The story features genuine characters and cuisine from the New Orleans culture, as well as an in depth look at the threat of environmental terrorism."
–**Gary Gerlacher, MD, MBA, Author of *Faulty Bloodline* and *Last Patient of the Night***

"Seyler writes with meticulous detail, creating a realistic and believable premise with a surprising resolution. Don't miss *A Place Unmade!*"
–**Travis Tougaw, Author of *Foxholes* and *Captives***

"*A Place Unmade* is an intricately researched novel exposing how dependent we are on organized crop production, which could be compromised quite easily by the correct formula of timing, technology, and human greed."
–**Anthony Viola, Author of *All Lies Begin with Truth***

"More than just a page-turner, *A Place Unmade* serves as a thought provoking thriller that captivates the reader and delves into the profound dangers that could jeopardize our modern food chain."
–**Troy Holland, author of *Clucked***

"This novel is as intriguing as its title."
–**Frances-Marie Coke author of *When Banana Stains Fade***

"Suspenseful and well-researched, with a touch of romance to lighten the tension, *A Place Unmade* will leave you awake all night, worrying about the ethics of the giant corporations that control "Big Ag" and the safety of your food supply."
–**Regina Buttner, author of *Absolution* and *Down a Bad Road***

"I loved this fast-paced environmental thriller that raises ethical questions about our modern food supply. Even though we suspect and then learn early on who the villain is, Seyler keeps the suspense going throughout as we watch our heroes' inch closer to the truth."
–**S.M. Stevens, author of *Horseshoes and Hand Grenades* and *Beautiful & Terrible Things - Coming July 2024***

"A Place Unmade is an exhilarating and thought-provoking experience that kept me engaged from beginning to end, and I would highly recommend it to fans of intelligent, well-paced thrillers."
–*Readers' Favorites*

A PLACE UNMADE

I go from the woods into the cleared field:
A place no human made, a place unmade
By human greed, and to be made again.
Where centuries of leaves once built by dying
A deathless potency of light and stone
And mold of all that grew and fell, the timeless
Fell into time. The earth fled with the rain,
The growth of fifty thousand years undone
In a few careless seasons, stripped to rock
And clay—a "new land," truly, that no race
Was ever native to, but hungry mice
And sparrows and the circling hawks, dry thorns
And thistles sent by generosity
Of new beginning. No Eden, this was
A garden once, a good and perfect gift;
Its possible abundance stood in it
As it then stood. But now what it might be
Must be foreseen, darkly, through many lives—
Thousands of years to make it what it was,
Beginning now, in our few troubled days.

–Wendell Berry

CHAPTER 1

Just after twilight, a man of medium height and build stepped inside an old metal building on the outskirts of town. Leased months ago, the space was abandoned years before when the welding shop went bust. An empty shell, all the equipment was removed long ago.

The man, known to his real estate agent as Richard Walters, offered a pleasant demeanor and little explanation for why he needed the building. The realtor was so glad to get the contract he didn't look closely at Richard, or his reasons.

In western Nebraska, where Richard was known as Dick Arlington, he was a hobbyist, needing space to work on his hot-rod rebuilds. In central Iowa, as Rick Simon, he planned to store supplies and accessories for a mail-order business. In North Dakota, it was storage for industrial parts. It was easy to find warehouse or industrial space at the edges of towns, where buildings emptied after commercial ambitions ebbed. Richard spent months quietly securing properties across the Midwest.

Sliding open the warehouse doors, Richard breathed in the sweet spring air, warm for that time of year. It had rained earlier in the day. With a tense smile, he turned back to his rented semi-trailer. Richard lifted the first of the four-trailer-door handles and pushed it to the left. Over the next few hours, Richard unloaded crates of automated drones. This was the last night, the last sector. Poised with predatory grace, more than 50 electronic raptors waited on the concrete floor. They were military grade, quad hybrids, custom designed for quiet and painted a dull charcoal gray.

The young woman who designed the drones had been hungry for Richard's business, the first large contract for her startup. What was her name? Helen, no, Evelyn—Evie—Lariott, that was it. Unusual for a woman to succeed in such a technical field, but Evie had worked with one of the leading manufacturers as their innovation manager. She developed a way to increase the flight range exponentially and enhance the flight automation. Breaking out on her own, Evie was excited about getting the contract and didn't ask many questions.

It was easy really. Richard explained he represented a large retail operation, Wisk Recreation, and sophisticated hobbyists wanted long-range drones. Evie signed the contract, her first as CEO of E-AeroSystems. Of course, it came with a confidentiality agreement. When Evie suggested ways to cut costs, like using less expensive materials, Richard told her he had a market for something pricey. Then he paid her half the contract cost in advance and chuckled at her naivete. An amateur—this job was full of them.

Richard operated the drone power distribution board and coordinated their pre-programmed flight. Once in a while, one of the drones didn't make it back. Usually, they returned safely for the next mission. The sophistication of the programming allowed him to set in motion 50 drones at a time. Designed to fly inches below 400 feet, these malevolent cyber locusts released their payload mission after mission over field crops all across America. Richard had the jamming device ready. Most drones would lift off only if their remote ID was operational, allowing for identification and tracking by any number of entities. Not these babies. Lips twisted in a sneer, Richard gave the software command. His programmed swarm lifted into the air and hovered. Their remote ID broadcast for less than a moment as he activated the jamming device to block detection by any ground monitoring stations.

With a faint whirring, the first drone row flew out the large open doorway, each device carrying a small biodegradable container. Richard watched with satisfaction as rows of more drones spread low across the sky.

Hours later, Richard dialed a number using a prepaid cell phone.

An elegantly dressed man, waiting in a black town car, picked up the phone and waited.

"It's done," Richard said.

"Problems?"

"I monitored radio traffic on all the channels." A sliver of irritation edged into Richard's voice. "A few reports of noise from the drones. This was their last flight. With the self-destruct, there's nothing to find if anyone goes looking. It just rained, so there's no chance of fire. We're secure."

"I'll release the last payment."

He listened to the click ending the call. At the next highway rest stop, Richard stopped for a cigarette. He casually tossed the phone in the trash, then used his lighter to set fire to the SIM card. Smiling in the glow of his cigarette, he took his time finishing his smoke.

CHAPTER 2

In a small office in New Orleans, Valentina Sorelli tapped her phone to call her cousin, Will. Arrows of sunlight reflected through the low hanging oak limbs and across her desk. Bouncing in her chair, she waited for him to answer. Where was he? This late in the day, Will should be home.

Hundreds of miles north, Will Torino pulled his phone from the pocket of grass-stained jeans. "Hey."

Finally. "Just 'hey'? Do you know you're speaking to the new marketing director of Winslow Park?"

"Hey, new marketing director. It's got a nice sound to it—congratulations."

"I'm so excited I can't stand it."

"It's wonderful news."

"I get my own office." Eyes wide, Valentina looked up from her desk. "It's the size of a closet, but it has a window."

"Moving up in the world. Will your day-to-day responsibilities change?"

"Not much. I'll still handle special events. The big thing is I'll have more say in programming. The job comes with a little more money, and, get this, tuition reimbursement for grad school."

"Oh, wow."

"It won't pay for everything, like books, but I can start paying off some of my school loans."

"That's so great," Will said. "How are your classes going?"

"Good. Interesting."

"I'm happy for you. Have you told our grandmother?" Will asked.

"Not yet. I needed a break. She keeps asking me when I'm going to fall in love and get married."

"Tell me about it. She wants to know when Susan and I are going to have a baby."

"It's horrifying,"

"She can't be serious. We're not ready, with just sorting out the farm."

"She's teasing—I hope." Fiddling with the pens on her desk, Valentina said, "Mia's feeling her age a little more. She wants us settled."

"She and Dean look so good I forget how old they are." Will paused. "Nothing's wrong, hmm?"

"Nah." For several years, Valentina lived with their grandparents after her parents passed. Will and Valentina had spent more time together than a lot of siblings. Four years apart, they were both only children, and close friends. "How are things going out there?"

"This is going to be our year, Valentina. The work never ends, but we should turn a profit once we harvest."

"Tell me what you see, right now."

"I'm looking out across the field, and the sunset makes it look gold. The sky is getting dark. Sometimes I can't believe this is mine. And the bank's, of course."

"It is amazing. How long has it been?"

"We're starting our third year."

"Mia says your love for farming comes from our Sicilian ancestors."

"I don't know about that, but I can tell you I love this time of day. You can hear the wind in the cedars. It smells so fresh, like growing things. The colors of twilight are just beautiful."

"Awwww."

"Okay, city girl, back to you. The promotion sounds great. What are you going to do with your newfound power?"

"I'll think of something."

After her talk with Will, Valentina stuffed her laptop in her bag and looked around her small office. It was a closet to be sure, but it was hers.

•　　•　　•

The sun dipped below the horizon as Will turned to go inside. A few miles away, a small biodegradable container struck the ground hard. It crumpled and a crack opened to the night. Melting ice crystals seeped into the dark earth. A microscopic community slept inside. Within the crowded chamber, they had no memory of the Indianapolis laboratory, the humming of equipment, or the burr of the Scotsman's accent. Frozen in place, they waited for the wind.

CHAPTER 3

Valentina, the newly promoted marketing director of the Botanical Garden at Winslow Park in New Orleans, took a deep breath. Corralling a group of schoolchildren on a tour, she counted them again. The children were excited to be on a field trip, especially since it was outside. The challenge was to keep track of them and not lose anyone. How could anyone not love this? On some days she arranged and publicized a plant show, on others she staged a twilight concert or coordinated vendors and artisans for the Winter Festival. Valentina enjoyed the variety. While two boys ran ahead, several stayed beside Valentina on the edge of the pollinator garden. A few lagged behind, enchanted by a butterfly that landed on milkweed at the edge of the ornamental iron gate. She couldn't blame them. It was all interesting.

Nudging them along, Valentina carefully moved the schoolchildren from place to place, enjoying their sense of wonder. But a couple of the kids were poorly dressed and seemed stunned by the park. For most of the tour, they had kept to themselves.

"Hey there, I'm Valentina. Tell me your names again, please?"

"I'm Maya and this is Keisha."

"Have you visited the park before?"

Both girls shyly shook their heads and looked down.

"When I first saw the park, I couldn't believe how big it was. How about you?"

"It's so green," Keisha said.

Maya added, "The trees are so tall. What's that gray stuff hanging down? It looks like my grandpa's beard – I bet it tickles!"

"In New Orleans, we call it Spanish moss. It needs the oak trees to hang on to because it likes the shade. It's called an air plant or bromeliad because it gets all its food and water from the air. Do you know that plants need food and water?"

"Just like people?" Keisha asked.

"Just like people." Valentina agreed. "Do you know that plants have families like people too? One of the cousins of Spanish moss is the pineapple plant. They're both part of the bromeliad family."

"I've never seen a pineapple," Maya said.

"Maybe you will one day." Valentina smiled at both girls. "Let's catch up with the others." She took both their hands and they hurried to the group.

"We were looking at the Spanish moss. Keisha, tell them what plant is its cousin."

"The pineapple!"

"No way!"

"Yes way!"

The kids laughed and Valentina jumped in while she had their attention. "We're going now to a very special place in the park, the Medicine Garden. We started our Medicine Garden with plants from another garden in western Louisiana. All these plants are native to Louisiana, or were brought here in olden times, usually the 1700's and 1800's," she said. "Native Americans and Acadians made remedies out of them when they were sick.

"Do you see these over here? Elderberry lowers a fever, and beebalm soothes an upset tummy. Feverfew helps with a headache. Groundsel bush or manglier gets you over the flu. For a long time, only people in Louisiana knew about that one. These are folk medicines that people used before there were drugstores."

"I have a fever! Can I have some elderberry?" one of the boys shouted.

His buddy coughed. "I feel hot. I have the flu. I need some manglow!"

"Manglier," Valentina slowly enunciated the French pronunciation. "You wouldn't like it. It tastes terrible. And the only parts of elderberry you can eat are the berries and flowers. Do you see berries anywhere? No? The birds beat you to them. What about flowers? Only the poisonous leaves and stems, hmm? And besides, if everyone ate from the garden when they came on a tour, we wouldn't have anything left. Some of these are very rare. Do you know what that means?"

"There aren't a lot of them," one child said.

With a worried look, a little girl asked, "What happens if all the plants get washed away by a hurricane?"

"I guess we would have to start over," Valentina said.

"But suppose all the plants in Louisiana are washed away?" she persisted.

"That would be a problem. But there have been a lot of hurricanes over the years, and they're still here, right?" Then, changing the subject, Valentina asked, "Do you see this plant here? It has three different names—goatweed, croton capitatus, and the last one is hogwort."

"Hogwort!"

"Did Harry Potter use it?"

"Maybe if he had chills or a fever," Valentina said.

As they reached the edge of the Medicine Garden, one of the rowdy boys complained, "We're bored."

"Yeah, there's nothing to do," his buddy said.

Valentina thought, time for the milk and cookie portion of the tour. "How would everyone like to race back to the concession stand?"

The kids took off running in a happy jumble. Valentina stayed behind long enough to send a quick message on her tablet to Beth in catering. At least they could get a head start with the refreshments.

●   ●   ●

Hundreds of miles north, a microcosm slept, impervious to its flight across the fields. The temperature slowly rose inside its small biodegradable container which broke apart on impact with the solid Kansas earth. The broken box rested among stalks of hard red winter wheat, planted last fall. Through a gaping chasm on one side, the sun reached through and gradually warmed the strike force within.

CHAPTER 4

Two years earlier

The town car glided silently at dusk, under a dark New Orleans sky softened by muted corals. Framed by the window, two men argued in the back seat. Bert, the driver, professional as always, ignored the rising volume of the conversation. Sam sat across from his father, Jack Stillman, who engaged the privacy shield with suppressed fury. Sam's mother sat on the other side of Jack, looking out the opposite window at Bayou St. John.

"How can you throw away everything we've worked toward?" Jack demanded.

"What do you mean, we've worked for?" Sam asked.

"Being a doctor provides a social standing that you never can achieve through business," Jack said.

"Dad, I applied to medical school for you and mom—not for me!" Sam shouted.

"But you got accepted. Doesn't that tell you anything?"

"It tells me I worked my ass off."

"You'll like it, Sam. How many people get accepted in their third year of college?" Jack said.

"I don't want to be a doctor."

Jack's eyes narrowed, and his lips thinned to a dark line. "I'm not going to pay for this crazy idea of yours."

"How is a doctoral program in biochemistry a crazy idea?"

"Not biochemistry, you want plant biochemistry." Jack spit out the words.

"*You should see it as your influence. Landever Industries was my first summer job. When I first walked into the labs to deliver some equipment, I loved it,*" Sam stared out the window, his voice softer. "*All the scientists, the technicians ... everyone was excited about what they were doing. The chance to create something new and better. Physiological research in plants, it's, it's the apex of science and creativity.*"

Jack scoffed. "*Those bozos in the lab don't know anything.*"

Incredulous, Sam looked at his father. "*Those bozos are responsible for every penny the company makes.*"

"*Are you kidding me? It's because of how I structure and control the product that we make record profits.*"

"*Sure, Dad.*"

"*I got you those summer jobs so you would want to stay in school. Sam, you think my career is something I wanted? I started in sales because I didn't have the education to become a director. I moved to management as soon as I could.*"

"*But look at where you are with Landever, Dad. You're in charge. You solve real world problems.*"

"*In the eyes of people that count, in business development I'm basically a peddler not a professional.*"

"*Forget it. You don't need to pay for anything. I'll use the trust from Grandmother. Or go to a state school—New Orleans University. NOU is a lot less expensive than an Ivy.*"

"*No, you won't. We have to sign off on any expenditure until you're 25,*" Jack reminded him.

Sam started to argue then threw himself back in the leather seat, seething.

For the first time, Elizabeth Stillman stirred. "*I'll sign, Sam,*" she said, still looking out the window.

"*Elizabeth, you wouldn't dare,*"

Beautiful, exquisitely dressed, Elizabeth turned slowly and looked appraisingly at Jack. "*Since my mother set up the trust for Sam, what exactly do you plan to do about it?*" Elizabeth turned to the window again, watching the last flickers of light striking the bayou.

"You're both going to regret this," Jack threatened.

Sam said nothing. There was no point. It had been like this for as long as he could remember. He was part of the game they played. No winners, no losers, and really, no family.

Jack lowered the privacy screen. "Bert, drop me off at the club."

"Yes, sir."

•　　•　　•

Later that same evening

Over a single malt scotch, Jack sat in an overstuffed leather club chair. Dim incandescent lights softened the ebony wood and jewel tones of the furniture and rugs. He swirled the ice in his glass and looked through the window down at the murky ripples of the Mississippi River. What happened to his family? They didn't listen to him anymore. He took a deep swallow of his drink, savoring the warm burn down his throat. For the first time in years, Jack signaled to the bartender for a second scotch. Maybe he would get drunk. To take his mind off Sam and Elizabeth, he looked at emails on his phone. One from Kiefer Abrams from Special Product Development caught his eye.

As Landever's business development director, Jack supported experimentation. Everyone at the company knew that R & D got anything they wanted. Five years before, Kiefer, one of Landever's youngest and brightest scientists, came to Jack and said he wanted to focus on wheat.

Jack remembered Kiefer's proposal.

"Mr. Stillman, wheat makes up 20% of the world's diet."

"I'm aware of that, Kiefer, it's one of our most important products."

"Wheat is vulnerable to a virus complex called wheat streak mosaic. Microscopic mites carry the disease. They damage the crop by feeding on the plants. Pesticides don't work because the mites hide in the crown of the wheat plant. They can cover an entire field before a farmer knows what's happening. If a farmer gets the virus, he stands to lose 80% of his crop. And not just the wheat. The mosaic virus affects barley, sweet corn, oats, rye, millet and sorghum."

"I'm aware of that too. What are you proposing?"

"There's a wheat genotype in Iran that's completely resistant to the virus. It's not marketable in its current form. But if you get me that plant, I will turn it into something that is."

"Kiefer, you know we don't have diplomatic relations with Iran."

"I know, I know. But we could get it through one of the international gene banks like CGIAR."

That stopped Jack short. CGIAR was a global partnership that funded research for food security. "We'd have to share the profits."

"Mr. Stillman, we could make so much money—so what if we have to pay them royalties. I'll get better yield and better resistance to pests of every type—insects, viruses, fungi."

"What about the baking quality? None of this will matter if we can't mill it or if it tastes bad."

"I can do this. Get me that cultivar, and I'll show you."

"Let me see what I can work out."

Jack sipped his drink, remembering how he mulled it all over. Wheat mosaic was the most economically significant wheat virus on the Great Plains, and worldwide in its reach. Seed companies across the globe were in a race to figure out how to combat it. Whoever came up with a long-term solution would make a pretty penny. Five years earlier, Jack decided he wanted in. Nevertheless, he had no intention of going through CGIAR—he wasn't about to pay them royalties. He found another way to go about it.

Jack obtained that very important original wheat genotype and four native cultivars with partial resistance. While the United States didn't have diplomatic relations with Iran, India did. An off-the-book payment to a biotechnician in Landever's Mumbai office managed the acquisition. Jack didn't ask questions because he didn't want to know. At the same time, Jack sent teams to Mexico, Cabo Verde, Turkey, Jordan, Italy and Tunisia to collect wild wheat plants or wild landraces.

Sure, he could have requested seeds or germplasm from CGIAR, but why get involved with material transfer agreements or pay royalties to support those institutions or the original source countries? And it could be done with very little risk to himself. If anyone was caught trying to bring the seeds out of the country, he would be well insulated. Enough layers were in place so no one would know of his involvement.

Once the plants arrived in Indiana, Kiefer started an accelerated cultivation program, with Jack pushing all the way. Groundbreaking greenhouse technology, mechanization and automation of seed preparation, coupled with enhanced LED lighting running over 20 hours a day spurred the growth and generational studies. Kiefer was able to use molecular markers to identify functional genes. With genome-wide association studies on the landraces and wild wheat natives, he identified best traits that he was able to quickly integrate into traditional wheat plants. Kiefer then asked for funding to do something called high through-put phenotyping. The same plant could act differently or become a different version of itself in a different place. The rest of it, well, Jack didn't really understand all of it, but it had something to do with accelerating the field measurements of the new plants to assess what traits were keepers and which ones weren't. Kiefer told him they would do high-resolution imaging to analyze a lot of plants at regular intervals in a short period of time. During their last contact, Kiefer thought they were close to a breakthrough.

In the dim light of the bar, Jack took another sip of scotch and opened his email.

Dear Mr. Stillman:

I am pleased to report that we have succeeded in breeding new wheat genotypes that are impervious to the mosaic viruses and most rust diseases. Through your support in the acquisition of new technology (high-throughput phenotyping, genome sequencing and genomic selection), we have realized productive, resistant varieties with excellent genetic diversity. Using cisgenic techniques, we have several superb varieties to put on the market. These cultivars have increased water and nitrogen use efficiency for significant drought resistance as well as higher levels of zinc and iron for nutritional support. Practical assessment of the wheat flour indicates top-notch baking quality.

We are quite satisfied with our results. It's been a long road, but we are beginning production now. As you directed, our research has been conducted with the utmost secrecy. I am quite certain that we are far ahead of all our competitors. I look forward to recognizing our team for their remarkable achievement and announcing their accomplishments.

Sincerely,

Kiefer Abrams, Special Product Development

Jack drank a little more scotch, then started making notes on the cocktail napkin, a habit of his. Even though he never used the notes, the process helped him think. He stuffed the paper in his pocket. Usually he found the notes later in the utility room, the wrinkles carefully smoothed out by the cleaning crew who saved them from the laundry. After a bit, Jack typed on his phone:

Great work, Kiefer. Keep this under wraps for now. Remind everyone of their confidentiality agreement. We'll need to get with our legal department to discuss the patent applications. Afterward, I'll arrange a special introduction of our new cultivars that will ensure their market dominance.

Look for a bonus in your next check as well as department funding for you to distribute to your staff as you see fit.

Jack Stillman

This was exactly what he was trying to explain to Sam. The lab guys were smart but had no business sense. They needed to wait for the right time to make the announcement, make it count. Market dominance. What could that look like? Landever was one of only nine mammoth seed producers in the world. Kiefer's breakthrough would make a difference, but suppose he helped things along a little? Jack settled back in his chair, swirling the ice in his glass. Across the river, the large cranes at the shipyard sat idle in the night. The Mississippi swirled past, dark and dangerous.

CHAPTER 5

Quick tapping steps echoed past 247-A, 249-A, 251-A. Valentina's run slowed to a walk as she arrived at the correct doorway. Pausing to catch her breath, she heard a low rumble of conversation spilling from the classroom.

Shoulders back, Valentina walked calmly into her class for business and ethics for biosciences, slipping into her seat exactly on the hour.

Tall windows illuminated the small conference room on two sides. Bookshelves lined the walls that led to a high domed ceiling. A thin, Asian man nodded. As always, Dr. Chen wore a suit and tie. Stacked neatly in front of him were several books and sheets of notes. Six students surrounded a large table centered in the room. One more student hurried in after Valentina and quickly found a seat—Leo Danekin, doctoral student in aquatics and marine biology. He caught her eye and smiled. Valentina's heart picked up again as she smiled back at Leo.

From the head of the table, Dr. Chen began. "What are your scientific principles?"

Sam Stillman, a little younger than the other students, leaned forward to answer. "Science must be evidence-based—"

Dr. Chen quickly stretched a hand out, palm down, and Sam stopped. That had happened at least twenty other times that semester. Sam memorized every reading assignment including the footnotes, perhaps a behavioral artifact of his elite private school education.

Clearing his throat, Dr. Chen asked again, "What are *your* scientific principles? How certain are you that you'll follow them? Have you experienced an ethical dilemma in your work or in school? I suspect that is the case, even if you did not recognize it or call it that. If so, what was your ethical decision-making model? Have you ever identified social injustice or inequality? What did you do? Do you follow a process when one of your colleagues does something disturbing? How do you respond if someone who is senior to you tries to influence your research or your conclusions? Do you have biases? Each of us does, but are you aware of yours? What are your compensatory strategies?"

"Dr. Chen, we could write a book about these issues," Sam Stillman said.

"There are books about each of these topics, and we will read some of them," Professor Chen assured him. "But for today, a few paragraphs will do. Near the end of our semester together, I will ask you to complete the same assignment. What will be your process for ethical decision-making several weeks from now? We will consider what we've learned and determine whether our thoughts have changed. Please take thirty minutes of our class time today to address these questions."

Valentina sat for a few moments, staring at the blank page in her notebook. No one else seemed to have doubts about what to write. She thought about the garden tour with the kids and the Medicine Garden. *I don't know if it qualified as a science dilemma, but it sure was a work dilemma. It was as though Maya and Keisha had never seen green space. That wasn't a research issue, although maybe... maybe it was.* Valentina started writing.

•   •   •

Far away, a box fragment tumbled across the North Dakota field, captured by the wind. It slowed and rested on light brown soil. An inert mass tucked inside responded feebly to the sunlight. The advance guard crawled slowly, clumsily to the edge. Weak, they needed to feed. Nearby, green shoots of wheat beckoned. Planted in late September, the sprouts held the soil in place during the winter storms that blew across the valley. Another gust caught the microscopic scourge. They flew.

•　　•　　•

Professor Chen collected their essays. "I hope that was thought-provoking and an opportunity for introspection. We will now begin our discussion. Please answer this question: Who owns plant genetic resources?" Pausing to shake his head slightly at Sam, Dr. Chen pivoted to another student. "Ms. Blackwell?"

"Professor," in a voice that rang across the room, Gemma Blackwell said, "I would imagine you're referring to the biological components of plants, so I would have to say the genetic resources are owned by whomever owns the plant itself."

"That is an *interesting* idea. Does possession of the plant determine ownership?"

"I would think so." Gemma was resolute. She wasn't backing down.

Seven other students straightened in their seats. Gemma's answer, announced with great confidence, lacked ... something.

"Thank you, Ms. Blackwell."

Dr. Chen turned his attention to Ellis Morrison, who always sat near the door. "Mr. Morrison, please expand on a term your colleague used: the biological components of plants?"

Valentina watched as Ellis took a deep breath. He was older than the rest of the class and always a little rumpled. His chinos were worn at the ends, as though he walked on them regularly. Valentina remembered that he retired from the aerospace industry. He seemed a little shy but always friendly.

In a low baritone, Ellis said, "Well, plants have roots, stems, leaves, fruit, flowers and seeds."

Speaking quickly, Sam interjected, "If we look deeper, the parts of the plant cell include the cell membrane, the cell wall, the central vacuole, the chloroplast, the chromosome, the...."

"Ah yes, the chromosome." Professor Chen stretched out his hand again. "Thank you, Mr. Stillman. Now, Mr. Danekin, what purpose does the chromosome serve? And we would appreciate your focus on our discussion as I doubt you will find the answer looking at your fellow students."

Valentina realized that Leo was staring at her and turned a bright pink.

Leo paled, and he looked anywhere except at Valentina. "Umm, right, the chromosome. It's what the chromosome contains that's important, which is both DNA and proteins. The DNA provides instructions to the plant, like a blueprint, to grow in a certain way. It's why when you plant a bean seed it doesn't become an oak tree."

"Where are chromosomes found in a plant, Ms. Sorelli?"

Looking steadily at Dr. Chen, Valentina said, "In plant tissue, the roots, the seeds...."

"Thank you," Professor Chen stopped her as he extended his hand again. "We could discuss the various kinds of proteins that maintain the chromosome, the organization of the DNA, its sequencing and replication, but that is not the purpose of our class. I am sure that you will explore these fascinating topics with Dr. Renfield during his lectures on molecular biology. What we are here to talk about is the essence of a plant and who owns it. We will focus on the germplasm, or the living genetic resources of the plant."

Valentina asked, "Do you mean one plant or are you referring to all plants in the same species, like all bean plants and all live oaks?"

"Excellent question. Does anyone have an answer for Ms. Sorelli?"

Sam volunteered, "The answer to your question would be both. In agricultural research, patents exist for the seeds themselves and the genetic resources. The company doing the research would own the resources and have rights to the future offspring. Any buyer of the seeds can't reproduce them and sell them independently."

"I never thought about it before, but where does the company get the seeds they use?" Leo asked.

"Another good question," Professor Chen responded.

"Professor?" Tala Vardeh lifted her hand.

"Yes, Ms. Vardeh?"

"Most scholars believe that agriculture first started in the Fertile Crescent many thousands of years ago. The land in the Middle East formed by the Tigris, Euphrates and Nile rivers was home to ancient cultures, such as the Sumerians and Babylonians. The very first seeds of agriculture came from that area."

"Do you think these ancient cultures own the plant genetic resources?" Sam asked.

Before Tala could respond, Sam answered his own question. "It's unrealistic to go that far back to find the original owners or their descendants."

"How can anyone own a plant?" Kai Prejean weighed in, with his broad shoulders, angular face and Cajun accent.

"Wait a minute," Sam said, holding up his hands. "That wasn't my point. Do you know how much money seed companies spend on research to improve seeds? They can't give them away for free."

"It's not fair to farmers to patent seeds," Kai insisted.

"How can you say that?" Sam said, his face getting red.

In his blunt slightly accented English, Kai said, "Farmers have been saving seeds from their crops forever. They pick the best plants, the ones that produce the most, the ones that don't die on them. Those are the ones they want to grow next year."

"Small farms save seeds. In large agricultural operations that wouldn't be practical. Because of research," Sam turned slightly away from Kai toward Dr. Chen, "yield per acre has grown exponentially in industrial agriculture compared to that of small, independent farms."

"And look at the chemicals they use on them, too." Kai bit out the words.

"It is not right." Tala said. "The culture that discovered the plant's usefulness should receive recompense."

"What do you mean?" Ellis asked.

Tala continued, "Consider Neem Oil. Do you use it to control, what do you call them, spider mites on your houseplant?"

"Sure."

"It's great stuff," Gemma said. "I use it all the time because it's not toxic."

Tala's gentle voice rejoined the discussion. "Its true name is *Azadirachta indica*, literally the free tree of India. It is considered of divine origin. For hundreds of years it was used to control pests and diseases. The genes of the tree are now patented by companies that had nothing to do with its discovery and development. So why is there no compensation to the poor farmers who no longer have access to the tree in the wild and whose ancestors taught the world how to use it?"

"That's exactly my point," Kai said.

"Not exactly," Tala said. "Shouldn't the agricultural company make reparations to the government or culture?"

"I understand what you're saying." Sam said. "But you can't expect a business to invest years of effort, not to mention millions of dollars, in improvements and then give its technology away. They changed the plant's genetic resources and have the right to patent it."

Except for the slight movement of her headscarf, Tala was perfectly still as her voice slipped back into the debate. "Plants are a product of nature. How can a company claim ownership of the genetic resources of a plant when it is openly accessible to all?"

"America's seed companies have fed the world through GMO crops and better fertilizers," Sam reminded her.

"GMO—genetically-modified organisms, *fou*, crazy," Kai muttered in disgust.

Professor Chen interrupted them. "Each of us needs more information for us to continue this discussion productively. In your handouts, you will find a link to the International Treaty on Plant Genetic Resources for Food and Agriculture. Review it carefully. Please also read the first two chapters of *Seed Wars*, your assigned text. This will be your homework assignment. Then write a paper explaining your views on the origins and ownership of plant genetic resources. We will continue our exchange of views in our next meeting on Thursday. Let us move on now."

•　　•　　•

A box shattered on a muddy field in north central Montana. Cryogenic gas slipped away, unobserved. An invisible vanguard shuddered from the impact. No movement was visible where half the outer edge was smashed. The wind caught the rim, tumbling it over and over across the field. When it stopped, infinitesimally small organisms crawled slowly to the perimeter that faced the sky. Their survival was measured in hours. Before their long sleep, they replicated again and again. Their multitudes would count for nothing if they could not reach their quarry.

CHAPTER 6

Heading home after class, Valentina found herself on her way to Mia's. She rang the bell and waited.

"Oh, you beautiful thing!" Mia said when she opened the door.

Since Valentina could remember, she would walk the ten blocks from the end of the streetcar line on Carrollton Avenue to her grandmother's two-story framed house at the edge of Hollygrove. It was her home too for several years. Often, Valentina arrived without notice, knowing whenever she rang the bell it would be the best part of both their days.

"How about some coffee? I just came in from the garden."

"Love some."

"It won't keep you awake tonight?"

"It'll be hours before I'm ready to go to bed. Where's Dean?"

"Right now? He's probably smoking one of his damn cigars. He's supposed to be going to the grocery. Should he grab anything for you? I'll send him a text. He'll be back after he checks on the rental on Joliet Street."

Valentina shook her head. "I don't need anything, but thanks."

Dean and Mia owned and managed a group of houses they rented throughout Carrollton, Mid-City, and Gentilly. Dean handled the maintenance, while Mia kept the books. It gave them a lot of flexibility in their schedules when Valentina was younger.

Mia made them both café au lait, boiling water then brewing the coffee fresh in the old white coffee pot. She heated the milk separately then poured it and the coffee together into a heavy cream-colored mug. Sitting at the small enamel table by the window, Valentina could see over the slate roof of the house next door, the gray and amber tiles reflecting the afternoon light.

"Tell me all about school."

"It was really interesting. Not sure if you remember, I have two classes, marketing and bioethics. Marketing has been helpful at work already. We're covering media relations, writing, like promotions and press releases, digital media and website analysis, how to analyze fundraising approaches, how to prepare a marketing plan."

"What a great fit, Valentina, for you and your job."

"I know!"

"What about the other class? What is it, ethics?"

"Bioethics. It's a required seminar for anyone in the biology department. Our teacher is originally from China, Professor Chen. He's at NOU for a research project. The class is small, only eight of us, and we discuss different questions. Today Dr. Chen asked us to write about how we would solve a work dilemma and describe our reasoning process for an ethical question. His question made me wonder whether we could do things differently with the kids who come to tour the park. Remember how you used to get Will and me to save seeds?"

"Of course. Some plants in my garden today are the descendants of those seeds."

"I started thinking that the kids should participate more in activities like that instead of just listening to me talk as we walk around."

"You and Will used to love that kind of thing."

As they talked, Mia got out some fresh French bread and butter.

"Real butter! How can you do this to me?"

"You didn't have time for lunch, did you?"

"Well..."

"When I first came to New Orleans, before Dean, I discovered French bread. It was my first love."

Valentina laughed. "There's nothing better."

They visited more then Mia asked her usual question, "Have you met anyone lately?"

"Maybe. I'll let you know if anything comes of it. I'm going to have to get home."

"Be safe driving. Text me when you're inside your apartment."

"Okay, love you."

"You're my heart, Valentina."

CHAPTER 7

Back at school a few days later, Valentina waited for her coffee at PJ's, part of a local chain of coffee shops.

"Hey, Valentina, over here."

Leo was waving from a table in the courtyard. She waved back, picked up her coffee and walked his way. Valentina couldn't help but smile. There was something about Leo—even 40 feet away, she was drawn to him. "Hey yourself."

Leo cleared a place for her to sit. "Sorry. My breakfast debris. How was your weekend?"

"Not bad, I worked some but not too much. What about you?"

"I work constantly," he said.

"That's right, you're finishing your dissertation."

"Let's say I'm moving in that general direction."

"What's the topic?"

"The effect of increasing salinity in the Pontchartrain Estuary as measured by Hydrachnidia."

Valentina looked at him skeptically.

"Well, you asked. How about: I'm using water mites as bioindicators in Lake Pontchartrain, to assess saltwater incursion, water quality, and contamination. Better?"

"Oh, clear as a bell." Valentina laughed and Leo joined in.

"We take and analyze water samples, compare the results to earlier data, and look for correlations. Depending on the condition of the water, we'll find different mite populations, or numbers of mites. We use a type of optical microscope, a stereomicroscope. The physical work isn't difficult, but the lake, or more accurately the Pontchartrain Estuary, is really complicated with a lot of moving parts. The analysis is taking a while."

"I've swum in that lake! Not exactly on purpose, but falling in 'accidentally' when I was little. There are mites?" she asked with a slight exaggeration of horror.

"Valentina, there are underwater cities, whole countries of mites in Lake Pontchartrain."

"I'll try to forget that the next time my grandfather takes me fishing."

He laughed and a beat passed. "How did you end up at NOU?"

"It's my alma mater. I'd thought about going back to grad school for ages, but have to work full time. I managed to save enough to start this January, and my boss is supportive. She's amazing, a true force of nature. She suggested an MBA, but I was thinking botany. I couldn't decide. When I met with the adviser, he signed me up for a combined major. So here I am."

"I'm really glad you're here." Leo said in a husky voice.

"Me too." Their eyes met for a moment, then Valentina looked away. After a slight pause she asked, "How did you pick NOU, and aquatics?"

"Well, I grew up in New Orleans. Spent a lot of time out by the lake with my dad. We'd walk along the seawall, and I'd be curious about something. Instead of answering he would make a game out of figuring it out. I love the water and science. Once I realized I could make a career out of two of my favorite things, it was a no-brainer." As he talked, Leo's face lit up. "As far as NOU, I went out to U.C. Santa Cruz for my undergrad work. I really missed New Orleans. Plus, the costs. Even with a scholarship, school in California cost a fortune. It's a lot cheaper here, and I get paid as a grad assistant for teaching a couple undergraduate classes."

"That's a lot. What do you like to do when you take a break?"

"You mean, that afternoon four or five months ago? Oh wait, was that Christmas?"

"I get the idea."

"Seriously, Valentina, I would like to ..."

Just then, Kai walked over from the food court and plopped his tray on their table.

Startled, Leo said, "Here, why don't you join us?"

"Thanks." Kai sat down and splashed hot sauce over his eggs.

"Hey, Kai," Valerie said.

"What did you think of the reading assignment?" Kai asked.

"Dr. Chen's question about the ownership of plant genetic resources makes a lot more sense now." Leo said. "Tala's point about reimbursement for native cultures, that's a serious question."

"I know. In class, I dismissed it as not being practical. But if you were the country that kept having its plants taken, it's a different story."

"It helps to have the context," Valentina said.

"It never occurred to me that a lot of plants didn't start out where they are now. Seeds are collected one place and brought to a different place," Leo said. "I hadn't thought about it before. When I mentioned this to my dad, he said that his grandfather, my great-grandfather, worked for that seed bank in Russia, the Vavilov Institute. I'm not sure what he did there."

"That's wild, Leo. Vavilov is famous. What do you know about his seed bank?" Valentina asked.

"Only that it's in Russia," said Leo.

Kai shrugged. "Never heard of it."

"I'm doing research on seed banks for my job. Although Vavilov didn't start the collection, he traveled the world to collect plants and seeds. Everywhere—Iran, Afghanistan, other parts of Asia, Africa, the Americas, China. Then he got into an argument with the wrong guy, and Stalin put him in prison. During World War II, a German blockade surrounded St. Petersburg, or Leningrad as it was called then. It lasted over two years, and all the Russians were starving. They couldn't get supplies in. No one had enough to eat. The scientists, who kept working at the institute without Vavilov, guarded the collection and actually starved themselves rather than eat the seeds. They saved the gene bank. Russia ended up needing to use some of the seeds years later to start over. It's an amazing story. I came across it in the stuff I'm doing for work. Do you think your grandfather would remember anything else?" Valentina asked Leo.

"Probably. I'm planning to visit him this weekend anyway. I know our family emigrated to the United States in the late 40s, after the siege of Leningrad, but that's all. Mostly my grandfather has talked about how cold it was, and how they ended up leaving. I hope he'll remember something his father said about Vavilov."

"Old people's stories are the best," Kai said. "It's like listening to a movie."

"I feel that way when I talk to my grandmother." Valentina took another long sip of her coffee. "Back to our class topic, I guess because I work at a park, the idea of collecting seeds doesn't seem strange to me. We swap seeds and plants with other gardens routinely. They're a resource you can share without losing what you have. What amazes me is the idea that you can patent a plant."

"I know," Kai said. "You can graft it, or modify it, and then own the rights to it. I started reading ahead, and the protections for the patent are unbelievable. If my patented, genetically modified corn pollen blows into your field and co-mingles with your plant pollen, you can't sell your corn."

"Kai, that's ridiculous," Leo said.

"Tell me about it. Genetically-modified seeds can be copyrighted. There was a farmer in Canada, Percy Schmeiser, who saved his canola seeds year after year and developed a custom strain that he sold locally. Monsanto sued poor Percy, successfully I might add, after their seeds invaded his farmland and had sex with his canola plants."

"Those hussies," teased Valentina. "That sounds pretty risqué for a corn plant."

"I know it sounds strange, but Big Ag has been pushing out the independent farmer for years. They've gone after the more lucrative crops, so there's less and less diversity. Then they compound the problem by getting patents on plants and seeds they've modified. Fertilizers too—it's bizarre."

"I think a worse problem is the pesticide that's getting into our water system. All that stuff from the upper Midwest is washing into the Mississippi River. All GMO research isn't bad," Leo said.

"True. I read some amazing reports about a scientist who developed one tomato with anti-cancer properties, and another that has more antioxidants than kale. Big Ag and GMO foods are twisted together in everybody's mind." Valentina said.

"Well, the thing about changing genetic interactions," said Kai, "is you really don't know what cascading effects might happen down the line. You make a genetic edit to a plant to turn off one characteristic, and the chemicals that produced that trait have to go somewhere else. You don't know if they're going to affect other traits."

"Couldn't that happen when a farmer does that independently?" Leo asked. "You really don't know what you're going to get."

Kai didn't respond immediately, so Valentina asked, "Your family has a farm, Kai? Is it organic?"

"We're not organic but close to it. Mostly Catahoula rice and crawfish." He grinned. "Plus Meyer lemon, pecan, fig trees. My mom and her sisters raise vegetables and have an herb garden. A little livestock. *Un peu de tout.* A little of everything."

"You think you're going to go back to farming?" Leo asked.

"Farming will always be part of me and my family," Kai said. "But I don't know that I want to do it full time. I've thought about working for the extension service or a conservation group. Not really sure."

"Where is your family's farm?" Valentina asked.

"It's a little southwest of Lafayette, off the Mermentau River, near a little town you've never heard of in Vermillion Parish."

Just then, Valentina saw Sam at the coffee counter. She stood and waved. "Sam, over here."

Sam's face lit up, then fell a little when Leo and Kai came into view. He headed their way with his coffee and blueberry muffin.

"Glad you could join us. So, how did you end up at NOU?" Valentina said. "What's your story, Sam?"

"It was a last-minute escape from my father's medical school dreams."

"It's tough to get into medical school," Kai said.

"Oh, I got accepted to Columbia, Indiana University and Tulane but it's not something I ever wanted to do," Sam said."

"Did you come to NOU straight from being an undergrad?" Leo asked.

"I did."

"Why did you pick NOU?"

"Cheap tuition. My mother would have helped, but my father hated my choice of graduate degrees. I felt like a volleyball between my parents. It's better to do it on my own."

"So, you're just a poor rich kid, right?" Kai said with condescension in his voice.

"Ha ha, Kai," Sam said, not laughing.

"*Mon cher*, are you a little sensitive?" asked Kai in an exaggerated Cajun accent.

Neither Valentina nor Leo laughed as they watched the interaction. Valentina glanced at the wall clock and picked up her coffee. "Guys, I need to get to work."

"Nice to see you all outside of class. I'm heading out too." Leo said, looking at Valentina.

"Me too," said Kai.

"Hey, I'll walk you to the parking lot." Sam quickly fell in step beside Valentina. Leo and Kai grinned as Sam subtly edged them out of the way.

•   •   •

Sunlight fell on an oblong container, the size of a box of salt. Crammed within, the murderous hoard was restless with hunger. Despite the impact of the landing, their box remained intact, and they were trapped. A large creature loomed, and the unit jolted with sudden, repetitive quakes. A red-winged blackbird pecked, looking for food. A seam broke then opened. A faint breeze stirred the stagnant air. Too small to be prey, the colony readied to launch.

Now there was only hunger, all-encompassing hunger. They found their quarry, a new food source. Using short stylets, they penetrated the epidermis and withdrew nutrients, quickly causing a distortion in its growth. As they fed, the virus passed into their sack-like posterior mid-gut, ready for transfer to a new target. Their ability to transmit the virus was unrivaled.

CHAPTER 8

As she drove home from work, Valentina kept thinking about Maya and Keisha. At first, they had been tentative, almost overwhelmed by the space around them, but they sparkled after just a minute of attention. Valentina reflected on how Winslow approached the tours. The children had such different backgrounds and experiences. She laughed to herself. One thing they had in common were dramatic claims of boredom. How could she add more hands-on activities to the tours? When she was little, Mia spent hours with her, showing her how to harvest seeds. After rinsing them, they spread them out to dry on a paper towel then put them in little glass jars. How many of these kids had a Mia? Winslow's outreach program targeted inner-city schools that had a large prevalence of single-parent households. It was hard enough for some of the moms to make sure the kids got something to eat and had clean clothes. That by itself often required more than one job. Sometimes there wasn't a lot of time or energy to explore the natural world or safely access green space.

Valentina thought about how much of their plant stock would be difficult to replace or replicate, and not only in the Medicine Garden. Although treasured by New Orleans residents, Winslow Park wasn't particularly well endowed. What if there was a way for the kids to do more hands-on activities that could help the park?

Once she got home, Valentina powered up her laptop. Over the next week, Valentina researched participatory educational programs, as well as seed storage systems. One of her friends, Amy, worked as a curriculum specialist with a local school group, and she called her to brainstorm. Supporting her cause, Amy told her nature-based instruction was associated with better attention and gains in learning, especially in disadvantaged students.

After hours of researching ideas, Valentina scheduled an appointment with her boss, Dee Claiborne, the director of Winslow Park. She asked Renny Plaisance from Maintenance to attend, as she planned to enlist him for the technical aspects of the project.

"What I'd like to develop is an interactive seed bank program," Valentina explained.

Renny listened quietly as Valentina outlined her plan to allow younger visitors the chance to participate in cleaning, drying, and storing seeds.

"Our goal would be to save seeds from at least 50 different or unrelated plants of the same species to make sure we have a diverse genetic representation. Some of the plants in the Medicine Garden we don't need to worry about, for example, manglier. It's everywhere and we wouldn't have difficulty replacing ours. On the other hand, something like wild yam or *Dioscorea villosa* is rare because of over-harvesting."

Dee interrupted. "How are we going to have time for this? You, Renny, all our crews have a lot of responsibilities already. How big an operation are we talking about, Valentina?"

"Not big, at least at first. I have some ideas for later—a vegetable garden where we offer training in gardening, how to grow vegetables. But right now, between the tour groups and the Master Gardener volunteers, I think we could harvest the seeds ourselves, particularly in the Medicine Garden. I found some basic designs for seed banks that don't depend on electricity. There are some pretty low-tech ways to handle the seeds that the kids could do themselves. We could heat rice in the catering oven to make it into a drying agent for the seeds. Renny could make a vacuum pump out of a bicycle pump to seal the seeds in plastic bags. We could use one of those excess metal cabinets with light bulbs as a seed germination chamber. The cabinets would work as seed dryers too, with small electric fans. Bathroom exhaust fans are pretty cheap. If we get school support, science teachers could help supervise and use the interactive seed bank as a teaching module. So, the major expense would be the refrigerated space to store the seeds."

"And our manpower," Dee reminded Valentina.

"Part of our mission is to help our visitors develop an appreciation of nature. Why not nurture that while we do something practical? Dee, when was the last time you had to corral a hyperactive ten-year-old? Let's get them engaged in some practical activity. It would be a different way of using our manpower."

"What happens when we lose electricity?" Renny asked.

"With vacuum sealing, and cooling the refrigerated storage area to a lower setting before a storm—35 degrees instead of 38 or 40—we would be pretty resilient. We can't store seeds forever, but this would give us back up if we lost the Medicine Garden in a hurricane or from a bug infestation. Even if another major storm like Katrina hits, we should be able to return while the seeds are still viable. Being able to store seeds between one and five years would keep the plant collection intact no matter what happened. We could sell the older but usable seeds as we harvest and keep newer ones."

"Sounds like a pretty good plan to me." Renny smiled at Valentina. "I bet I could find a YouTube video for that pump."

Dee nodded. "It would be a new direction for us, but I like the idea. You may be a little unrealistic about how much time this is going to require but some of the larger botanical gardens have had their own seed banks for years. I'm not sure any of them allow the public, much less schoolchildren, to participate in collecting, but what an excellent idea, Valentina. Let me talk to my contacts in the Botanical Gardens Consortium. They may have ideas where we can find the money."

A few days later, Dee called Valentina into her office. "Blakestone Partners, Jamison Botanical, Kellington Foundation," she announced.

Valentina, accustomed to Dee's sometimes unpredictable pronouncements, just waited.

"Drum roll, please. I found potential funding sources for your seed bank."

"Really? That's wonderful, Dee."

"Take a look. I've sent you links to each of the grant applications. It looks pretty involved. This will be a lot of work."

Opening Dee's email on her tablet, Valentina quickly downloaded the applications. "Blakestone's application seems to be oriented to research. I'm not sure this project really fits, Dee. And they want my first unborn child."

"Maybe your second." Dee laughed.

"No really, look at section 7.1: 'Provide the ensuant and sequent expectations of a successful relationship ...'"

Dee snickered. "They're looking for measurables. We have to identify the objectives and place them in the context of our social vision. Valentina, you may not have articulated it, but you know what you want to accomplish. What do you hope the kids will get out of this? Will we be able to point to a difference in the children's behavior after they participate in your program? I think we could work with our school partners to administer assessments before and after the kids' visits. We could get input from the parents and the teachers. I bet they would help us identify outcome measures."

"Dee, do you remember meeting my friend Amy Benoit? She's the curriculum specialist for the Parish Schools Alliance. When I talked to her initially, she told me tons of studies exist about the positive effects associated with outdoor learning. Nature-based learning has been found in some cases to work better for disadvantaged students. Would you be open to getting her involved?"

"I'm open but a little cautious. I know you're busy, Valentina, but I think we can do this in-house. We have a cooperative relationship with Perrier Elementary and McLarin Urban Prep. I think they would be willing to work with us to develop measurement tools. Involving the school system in an official capacity would make this much more complicated."

"Let me talk with her again. I think she can advise us informally."

"That would be better," Dee said. "Let's talk in a few days.

•   •   •

Before the alarm blared, Valentina rolled over, checked the time, and texted Amy, her running buddy. *6:00?*

A second later, Amy texted: *I hate you. But yes*

Three mornings a week for the past five years, Valentina and Amy had jogged in Audubon Park. The 30-minute loop gave them time to catch up. Their default time was 6:30, but if either was awake earlier, she checked and some mornings they started earlier.

See you in a few minutes, Valentina confirmed.

Valentina waited for Amy at the park entrance on St. Charles Avenue, where the fountain was backlit against the sky. The tree limbs were silver, and the leaves shifted in the glow from the ground lighting, beautiful and clear.

Amy walked up. "Sorry I'm late."

"What, an entire minute-and-a-half? You're really slipping. How are you?"

"I'm still asleep. Tell me again why we run before seven o'clock in the morning?"

"Um, because we have jobs?" Valentina said.

"Oh, right."

As they started their run, Valentina said, "I'm going to impose on our friendship."

"Again? What a leech. Seriously, what's up?"

"You know the seed bank project I mentioned? You talked about how outdoor learning can be beneficial for school kids?"

"Mm-hmm. Being outdoors and hands-on activities are better for kids."

"Remember my boss, Dee Claiborne? You met her at the plant sale last year. She's found three different organizations that award grants for projects that demonstrate enhanced learning in elementary age children. When I first had the idea for the seed bank, I was thinking we would pay for it through our regular funding sources. Dee wants to try for a grant."

"That's not a bad idea. A lot of time, the recognition that comes from getting a grant will increase donations from your regular supporters."

"Really? Hmm. Could you email me the links for the studies you mentioned? Right now, I have a gut feeling outdoor, interactive activities lead to better communication skills and critical thinking. I can't find anything concrete to back that up."

"There are a ton of studies that show a strong correlation between access to greenspace with improved performance and better physical and mental health. I'll send you the links."

"Thank you, Amy. You're a star."

"That's right."

•　　•　　•

In South Dakota, the empty shell of a biodegradable container rested against short green stalks of wheat, the color of spring. Microscopic assassins crawled deep within fecund emerald caverns to feed. Hidden inside leaf whorls, they pierced tissue-like epidermal walls with their short fangs. Once sated, they looked for their next victim, crawling to the upper leaf margins. Leaving their venom behind, they waited for the next gust of wind. It took less than 30 minutes.

CHAPTER 9

Professor Chen waited in the conference room as the students arrived. He nodded as they placed their papers before him. Finding a seat next to Gemma, Valentina smiled at Tala and Ellis. With satisfaction, Sam sat down on her other side. Leo and Kai grabbed chairs on either side of the conference table near Ellis. Another student, Xavier Richard, arrived as class began.

"Welcome to you all. If you completed the reading assignments, you may have your own thoughts regarding the ownership of plant genetic resources. Now we will further inform our opinions by discussing an ethical decision-making model. First, let us consider the term beneficence. Ms. Sorelli, what do you think beneficence means?"

Valentina looked up, startled. "The Latin root, bene, means good or well, so I would expect that beneficence has to do with goodness."

"That is correct. It is the quality or state of doing or producing good. In ethical theory, beneficence is more broad. It is a reflection of our goals, our attitudes, cultural expectations, what we do, how we think about doing something, all with the intent of promoting the good of others. In beneficence, there is a continuum between conscientiousness and obligation. It is the core of all ethical theory and reasoning. We start with this point because it differs from religion, from morality, and from law."

"Let me pose a different question." Dr. Chen said. "How does one know when one has an ethical dilemma?"

"It's when there's no perfect answer." With his pressed blue jeans and military bearing, Xavier was calm, cool and collected. "Whatever we choose to do, we risk causing harm."

"Exactly. It is a choice between two or more unsatisfactory alternatives. We can consider the mantra 'Do no harm' as the baseline. Across many disciplines, we find similar ethical decision-making models. I distilled this information to provide an easy reference for our class discussion. The assigned readings will review these steps in more depth and provide context." Professor Chen handed papers to Sam and Xavier to pass out.

Valentina looked around the small conference room. Graduate school was different from being an undergrad. Everyone around the table was focused, intent, listening to Dr. Chen and taking notes by hand or on computer.

"Our first step is to recognize whether there is an ethical dilemma. We have a situation, as Mr. Richard said, where there is no perfect answer." Dr. Chen looked at each of them. "Perhaps there is no choice that is all right or all wrong.

"Our second step requires us to gather more information. Sometimes all we need to make a correct decision or judgment is to gather all the facts. Though after collecting all possible evidence, we may be left with an uncomfortable feeling. This confirms that we have a dilemma.

"The third step is to identify who is affected by this problem, who are the stakeholders. How do the circumstances affect the people or entities who are involved? How do we weigh their interests?"

As Dr. Chen made this last point, Tala looked over at Sam who had a laser-like focus on the lecture. She sighed a little as he wrote down the professor's comments.

"The next step is to identify the possible solutions, the alternatives for what can be decided. We must evaluate these options by asking ourselves: what will create the most good and do the least harm? Which option is respectful of the stakeholders and their interests? Which one treats the parties involved equally? Which option is the best for the many and not only the few? Is this choice consistent with my values?

"Step five. Along the way, it is appropriate to consult others who have familiarity, wisdom or skill regarding the problem. Who can guide us in our decision? Perhaps our peers?" Dr. Chen stared at each of them. "If nothing else, they can listen as we articulate the problem to better understand it.

"Our sixth step is to come to a tentative decision. Make a choice about which of these options is best. It may be time to consult again with your peers. Imagine how you would feel if your decision became public knowledge. Would you be comfortable with the scrutiny or embarrassed? Do you think others would find your argument compelling?

"Finally, we complete this process by returning to the beginning. How is that uneasy feeling? Have we done the best in accordance with our values and by all involved?"

Stretching her arms overhead, Gemma leaned back and stifled a yawn.

"Are we keeping you from more exciting activities, Ms. Blackwell?" Dr. Chen asked.

"Oh, no sir."

•   •   •

While Dr. Chen and his students explored the underpinning of ethics, pieces of a small container blew across a north Texas field. Balanced at the edges of the box, wormlike organisms stood erect. Like small flags, they caught the wind with their front legs and dispersed, an unseen, lethal menace. Microscopic corruption swept across the air. They were free.

A single mite laid 15 - 25 red eggs along leaf veins in straight parallel lines. Its eggs hatched in seven days. In 60 days, every microbe would have three million descendants. Like a tsunami, light and dark green mosaic patterns rolled across the newest wheat leaves. The oldest leaves that first emerged in early spring lay prostrate on the ground, diminished and yellowed.

•   •   •

Dr. Chen picked up where he left off. "Some variation of these steps has been explained more eloquently by many others: writers, philosophers, political leaders, physicians and exceptional individuals in different professions. For our purposes, we will follow this sequence in our class discussions. It is my hope this will allow us to remain true to our values as we evaluate our actions.

"Now that we have an ethical decision-making model, we will consider the question of plant genetic resources. Ah, Ms. Blackwell, please state the dilemma."

Gemma paused before she answered. "Who can claim ownership of plant genetic resources."

Uncharacteristically drawing attention to himself, Ellis asked, "Is it the right to claim ownership or who actually owns the plant genetic resources? Lots of entities: individuals, farms, corporations, seed banks, countries—any of them could say they own the plant genetic resource."

"I can go with that." Gemma caught Ellis's eye and smiled her thanks.

"You would like to define the dilemma as who actually owns the plant genetic resource. And?" Professor Chen encouraged the class. "Ms. Sorelli?"

"According to our model, the next step is to lay out the information, consider the facts. Ellis, Mr. Morrison that is, outlined several stakeholders. There is some legitimacy to most of their claims. The first would be the country where the plant was discovered, which is usually a less-developed nation or culture." Valentina said.

"Mr. Prejean, why don't you continue?" Professor Chen said.

"I guess the next group with a claim on the plant stock would be the individual farmer or group of farmers who saved seeds from their best plants—the ones that grew the best, were stronger, or taller, produced more and were more resistant to pests and disease. That's the way they come up with better plant varieties."

"And from there, Mr. Danekin?"

Leo was prepared and ready with a nuanced answer. "From there, does the explorer or visiting botanist who gathered the seed have a claim? I'm not sure about that. He or she seems opportunistic. Sometimes there were laws prohibiting the collection of the plant genetic resource, like in Brazil for their rubber trees. Plant collectors deliberately broke the law and stole some rubber trees. Over time, Brazil's share of the world rubber market collapsed. It affected the economy of the whole country. Sure, the plant collectors had to develop the new plants, and a lot of hard work was involved, but they stole the original resource. It doesn't seem fair. There was never any payment to Brazil for the loss of a whole industry."

"Another stakeholder, Mr. Richard?"

"I guess governments would be next. They formalized the collection process and distributed new seeds all across the country to many different farmers. So we have the farmers again and botanical gardens and seed banks that experimented with new seeds and developed varieties that did well on the farm."

"Mr. Stillman, can you complete the list of stakeholders?"

"It would be the agricultural companies that developed new varieties or modified the plant genetic resource to make it more productive and more disease resistant."

"To summarize," Dr. Chen stated, "there are at least five distinct entities or stakeholders."

Sam looked troubled.

"Yes, Mr. Stillman?" Professor Chen asked. "Do you disagree with this analysis?"

"I'm having trouble with the balance of stakeholders. If we look at the developments made possible by agricultural companies, the research they've underwritten, the incredible advances in increased productivity, how can we place the same value on their enormous investment compared to the work of an individual farmer or the source country?"

"Let me pose a question," Tala interjected. "Does the agricultural company profit from its investment?"

"Of course," Sam said.

"Billions of dollars, am I correct?"

"Well, yes."

"Has any attempt been made, not for parity, but to provide resources to the originating country or center of origin? Where is the morality in this? I am not suggesting a commensurate payment, but perhaps one that is a fraction of the monetary profit the agricultural concern realizes each year," Tala said.

"But large agricultural companies invest in less developed countries. Look at the jobs created through agricultural research and production."

"Mr. Stillman, what about the use of plant varieties from less developed nations that allowed the companies you mention to develop disease-resistant crops? This continues to save American agriculture millions of dollars annually," Tala said in her calm, accented English. "The transmission of original plant germplasm is always to more developed nations. Plant genetic resources are collected freely from less developed countries under the guise of protection. I must ask you, Mr. Stillman, protection from whom? And you question the value of the investment by less developed countries? Improvements to industrialized agriculture have come at great cost to poorer nations."

Sam sat stiffly in his seat, a faint flush on his face. "How has it cost less developed nations to share their seeds? The world population would starve if it only had access to the original germplasm. Look at Henry Wallace. In the 1930s, his hybrid seeds increased the yield for farmers and helped them make a better living. America practically feeds the world now. And how can you completely disregard intellectual property rights?"

"I do not disregard them, yet you do not seem to acknowledge the sovereign rights of other nations," Tala said serenely.

"When and where did these sovereign rights begin, Ms. Vardeh?" Sam asked

"It is a simple matter to identify the location, Mr. Stillman." Tala persisted. "I suggest you review a map of the southern hemisphere and the Middle East. An incomplete list would include Africa, Brazil, Egypt, India, Iran, Iraq, Mexico, Panama, Peru, Uruguay."

"Plants are part of the common heritage of mankind."

"You consider them free for the taking. Agriculture companies 'improve' the plant's genes or seeds." Tala said, making air quotes. "Then you patent them. Only the 'improvement' is oddly beneficial to the company. You asked what is the harm. If a farmer saves seeds from this modified plant, his yield will be much less. The seed is viable for only one season. That means the farmers, including those in less developed countries, have to keep buying seeds each year."

"It's true that the Third World has to import more seeds now, Ms. Vardeh, but that's mainly the breeders who don't want to go to the trouble of finding them in the wild. The other problem is there's a lot less diversity in the individual countries so they wouldn't be able to feed their population with what grows there." Sam said emphatically, "The U.S. has imported more original plant genetic resources from third world countries, but now exports more to them. Most breeders get their plant genetic resources from seed banks."

"Um, could we use the term 'less developed' instead of 'Third World'?" Xavier asked. "That's a little insulting."

"Sorry, I was not being intentionally offensive." Sam paused then continued more calmly. "And there is a system in place through the Plant Treaty to pay a portion of royalties to CGIAR, an international global partnership for agricultural research."

"Really?" asked Tala with quiet bitterness. "Do you know how many organizations have given royalties to CGIAR?"

"Well, no."

"One, Mr. Stillman. In the fifty years of CGIAR's existence, only one."

Sam looked down as he twisted his pen.

Dr. Chen allowed the silence to continue for a moment. "Although this discussion has been quite interesting, I suspect that we cannot resolve these differences in our remaining class time."

Sam raised his hand.

"Yes, Mr. Stillman," Dr. Chen said with resignation.

"Sure, sorry," said Sam. "But we've gone from producing 35 bushels of corn per acre to 200. By increasing the yield, there's less need to cut down forests for farmland to feed a population that only keeps growing. Better fertilizers and crop genetic improvement prevent starvation in many less developed countries. With increased production, prices go down and people don't have to spend as much money on basic foods. They have money to do other things. You have to admit that there is a lot of benefit to what the large agricultural companies are doing."

"I'm not sure they are that benign," Kai said. "In the 90s, Delta & Pine Land Company, in partnership with the USDA—yes, our Department of Agriculture—created seeds with an off switch. It's called Genetic Use Restriction Technology or GURT. By applying a chemical or not using a chemical, Big Ag can tell the seed whether or not to reproduce. Luckily, a moratorium was declared so they haven't been able to use it yet. The slang name is Terminator."

"Whoa," said Leo. "How do you know that?"

"I keep reading ahead."

"No ethical company would ever try to harm a third, I mean, less developed country," Sam said.

"Why do they keep developing new related patents to maintain access to the terminator technology?" Kai asked.

"There's a valid reason for that," said Sam. "Most of the current research is focused on controlling a specific gene in the plant, like a switch. All the other genes aren't changed. The plant will still reproduce, but without that one genetically engineered trait. It protects future plants. Another benefit is that the bio-engineered crop can't reproduce itself. That protects surrounding areas—say for example—an organic farm from accidental pollination or fertilization."

"I wasn't aware of that." Kai said. "I'm still not sold on it."

Sam pressed his point. "The goal is to produce crops that are more tolerant of drought or saltwater incursion, or that have increased nutrients to better address hunger issues."

"A worthy aspiration," Ellis said quietly.

"Another benefit is that certain varieties of plants can be made resistant to certain pesticides, so that farms can use it without harming the crop," Sam said.

"Glyphosate?" Leo asked with a wince.

"Sure, among other things. That's one tool in the toolbox."

"There's a lot of research that says glyphosate affects marine life adversely," Leo said.

"I read somewhere that bioengineered crops can spread herbicide resistance to the weeds themselves, making the pesticide useless." Gemma said. "Is that true?"

"Weeds will always become resistant to a pesticide. Using a combination of different ones helps avoid that," Sam said.

"What about not using it at all?" Kai glared around the room.

"That's not practical," Sam said. "Without crop-protection methods, farmers would probably lose half their produce, if not more. Glyphosate is one of the tools, along with other herbicides, insecticides, fungicides. The exciting area of research now is in naturally-derived products, biological control agents, and bio-stimulants. Things like plant extracts, insect pheromones and predatory insects to control for pests and diseases. Bio-stimulants, things like amino acids or seaweed kelp, protect the plant naturally. Data science has the answers."

"Wait a minute," Kai said. "Another side to the pest control problem is the question of genetic diversity. In the early '70s, a fungus wiped out 15 - 25% of America's entire corn crop. Almost two thirds of all corn plants were from only six cultivars. In 2006, it was only seven. For wheat, most acreage is planted with the same five to ten varieties. Breeders keep using the same hybrids. Our food supply is too susceptible to a bug or disease because there's too much genetic uniformity."

Tala cleared her throat softly. "I must agree with Mr. Prejean. To save the corn crop in the 1970s, agricultural scientists collected wild corn from Mexico and crossed it with hybrids. We have lost many valuable traits through large-scale domestication of the original plants. And we should consider another point. Engineered plants can require too much pesticide use, which causes grave harm to the environment. As Ms. Blackwell said, we are developing glyphosate-resistant weeds. This is why it's critical that we protect the wild crop relatives found in less developed countries."

"But Tala, um, Ms. Vardeh," Sam began.

Professor Chen intervened with a characteristic lift of his hand. "We have come full circle. Perhaps it is sufficient to agree that both the nations where the original germplasm is found and the agricultural corporations are stakeholders, yes? And may we consider the determination of the weight of their contribution part of the ethical dilemma? We have adequately identified the stakeholders. This brings us to step four in our decision-making model. I would like you to use the rest of the class time to identify proposed solutions to our dilemma."

CHAPTER 10

One year earlier

Jack Stillman's shoulders relaxed as he made the turn onto Highway 30A toward the beach in Santa Rosa. He rolled down the windows and listened to the waves. He could breathe for the first time in weeks. After several miles, he parked the Jeep underneath the raised house. Since Jack was a kid, he had been coming to the Florida panhandle. He was thrilled when he and Elizabeth were able to buy this place. Jack grabbed his bag and climbed the stairs slowly, inhaling the salty night air. He couldn't wait to walk out on the beach the next morning.

Sugar sand, he thought. Images flashed through his mind. Lazy mornings with Elizabeth after sweet, cool nights cuddled on the sleeping porch. Sam as a baby, starting to walk, flinging himself face forward on the powdery sand to feel it with his whole body. Looking for shells with three-year-old Sam, the sun rising over iridescent waves while Elizabeth slept in. Holding hands and running between fiddler crab convoys, Sam at five, giggling uncontrollably. Body surfing with a slightly older Sam, a huge smile gleaming from his tanned face as the water churned around him. Elizabeth, slim and graceful, taking pictures from the deck. He treasured their beach trips, down time from his all-consuming job at Landever Industries.

He wasn't sure how or when it happened, but imperceptibly over time, Elizabeth stopped making the trip, and it was only him and his boy. The first time she didn't come, it was an adventure. They had leftover pizza for breakfast and stayed in bathing trunks all day. The days passed with sandwiches on the deck whenever they were hungry, and at night they stayed up late to find the constellations in the stars over the Gulf. Later, every once in a while, Elizabeth joined them, and it was almost like old times.

Gradually, Jack realized that Elizabeth would rather visit her mother and friends in Denver, where she grew up. She was an only child, indulged by her father. Her mother needed her after her father passed. Sam got older, and Jack traveled more as he was promoted. He spent a lot of time in the Midwest at the corporate office. They eventually bought a place in downtown Indianapolis since he was there so much. Of course, Elizabeth never visited. Sam became accustomed to only one of his parents being around at a time. He stayed at the house in uptown New Orleans, which was less and less like home. One of the last times they were all together for an extended period was when they drove Sam to Emory for his first semester in college. For Sam's college graduation, Jack flew to Atlanta from Indianapolis while Elizabeth caught a flight from Denver. They returned to New Orleans to spend the holidays, to celebrate Sam's birthday, and for a couple of Mardi Gras balls they agreed they should attend.

When her mother died, Elizabeth met several times with the estate lawyers and went through things at her mother's house. The estate was considerable. With the exception of the trust for Sam and a few bequests, everything went to Elizabeth. She stayed away for longer periods. Jack remembered when she bought the condo in Vail. Cold fury, like a wave, swept through him. There was no discussion. Elizabeth presented it as a fait accompli. She needed a mountain retreat away from Denver. Her friends all had places in Vail. After all, he had the condominium in Mile Square, a superb location in Indianapolis. Sam might want to have friends join him to ski at Vail Mountain. Since she was only using a small part of her inheritance, why should he care?

Jack tried not to care. Sometimes he wondered what else he could have done. Elizabeth found the idea of seeing a counselor invasive and distasteful. He brought up divorce, not for the first time. She didn't see the point and would throw him a bone to keep him in line—unexpected sex, an affectation of affection, a gesture, but in a predictable pattern. She liked *their image. Elizabeth always thought they looked good together, a power couple. Jack Stillman, lean and polished, with an important position in the corporate world. Elizabeth Ross Stillman, the lovely philanthropist, wielding the control her parents' money provided.*

Jack decided it was time to change the dynamic.

On his rare time off, Jack flew into Panama City, Florida and was on the beach in less than two hours. With the Labor Day holiday that week, he had a long weekend. Unlocking the door, Jack dropped his bag in the entryway. He walked into the expansive living area and opened the French doors to the Gulf. He didn't get farther than the oversized couch facing the night sky and the water. The one drink he allowed himself each day could wait. Dinner could wait. He fell into a deep sleep listening to the sounds of the waves.

Early the next morning, Jack woke up to the persistent ringing of his cell phone. He recognized the number. The sky was still dark.

"Yes, Angus?"

"Mr. Stillman, we've achieved stasis."

Jack was buoyed by the clipped Scottish accent of Stephen Angus, one of Landever's entomologists on special assignment. He grabbed paper from the coffee table to take notes. "Remarkable, Angus. At what temperature?"

"Using a slightly different approach than Kuczynski, we have an 82 percent survival rate of the Aceria tosichella at zero degrees Fahrenheit for five days, much longer for the virus complex."

"How long?"

"Viruses can survive for 700 years in ice and remain transmissible. If the host survives, the virus will."

"Which lineage of mite? There are what, about 30 different biotypes?"

"As we expected, both the Type 2, also called MT-1 and Type 1 or MT-8 mites. These two genotypes are the best transmitters of the virus, particularly Type 2. When identified in Nebraska, it had a transmission rate of 64 %."

"If it takes time to reach the plant, can the mite survive independently? I understand that it can do considerable damage even without the virus."

"Yes, but only for about 48 hours without a living host," Angus said.

"What is their lifespan?"

"No one really knows. The complete life cycle from egg to adult requires seven to ten days. They may live up to 20 to 30 days under ideal conditions."

"That doesn't give us much time."

"A single female produces 12 to 20 eggs, or three million descendants in 60 days."

"Busy little buggers."

"Yes," Angus agreed. "Randy bastards. They acquire the virus after feeding for 30 minutes, and can transmit it for about seven days. The rate of transmission accelerates. After 14 days, the mites on each new plant have a 25% higher density."

"Impressive. Can the virus be transmitted through seeds?"

"It's possible, but the rate of transmission is very low, almost insignificant, unless the mite vector is present. Now that we have a ready supply of the mites, we are ready to proceed with the next phase of our research, to change their genetic markers."

"Well done, Angus. I'll process the incentive we discussed. I'm at the beach in Florida, but it will happen once I get back."

"Sorry to disturb you on your holiday, Mr. Stillman."

"You haven't disturbed me, Angus, not at all. This is great news. I asked you to call day or night. I'm on a quick break at our home in Florida."

"Very good, sir."

Stephen Angus thought that Landever was studying the mites to develop a genetic means to stop their replication. What a chump. Angus was book smart, but he didn't know anything about grabbing hold of the entire world grain market.

Jack stood and stretched. All the pieces were in place now. A breeze from the open doors blew his notes off the table. Reaching down, Jack stuffed them into his pocket, then walked out to the early morning on his deck. The lights of a small sailboat glowed softly on the horizon.

The next morning, Jack left early to return to the airport. As usual, he left behind an array of dirty clothes on the floor of the main bedroom, notes crumpled in a pocket. After all, that's what maids were for.

CHAPTER 11

Valentina arrived early at the school library. She found a table near a window that opened to a row of crepe myrtles. Valentina loved the quiet and the light rain streaming past the windows. In a bit of serendipity, one of her marketing assignments was to develop a fundraising plan for a non-profit entity. She had the perfect candidate. Winslow's annual soiree wasn't too far away, and was a significant revenue source. Although Valentina had helped in the past, Dee put her in charge this year. She had gotten an early start and had done the preliminary organization and marketing.

But Valentina quickly learned she wasn't early at all. One article recommended planning a first-time gala 18 months in advance. When she stopped hyperventilating, Valentina realized they weren't far behind. Although it was her first soiree, it wasn't Winslow's. She could tap the volunteers from last year for different tasks—getting more sponsors, increasing ticket sales, as well as helping with the raffle and auction. Food and drinks weren't complicated since the catering staff handled so many weddings. She was shocked by the advice—evaluate whether a gala is the best way to go about raising money. Question whether to have a party? Heresy to a New Orleanian. There were recommendations about doing a cost-benefit analysis and keeping costs below 40% of the revenue. Valentina made notes and planned to review the records of past soirees. Dee said they generally cleared about $200,000 from the event. Realizing the time, Valentina gathered her things and headed for the front doors.

By that time, the rain was coming down in sheets. Valentina waited with a small group of students on the steps underneath the large overhang. Sam saw her, stopped short on his way out the door, and smiled from ear to ear.

"Valentina! Happy Friday! Good to see you. How about a cup of coffee? What are you working on?"

"Hi, Sam. A marketing assignment. I have to develop a fundraising plan for a non-profit and I'm responsible for the park's gala in late spring—definite synergy. But look at the time. I have exactly 15 minutes to get to work. Don't you have another class right now anyway?"

"Umm, yeah. Okay, see you Tuesday. Want to have coffee before?"

"I am totally jammed right now. How about after my gala?"

"Great, it's a date."

No, it's not, thought Valentina as she grabbed her keys and ran for her car. Sam was cute, scary smart and more like a puppy than a grad student. A few years younger than Valentina, he was fast-tracking to a doctorate in plant biochemistry. At any given moment, it's was toss-up as to whether Sam would utter something brilliant or completely moronic, she thought. She wasn't sure how she felt about him. Walking with Sam the other day, Valentina learned a few things. He graduated from an expensive private college in biochemistry. Sam's father pushed medical school, and Sam pushed back. Despite a 4.0 grade point average, he had no intention of becoming Dr. Sammy. He wasn't the typical New Orleans University student. His clothes and mannerisms suggested a more comfortable background than was common at NOU. But it was strange that his dad wouldn't support Sam's focus on phytochemistry and bioengineering. A mystery for another day, Valentina thought. Right then, she had to get to work.

When Valentina arrived at her office, she pulled up the grant application for Jamison Botanical. Once Dee threw her support behind an idea, she was all in. After she bought into Valentina's idea for a Winslow seed bank, Dee gave Valentina a five-page list of things to do. Dee found a boot camp for grant writing that she needed to check out. Today would be intense, and she was only on page one of Dee's list.

CHAPTER 12

Valentina: *It's going to rain*

Amy: *Not till Wednesday. In case you hadn't noticed, it's Monday. Let's go - 6:15?*

Valentina: *I need my coffee*

Amy: *Who else is going to resolve world affairs in 30 minutes? The country needs us*

In a little while, Valentina and Amy were jogging under the oak trees. That morning, they solved all the current political crises and were avoiding a discussion of their non-existent social calendars.

"No date material in either of your classes?" Amy asked.

"I don't know. There's a guy, really a couple of guys, who are interesting. Then there's a younger student, Sam, who's like a puppy. And smart. Sweet, very Uptown, but not stuck up. You can tell he's had a lot of advantages."

"And the other two?"

"Leo is in the doctoral program, working on getting his thesis done. He might be too busy to date right now. Kai is the other guy. Nice looking, a bit of an edge to him."

As they rounded the curve of the track near Magazine Street, Amy said, "Come on, that's it?"

"I've run into them both outside of class a few times. I enjoy talking with Leo. He makes me laugh. Everything sort of clicks when I'm around him. It's easy and fun—we're in sync. There was an instant connection ... It's hard to put into words." Valentina shrugged. "He teaches one of the intro classes for undergrads. Earlier in the semester, I saw a bunch of younger students trying to get his attention. They hang on his every word, but he's not full of himself. He seems kind. I think he wants to get together after the semester ends."

"And Kai?"

"He's from a small town near Lafayette and has that sexy Cajun accent, dark hair. He's a few inches taller than me. Built, but his muscles aren't from the gym. Opinionated, a little impatient."

"All three are in bioethics?"

"Yep. My marketing class is huge. More people work full time. Everyone runs out of the room like it's on fire. At that time of day, they probably need to get to their jobs afterwards. It's a little harder to make a connection."

"There's more opportunity to meet someone at school than at your job. Speaking of which, how's it going with the soiree? You haven't mentioned it in a while."

"I think it's all coming together. Food, flowers, decorations, auction items, waitstaff, invitations ... I know I'm forgetting something, but I'm not sure what."

"What are you going to wear?" Amy asked.

"I don't know. Maybe I could borrow your black silk skirt?"

"You must be kidding. I love that skirt, and of course you can borrow it. But this is one of your most important events of the year! Trust me, you need a new outfit."

"I could wear my beige cocktail dress. I haven't worn that to a function lately."

"Valentina, beige looks better on you than anyone else I know." Amy sighed. "But you are not wearing an ancient bland dress to a soiree with 300-zillion-dollar guests, especially when you want to ask them for a little of their pocket change."

"It's less than four years old and a classic."

"In the world of St. Charles Avenue and the New Orleans Country Club, a dress you bought a year ago is dated, two years is really old, three years is ancient and four years ago, simply too embarrassing to contemplate. We are going shopping."

"Let's compromise. We'll look. I really don't want to spend anything right now. That's textbook money."

"You won't have to spend that much. Becklin's has great buys, and we could also try Ashbury on Magazine. Come on, Valentina."

"You know I'm going to fold. Okay, what about Saturday?"

"Eleven?"

"Deal."

•　　•　　•

After a quick shower, Valentina drove to the park. "Hi, boss."

Dee waved Valentina into her office. "Let me show you an old trick, updated for the digital age. Got your computer?"

"My tablet."

"That works. We are going to review our guest list."

"I have a tally of everyone who has RSVP'd."

"Take the first names on the list, Cameron and Sheryl Walker. Look them up."

"We're going to cyberstalk our donors?"

"It's not cyberstalking, Valentina. We are preparing to be gracious hosts, and it's important to be able to greet our guests with the recognition they deserve. Let's look at a few of our attendees. We'll start with the top donors that we know are coming Thursday evening."

"I'm not sure about this."

"Trust me. You'll appreciate it later. My father did this before his business functions. Really, it was an ongoing thing. After meeting with a potential client, he would jot down notes on index cards to help him remember the person, where they worked, their hobbies or interests, the name of the spouse, and if anything significant was going on in their lives or with their kids. If the newspaper published a story about a client, he would add a short note to the card. He kept the index cards in a little wooden file box and reviewed the notes before events. Usually it's flattering when someone remembers something personal about you. It's much easier now with the internet. You know, I still have his little file box, although I keep my USB flash drives in it now. It reminds me how success is based on a series of small steps, day by day."

CHAPTER 13

Valentina stopped at the food court after her marketing class. Leo was at a table in the back, talking earnestly with an older man over coffee. She loved watching him—the way he listened intently and then laughed. After a little while, Leo and his companion walked toward the exit together. Leo was dwarfed by the older man who had to be six feet five and robust.

A few minutes later, Leo appeared next to her table, carrying a food tray.

"Mind if I join you?"

"Have a seat. I saw you in the back, but it looked like a real meeting."

"Yeah, that was Dr. Olson. He's first rate. We were planning my next data collection."

"For your water mites?"

"Yep. They definitely have lives of their own. I'm trying to keep up. We have ten different sampling locations on the lake. Once every few weeks, usually Devin, another grad student and I, ride around in a boat and collect them."

"The secret lives of mites?" Valentina asked as she tilted her head slightly.

"Exactly."

"Do you have other secret lives? Or secrets?"

"I might." Leo smirked. "Ask me anything."

"I feel so empowered."

"You have all the power, Valentina."

Valentina looked up, and he gazed back at her steadily. "I'm all in. I want to get to know you better. Let me finish the semester, okay?"

Just then, they heard someone call, "Valentina, Leo!" Kai waved as he approached their table.

"We've got to stop meeting like this," Valentina laughed. "Sit. We were talking about water mites."

"Hydrachnidia?" Kai asked.

"Oh, my man!" Leo exclaimed.

"Really?" Valentina said in disbelief.

Kai shrugged and started on his tacos.

"Speaking of Arthropods," Leo said, "I had the shrimp tacos. They weren't bad."

Kai and Valentina laughed.

"They are pretty good," Valentina said.

"Not bad at all," agreed Kai.

"What are you working on?" Leo asked Valentina.

"I'm knee deep in grant proposals."

"Is this for work or school?" Kai asked.

"Work, but I got the idea during bioethics. Dr. Chen said something that gave me the idea of a seed bank for the park. I pitched the idea to my boss, and she was supportive. She found a few philanthropic groups that offer grants. At the moment, I'm figuring out different ways to beg for money."

"That's a practical skill to develop. Success in grad school is all about getting funded. What did Dr. Chen say that gave you the idea?" Leo asked.

"Do you remember when he talked about an ethical dilemma?"

"Sure."

"I took a closer look at how we're handling school visits. All we've done with the kids on the tours is walk them around the different gardens and talk at them. A lot of them live in Central City and probably don't have yards. They're not engaged, and that's on us, not them. I've been thinking we need to have a way to get them more involved."

"When will you know if you get the grant?" asked Leo.

"We're applying to three different groups. The deadlines are coming up in a few weeks."

Kai watched Leo, who was looking steadily at Valentina. "I'd be glad to help," Kai offered gallantly.

"If you don't get funded, I bet there's a way to do an interactive seed bank on a small scale. I'll have more time this summer to help," Leo said.

"Really? That would be amazing, you guys."

"Saving seeds is an independent farmer's way of life. It's something my family has done for generations," Kai said.

"Apparently, it's something the Danekins have done too," Leo said. "Remember how I found out that my great-grandfather worked at Vavilov?"

"Yeah," Valentina said.

"It's strange to me we never talked about it before. I knew my grandfather had emigrated to the United States from Russia around 1950. He was only about eight when he left Leningrad with my great-grandparents. They had to live in a displaced persons camp in Germany for months. I'd heard the name Vavilov, but I thought my great-grandfather worked on a farm, because they said he took care of potatoes. But he worked at Vavilov." Leo's voice rose and his eyebrows lifted. "He dug up potatoes during the siege of Leningrad. He kept thousands of different varieties of potatoes for their diversity. The danger came during the winter of 1941-1942. The entire city was starving, so they had to guard the potatoes. Since the building wasn't heated, they burned furniture, papers, boxes, anything to keep the collection from freezing. Once Lake Ladoga froze, they were able to transport the collection over the ice out of Leningrad."

"Leo, that's amazing," Valentina said.

"Wow," Kai looked across the table, apparently noticing Leo's laser focus on Valentina.

"My grandfather wouldn't talk much about the camp where they had to stay after they left Leningrad. I'm going to see him again as soon as I can."

"Grandparents are amazing," Kai said.

Valentina's phone beeped an alarm. "I'm sorry, guys, I've got to get to work."

Leo waved, "Later."

Kai stood and helped Valentina gather her computer and books. He moved closer, smiled and said, "Great to see you."

Valentina felt a warmth down to her toes. "You too." Valentina hurried to her car. That was interesting, she thought.

CHAPTER 14

Six months earlier

Jack Stillman had set up the meeting carefully. He invited Stephen Angus to join him in the dining room reserved for Landever's corporate officers and their guests. Since Angus got to work early, Jack suggested an early lunch. The added benefit was that no one else would be around when he met with the entomologist. Key Landever officers ate later, usually at 1 pm, after their days were well underway, when they could relax and network with other department heads. An unsophisticated research nerd like Angus wouldn't realize the big players weren't in the dining room.

Jack remembered his excitement when the CEO invited him to the private dining room for the first time several years before. He had stepped into the private elevator that led to the 30th floor and the doors opened to tall windows with their panoramic view of Indianapolis. Jack recognized important company players quietly talking at white linen tables across the elegant dining room and thought, I have finally arrived. That same awestruck wonder should help in his meeting with the entomologist.

Angus stepped out of the elevator wearing a slightly rumpled wash-and-wear shirt, khakis and a bemused facial expression. Jack rose from his seat and waved him over. As always, Jack was impeccably dressed, wearing a custom-fitted stylish jacket, linen dress shirt, and tailored slacks.

A master of small talk when he chose, Jack related humorous stories about his first days with Landever. He recalled that Angus grew up in Scotland before completing his doctorate in the United States. They briefly discussed the cryogenic studies on the mites that Angus was carefully developing in his lab. He was about to begin a critical phase, but he had a little time. He needed to complete some routine preparations before that got underway. Angus mentioned he met Sam, Jack's son, during one of the summers Sam worked at Landever. Jack imagined a much younger Sam being captivated by Angus's Scottish accent, his enthusiasm for research, and his dry sense of humor.

After they ordered, Jack leaned forward in his seat. "Angus, I'd like to talk with you about another project. This one is quite short term, and you're the best person to handle it. Our operations in India require assistance in developing a weapon against a coconut mite, Ace ..."

"Aceria guerreronis?" Angus asked.

"Exactly!" Jack clapped Angus on the shoulder. "As you may know, this bug is presenting major issues for our worldwide coconut crop. Our Mumbai office has had considerable delays in completing a research study design. Frankly," Jack paused, as he looked meaningfully around the room, "upper management is a little concerned with our Mumbai team. We want someone we trust to evaluate things in person. As Landever's expert on mites, we know we can count on you to determine what's actually going on there."

Angus looked a little puzzled then asked, "You want me to go to Mumbai to check up on them?"

"Exactly," Jack said definitively. "And help them with the research design."

"What specifically are they trying to study?"

"Why don't you reach out to Anand Darsh, their head of research, to discuss that. Much better to talk scientist-to scientist. We'll explain your visit as a desire to learn about their study design to assess whether it will be applicable in the States. Of course, you must be tactful and not disclose our concerns."

"Any study, Mr. Stillman, must be replicable."

"Yes, yes, of course. We'd like you to evaluate the rigor of their approach, documentation, you understand."

"Certainly. When would you like me to go?"

"Immediately. My assistant will help you with your travel arrangements. First-class, Angus. Our appreciation for your helping us out here."

"Thank you, sir."

* * *

If Angus was surprised at the speed of the arrangements, he didn't say a word. The next few days were a whirlwind. On Friday afternoon, Angus found himself in the first-class lounge at Indianapolis International being offered a scotch. After boarding the sleek airliner, he thought back to the fancy lunch with Stillman in the executive dining room. It was odd. He expected—no—was looking forward to discussing the next phase of his research. Being able to put the Aceria in a state of suspended animation was only the first step, although by itself was groundbreaking. Stillman wasn't a scientist, but he would have recognized the significance. Angus wondered why the executive hadn't taken credit for it in a press release.

Angus had a lot of ideas about how to control the mite in its natural habitat. Having a sufficient sample size in his lab was critical. He finally produced enough of a mite population to begin testing his theories. Stillman wasn't interested in talking about that at all. Not able to make sense of it, Angus stretched out and slept for a few hours.

Later, Angus sat quietly looking out the window in the best aircraft seat he ever experienced, enjoying the leg room. He turned down a glass of champagne and then a single malt scotch a few hours later. Something wasn't right, and he wanted to think. What was he doing on this flight? If there were problems in India, why pull him in? Other entomologists at Landever were closer. Why hadn't they brought someone over from Belgium? Landever was spending thousands on this expedition. None of it made sense. Angus shrugged off his concern. He was curious about Mumbai, the exotic city that used to be called Bombay.

Secluded in his office, Jack confirmed when the flight left. He knew Angus was on the plane because he had an executive service pick him up in one of their town cars for his afternoon flight to Mumbai, and they helped him check in. After takeoff, Angus would arrive over 20 hours later and spend about a week in India. Jack insisted Angus get there a few days early to acclimate before going to Landever's lab on Monday. It was the least they could do. Jack told Angus to do some sightseeing, enjoy himself. He was doing a great service for the company.

On Friday evening, Jack worked late as usual. If he wasn't heading south to New Orleans or Florida, Jack spent weekends at Landever, or in his apartment going through stacks of reports. Typical for the beginning of the weekend, only a skeleton crew was on duty. Jack walked through the complex, past the glimmering rooftop greenhouses, to the industrial-looking brick buildings that made up the research sector. They didn't guard Entomology as heavily as other research areas, like the department for development of new seeds and plant genetic traits.

Jack wheeled what appeared to be large, stacked briefcases down the hallway into a less traveled wing. Entomology was not one of the prestigious departments at Landever. Necessary, minimally funded, and definitely not high-profile. Bug research was never at the front of the line for research dollar—until recently. Jack walked into Angus's well-organized lab. Everything was carefully labeled. Jack opened the top storage case in his stack, a specially designed container to maintain below freezing temperature. Turning to one of Angus's new freezers, thousands upon thousands of Aceria tosichellae waited in synthetic torpor, harboring Wheat Streak Mosaic Virus within their microscopic bodies. Jack put on gloves then quickly loaded the mites into the refrigerated containers, and headed downstairs. He told the security guard that he would be back for two more groups of boxed files, as he planned to get a lot done over the weekend.

"Sure, Mr. Stillman. Need help with that?"

"No, George, I've got it. Thanks though."

After loading everything into his rented SUV, Jack returned for the second and third loads of mites. He unplugged Angus's state-of-the-art freezer, smashing the prongs of the electrical plug to one side, an accident that would be attributed to an overzealous cleaning crew. Wheeling the final cargo of mites out the building, he marveled that something so small was going to allow Landever to corner the grain market. He'd make millions trading in commodity futures.

Jack drove exactly the speed limit to west Indianapolis, crossing the White River. He turned onto a nondescript street near the old General Motors stamping plant. A new development was in the works, but for the time being, the area was quiet and deserted, as it had been for years. An identical black SUV with tinted windows drove slowly up the street, and both stopped by the side of the road. The other driver looked across at Jack, waiting. Jack turned his face away and sat for a moment, swallowing hard to clear the taste of bile in his throat. *If I do this, there will be no going back. Up to that point, everything could be explained, even lauded, with no adverse consequences ... the new wheat cultivars, the cryogenic research with the mites. He could call it off, drive away.* He froze.

A street light came on at the end of the block. The road was empty adjacent to the industrial site, with weeds growing through the broken concrete. The rusted metal husk of the old stamping plant loomed in the distance. Taking a deep breath, Jack pulled a face mask over his head. He opened the door of his vehicle, stepped out, and waited. The other driver, a man of average height and weight, got out of his black SUV. He could be anyone, but this must be Richard Miller. A chameleon. Jack hesitated.

"Any problem?" Richard asked.

"No, no ..."

"I don't have all day."

"Right." Jack pulled the first freezer container from the back of the SUV.

CHAPTER 15

Valentina's hands tightened on the steering wheel as she pulled onto Park Avenue. *You've got this. Just because over 300 of our most significant donors will arrive in less than seven hours is no reason to panic.* Especially because everything was not ready!

Valentina tried not to yell into her phone, "Allison, where are you? You said the flowers would be here by now."

"Chill, baby."

With more than a little dread, Valentina almost pleaded, "Tell me that means you're outside the pavilion with 30 table arrangements, garland for eight doors and ..."

Allison interrupted, "I am."

"On my way. We'll help unload."

Valentina hurried outside through the pavilion where Renny and Ike were blowing the leaves from the walkways.

"Hey guys, can you give me a hand?"

"Sure, Valentina. Whatcha got?" asked Renny.

"The floral arrangements just arrived."

"Come on, Ike, let's go." For the past 16 years, Renny had worked at Winslow. Like Valentina, his part-time job evolved to become much more. Renny picked up trash and raked leaves as he did in the beginning, but now he was in charge of maintenance for 550 acres in the heart of the city. The three of them walked out past the wrought-iron gate to the back of the Mariposa flower truck parked outside.

"Allison, these are lovely," Valentina said softly as she lifted a box of centerpieces from the truck and handed it to Ike. "Are we your last delivery?"

"No, I'm going back to the shop. Can you handle hanging the garlands after we get everything unloaded? There's an after-play party in the Warehouse District. I wanted to get the arrangements to you, but I really need more time on the party."

"No worries. We'll get them out in no time. I'm going to head inside and start putting the centerpieces on the tables."

As Ike unloaded more of the arrangements, he turned to Renny and said, "These look cool."

"Valentina knows her stuff." Renny winced. "Um, you too, Ms. Allison!"

"That's all right, Renny. Valentina definitely knows her stuff. She thought of trying these flowers together, and they look beautiful. Local, and not too expensive. A win-win."

About ten minutes later Allison said, "That should be everything. See you later, gentlemen. I've got to run."

"You be careful, Ms. Allison. Ike, I'll get the rest of this. Why don't you get that ladder."

"Sure, boss." Ike looked around at all the flowers. "This place is going to be tricked out."

Before long, night lanterns hung from the oaks on the far side of the rose garden, glimmering softly in the distance. Several tables draped in white linen were spread across the room, topped with discreet reservation cards. When the candles on the tables were lit, the room would glow inside and out. Rows of delicate glasses sparkled at the wine bar.

Valentina saw her boss walk through the front entrance and take a deep breath.

"Hi, Dee," Valentina called from a ladder near the front entrance, her hands full of garland.

"The wreaths look gorgeous! Did you remember to bring the programs? Where is the insert for the programs? What about the cards for the silent auction? Remember we need a sign-in sheet. Oh, my goodness, the centerpieces!"

Since that was delivered almost without a pause, Valentina waited until Dee took a breath before jumping in. Looking lovely, Dee wore a long, flowing cocktail outfit that shimmered with gold threads.

"Thank you. Yes. Programs, inserts, and sign-in sheet are all on the table by the entryway. The cards are near the podium. See those tables, that's where we'll set up the auction items. Allison did such a nice job with the flowers. Aren't they wonderful?" White roses nestled between dusty blue hydrangeas and soft sage, accented by small candles on each of the tables. "Spring is one of the best times of year in New Orleans. I wish we didn't have as much competition for the weekends. Allison ran out of time. Since she's practically working at cost, I couldn't argue."

"I wondered what you were doing on that ladder. Need help?"

"No, I've got this." The thought of Dee on a ladder was pretty scary, probably for both of them. "This is the last one." Valentina quickly changed the subject. "How was your flight?"

Dee turned from the auction table, where she was arranging the boxes. "Oh, Valentina, it was exciting."

"The flight was exciting? I know how much you love to fly." Valentina said with a wry smile from her ladder.

Dee had flown to meet with representatives of the Jamison Botanical, a philanthropic group based in New York, to follow up on their grant proposal.

"No, silly. The flight wasn't late and that's about the best I can say for it. The meeting went well. They listened, asked questions, and were familiar with the materials we sent. We're not home free, but I think they're interested."

"Getting the grant would be amazing."

"We don't have time to think about that now. What else has to happen? You need to go get changed," Dee reminded Valentina.

"Could you check with catering? Everything should be coming out now."

"Will do. Now scoot."

Valentina grabbed her dress and tote, and did as she was told. She wrangled her curly hair into an elegant upsweep. Valentina never regretted her Sicilian background, except when the humidity was above 80 percent. *Who am I kidding? The humidity is above 80 percent for at least half the year in New Orleans.*

CHAPTER 16

Valentina was glad Amy talked her into the new dress. She loved it: silk, sage green, form fitting, with a V-neck that didn't show too much cleavage. She checked her makeup in the staff bathroom then leaned on the sink and told herself to relax.

As she circulated through the pavilion, Valentina smiled, introduced herself, and mentally thanked Dee for insisting she do her homework on the guests. She recognized Sophie Benfield, a widow who was usually accompanied by her son Harold to local social engagements. The Benfield's were generous contributors to Winslow. Their company, Sterna Shipping was based in New Orleans and carried freight all over the world. Harold Benfield was considered quite the catch. His father, Andrew Benfield, passed away two years before, and Harold assumed control of Sterna. Barely five feet tall, Mrs. Benfield was a little plump in her couture gown. She was standing alone, looking bored. Before she could eye the exit and escape, Valentina grabbed two glasses of sparkling wine.

"Hello, Mrs. Benfield, a glass of champagne?"

"Yes, please. How thoughtful of you."

"Your dress is lovely. I'm Valentina Sorelli. I work here at Winslow with Dee Claiborne. Will Harold be able to join us a little later?"

"You are so kind. Yes, Harold will be here by eight. He's delayed by a logistics issue at the office. He's exactly like his father, so conscientious."

"I'm sorry for your loss, Mrs. Benfield. Your husband was involved in so many organizations in the city."

"I miss him every day."

"I hope to feel that way about someone, someday," said Valentina.

"If I may be personal, how old are you, Valentina?"

"Twenty-six." Somehow having someone older ask such personal questions didn't bother her.

"There's time. Are you seeing anyone?"

"No, not anyone special."

"I met my Andrew when I was 27. We circled around each other for a couple of years and got married when we were 30. Then we started having babies right away."

"I didn't realize you had other children besides Harold."

"Only one. Harold has a sister, Leanne, who lives in the Midwest now.

"That's nice. Has Harold taken over the local operations?"

"Yes, and he's automated everything. Despite that, all he does is work. We've done things the same way since I can remember. Harold is shaking us up quite a bit, dragging us into the 21st century. We have partnerships now with rail lines and trucking companies across the world."

"Those are wonderful steps forward. Didn't your grandfather start Sterna Shipping?"

"As a matter of fact, he did. He was a deckhand on another line. Then he got into a high-stakes poker game and used his winnings to buy his first boat."

"What a gamble! I never heard that before."

"He was quite the card player. Thank goodness he won. Of course, it wasn't until years later that he told my grandmother he had bet her jewelry on the game."

"You two look very chummy." A tall, distinguished man in his early 50s walked toward them. Wearing a bespoke suit, he kissed Mrs. Benfield on both cheeks. "How are you, Sophie?"

"Oh hello, Jack. I didn't know you had an interest in Winslow."

"Of course, I do," he smiled at Mrs. Benfield, then looked at her and Valentina expectantly.

"Oh, you haven't met?" Mrs. Benfield asked.

"I haven't had the pleasure," Jack said.

"Valentina, this is Jack Stillman with Landever Industries. Jack, this is Ms. Sorelli."

"Mr. Stillman, it's nice to meet you. I'm Valentina. I'm with Winslow. We are grateful to Landever for all your support."

"Landever is glad to help."

"Have you seen the summer flowers? They're gorgeous."

"As lovely as Winslow's staff." Jack leaned in to Valentina with a lascivious smile.

Valentina tried to deflect Jack's apparent interest. She laughed and said, "Our crew started your company's seeds in the greenhouse some weeks ago."

"Landever is always willing to help a good cause or a pretty woman." Jack continued in this vein for several minutes, flirting and flattering Valentina.

Finally fed up, mega donor or not, Valentina asked, "Mr. Stillman, are you related to Sam Stillman?"

Jack stood straighter and backed up. "Why yes, he's my son. How do you know Sam?"

"We have a class together at NOU. Sam is so bright, and passionate about bioresearch."

"He is that," Jack said through a false smile.

Valentina wasn't sure what to say. "I definitely see the resemblance."

Changing the subject, Mrs. Benfield asked, "Valentina, did you have anything to do with the decorations?"

"Allison Sanders with Mariposa put these together for us."

"Beautiful," said Jack. "Valentina, what is your role at Winslow?"

"A little bit of everything. I work closely with Dee Claiborne on special events and marketing. I started at Winslow in the gift shop while I was in high school. I love the park and can't imagine working anywhere else."

"It looks like you have some interesting items in the silent auction," Stillman said.

"I'm bidding on the week at the beach house," Valentina said.

"You like the beach?"

"I love the beach, especially somewhere like Gulf Island. It's less frenetic than Destin."

"I know what you mean, Valentina. Sam and I like to spend time on Santa Rosa Beach for the same reason. Sophie, how about you? Are you going to bid on anything?"

"There's a spa day extravaganza that has my name on it." She winked at Valentina.

"Something for everyone," Stillman said. "There's a cigar cabinet I plan to check out. It has an active humidification system."

"Corojo donated that to us."

"One of my favorite restaurants. We should all go sometime. What's your next project? I imagine getting things ready for this soiree took a bit of your time," Stillman said.

"We're applying for a grant to start an interactive seed bank in the botanical garden," Valentina said.

Jack Stillman stiffened and nodded carefully. "Tell me more about this seed bank, Valentina."

"Seed banks are a way of preserving our resources in the event of a cataclysmic event. Hurricanes or a plant parasite could decimate our botanical collection."

Stillman's light-hearted demeanor had changed, and he seemed almost agitated. "Yes?" he motioned for Valentina to continue.

"Initially, we plan to harvest and store the seeds from the Medicine Garden. We have a lot of native plants in there that would be difficult to replace if we lost them in a storm. As an added bonus, we want to add more hands-on activities to the children's tours. So, we plan to work with our school partners on the academic requirements and have the kids help establish the seed bank. We'll have to see where we go from there."

"What a splendid way to involve the children. Valentina, I've never seen the Medicine Garden," said Mrs. Benfield.

"Let me take you on a personal tour. It's lovely this time of year," said Valentina.

"I may take you up on that."

Stillman narrowed his eyes as he stared at Valentina. "When is this seed bank going to come online? Will you store grains or other crop seeds in this seedbank?"

"Oh no, just local plants. Grains are a little beyond our scope," Valentina said. "We're not sure of the timing. We just finished the grant applications." Before she could ask about his curiosity, Dee walked to the microphone. "Ladies and Gentleman, on behalf of Winslow Park, welcome to our spring soiree!"

"I'm getting a little tired. Valentina, come sit with me?" Mrs. Benfield asked quietly. "Excuse us, Jack."

They quickly found a table, leaving Jack Stillman. Mrs. Benfield shrugged and said, "Jack is a little intense. His wife doesn't always accompany him to these types of events. She seems to be out of town a lot."

Valentina nodded and focused on Dee's talk.

After Dee's remarks, the rest of the evening passed quickly. Valentina checked on the volunteers at the auction tables. Several people were standing near each item, joking amongst themselves and the volunteers.

"Gerri, you and your crew have this down," Valentina said.

Gerri, a pretty strawberry blond, blushed. "This is the fourth year that I've volunteered, so we've had some practice. A little different than managing the gift shop!"

"You've been at Winslow almost as long as I have, Gerri."

"Not quite, but I can't imagine being anywhere else."

"You're saving the beach vacation for me, aren't you?"

"Get in line," said Gerri. "That's one of our hottest items."

"It looks like it's going well."

"It is, Valentina. We have bids higher than the minimum suggested, and multiple offers on all the items. Well, except for the cigar cabinet. Two gentlemen seem to be in competition for it. One of them seems pretty tightly wound. We've had a few others make offers, but for the most part everyone else is staying clear."

"Let me see the bid sheet." Valentina glanced at the names and said, "I know Ferris Jefferson. He's lovely."

"It wasn't him. Here's his name: Jack Stillman. Do you know him?"

"I just met him. Not exactly Dr. Jekyll and Mr. Hyde, but he was a little abrupt."

"Mr. Jefferson may be an old softie, but he doesn't give up easily, from what I remember of last year."

"Oh, that's right. He wanted the Panama hat for his son-in-law," Valentina recalled.

"And got it, too. I think he beat out Ralph Neeley. The bidding went stratospheric," Gerri laughed. "We made a lot of money, but it was more entertaining than serious. Let's hope this goes as smoothly."

It didn't.

Instead of the lighthearted banter between Mr. Jefferson and Ralph Neeley, the battle for the humidor became a fierce bidding war with an undercurrent of spite. Jack Stillman won the auction for the cigar cabinet, which went for ten times its value. Mr. Stillman held on to the bidding sheet until right before the auction closed.

Mr. Jefferson said, "Now, young man, that isn't very sporting of you."

Gerri tried to mediate, but Jack Stillman waved her away, saying, "I've got this."

Several of the other guests watched from the sidelines, shaking their heads and raising eyebrows. Valentina looked at Dee across the room. No matter what additional money they realized from the auction, it wasn't worth such a scene. Normally when they announced the winners of the silent auction, there was laughter and good-natured teasing. This evening, after a smattering of polite applause, uncomfortable murmurs arose from corners of the pavilion.

Valentina walked quickly to the band, and asked them to play a little longer. The young female vocalist agreed and turned to the other players. After they played a few chords, the singer turned back to the mic and sang almost in a whisper, "Do you know what it means to miss New Orleans, when that's where you left your heart..."

Valentina found Gerri, monitoring the volunteers as they completed credit transactions for the auction items. "Do me a favor, please."

"Sure, Valentina, what do you need?"

"Something to make everyone forget that pompous ass. Let's try to end this evening on a positive note. Can you dance?"

"Um, yes?"

"Come with me and ask Harold to dance."

Valentina led Gerri to the lately arrived Harold Benfield and quickly made introductions. Valentina was glad to see a spark of interest in Harold's expression.

Gerri smiled at Harold. "I've wanted to dance all night. Would you join me for this one?"

Harold chuckled and offered Gerri his arm. "I thought you'd never ask."

Valentina turned quickly and found Ferris Jefferson.

"Mr. Jefferson, I've been pining for a dance with you."

"Oh, Valentina, don't you have a young man waiting for you?"

"Do you see any lurking about? Come on, one little spin."

The singer continued, "The Mardi Gras memories of creole tunes that filled the air, I dream of oleanders in June, And soon I'm wishing that I was there ..."

As they danced, they passed near Mrs. Benfield's table. Sophie smiled and waved. Valentina thought she looked a little wistful.

"Mr. Jefferson, have you met Sophie Benfield?"

"No, I haven't. I know Sterna Shipping, of course. Always heard good things about Sterna and the Benfields. I was sorry to hear about Andrew. When we finish this number, why don't you introduce me."

"Only if you ask her to dance," Valentina said, smiling.

"Young lady, are you getting a commission from some dance studio?"

"Now that's an idea. Seriously, it's a party, Mr. Jefferson. There should be dancing."

In short order, Ferris Jefferson and Sophie Benfield were carefully waltzing to "Someone to Watch Over Me." Valentina moved gracefully through the room, encouraging other couples to dance. Through the crowd, she glimpsed the sway of Gerri's pale blue dress and an animated expression on Harold's face. Valentina walked over to the Walkers, but Sheryl Walker said, "Not this time, Valentina. Go ahead, Cam, my shoes are killing me. Dance with Valentina, you love this song."

Dee floated by, the hint of gold in her dress winking in the soft glow of the lights. Over her partner's shoulder, Dee lifted her eyebrows at Valentina and nodded with approval.

The evening would end well.

Jack Stillman frowned at Valentina from across the room then turned and left.

CHAPTER 17

Following the gala, Valentina had a "date" with Sam before class. She planned to set things straight. She headed toward the counter at PJ's. Sam spotted her and joined her in line. "A small cappuccino," Valentina said to the server. "Yum, look at those biscotti. But I can resist."

"Who are you trying to convince—you or me?" the barista asked.

Valentina laughed and waved off the biscuit.

"I'll get your coffee," Sam said. "Thanks for coming."

"I've got it," she said while tapping her credit card. "Nice to see you. Look, there's a table over there. I'll go grab it."

Sam got a mocha and muffin for himself and a biscotti for Valentina. The barista grinned. As they sat down, Valentina noticed the biscotti. "You knew I really wanted one!"

Valentina dipped the biscotti into her coffee. "My grandmother makes these, and I love them. She doesn't coat them with chocolate, so I wanted to try it." Valentina took a bite.

"Well?"

"Not in the same class as Mia's, but the chocolate makes it a contender."

"Do you like Italian food? I would love to take you to Irene's."

"I've heard it's excellent, and I love Italian food. We could get a group from class and go together. That would be a lot of fun."

"But ..."

Valentina immediately asked, "Besides bioethics, what are your other classes?"

"Advanced genetics, biochemistry and advanced statistics. I also have a biochemistry lab and a research seminar on Tuesdays."

"That sounds like a heavy load."

"It's a little intense but not bad. Math has always come easy for me, so I'm enjoying it. I haven't narrowed down my area of research yet, but I plan to pursue some aspect of plant genetics."

"Very cool. What got you interested in the field?"

"My first summer job. My dad got me on as a courier at Landever when I was fifteen. I saw the research labs and was hooked. Besides the slick equipment, the researchers and techs were so into the work. It was obvious they respected each other and were pumped by what they were doing."

"When you meet people who have a real passion for their work, it's contagious."

"Exactly. I wanted to feel that, and thought I'd work with one of the large seed companies. Since our bioethics class, I've halfway considered CGIAR."

"Oh, right, that's the group of international seed banks. They protect the genetic diversity of the area."

"I'd be more interested in their research. They do a lot of genome sequencing to identify and improve plant lines."

"Aren't all the centers in foreign countries?"

"There's one in DC, but most of the research takes place in Central and South America, or Africa and Asia. Sometimes I think it might be interesting to live somewhere else for a while, but I'll probably end up with one of the ag companies in the States."

"Have you traveled outside the country?"

"Mostly Europe. If my dad had a business trip overseas, sometimes I would meet him in London. We did go to Oslo and Svalbard in Norway."

"I have a serious case of envy about Europe, but Sam, you've been to the Svalbard Seed Vault?"

"About two years ago. When my dad and I were still speaking." Sam laughed, a little bitterly. "Landever was scheduled to make a deposit of seeds at Svalbard. My dad got permission for me to go with him."

"It must have been amazing."

"Being at the Arctic Circle was amazing. And a lot of work. We took a boat tour of a wilderness area on a Zodiac, a really fast, rubberized boat that's almost unsinkable. It was exciting, but we weren't able to see a lot. The ice, Valentina, it was blue. And it sounded alive, knocking and cracking, moaning. The thing is, everything you wear has to be sterilized, your boots, the inside of your pockets. It's crazy. They even go through the Velcro on your jacket with tweezers to make sure you're not accidentally bringing in seeds or foreign material."

"What was the seed bank like?"

"From the outside, Svalbard looks like a huge trucking container tucked into the side of a mountain. With crazy, fiber optic lighting. The inside is pretty industrial looking with shelves and shelves."

"Just think, Sam. You were literally at the repository of life for our entire civilization."

"That's an idealized way of looking at it. You've bought into the idea of it being the 'Doomsday' Vault?"

"You haven't?"

"It's hard for me to imagine a catastrophe that could destroy agriculture as we know it."

"I hope you're right. Svalbard is the ultimate backup for seed banks worldwide. They have a collection of what, a million seeds? If something happens to a crop, there's a way of regenerating it. I've been doing research for grant applications at the park. I read that the civil war in Syria threatened their gene bank and Svalbard saved their collection. Seeds from the beginning of their culture could have been lost. Some go back ten thousand years. They're the basis for developing plants that are disease or drought tolerant."

"I guess. Oslo had a neat vibe. We did a little skiing. Kind of unexpected for my dad to want to go and to let me go with him."

"By the way, I met your dad. He came to the Winslow gala. He's a generous donor to the park. I didn't connect the two of you until I saw him in person. You look alike."

"Oh, you met him? You've seen him more than I have then. We're avoiding each other right now. He wasn't too pleased with my choice of graduate programs."

"If I remember right, he wanted you to go to medical school. But I'd still think he'd be happy you're following in his footsteps."

"You do remember right, and not exactly, on both counts."

"What do you mean?"

"My dad is responsible for business development at Landever. A scientist will never be in charge of that company. Only money guys make it to senior management. So, I wouldn't be following in his footsteps. And my father has it in his head that being a doctor is more important than doing something I really like." Sam changed the subject. "How was the gala?"

"It was good. Crazy good. The soiree is one of our main fundraising events of the year. This was the first year that I was in charge. I had tons of support from Dee, my boss, but it was my baby. Based on the preliminary estimates, we'll more than hit our targets. I'm relieved and pumped at the same time."

"That's fantastic."

"Your dad bid on a cigar cabinet. He seemed really intent on getting it."

Sam hesitated. "He's pretty intense about everything he does."

"The silent auction is one of our best fundraisers, well, especially this year, in part due to your dad. I tried for the Gulf Island beach vacation, but someone outbid me."

"I love the Florida Panhandle. My family has a house on Santa Rosa Beach. The coast is so beautiful with that white sand and blue-green water. A friend of mine is a paleontologist. She says the sand particles look like diamonds under a microscope. It's actually quartz that began as granite in the Appalachian Mountains."

"That's amazing. I love walking on the beach in the early mornings and evenings."

"I love body surfing too. Santa Rosa was my favorite family vacation. My dad would relax. Even when my mother didn't come, it was a lot of fun. I still enjoy it. We could go one weekend."

Valentina sighed to herself and realized she had to be blunt. "Sam, you're a great guy, cute and smart, but I'm not sure that I feel that way about you."

"I understand." Sam looked down at his mocha, his face reddening slightly. "Well, not really."

"I ..."

They both looked up as someone dropped a tray across the room and his table mate yelled, "You dork!"

Saved by the dork. In the brief laughter around the food court, Valentina struggled to find something else to talk about. "I'm enjoying our class together. Everyone has such different backgrounds—the discussions are really interesting."

"You know, at first, I thought everyone was anti-industry. Except for Tala, everyone seems to have an open mind."

"Tala seems as though she's had a very different world experience than ours. I'm curious to know her story. You know, I'd like to get everyone together, outside of class. My apartment has a huge patio."

"That sounds nice, Valentina."

"I'll check with everyone in class. What about next Saturday evening?"

"I can make that work."

A little while later, Valentina and Sam walked to class together. Except for Dr. Chen, they were the last to arrive. Valentina quickly spoke up. "Hey everyone! I'm having a class get together next Saturday night, a week from this Saturday. Anyone interested in potluck on my patio? The weather is supposed to be great. I could make gumbo."

"Homemade gumbo," Ellis said reverently. "How about if I bring the wine?"

"Perfect, Ellis."

"Gumbo would be awesome. I'll bring a salad," offered Gemma.

"I'll pass around a paper with my address, number, and email. Write your contact information and what you plan to bring, and I'll email everybody."

"I'm in. What time?" asked Leo.

"7:30?"

"Aw, *cher*, I'll be there," Kai said with an exaggerated Cajun accent.

Everyone laughed, and at that moment, Dr. Chen walked into the classroom. He glanced around the room. "I am going to pass out an example of an ethical dilemma. Find a partner and begin your discussion using the decision-making model you have learned."

•   •   •

A few mornings later, Valentina and Amy met at the fountain. As they jogged, Valentina asked, "What was I thinking? Ten people are coming to my apartment next Saturday night and I promised to feed them gumbo."

"I don't know, Valentina. What were you thinking? And I thought there were only eight of you in the class."

"Ellis and Xavier are each bringing someone, and Gemma might, so there could be eleven of us."

"Don't worry. You make great gumbo. I can't figure out why you decided to do this now. You just finished with the gala."

"I was fending off Sam."

"The brilliant puppy."

"Yes. The hurt, brilliant puppy. He wanted to buy me dinner at Irene's, so have some respect for my ethical decision making."

"I think bioethics is going to your head."

"It was when he invited me to his family's house on the beach that I confronted my true ethical dilemma."

Amy groaned. "He didn't."

"He did."

"I am in awe of your strength of character."

"Me too!"

They both laughed as they rounded the curve toward the fountain.

"Back to the class party. It's a neat group, and I'd like to get to know them better," Valentina said.

"Fess up, is it Leo or Kai?"

"I haven't spent enough time with them to say. And who knows if either one is really interested or only flirting a little. They both seem like great guys. Anyway, I hope to get to know them both."

"I might bet on Sam as the dark horse."

Valentina laughed. "Not to change the subject, but how was your board meeting last week?"

"It was all about the budget for next year. Luckily, they still like having a curriculum specialist. Let's go back to your party plans. They're more interesting. Come to think of it, you always have a party or a gala to plan. By comparison, I lead a very dull life."

"Ha!"

"Besides gumbo, what's on the menu?"

"It's potluck. Gemma is bringing a salad. Xavier said that he and his wife will make South African pumpkin fritters. On the sign-up sheet, he wrote '*pampoenkoekies*.'" Valentina counted off the rest of the class on her fingers. "Sam—dessert, Leo—French bread and beer, Ellis—wine, Tala—a fruit salad, and Kai said an appetizer, but he didn't say what."

"That sounds wonderful."

"I'm going to the Westwego Seafood Market early next Saturday morning. Do you want me to pick up anything for you?"

"Maybe two or three pounds of medium shrimp?"

"You got it. I'll drop them off on my way back home."

"I'll be there. I have a date with my vacuum cleaner."

"Great. See you then."

CHAPTER 18

Until then, it had been a warm, wet spring, but that day the air was cool and dry. Will Torino stepped down from his Ranger to get a closer look. He noticed a yellow cast to the winter wheat in the north field. Bending down, he touched the leaves. Streaked with yellow, some leaves curled inward along the spine. Walking along the rows, Will saw the same discoloration near the base of every plant. "Blast!" He climbed back in the truck and pressed his fingers hard into the bridge of his nose. He rammed the truck in gear and drove quickly to the sweet corn, where a yellow wash stretched as far as he could see. Will kept driving, stopping, and inspecting the ruin of his entire season. Stunted roots, yellow stripes on what should have been solid green leaves. Everything, everything was ruined.

Before reaching the house, Will stopped and pulled out his phone. He punched in the number for his insurance agent.

"Hello? Will?"

Will managed a low growl, "Ian," and stopped.

"What's going on, Will? You sound bad, buddy."

"Something has infected my crops."

"How bad is it?

"All the wheat, all the sweet corn, the whole farm."

"You cleared the fields before planting."

"Yeah, I did. We've had a lot of rain. I heard that makes things worse."

"It's been real windy, too. Will, you're the fifth call I've gotten in the last two days. I was going to call you."

"Mitch?"

"Yes."

"Norris?"

"Yeah."

"James?"

"Why don't you ask me who wasn't hit. From what I've heard, it's the whole county. I can come out tomorrow afternoon, right after lunch. I'll start the paperwork this evening."

Will ended the call and drove the rest of the way to the house. If his farming practices weren't found lacking, insurance would pay 65% of the historic yield for the wheat. But he only covered the corn for 50%. The mortgage on the new building would eat that up in no time. Will wasn't sure how he was going to tell his wife, Susan. He was relieved he hadn't agreed to buy the new tractor. He never could have dug his way out of that hole.

After turning off the motor, Will didn't get out of his truck. If Susan didn't know, it wasn't real yet. The wind picked up, and he saw her walking toward the house from the kitchen garden. She looked up, carrying a bucket of soft pink peonies. Last September they had planted the tubers and early spring bulbs together on a beautiful sunny day, with a touch of fall in the air. The ache in Will's neck eased a little. Things were bad, but Susan was his everything.

He walked to Susan and reached for her hand. "We have to talk, babe."

"I got a call from Erin. She said Mitch is beside himself. What's going on?"

"All our wheat, the sweet corn, it's infected, Susan. It may be a wheat virus the Extension office talked about a few years ago. John Beryl gave a presentation. He said they've had problems in western Kansas. If you unroll the leaves, there's nothing to see. I want to get my hand lens to look for mites, which I understand cause the virus. Though from what I remember of the talk, there are three or four viruses. Wheat streak mosaic is the one I remember. Caleb called it yellow mosaic. I'm going to drive into town early tomorrow morning and take the leaves to the Extension office. John usually is in the office then and I'll get him to take a look. It's all over the county. I called Ian, and he's starting the insurance claim tonight."

"Will, isn't there something we can use, something we could spray?"

"If it's one of the mosaic viruses, there's not a darn thing we can do. I may stop at the bank after talking with John."

Susan glanced toward the new storage building, blinked rapidly, straightened her shoulders, then looked back at Will. "They can't foreclose on the whole county, can they? Let's go in and have dinner. I did that chicken stir-fry you like."

•　　•　　•

The next morning, Will arrived at the Extension office as they opened.

"Hey, John. Got a minute? Will Torino, you may not remember me. I took over Caleb's old place a few years back."

"Sure, Will, how's it going?" asked John as he unlocked the door.

"I've been better. Could you take a look at something for me?"

"Sure, come in the back."

As John settled behind his desk, Will pulled out two Ziplock bags.

John sighed. "Let me see. If this is anything like what's going on in the rest of the county, neither of us will be happy."

John reached for a shallow plastic bin and turned on his desk light. He carefully opened the contents of the first bag, leaves and small bits of mud falling into the bin. After looking at it for a few moments, John opened the second bag and looked inside. "These came from different fields?"

"Yeah."

"It really doesn't matter. I think this is wheat streak mosaic or high plains virus. I've done tests on some samples that came in earlier. They looked the same.

"Will, let me ask you something. Did you find this concentrated in spots, or at the edges of the fields?"

"No, it was throughout every field, all the crops."

"That's what I've been hearing, but it's downright strange. When we've seen this before, it's usually more severe on the margins of the fields. Or we'll see differences in the symptoms depending on where the infection started. The wheat curl mites are tiny, with two legs. The adults stand on their tails, wave their legs and get picked up by the wind. They get blown into the field, so the damage typically isn't uniform. It usually starts along the edges."

"My fields, they all looked the same. I remember the talk you gave a while back. Mites caused this? I didn't see anything with my hand lens."

"It's likely." John nodded. "The young mites carry the virus, and the wind carries the mites. A strong wind blows them up to a mile and a half, two miles away. When did you plant?"

"I may be fairly new to farming, but I know enough to plant after the fly-free date."

"Then we can scratch that off the list." Saying more to himself than Will, "It has been pretty warm. That makes it worse."

"There's no new treatment that will work?"

"Not a thing. The mites mostly stay in the leaf whorl where a pesticide can't reach them. The virus suppresses the RNA in the wheat, the corn, barley, soybeans, whatever, and then it overcomes the plant's resistance to disease on a molecular level. We're only now starting to understand this, and have nothing to compensate for it. Carbofuran controlled it, but the EPA revoked its use on food crops in 2009."

"I don't get it. Everybody I know cleared their fields."

"Did you clear the areas surrounding the fields at least two weeks before you planted?"

"Yep."

"I'm sorry, Will. I don't know of a farm in this county that isn't infected. It's more involved because it seems to be a virus complex. If it's the mites, you can't see them without significant magnification. They're one-one-hundredth of an inch long."

"Dang."

"Let me send this to the lab. It could be any of several viruses. Wheat streak mosaic—air or soil borne—high plains, *Triticum mosaic*, wheat spindle streak. A virus complex or a combination, but I can't be sure."

"I guess it would be helpful to know."

"Another problem is that everyone uses the same seed. Wheat has very little genetic variance to begin with. If we get a bad bug in the county, it's going to spread. It makes our crops too vulnerable."

"What do I do now?" asked Will.

"Are you insured?"

"Not enough."

As Will was leaving, John said, "We're hearing a few rumblings from other parts of the Midwest, not just here. It doesn't help with the loss, but you're not alone in this."

Will drove to the bank, where he saw James's truck and four others he didn't recognize. He had never seen more than one or two customers at a time at the bank. When Will walked into the lobby, a representative told him he would need to schedule an appointment unless he wanted to wait a few hours. As he left the bank, Will decided to stop and see Mitch before heading home. He found him in one of his fields near the county road, sitting on his old tractor. Will left his truck by the gate and walked over.

"Hey."

"Hey yourself."

"I just left the Extension office."

"John have anything enlightening to say?"

"It's what he didn't say: 'You're screwed.'"

Mitch snorted. "Ya think?" He swung his leg over the seat and jumped down from the tractor. "You called Ian?"

"Yeah."

"What did he say?"

They turned to each other. "You're screwed!"

Smiling slightly, they moved slowly through the rows of green and yellow striped leaves.

"Seriously, Ian's a decent guy. He'll do what he can," Mitch said.

"You've been up here longer than I have. Have you seen anything like this before?" Will asked.

Mitch shook his head. "I've never even heard of anything like this happening."

"I remember Caleb and some of the old timers talking about yellow mosaic when I first got here. My impression was that it was a long time ago and affected only a few farms, usually next to each other. But John said this is all over the county.

"That's surreal."

"I can't believe it."

Neither spoke for several minutes as they continued walking. Will was glad for the company.

"John said it was by mites or aphids. He's sending it to the lab. Because of the color, he thinks it's the wheat mosaic. If it was high plains there'd be more white spotting, but it could be both." Will said.

"You know, I thought I noticed a lighter green or yellowing in the fields a little earlier, but thought it was a trick of the light. If anything, I thought it might be a pH or nutrient problem, but it didn't seem out of hand. I considered adding nitrogen. Yesterday, when I realized how bad it was, I called Norris. He told me nitrogen would increase the spread," Mitch said. "Then he said be careful and check our onions and garlic because the mites migrate. In fact, he wonders if that's how this whole thing got started." Hands in pockets, they stood quietly for a minute.

"I'm going to plow those suckers under."

Mitch turned to head back to his tractor. "Yeah, die you bastards."

"Are you going to plant anything after you plow?" Will asked.

"Norris told me to consider alfalfa or clover to avoid an erosion problem. Or pennycress."

"That's what I was wondering about. If we leave the fields bare, the wind could blow half our topsoil to Georgia or at least Missouri."

As they walked back, something crunched under Will's work boot. He bent down, and picked up something dark gray and flat. "What's this? Plastic?"

Taking the piece, Mitch held it closer. "Yeah, I guess. Can't tell what it's supposed to be."

They both stared at the small flat piece of cracked material that was a little longer than a playing card and a little thinner than a deck of cards. A small round metal thread attached to its vertical edge.

"How'd it get in the middle of your field?" Will asked.

"Kids?"

"If it was kids getting baked, we'd see papers, beer cans, something more."

"Hey, here's another," Mitch said. He picked up a piece of angled material about four inches long. The edge looked as though it had melted.

Mitch and Will both searched the ground and nearby plants. After about fifteen minutes, they each found a few handfuls of small fragments.

Will's phone started to ring. He looked at it, and said, "I better get this. It's Valentina."

CHAPTER 19

Valentina and Mia had planned this visit almost two weeks before. With clean-up, thank you cards and post-event party analysis done, Valentina could spend the next few hours with two of her favorite people.

"Mia, Dean! I'm so glad to see you."

"Tell us all about it, Valentina. We want to hear everything," Dean said.

"Come inside, sweetheart." Mia hugged her close. "I just made fresh coffee."

Valentina relaxed as they settled around the kitchen table, covered by one of Mia's seasonal tablecloths. She ran her hand over one of the blue irises across a creamy white background. Over the years, they had countless talks and thousands of casual meals in that very spot. Valentina had some memories of her parents, but her mom's illness and dad's disconnection colored those recollections. Mia and Dean were home for her, and this kitchen its core.

"Over 300 patrons attended. Our goal was to clear $200,000, and we hit $320,000."

"Woohoo! That's our girl. What made up the difference?" Dean asked.

"Besides my brilliance?" Valentina laughed. "Seriously, it was a few different things. We had more sponsors and attendees and more popular raffle items. My marketing class actually helped. I was more aware of the financial analysis than I would have been. We kept the costs lower. Do you remember Allison Sanders?"

"Mm hmm. You had a lot of classes together early on."

"After we finished college, she opened a florist business, Mariposa. She gave us a great deal on the flowers. Renny connected us with a jazz group, the Transport Jazz Trio, not too well known, so a little less expensive. Their female vocalist was amazing. She has an incredible range. I think both Allison and the band want the exposure. It's an influential audience. Mostly, I think we did well because of the silent auction. The bidding got crazy high."

"Well, that's great, honey." Mia looked closer at Valentina. "What are you not telling us?"

"It's nothing." She hesitated. "There was one guest, Jack Stillman, who was pretty overbearing."

"Did he get drunk?"

"No, I don't think I ever saw him take a drink. Earlier, Mr. Stillman seemed a little off. I was talking with Sophie Benfield, one of our sponsors, and he came to say hello. At first, he was pleasant, a little too flirty, but nice, and then his demeanor changed abruptly. I think he embarrassed Mrs. Benfield. She didn't seem to like him very much. His company donates a lot of plants and money to us, so I had to be careful. Then he became aggressive about a cigar cabinet we had in the silent auction." She shook her head at the memory. "It really started to affect the evening, but we got the musicians to distract everyone. A lot of people wanted to dance but hadn't yet."

"There's nothing like a good cigar." Dean looked at Mia and grinned. Mia's efforts to get Dean to give up his cigars were legendary.

Mia scowled at Dean and pointedly ignored his comment. "It sounds like you handled it. What kind of music did they play?"

"Traditional jazz with contemporary pieces mixed in. I loved their version of the old classics "Stardust" and "My Funny Valentine." That reminds me. I introduced Gerri to Mrs. Benfield's son, Harold. He apparently works all the time. They're both a little shy, but I got them to dance together."

"That's sweet. Can you stay for lunch?" Mia asked. "How about spaghetti and meatballs? We have some left over from Sunday."

"Love some! But only if we call Will so I can brag. Then I'm going to have to run right after we eat."

"You two," Mia shook her head. "You know I've sent Susan the recipe." Mia got her red gravy and meatballs out of the fridge to warm up then started water boiling for the pasta.

"It won't be the same." Valentina said with a smirk.

After lunch, Valentina found Will's contact on her cell phone and put the call on speaker.

"Hey, Will, guess where I am?"

"What's up, Valentina?" he asked, sounding distracted, maybe a little impatient.

One thing in her life Valentina could always count on was Will being glad to hear from her. They talked by phone almost every week, and sent texts and emails in between. Since it was just the two of them, they were close like siblings. Shocked by his tone, Valentina realized something was wrong.

"Will, I'm visiting with Mia and Dean."

"What's going on over there?" Dean asked. "Something's happened."

In the background, Valentina heard another voice say, "Found some more."

"Is that Mitch?" Dean asked.

"Yeah, we're in a mess." Will hesitated. "A bug affected all our crops—the wheat, the sweet corn. Total crop failure. We're filing with our farm insurance, but it's not going to cover everything."

"Has it affected both your farms? Your fields aren't close to each other," Mia said.

"Mia, it's hit everybody. Every farm in the county has it. The Extension agent said other parts of the Midwest are having problems too."

"What was Mitch saying? Y'all found some of the bugs?" Dean asked.

"No, we found little pieces of plastic or metal. I don't know. It's strange."

"Have you talked to your parents yet?" Mia asked.

"Not yet. We only realized something was wrong yesterday," Will said. "Look, I've got to go."

"Send pictures of the pieces," Valentina said.

"Coming your way. I'll call soon."

In the silence, Valentina, Mia and Dean sat for a minute looking at the cell phone as it went dark.

"Wow, that's awful," Valentina said.

"It is awful." Dean agreed. "They took out a loan for the new storage building. Will was counting on a good harvest to pay down the loan."

Valentina's phone signaled a text. "Look, here's the picture."

They crowded in to see the photo on Valentina's phone. It chimed again as Will sent more pictures.

"One piece reminds me of something you'd see in a model airplane kit," Dean said. "Check this one out. Looks like part of a propeller."

"Really, Dean? It looks like plastic to me."

"A guy in my class worked in aviation. I'll show him the picture and see what he says. But what can we do for Will?" Valentina asked.

"He'll let us know what he needs when he's ready," Dean said.

Mia got up and began clearing the lunch plates, dropping one with a clatter.

"Here, let me help." Valentina brought their cups to the sink. She hugged Mia. "Will and Susan will be okay. He always is. This is Will we're talking about."

Mia hugged her back, close to tears.

"I've got to get back to work," Valentina said. "We're still working on one of the grant applications."

"Focus on that. We'll see you later." Dean walked her to the door. "We'll figure out what we can do to help Will."

"Love you, Dean. See you later."

"Love you too. Your grandmother will be all right. But check in with her tomorrow."

•   •   •

The next morning Valentina called Mia about seven, knowing she'd find her in the garden. Mia spent the sunrise hours there, watering, weeding, trimming, and tending her plants.

"Good morning." Valentina could picture her grandmother in the yard, surrounded by her pots filled with flowers and rows of tomato plants, snap beans, squash and peppers.

"It is a beautiful morning. Aren't you up early? How are you, sweetheart?" Mia's voice was bright and steady.

"Fine, Mia. Calling for two reasons. The first is to check on you. That was pretty hard news from Will."

"It was. But they have insurance. It's going to set them back, but it's not the end of the world. My grandfather had tough times on his farm. And we both know there are worse things. Once Will knows more, he'll have to weigh how he feels and decide if he wants to keep the farm going."

"It's such a bad break."

"It really is. I felt, what's that word? So—gobsmacked. That's it. He and Susan were doing well. I've had time to think since then. Dean's right. We have to trust Will. He'll let us know what he needs when he's ready. Now, what was your second reason for calling?"

"May I borrow that big folding table and chairs in the shed? I'm having my class over next Saturday night."

"Sure, I'll get Dean to bring it by next Friday while you're at work. Just leave your gate unlocked."

"Fantastic, thanks. I was a little gobsmacked myself yesterday and forgot to mention it."

"Sure, what are you doing?"

"Hosting a class party next weekend. It's potluck, and I'm making gumbo."

"Where are you getting the shrimp?"

"The Westbank, of course."

Mia nodded in approval. "Pick up a couple pounds of the jumbos for us? I'll get Dean to make his barbeque shrimp."

"Definitely. I'll drop them off Saturday morning."

Valentina spent the next few evenings after work cleaning her apartment and collecting the ingredients for the gumbo. While she was at work, Dean set up the large, round folding table and chairs in the center of the patio. Mia sent one of her oilcloth table covers, the one with beautiful yellow freesias. Late Friday, Valentina hung string lights between the trees over her patio.

On Saturday morning, it was a quick drive over the Crescent City Connection to the Westbank Shrimp Lot. She remembered when Mia and Dean first took her there on the ferry to introduce her to the best shrimp in the city, fresh off a boat docked at the end of the lot. She didn't have time for the ferry today, but promised herself she would soon. Valentina loved looking out over the railings at the Mississippi, the water moving fast, reflecting brightly in the sunlight. On the way back, the three silver-gray steeples of St. Louis Cathedral would rise from the thin strip of land on the river bank.

The open-air market reminded Valentina of a school fair with its small stalls and bright signs. Many of the stands were operated by the fishermen's families. She stopped her car in the center of the lot framed by two rows of stalls, where other customers had parked with casual abandon.

"Hi there."

"Hey, whatcha need?"

"Seven pounds of medium shrimp, two pounds of the jumbo."

The woman behind the counter gave her the price.

"Sounds good. Do you have crabmeat?"

"I don't, but Wade does, at the end of the row. You need ice?"

"Yes, please. I have an ice chest right here."

After getting the shrimp, Valentina walked a few stalls down to Wade and got her crabmeat. Once she loaded her car, she drove back over the Crescent City Connection to the east bank of New Orleans. She dropped off two pounds of the mediums to Amy, the jumbos to Mia, and headed home.

With the Neville Brothers band streaming and the day stretching before her, Valentina peeled and de-veined the shrimp. She heard Mia's and Dean's voices in her head. "You've got to keep the shrimp cold!" After putting the clean raw shrimp in a bowl of ice water, Valentina started on her stock. She roasted the heads and peels in a pan, then brought them to a boil in a big pot of water with onion, celery, carrot and garlic. While it cooked, she sautéed the okra and prepped the rest of her ingredients. Then, with the stock strained and set aside, Valentina started the roux. She browned the flour and oil to the color of dark caramel until it gave off a nutty scent. Valentina added the vegetables, then the stock and seasonings. She would wait before adding the shrimp and crabmeat.

CHAPTER 20

Hours later, the gumbo quietly simmered next to a large bowl of warm rice. Freshly showered, Valentina sat outside enjoying the cool spring evening. The patio and backyard were the reasons she rented her pocket-sized apartment. In an old Mid-City neighborhood, it had one large room with high ceilings, old pine floors and vast windows. The bathroom was the size of a closet. But two huge live oaks shaded the brick patio. A few old Adirondacks and mismatched metal chairs leftover from previous tenants rested underneath the branches. Camellias, Savannah hollies, and crepe myrtles surrounded the yard that stretched fifty feet from the house. When Winslow threw out seasonal or sickly plants, Valentina rescued the shade-loving varieties and found homes for them all. Impatiens, ginger, begonias, lacecap hydrangeas and maidenhair ferns spilled over between tree roots and at the edges of the patio and fence. A small grove of native milkweed grew at the back fence, calling to butterflies.

Everything seemed ready. Valentina's thoughts returned to Will and what she could do for him. Footsteps on the path soon distracted her. A smiling older woman approached, followed by Ellis, who introduced his wife, Annie.

"Annie, it's nice to meet you."

Annie grasped her hands and said, "At last, an introduction to one of the famous bioethics classmates."

Valentina laughed. "As long as we're not infamous, I guess that's good."

"Hi, Valentina. What a wonderful yard!" Ellis beamed. "Where should I put the wine?"

"I have a tub there with ice for the cold drinks and you can put the red wine on the table. There's water and soft drinks. Annie, what would you like? Ellis?"

"Valentina, I'll get our drinks. You cooked gumbo for us. We should carry you on our shoulders."

"It wasn't that complicated."

"We never make it ourselves." Annie said. "My family moved from New Orleans when I was young, and Ellis is originally from the Midwest."

"What brought you back?"

"When Ellis retired, there was nothing keeping us in Fort Worth. We thought about the Midwest, but ... we said, 'Cold winters or New Orleans!'" Annie gestured with each hand as though she was balancing a scale. "There was no contest. We're getting older, and we weren't looking forward to that ice and snow. I'm a nurse, so it wasn't hard for me to find a job. And I still have a little family here."

Ellis returned with a glass of wine for Annie and a glass of water for himself. "Did you need anything, Valentina?"

"I'm good. How's retirement?"

"A little different from making propellers. I haven't wanted to commit to anything long term yet. After 20 years in aviation, I'm thinking of opening a plant nursery, or teaching high school. I don't know. Still exploring my options. Taking the class buys me time. At least I'm doing something. When I registered, there wasn't a lot open, and bioethics seemed more interesting than the other classes that were available."

Valentina began, "Ellis, I have a question..."

At that moment, Gemma walked onto the patio, threw her arms wide and exclaimed, "I love it!" She put a huge bowl of salad on the table with a small bottle of dressing. "Look at all the flowers." She came over to stand with Valentina, Ellis and Annie. "What a nice idea to get everyone together, Valentina. Hey, Ellis. You must be Annie? I'm Gemma."

"Good to meet you, Gemma," Annie said.

"May I get you something to drink?" Ellis asked. "Valentina has an ice bucket of non-alcoholic drinks, and we brought wine."

"I'd love a glass of white wine. Thanks Ellis."

As Ellis turned to the drinks, Sam walked in carrying a large bakery box.

"Hi, everyone," Sam said, only a little awkwardly.

"Hey," Ellis said. "Nice to see you outside of class."

"Hi, Sam, I'm Annie."

"Hi."

"Gemma, Sam, good to see you both," welcomed Valentina. "Sam, does that need to be refrigerated?"

"Yeah, it's a doberge cake."

"Ooh." Valentina smiled at Sam and took the box inside.

Ellis looked at Annie. "A what cake?"

"Oh Ellis, you just wait. Sam, what a wonderful treat. I haven't had a doberge cake in years," said Annie, pronouncing it "dough bash."

"Me either. It seemed like the right occasion."

"What bakery?" Annie asked.

"Haydel's, of course."

Sam, Gemma and the Morrisons continued their conversation, settling into the chairs under the oaks. A few minutes later, Xavier and a tall Black woman came up the walkway. Valentina heard laughter behind her as she approached her new guests. "Hi, Xavier. It's great that you could come. I'm Valentina," introducing herself to his wife.

"Valentina, thank you for inviting us. This is Bailey."

"Bailey, I'm glad you're here."

"It's good to meet you. Where can I put the *pampoenkoekies*?"

"Oh, the pumpkin fritters! Is it a complicated recipe?"

"They're not hard to make. We used an air fryer this time."

"I've thought about getting one of those. Here, I'll take them—go meet everyone."

Kai walked down the sidewalk with a big smile, carrying a bowl and crackers on a tray. As he drew closer to Valentina and the Richards, Kai put his hand behind his back while bowing slightly. He held out his appetizer saying, "*Mes amis?*"

"Did you make that?" asked Valentina, motioning to his bowl.

"Of course, *Chere*. Any real Cajun knows how to cook. It's pecan cheese spread. The pecans are from our farm, and I toasted them myself."

"Let me see," Valentina teased, and tried a cracker with the dip. "Pretty good, Kai."

"*T'es très belle ce soir.*"

"Ah, *merci*, Kai. *Pardon*," Valentina said as she walked up the steps to her apartment.

At that moment, Tala came up the path, followed by Leo with his hands full of bottles of beer and French bread. Valentina turned as she heard everyone say hello, feeling Leo's intense gaze from across the patio. She smiled. He looked back steadily, then smiled and nodded. Kai watched their non-verbal interaction, a calculating expression crossing his face. Tala took her fruit salad and Leo's French bread to the table, where Sam was pouring a glass of wine.

"Hello, Ms. Vardeh."

Smiling, she said, "Since we are not in class, perhaps you could call me Tala?"

Sam grinned. "Hi, Tala."

"Why don't you go sit with the others," said Valentina, shooing them off to join Ellis, Annie and Gemma under the oaks, their branches lit by hanging lights. Turning back to get the wine and drinks, she found Leo at her elbow.

"Hey, Leo. I'm glad you could make it."

"Me too. Your patio is amazing. Did you do all the flowers?"

"This is the Valentina Sorelli home for unwanted and withered flora. Winslow updates their beds periodically, and the employees can take home what can't be used or what's on death's door."

"It's amazing."

"Thanks, I love to garden. Were you working in the lab today?

"Nah, I was out on the water for a few hours to take samples. We left a few mites for your next fishing trip."

"Oh, well, thanks. Let's bring these drinks over to everyone."

Valentina relaxed as the conversation flowed. She learned Bailey was working in the Peace Corps in South Africa when she first met Xavier. He was assigned there for several months with the Marines. They were both on leave when they found each other on the beach in Cape Town.

Tala was from the Middle East and emigrated to the U.S. a few years previous. After all her travels, she wanted to have a role in addressing the problems she saw across the world, particularly food insecurity. She hoped to work in research for one of the international seed banks, like CGIAR. Gemma's focus was medical school. She enrolled in the graduate program to improve her grade-point average because she had had a little too much fun during her first year in college.

When there was a lull in their discussion, Valentina asked, "Anybody ready for gumbo?"

"At last!" Ellis cheered.

"Everyone go in and help yourself. You should see everything you need by the stove."

After a few minutes, they settled around the table on the patio where Valentina had placed a low vase filled with late-season camellias. Leo entertained everyone with his day on the boat. He had a new grad student helper, who fell in the water while trying to get a sample. He said, "I'm lucky he can swim. And there was time for me to take a shower."

"I think we're the lucky ones!" Kai laughed.

"You too could have experiences like these if you changed your graduate program to aquatics and marine biology."

"Yay, Aqua Man!" exclaimed Gemma.

"Valentina, this is perfect," said Ellis.

"Ellis is in his happy place," Annie said. "The man can't get enough gumbo. We're going to have to learn how to fix it ourselves."

"I could teach you," said Valentina.

"Be careful what you say, I may take you up on that," Ellis warned.

"Valentina, if you have a cooking class, I want to come," said Gemma.

"Okay! But for now, I'm going to get the dessert. Sam brought a fabulous doberge cake." Valentina headed back to her apartment, and Leo jumped up to help. As they walked inside together, he held the door for Valentina.

"Are you enjoying yourself?" Leo asked.

"I really am. I like our class. Are you?" Valentina asked.

"Enjoying myself? Very much. It's nice to see you on your home turf. Everyone is having a nice time."

"I'm glad you could come."

"I'm looking forward to spending more time with you this summer."

"That would be great. Until then, here's the cake. As good as a date."

Leo looked at Valentina and said, "We're going to have to find that out."

"Here, can you bring that out? I've got the plates and forks."

"Got it."

Everyone wanted a piece of the "dough bash" cake.

"Sam, this is incredible!" Ellis almost swooned over the doberge cake. "Annie, you've been holding out on me." It was a half-and-half cake, six layers of chocolate on one side and lemon-filled buttermilk cake on the other, both with custard filling and icing.

"If we want to eat like this, you've got to come to the gym with me," Annie said.

"This I have not come across in my travels," Tala said. "It is excellent, Sam."

"Doberge cakes are original to New Orleans. That's probably why you've never run across them," Sam said. "How long have you been here?"

"Only a year."

Tala and Sam continued their conversation with apparent enjoyment. After dessert, the class migrated with their glasses back to the chairs under the trees, talking softly in small groups.

Sam broached the idea of a beach party. "Would anyone be interested in an after finals celebration in Santa Rosa? My parents have a beach house there we could use. There's plenty of room for everyone."

"You're thinking of the third weekend in May?" asked Gemma.

"Yeah," Sam said.

"That sounds stupendous," Gemma said. "Is there room for partners?"

Sam looked confused for a minute, then said, "Sure."

"That's a nice idea, Sam. We could all bring food," Leo offered.

"I love the beach," Valentina said. "I'm in."

"I'll make that work," Kai added.

"Beach time ...those are magic words for Bailey. We're in," Xavier said.

Annie looked at Ellis, who shrugged. "The Panhandle was on our list of things to do this year," she reminded him.

"We'd like to come, if you don't mind a couple of old geezers tagging along."

"It wouldn't be the same without you," Sam told Ellis. He looked at Tala.

"I would like to come," Tala said.

A relaxed conversation continued. Valentina went to sit near Ellis. Before it got too late, she wanted to ask him about Will's pictures.

"Ellis, would you mind looking at a few photos? My cousin took pictures of debris he found in his field, and we've been trying to figure out what it is. My grandpa thinks it looks like pieces of a model plane kit."

"Sure, Valentina," Ellis said. "Is this what you started to ask me earlier?"

"Yeah. My cousin, Will, lives in Nebraska. He has a weird problem with his crops. Here, let me send them to your phone."

Ellis studied the pictures then suggested, "Why don't we pull Xavier in on this, okay?"

Valentina looked confused.

"Xavier worked in aviation when he was in the service."

"That's right. Okay, sure." Valentina called, "Hey, Xavier, got a sec?"

Xavier walked over. "Whatcha got?"

"We want to call on your military experience. Didn't you work in aviation?" Ellis asked.

"I was a UAV operator."

When Valentina seemed puzzled, Xavier said, "Unmanned Aerial Vehicle—I operated drones in the Marines."

"Wow. Let me forward these pictures."

Ellis continued looking at his cell. "This is pretty interesting. Look at this one, right here," he said, gesturing. "You see how the piece bends outward? That looks like part of a propeller."

Xavier's phone pinged as he received the pictures from Valentina. "Which one are you looking at, the second one?"

"Yeah."

"Take a look at the first one, Ellis. The bit to the far right. You think it could be part of a flight controller?"

"Does he have anything for scale?"

Valentina looked through her pictures. "There's one I didn't send. He got a shoe in the frame. Would that help?"

"Yeah."

"Sent."

"Look at the fourth pic. I think that's part of a motor mount." Xavier said.

"Yep. In the foreground of the first picture, you think that's a piece of an antenna?"

"Could be." He and Ellis continued to scan the photographs, murmuring to each other. They lapsed into a technical jargon Valentina didn't understand. After a minute, they both looked up.

"Valentina, we think these are the remnants of a UAV or drone explosion," Ellis said. "Where did your cousin find them?"

"His friend's wheat field. Maybe kids?"

"Maybe a hobbyist," Xavier said. "Pretty expensive equipment for kids."

"What makes you say that?" Valentina asked. "I thought drones were pretty cheap."

"Not this baby. Some of the material looks like carbon fiber composite," said Xavier.

When Valentina still looked uncertain, Ellis explained. "That's not something you typically see in a birthday present for little Joey. It would cost a pretty penny."

"Okay. I'll pass that on to my cousin." Valentina nodded thoughtfully. "Thanks, guys. I've taken enough of your time with this. Let's get back to the party."

While Ellis left to refresh everyone's drinks, Xavier turned to Valentina, "Let me know if you want me to look into this further. I have some buddies who could pin the parts down. And Ellis has some Fort Worth connections where he worked before. What's going on with your cousin?" Xavier asked.

"Will has been farming in Nebraska for the last couple of years. He and his buddy Mitch both graduated from LSU in agriculture. Things were going really well, but a strange bug hit all their fields at once. It seems really weird. Thanks, Xavier. I'll tell him what you said."

"Okay, not a problem."

Lost in thought, Valentina grabbed a chair between Kai and Leo. "Everything okay?" Leo asked.

"Mm-hmm, thanks."

"Have you heard anything about your grant applications?"

"Jamison Botanical asked for an in-person presentation, which means we're in the semi-finals."

"That's fantastic, Valentina. How did it go?"

"My boss, Dee, met with them a few weeks ago. The only time they had available was the same day as our gala, and I was involved in the prep. She thought it went pretty well, so fingers crossed."

Leo toasted her with his beer. "Fingers crossed."

At that moment, Ellis and Annie got up from their chairs. "Valentina, everyone, this has been exceptional. Annie has to work tomorrow, so we're going to head home. Don't get up, you guys. We'll bring in some of the dishes as we leave."

"I've got to get going too. I'll help." Gemma started gathering glasses and dishes.

"I must leave now too," Tala said.

"It's time to call it a night," agreed Leo. "Valentina, thank you so much."

Everyone carried in the debris, echoing Leo's thanks. Gemma rinsed all the plates and bowls while Leo checked the patio for forgotten dishes and silverware.

"I'm glad we did this. Thank you all for coming."

Good nights sounded across the yard and sidewalk. Sam was the last to leave. "Oh, Sam, I'll go get the rest of your cake."

"You keep it. It's just me at the house, and I don't need to eat it by myself."

"I'll take some to my grandparents. Thanks, Sam."

"I appreciate you putting this together. It was magic. I'll start working on that class beach trip after finals."

"I'd love that. Be safe going home."

"Good night, Valentina."

After Sam left, Valentina sat with her glass of wine under the oaks. The air was cool across her skin. She'd throw everything in the dishwasher in a bit. She needed to process what she learned from Ellis and Xavier.

It was too late to call Will tonight. She wasn't sure what she would tell him. How about—my new friends think a drone exploded in your friend's field. Not just any old drone, a fancy drone. They have a lot of experience with, what's the word? Rotorcraft, and they think the one in Mitch's field was expensive, possibly military grade. That was going to go over well—ha.

Valentina consciously made herself step back from her worry over Will. She thought about her party, which she loved. Whether it was only luck or coincidence, Valentina felt she was making real friends. The class discussions were about issues she cared about. Sam was sweet. She thought about Kai and Leo, different and both appealing. Kai was charismatic, but there was something about Leo, a lightness to him with a simmering intensity. She felt as though she'd known him a long time. Valentina reminded herself she didn't need to do anything but could see what developed. She had dated, but never felt that connected to anyone. This was different. Anticipation, even excitement, that she hadn't experienced in the past. She wanted to get to know both of them better. Whether either would become more, she told herself sternly, it was too soon to tell. Finishing her wine, Valentina walked up the steps to her apartment—time to call it a night.

CHAPTER 21

Valentina had set an alarm to catch Will before he left the house.

"Hey."

"Hey yourself."

"How are your folks?"

"They're doing okay. I haven't talked to them about the virus yet."

"So, your bug is a virus?"

"Yeah. Wheat streak mosaic virus, to be precise. There's also a little high plains virus mixed in, and who knows what the else. The testing came back from the Extension service. They're calling it a virus complex. We're plowing everything under."

"Oh, Will."

"This was supposed to be our year. We had two okay seasons, and we made mistakes. This year, we did everything right. It came out of the blue."

"Isn't farming like that?"

"Not like this, Valentina. Not like this. When I told you it was the whole county, I wasn't exaggerating. Every single farm around here has lost all their wheat and sweet corn. We found mite damage in the kitchen garden too. The old-timers have never seen anything like it."

"Those pictures you gave me, I showed them to two of my classmates."

"Why in the world would you do that? Letting them know that your stupid cousin is a farming disaster?"

Reminding herself that he was under a lot of pressure, Valentina said, "Come on, Will. I'm trying to help. There are two guys in my class who worked in aviation. One of them, Ellis, is an engineer and worked at Bell Helicopter in Fort Worth. Xavier is the other guy. He was a pilot of UAVs or drones in the Marines. They think that the pieces in Mitch's field are from a drone that exploded."

"What do kids playing with model kits and firecrackers have to do with anything?"

"Maybe nothing. But Xavier, the pilot, said that wasn't an ordinary drone. From what he and Ellis could see of the material in the pictures, it was an expensive piece of equipment, not something that a kid could access. Possibly a hobbyist with a lot of cash. They think they see a burn pattern. At least some parts are a carbon fiber composite."

"I can't see how it's related, Valentina. I appreciate what you're trying to do, but leave it be."

"Okay, cuz. You know what I know now. I've sent you an email with notes on what they think the pictures represent."

"Valentina ... thanks. This is hard. Sorry I was short with you. I have a meeting with the bank today, and I'm waiting to hear from Ian, our insurance guy. When I have more information, I'll call."

"I'm here for you. Whatever you need."

"That's a two-way street. I'll talk to you soon."

•　　•　　•

After ending the call, Will thought about what Valentina said about the drone. He read her email about the pictures on his phone. She wanted him to do what? Post them on Facebook—Oh, Valentina, have you lost your mind? After staring too long at the photos, he sent Mitch a text before he left for the bank.

You still have those plastic pieces we found?

Think so. Probably on my workbench.

Hang on to them. I'm going to come by on my way back from town.

Ok

Will called, "Hey Suse, I'm heading into town. We need anything?"

"No, I don't think so."

Once she learned of the crop loss, Susan shifted into austerity mode. She had grown up poor and knew how to stretch a dollar. Will doubted she would say they needed anything from town ever again. Will kissed her goodbye.

"I'm going to take your car. It uses less gas. It's going to be okay."

"I know, honey."

Susan worked from home as a medical bill coder. She entered codes for medical diagnoses and treatment into a computer program, so that health care professionals could get reimbursed. Following her training and certification, Susan worked in a large hospital for a few years. Once they moved to the farm, Susan began working from home. Once in a while, she had to make a trip to Omaha for a meeting. There was flexibility in her work hours, as long as she got the job done. Unfortunately, they'd have to depend on her salary and Susan had contacted her company to ask for extra work. Luckily, another coder recently left, so plenty of overtime was available. Although grateful, Will didn't like that she needed to carry all the weight for a while.

Driving Susan's eleven-year-old Corolla into town, Will dreaded the meeting with the loan officer. If things were as bad as he was hearing, the bank might be in trouble too. He and Susan worked through all the math, and they could manage a reduced payment on their note. He hoped it would be enough.

When he walked into the lobby, a clerk with a serious expression greeted him. "Mr. Torino, please have a seat. I'll let Ms. Franklin know you're here."

A few minutes later, a middle-aged, professionally dressed woman with direct green eyes approached. "Will Torino?"

"That's me."

"I remember you," she said. "I'm Sarah Franklin. We met some time ago."

"That's right, Ms. Franklin. It was almost three years ago that I applied for the loan to buy the old Jennings farm."

"Caleb ran a good operation."

"It's a great place to live, Ms. Franklin."

"Call me Sarah. Please come into my office."

It was a plain office, filled by a desk and a few chairs. A small painting of a farm at twilight, a glow surrounding the house in a darkening sky, hung on the wall. Sarah sat behind her desk where one folder rested next to her computer. She motioned to the chairs. "Make yourself comfortable."

"Will, you asked for this meeting to talk about your loan. What can I do for you?"

"A virus infected our crops, and we've lost both our wheat and sweet corn. I'd like to restructure our loan. My wife and I, we went through the numbers and would like you to consider a smaller monthly payment. We understand it would add time to the life of the loan." Will took a piece of paper from his pocket and unfolded a spreadsheet he and Susan had put together.

"Here, let me see that."

Sarah studied the spreadsheet for a minute. She opened the folder on her desk, and entered information on her keyboard.

Will waited an eternity.

Sarah looked up. "We can work with this. You've never been late on a payment. We'll make the necessary changes. We'll roll in the closing costs so you won't have out-of-pocket expenses to refinance."

"Whew. I can't tell you how relieved I am."

"Me too. I've had a lot of meetings in the last week or so, and some of them haven't gone as well. You crunched the numbers and have a plan. To be candid, we've had a few defaults."

"It's not time to give up."

"I'll get the paperwork together. Do I have your email address?" She looked through her folder. "Here it is. I'll shoot you a note when we're ready for you to come in and sign."

"Thank you very much. I appreciate your understanding."

Sarah walked with him to the door of her office. "I grew up on a small farm, Will. It's not an easy life. It's one we want to support."

Will left the bank, feeling his shoulders relax for the first time in days. Several minutes later, Will arrived at Mitch's farm. Erin's car wasn't there.

"Hey, Mitch!" Will called as he unfolded his legs from the old Toyota. As much as he appreciated the reliability and gas mileage, he wished it was twice its size.

"In the barn," Mitch yelled.

He found Mitch working on his tractor. "Frozen clutch?"

"Yeah, almost done. Can you move the C-clamp?"

"You want me to try the pedal?" Will asked, as Mitch moved the drain pan out of the way.

"Sure, let's see if it works."

Mitch took a swig from his water bottle and watched with satisfaction as the clutch pedal moved.

"Where's Erin?"

"She drove into town."

"I must have just missed her."

"How did it go at the bank?"

Will jumped off the tractor. "They agreed to refinance."

"Amazing."

"Have I thanked you already for talking me out of getting that new tractor?"

"About ten times. We both should thank Norris. The first thing he asked me was, 'Do you know how to fix a computer?' when I thought about buying one. Then he said, 'Even if you can, it would void the manufacturer's warranty. And if you depend on the manufacturer to fix it, you'll be waiting a week for them to come out in the middle of planting.' You know how he looks at you when you're thinking of doing something really stupid, like you have three heads?"

"I have to confess I am familiar with that particular Norris expression." Will laughed.

"So, I went online and read more about those fancy tractors. A broken piece of electronics could have shut me down in a heartbeat, and I wouldn't be able to fix it myself. The last thing Norris asked me was how I'd like having a $400,000 slick-looking piece of junk stuck in my field," Mitch recalled.

"Ouch," Will said.

"I'm grateful, believe me. I just wish it wasn't so painful."

"Mitch, I don't want to hold you up, and I've gotta get back. Do you have those plastic pieces?"

"My hands are a mess, so help yourself. Look on the workbench. I put them in that paper bag. What are you going to do with them?"

"Valentina called me this morning. She knows a couple of guys who worked in aviation and showed them the pictures. Get this—they think these plastic bits are part of a drone that exploded. And the material probably is a carbon fiber composite which is really expensive. I'm going to post them on that Facebook group for farmers. It's worth checking to see if anybody else found anything. A stretch, but ... who knows? What do I have to lose?"

"Only a little time," agreed Mitch.

"That and my reputation for being more or less normal. I should call it a flying saucer and we can get our own UFO museum."

Mitch guffawed. "Let's visit soon. I know Erin would love to see Susan."

"Looking forward to it. We'll put something on the grill."

"Okay, man. I'll catch up with you later."

•   •   •

When he got home, Will spread out the pieces on the kitchen table. Using his phone, he took several more pictures. Feeling more than a little foolish, Will uploaded the pictures to his computer. When he opened the farmer's Facebook site, Will saw more than 40 posts about total crop failure from all over the Midwest. It wasn't only happening in his county or southeastern Nebraska. Anywhere winter wheat grew, farmers were experiencing the same problem. It had the potential to be a national emergency. There was a post from Canada. Considering the amount of wheat exported, it could be an international disaster. Wasn't anybody looking at this? Not most farmers, who were usually too busy to eat lunch, much less check out Facebook. Will posted the pictures with the heading, "Possible Drone Crash in Failed Wheat Field," and asked if anyone had found anything similar. Will turned off the computer. This couldn't be a coincidence. Something was off.

CHAPTER 22

On Monday, Valentina arrived at the fountain to meet Amy and stretched as she waited. Amy's car skidded to a stop and she leapt from her car. "Good morning," Valentina called.

"Hey."

"I have doberge cake for you." Valentina said as they started jogging, "In an ice chest in my car."

"From your party? Be still my heart. We should run two laps today."

"Not a bad idea."

"Who brought the doberge cake?"

"Sam."

"Of course. The Sam who has the beach house and wants to take you to dinner at my favorite Italian restaurant. That Sam. Can you introduce me to this guy?"

"I took some cake to Mia and Dean when I returned their table and chairs. They offered to rent them to me next weekend for more doberge."

"How was the party?"

"Everyone seemed to have a good time. One thing I enjoyed is that Sam and Tala got to know one another a bit. They come from such different backgrounds. They're always talking past each other in class. Tala's had interesting experiences. She's originally from Afghanistan and worked as an interpreter in the Middle East during the Iraq War."

"Wow. Do you think she might be open to giving a presentation? We're trying to introduce global awareness to kids at all levels in the curriculum."

"She might. I think she would enjoy helping other people understand or at least be open to other cultures. I'll ask. If she's interested, I'll do an introduction. I'm not sure what her time commitments are besides school, but she's an effective speaker in class."

"Great, let me know."

"You know, Xavier's wife worked in South Africa in the Peace Corps," Valentina said. "Would you be interested in contacting her, too?"

"Definitely! That would be fantastic."

Neither spoke for a few minutes as they run.

"Sooooo, Valentina," Amy said with exaggerated slowness and a wicked smile. "Let's talk about the two elephants in the room, er, park. How did it go with Kai and Leo?"

"Well, Amy." Valentina smirked. "Pretty well. How was your weekend?"

"Oh, come on!"

Valentina laughed. "They were both fun. We flirted a little. Leo told funny stories and Kai was adorable. I can't say who I like more, or if anything will happen, but I'm having a great time."

"Good enough."

"How was your date with Charlie, the lawyer?" Valentina asked.

"Please, *Charles*, not *Charlie*. That's kind of how it was, a date with a lawyer. Not so fun, not so adorable. He was more impressed with himself than I was. A little controlling."

"Oh, well."

"Yeah, oh well," agreed Amy.

They jogged for several more minutes before Amy asked, "Any news from Will?"

"I talked to him yesterday. He's refinancing their loan, and Susan is doing a lot of overtime. At least for now, they'll be okay."

"Do they have any idea what caused the crop failure?"

"Besides the wheat virus? No, it's strange. Remember how I told you about those plastic bits he and Mitch found in the field? I showed Will's pictures to Ellis and Xavier, the aviation guys from class. They think they were from a military grade drone."

"A drone?"

"Yeah, an expensive drone. Anyway, there's a Facebook group for farmers, so Will posted them there. He's going to check back in a few days to see if anyone else has found anything like that."

"That is strange."

"He saw posts from other farms with the same type of crop failure across the Midwest."

"Even stranger."

Just then, they heard someone call, "Hey, Amy!" They turned back to see who it was. A fit, muscular man jogged up to them.

Amy looked surprised and not altogether pleased. "Oh hi, Charles."

"What luck. I never thought I'd run into the two of you. You must be Valentina," he said. "Amy told me you jog some mornings at the park."

Amy looked at Valentina with a flat expression. "Valentina, this is Charles Emerson. He and I met during my appointment with the city's human resource department."

Valentina started to ask, "Oh, was that for the job skills training ..."

Charles interrupted. "With my position in the city's legal department, it was critical that I be there. And then I saw Amy, representing Parish Schools. She looked so cute at the meeting."

Valentina heard Amy make a choking sound.

"Do you ever use the fitness stations on the perimeter?" Charles asked. "It would make your fitness routine more productive."

"Charles, Valentina and I use this time to catch up with each other."

Ignoring the hint, Charles jogged alongside Amy. "You could get your cardio and strength building in during the same session. It would really tone your arms."

"I'll put it on my list," Valentina said, wondering who would talk like that besides a personal trainer.

Charles smiled with satisfaction and told Valentina, "We had our first date last night." He looked down with affection at Amy. Their run had taken them back to the fountain, where several people were talking or warming up before a run.

Amy looked at Valentina and said, "Why don't you let me visit with Charles for a bit here at the fountain? I'll catch up with you later."

Charles preened.

"Sure, Amy." Valentina left for her car, which was parked less than a block away. As she drove away, Valentina decided to circle around the park to make sure Amy was okay. More likely, she would need to call the paramedics for Charles once Amy finished with him. As she made the turn again onto St. Charles Avenue, Valentina saw Amy about to reach her car. She pulled over, and Amy walked over.

"Everything okay?"

"Yep." Amy said emphatically.

"I see why you like him."

"Can't you just? See you next week," Amy said. "Without Charles."

"Oh shucks."

Valentina started to drive away. "Wait! Your cake!"

"Darn that Charles. He almost made me miss my doberge."

"But we didn't let that happen."

"That's right."

•　　•　　•

After a quick shower, Valentina left for Winslow. She always enjoyed the drive from her apartment. She took different routes, sometimes down Carrollton, other times she found her way through smaller neighborhood streets. Each block was different. Prim, traditional homes painted white with dark green shutters stood right next door to splashes of Caribbean blues, greens and orange. Valentina loved the deep porches, the ceilings painted pale blue, some with ceiling fans and striped awnings for warm summer days.

Valentina walked through the gates to her small office. She powered up her computer and checked her inbox. With the gala wrapped up, Valentina was focusing on Winslow's routine events, like Wednesdays at Winslow. Every Wednesday evening, they held performances by local musicians in the sculpture garden. She was glad to see a confirmation email from the musicians for the upcoming Wednesday. The events were well attended and becoming more popular. Although it meant she worked late, Valentina loved introducing the performers and welcoming the audience. The music seemed to float up from the low stage, past the elegant art déco statues, and into the oak trees. She sent a quick reminder to Renny in Maintenance, and Beth with Catering. It was a simple event. Renny's crew put out chairs, and Beth rolled out a beverage cart. Valentina arranged for two different food trucks each week, and they gave the park a small percentage of their sales. Between that and the small admission fee, Wednesdays at Winslow supported small local entrepreneurs and made a little revenue for the park. Sometimes, they partnered with local chefs, restaurants, or neighborhood associations.

A plant sale was two weeks from Saturday. Valentina checked that her posts on all the social media platforms were online for both events. Winslow was listed in the calendar of events for the *Times Picayune* and with other local publications like *Gambit* and *New Orleans Magazine*. She placed public service announcements on local radio and tv stations.

Registrations were coming along nicely for the summer camp program. A local teacher, Karyn Meyers, had directed the program for the last five years. Valentina would meet with Dee and Karyn on Friday to finalize the camp counselor positions.

A note from Dee popped up on her computer. "Come see me." Valentina grabbed her tablet and walked over to Dee's office, where Dee was typing madly on her computer while talking on the phone. Valentina stood at the door waiting, enjoying the view through the large open windows. It was a beautiful spring day, cool enough in the morning that they didn't need air conditioning yet.

"Are you ready for this?" Startled, Valentina realized Dee had finished her call and was directing her formidable energy her way.

"Sure, what's up?"

"Come in. Have a seat. You should be sitting down when you hear this."

"Umm, do I still have a job?" Valentina asked half facetiously.

"I think you have two jobs. Valentina, we got it. I just got a call from Naomi Ruli. Jamison picked Winslow and four other programs. We'll get the official Notice of Award in the next few days. It's for $60,000 over a three-year period."

Valentina sank back in her chair, shocked. In her wildest dreams, Valentina hadn't expected that. Once Dee bought into Valentina's idea for a Winslow seed bank, she was all in. Many first-time applicants didn't get funded, but they had done their homework, and it helped. They also learned that getting an award was only the beginning. Administering a grant was a lot of work.

Dee immediately shifted into planning mode. "We'll need a press release. Before that, we need to send Jamison a thank-you letter. Let's get that done first. We should notify the board. The chair may want to make the announcement personally. In fact, why not see if one of the TV stations will give you a few minutes? We have to let our partner schools know, Valentina. Put that on your list. Do you know where you'll purchase the refrigerated storage unit? I'd like to see a schedule for the seed bank, which plants, when the seeds for each need to be harvested, you know. And let's talk about record keeping."

Valentina sat back in her chair, speechless.

"Valentina?"

"I can't believe it."

"You came up with a creative idea, and we put it together. Now we have to deliver. You have about," Dee looked at her watch, "five minutes to be flabbergasted. Then let's get busy."

"Yes, ma'am."

"Go back to your office and write the thank-you letter and the press release. Naomi will send an acceptance letter for me to sign with the funding agreement and specific grant guidelines. Come back in two hours with a very general outline for implementation. It's not enough money to hire a full-time staff person. Maybe we bring on a part-timer, or buy a little guidance from our boot camp consultants. Think about our in-house strengths and what we might need. Remember accountability, record keeping, reporting." Dee continued, ticking points off on her fingers. She grinned. "Be careful what you wish for. See you back here at noon. I'll order lunch."

Valentina walked back to her office in a daze. She called Mia and got her voice mail. She sent a quick text instead. *We got the grant!!!* For a split second, she thought about texting Amy, or maybe Leo or Kai, and didn't. Then Valentina got to work.

After drafting the letter, Valentina worked on her plan for implementation. She left messages for her school contacts. Since they both taught classes, she didn't expect to hear from them until the end of the day. Valentina prepared a press release to send to the producers at all the news stations. Jamison had a grant management officer, Liz Wilder, who would supervise their reporting and release of funds. Valentina decided Liz would become her new bestie. She reviewed the application they submitted in depth, and the emails back and forth. She went to Jamison's website to commit to memory the general guidelines and the discussion of grant sanctioned activities. With a basic framework beginning to come together in her head, Valentina started her outline. Some time later, Valentina heard a noise and looked up. Dee was standing in her doorway.

"Do you want to eat today?"

Valentina paused for half a second. "Yes! I'm starving. What time is it?"

"Two o'clock. Come on."

"You have food?"

"Girl, what do you think? Although if you don't hurry, maybe not." Dee twirled her graceful but ample figure, heading back to her office.

Valentina grabbed her laptop and notes then tore after her boss. "What's for lunch?"

"Vietnamese," Dee tossed the word over her shoulder.

"Mopho?" Valentina loved Asian food, and Mopho was one of the best neighborhood restaurants. It was close enough to the park to meet friends after work as a special treat.

"You deserve it. But you know what I'm going to ask you after lunch?"

"Something along the lines of 'What have you done for me lately?'"

"You got it."

"I have some ideas."

CHAPTER 23

At 7 am, Jack Stillman was on his third cup of coffee at the Landever office in Indianapolis. Jack always got a lot done in the morning before the papers arrived. He reviewed and responded to everything in his inbox, except for a couple of items requiring a more in-depth response. For instance, Stephen Angus was still pestering him about the accident in his lab. That was months ago. Angus couldn't understand why it had been necessary to dispose of his mites. The storage compartments of the state-of-the-art freezing equipment were gone. What did Jack mean that he was "not optimistic" that he would be able to get authorization for an entirely new unit from Landever's board. Throwing a few research bucks to Angus had pacified him for only a little while.

Jack thought back to his early morning visit to Angus's lab. In place of the purloined mites, Jack substituted freezer containers filled with rotting insects. Workers from nearby work stations and labs discovered the mess by the foul smell coming from the unplugged freezer, presumably the decay of thousands and thousands of mites. They blamed the cleaning crew. No doubt their cart accidentally dislodged the electrical plug in the outlet. Naturally, everything had to be thrown out, quickly too, in the fetid air. No one had wanted to examine the containers too closely, or took the time to notice they were cheap imitations of the original, specially designed equipment.

Jack had reminded Angus that he was one of the few entomologists to preserve mites in a laboratory setting that were viable after freezing. Angus automatically corrected Jack's description of his research method, explaining again he had used cryopreservation. Cryopreservation or cryoconservation was a specialized process allowing flash freezing of materials. Angus used liquid nitrogen to prevent enzymatic or chemical activity that would have damaged the mites or allowed ice crystals to form.

And yes, Angus agreed. He did groundbreaking research. Besides his lab, there was only one other that successfully froze mites, and those were adult red velvet mites, *Allothrombium*. In a natural setting, only one or two known mite populations survived freezing, but that was in permafrost. Jack said that should be worth an article or two in the scientific journals, at least. Angus had all his original notes and research data, didn't he?

Angus admitted grudgingly that accidents happen. But he raised a lot of annoying questions. In his latest email, Angus ranted about Landever's reluctance to fund the replication of his original research—they could purchase a used cryopreservation machine for less than $30,000. Jack planned to tell Angus that he'd do his best to convince the board. He'd find a few more dollars to throw his way and Angus would go back to burrowing in his lab.

With that settled, Jack began his daily perusal of the news. He was old-fashioned and liked the newspapers delivered each morning. Of course, he used online publications, but there was nothing like reading an actual newspaper. He checked the papers at least once a day for any mention of crop failure. Today, at last, a small item.

Crop Watch—Indiana Farms

Wheat streak mosaic virus (WSMV) has been spotted in several communities across Indiana. Aceria tosichella, commonly known as the wheat curl mite, is a vector for viruses adversely affecting wheat and a number of other cereal grains. WCM can transmit four separate viruses: wheat streak mosaic virus, high plains wheat mosaic virus, Brome streak mosaic virus, and Triticum mosaic virus. The Department of Agriculture asks growers to pay particular attention to symptoms of crop infection, which include yellowing as well as rolled and trapped leaves. Prevention is the only weapon against this pest. Heavy crop losses are feared. Contact your Extension office for further updates.

Jack smiled and leaned back in his $5,000 executive chair. He pulled out his cell phone, put his feet up on his absurdly expensive desk, and called his stockbroker. Now that he had the USDA's World Agricultural Supply and Demand Estimates, he wanted to discuss grain futures. Time to leverage his future gains.

•　　•　　•

That same day, long into the evening, in the oldest section of Landever's multi-block complex, Stephen Angus sat quietly in his entomology lab. Out of sorts, unsettled, just like the equipment area, unbalanced by the missing freezers.

CHAPTER 24

When she left work on Friday, Valentina had a bucket of discarded plants. Renny's crew pulled out last season's hangers-on, cut back the star jasmine, and divided their crinum lilies. Valentina had a few spots in mind for all of them. On Saturday morning, she pulled on her baggy gardening pants and an old T-shirt. Although a lot of her yard was shady, there were pockets of dappled sunlight where the newbies could grow. Valentina was well into the planting when her phone pinged with a text. She pulled off one of her gardening gloves to grab the phone. It was Leo.

May I stop by?

Having anticipated this moment, Valentina didn't need to wonder any longer whether it would happen. That it arrived didn't mean anything, other than that things would change. She was on the brink of something new and laughed a little.

Sure. I'm in the back—come in through the gate.

A few minutes later, Leo walked through the gate under the tree canopy.

"Hey. Nice to see you," Valentina said.

"Good to see you. You look comfortable."

Valentina looked down and remembered she was wearing the oldest, least flattering clothing she owned. Too late. But Leo didn't look too put together either. He was wearing cargo pants that were a little damp and a Saints football jersey that had seen better days.

"So do you."

"I'm a mess. I've just come from an early morning trip on the lake. I brought you something." Leo opened a bag filled with bulbs with long thin leaves and a few deep blue flowers attached. "They were growing by the edge of the water. I thought you might like some iris. You didn't seem to have any."

"I love blue iris. They're probably *Iris brevicaulis*," Valentina said. "Do you think I've got enough sun?"

"Mm hmm, come see." Leo tugged on Valentina's glove and pulled her toward the back fence, far from the outstretched limbs of the oaks and the crape myrtles, where only the milkweed grew. "There's sun right here. And see how damp the ground is? There's a slight depression. Your yard and the neighbor's slope toward each other. I noticed the other night when I was looking for stray glasses. This must be swamp milkweed, otherwise it wouldn't like to be as wet."

Looking down at the bulbs, Valentina said, "Let's give you a new home, hmm?" She took a few from Leo, who knelt down beside her. "I've got an extra trowel on the steps. Why don't we do it together?"

"I'll be glad to do that."

"How far apart should they be?"

"About a foot. They'll multiply, so if you move, you can take some with you."

Valentina looked around. "They'll fit right in. My yard is the second or third home for most of the plants here. The park updates the beds most seasons, and our maintenance chief, Renny, is constantly thinning or cutting things back. A few of us like to garden, so he puts things aside for us."

"Nice. Your yard is beautiful."

"My grandmother is always giving me cuttings, too. I covet her roses, but there's too much shade."

As they planted the bulbs, Valentina recognized a quiet contentment, as warm as the sunlight on her shoulders and back. It felt right. They started at opposite ends of the back fence, digging small holes in between the milkweed, and slowly worked their way closer.

"I've been here for years," Valentina said. "The apartment isn't much to look at, but I couldn't pass up the yard—well—the trees and the space."

"You'll be able to see the blooms when you're sitting under the trees."

"We have enough bulbs to group them a little. It'll be a big splash of color in the spring. Thanks for thinking of me."

Carefully digging space for another bulb, Leo nodded as he set it gently in place. "You mentioned your grandmother. She's a gardener too?"

"The best. If she sticks a twig in the ground, it'll grow."

They continued planting the bulbs in a comfortable silence.

"Your grandmother is Italian?"

"Mia is Sicilian. There's a difference."

Leo looked at her questioningly.

"Much better cooks, of course."

"Of course."

"She's my rock. After my parents passed away, I lived with my grandparents until I graduated from college."

"That must have been hard."

"Yeah, at first, but it's been a long time. I was pretty young. My mom had cancer and was really sick for a long time, so I had been spending more and more time with my grandparents. A little while after that, my father died. Mia and my grandfather have always been there for me."

"I'm sorry."

"Like I said, it was a long time ago," Valentina paused. "You know, Mia spent her first few years on a farm. It's strange. I never thought to ask Mia much about the farm until recently. There's a long history of small-scale farming in my family, but it must skip a generation here and there. I have a cousin, Will. He farms in southeastern Nebraska. I guess he came by that naturally. Will is more like my brother. We spent a lot of time together growing up and always stayed close."

"What does he grow?"

"At the moment, nothing. All the farms in his area got a virus and they had to plow everything under. I think he's planting alfalfa or clover as a cover crop. He was growing wheat and sweet corn. It's a disaster. I think he called it wheat streak mosaic, or something like that."

"Wow. There're a bunch of different mosaic viruses. They attack fruit, vegetables, grains, you name it."

Not wanting to think more about it, Valentina changed the subject. "How's it going with your research?"

"All consuming, but it's great."

"What do you like most about it?"

Leo leaned back on his heels and looked at Valentina. "It's a chance to figure out what's going on in the estuary. Really, I feel lucky because Dr. Olson bought into my idea, and I'm getting to do original work. Getting paid to be out on the lake doesn't hurt either."

"Nice." Valentina loved how Leo totally focused on her when they talk. She felt his gaze as she continued to plant the iris. "Oh, I haven't had a chance to tell you, we got the grant."

"For the seed bank in the park? Fantastic!"

"I'm still in shock." Valentina shook her head. "It's going to be different. I'm neck deep in documentation, coordination with our partner schools and park personnel, not to mention the plain physical labor getting it all set up."

"You'll make it work." Leo stood up as he looked at his watch. "Valentina, I'm going to have to run."

"Do you want coffee or anything before you head out?"

"I'd love that, but right now, my time isn't my own. I'm going flat out trying to finish my dissertation. I saw the iris earlier this morning and felt compelled to bring you some."

"Compelled, huh?"

"Just know that I'm looking forward to spending more time with you."

"I'll see you in class,"

"See you then." As he started to leave, Leo stepped back toward Valentina and kissed her on the cheek.

"I'm glad you stopped by."

"Me too."

Valentina went back to her gardening. A little while later, another text arrived, this one from Kai. *Oh my goodness.*

Hi, have time for lunch? Valentina looked at the time, 11:30. She couldn't get cleaned up that fast.

Can't, getting together with my girlfriend

What about this evening?

That works

BeauSoleil, one of my favorite Cajun bands, is playing at Tipitina's - want to go?

Love to

Would you like me to pick you up?

Sure

I'll be there around 7

Valentina immediately called Amy, who didn't answer. Still a little stunned, she sent a text: *SOS!*

A couple of minutes later, Amy called. "Hi! What's up?"

"Be still my heart."

"Which one, Leo or Kai?" Amy asked.

"Both! And you and I are spending time together today since I used you as my excuse not to have lunch with Kai because I am a total mess. Instead, we're going to hear BeauSoleil tonight at Tip's."

"Wait, we're going to Tipitina's tonight?" Amy teased.

"Not you, me and Kai!"

"Just kidding. Whatcha going to wear?"

"That is how we're going to spend time together today."

"Shopping?"

"Let's stick with what I have. Remember, one of us is on a budget."

"Okay, I'll see you this afternoon, maybe 5:30?"

"Thanks, Amy. What did I interrupt on your end?"

"Another fascinating conversation with Charles. The guy doesn't take no for an answer."

"Ick. Are you concerned at all?"

"No, Valentina. He's a pissant."

"Okay, see you later."

CHAPTER 25

Will and Susan sat together on the window seat by the kitchen table, finishing their sandwiches. Although he had more plowing to do, Will came back to the house to meet Susan for lunch. She was working such long hours. Will liked to make sure she took a break, even if it was only fifteen minutes.

The kitchen was light gold in the noonday sun. Will loved their old house, with its steep, pitched roof and deep porch. When Mr. and Mrs. Jennings put it up for sale, it needed a lot of small repairs, and a few significant ones the older couple hadn't been able to handle. The first-floor windows leaked and some walls showed water damage. Mitch had helped Will install large insulated windows along the south side. They took down the walls between the kitchen and family room so now a wide open area looked out into the side yard and back garden. Will and Susan refinished the battered wood floors and found colorful rag rugs at yard sales. The Jennings left behind their old drop-leaf table, which stood ready against the interior wall, waiting for family and friends to gather. Will wanted time to stand still. They had been here barely three years and it would break his heart to lose the place.

Susan stood up and stretched. "This has been nice, but I need to get back to it." She reached for their lunch dishes. "It's different to see you in the middle of the day—a good different, of course."

"That's a relief. I've got the dishes—go on." Then he said, "Wait," pulling her close. Will stood with his arms around her for a minute, resting his chin on her shoulder. "Okay."

"Okay," Susan said.

After wiping down the counter, Will started to head to his tractor, then stopped. He hadn't checked Facebook since he posted the pictures of the drone parts. He doubted anyone responded seriously but best to check. Will opened his account and steeled himself to be laughed out of the farming community group. Instead, he was amazed. There were now hundreds of comments about total crop loss. His drone post had garnered eight replies—well, 10 if he counted the two people calling him a nutcase. Two people found parts of propellers, one person had what he thought was an electric motor and another had a battery. Three others had bits and pieces they couldn't identify. *Holy Cow, somebody found an entire drone.*

Will's phone gave off the special ring for family members. It was Valentina. "You were right."

"I am always right."

"No, really. Valentina, somebody found an entire drone," Will said, astonished. "Seven other people found parts like Mitch and I."

"Oh, my goodness! Ellis and Xavier knew what they were talking about."

"They sure did. I posted the pictures about a week ago and checked just now when I came in for lunch. There're probably hundreds of posts about total crop loss."

Valentina couldn't say anything at first. "Will, what does it mean? Do you think drones have anything to do with the crop failures? How can so many people have lost everything they planted?"

"I'm not sure what to think. If it's deliberate, and it's beginning to look that way, who would want to do that?"

"Who has anything to gain?"

"I don't know. The only reason we'll get through this is because of Susan's income. We've been able to refinance. A lot of farmers can't. I think the bank was glad I wasn't there to hand them the keys."

"How is Susan?"

"Working constantly. I'm trying to lighten the load where I can, but I have to get the cover crop planted so we don't have an erosion problem. Susan would normally do the vegetable garden, but I'm doing that. We're grateful her company has the overtime, but she barely has time to sleep. She had just started feeling more comfortable. I hate how this is bringing everything back."

"You mentioned she had a tough time as a kid."

"She did, but that's Susan's story to tell. So, what's up with you?"

"I have a date tonight."

"You're kidding! Wait, I didn't mean that the way it sounded."

"Will, I'm crushed."

"I'm sorry ..." Will began a serious apology, which was interrupted by Valentina's peal of laughter.

"You goof. We both know I've been in the dating desert for a while now."

"From what I hear from Mia, that's been your choice."

"I hadn't met anyone that I wanted to see more than once or twice."

"But now you have?"

"I think so. Actually, I'm interested in—well, curious about—two guys from school."

"You're seeing both of them tonight?" Will joked.

"That would be entertaining. One stopped by earlier and the other asked me out."

"And?"

"The date is with Kai Prejean. He's from a small town in Acadiana. Attractive, confident, a little too confident? The other guy, Leo, I don't know, there's something about him. He came by earlier today. When I'm with him, I feel relaxed and energized at the same time. He's nice, really smart, and a lot of fun."

"Do you have a preference?"

"I'm not sure. Leo doesn't have a lot of time right now because he's working on his dissertation," Valentina said.

"That's not really an answer."

"Well ... being around Kai is exciting."

"Are there any little voices in your head saying, 'Wait a minute' about either one?"

Valentina paused before answering. "It's hard to tell. A couple really loud ones are saying 'Ooh, baby' and 'Let's go.' But as you tactfully pointed out, I haven't dated anyone in a while. Those voices may not be too discriminating."

Will laughed.

"Leo brought me bulbs today."

"Bulbs?"

"Louisiana native iris blues."

Will smiled. "Not so exciting, but Leo seems to know you pretty well. You'll have to keep me posted."

"It's not that Leo isn't exciting, it's ... different."

"What are you and Kai doing tonight?"

"BeauSoleil at Tipitina's."

"Now I'm jealous. That's when I miss New Orleans. You think he can dance?"

"I intend to find out."

"It's good to catch up, but I have to get back to work."

"Hey, one more thought about your drones. Are they regulated?" Valentina asked.

"I don't know. Let me see." Will typed for a minute. "It looks like it's the Federal Aviation Administration, the FAA. They have something called a Drone Zone."

"These are the same folks who monitor commercial aircraft?"

"Right." Will was silent for a minute while he skimmed the website. "It looks as though a drone has to be registered with the FAA if it weighs more than about half a pound. The registration number is supposed to be on the outside of the drone. Let me try that. I'll send a message to the guy that found the intact drone. At this point, there's no connection between the drones and the virus that took out our crops. I don't know if it means anything, but it's worth pursuing."

"Let me know what happens."

"Of course. You pushed me in this crazy direction."

"Love you."

"You too, Valentina."

Before heading outside, Will sent a message to the eight farmers who found drone parts and invited them to join a group so they could communicate directly.

(1) Did any of you see a registration number on the drone or the parts that you found? Drones are supposed to be registered with the FAA.

(2) Has anyone connected the drones to the crop failures?"

Will logged off his Facebook account. His tractor was waiting.

CHAPTER 26

Valentina picked up her gardening tools and swept the patio. Saturday was for chores and errands. She had time to make it to the farmers market and she needed to wash clothes, the floors and her car, not necessarily in that order. Valentina checked in with Mia, who invited her for Sunday dinner, which in the Sorelli family, took place at noon on Sundays.

"Can I bring anything?" Valentina asked.

"How about dessert?"

"You got it. I've been watching a baking show. How about a flourless chocolate cake with a fruit coulis sauce?"

"Goodness, Valentina, I was going to ask you to pick up some ice cream. That sounds wonderful. Any plans for tonight?"

"As a matter of fact, I have a date."

"Really?"

"Between you and Will, a girl could get a complex."

"Is this someone from your class?"

"Mm hmm. A nice Cajun boy, Kai Prejean."

"Tell me about him."

"Let me find out tonight if there's anything to talk about and I'll tell you tomorrow."

"That's a deal. Is Will okay?"

"He is. They were able to refinance and Susan's working a lot of overtime. Look, I'm going to have to run. Let's visit tomorrow."

"Okay, see you then."

Valentina was able to catch the end of the farmer's market. Too late for the tomatoes, she scored some raspberries and fresh eggs. She spent the afternoon cleaning, then hopped into the shower. At 5:30, Amy kicked on her door, clothes draped over each arm.

"Hey."

"Wow, I feel like Cinderella," Valentina said as she opened the door and grabbed some of the clothes.

"Half of these are yours. They need to be repatriated."

"I was wondering where that skirt was. Oh, these are from that weekend for your date with Charles."

"Please, he is ever after to be known simply as the pissant."

"Right. He seems like a real creeper."

"That's because he is a creeper." Amy shuddered. "The other reason I brought all this is because I also have a date tonight, but not with the pissant."

"Cool. You notice I am not acting surprised like my family did when I told them I was going on a date."

"Thank you for that."

"Who is he?"

"His name is Mike Fernandez. He's an adolescent and child psychologist in private practice here. We both had appointments at the State Department of Education in Baton Rouge. We talked and talked. I've never had such a good time in a waiting room. When I was leaving, he was watching for me in the lobby. We swapped contact information and visited a couple of times by phone. Then he asked me to dinner."

"Wow. Where are you going?"

"Big splurge—GW Fins."

"Nice. What's he like?"

"He's smart but doesn't take himself too seriously. It was easy to make each other laugh. I feel alive when I talk with him. Our work is different but there's enough common ground that we appreciate what each other is saying. He's interesting. It's more than that. It's like when you volley the ball and you know it's going to come right back." Amy's eyes sparkled while she talked.

"You haven't said that about anyone in a while."

"Tell me about it. So how did the date come about with Kai?"

"He sent a text this morning. That was after Leo stopped by and we planted iris bulbs that he picked up early this morning."

"It must be love," Amy said, fanning her face.

"I'm easy."

"No, you're transparent, to me anyway. We've known each other forever. How do you feel about Kai?"

"He's exciting to be around."

"So there's chemistry."

Valentina shrugged then nodded.

"Let's look at these clothes." They spent several minutes pulling and trying on clothes from Valentina's closet and Amy's piles.

"I think I want a skirt for Tip's," Valentina said. "Not too short but a flippy skirt, with my low cowboy boots."

"Then wear this skirt, with the white shirt, and your jean jacket," Amy said.

"Not this Tee? Or this one?"

"No, it looks too … something. This is better."

"That works. Okay, now let's go back to you. What about this shift dress? It's a great color for you."

"Too dressy?"

"Not if you wear your platform sandals with it. And some chunky bracelets?"

"Not the jeans?"

"You could. But why not show some leg? The dress is more feminine."

"Okay."

"What are you going to do with your hair?"

"Leave it straight, wear it down."

"Good."

"Yours?"

"I'm going to wear it pulled back and up and let it curl down. It gets warm at Tipitina's. With the humidity, it would get huge if I left it down. See the headlines: Man smothered by date's hair. Bad form."

"I can't argue with that," Amy said.

"It's been a while since both of us had a date on the same Saturday night."

"You think?" Amy said as she separated their clothes.

"Let's not go there." Valentina walked with Amy to the door.

"We'll have lots to talk about on Monday during our run."

"See you then."

"Have fun tonight!"

"You too."

Valentina put everything away and then sat. She really couldn't remember the last time both she and Amy were excited about their dates. Maybe when they were 16?

CHAPTER 27

Valentina's door chimed a little after seven. Okay, deep breath, she told herself. "Hi."

"*Bonsoir, chère.* You look great," Kai said.

"Thanks, so do you." And he did, Valentina thought. Freshly shaved, wearing jeans and a crisp white shirt, Kai topped her height by two or three inches. His dark brown hair was a little damp from his shower. Valentina felt almost blinded by his smile and realized she was grinning just as much. Simmer down, Valentina, she told herself. It wasn't all about chemistry. You don't know this man well. Valentina stepped out and locked the door. They walked to Kai's truck, where he opened the door for Valentina then settled behind the wheel.

"You like BeauSoleil?" Kai asked.

"Love them. I saw them at Jazz Fest a long time ago and have been hooked ever since. I've thought about going to one of their shows in Lafayette, but mostly I try to catch them in New Orleans."

"I heard an interview once with Michael Doucet, the lead singer. He's kind of my musical hero, *mon héros musical.*"

"I know who he is, and I love their music, but that's about it. They've been around a while. Tell me about him."

"Doucet's family is French, and when he was young, he took a trip to France. He recognized the music he heard there as being songs his family and friends play. When he returned to Louisiana, he got grants to find and record a lot of the old French singers here.

Then he transcribed their music. Music from 17th century France that's evolved over time."

"Wow, I had no idea," Valentina said.

"He talked about the culture and how tenacious the Acadians were. You know the story of how the English exiled the French from Canada—well, what's now Nova Scotia. You know many came to Louisiana?"

"Mm hmm."

"Doucet said the music tells a story like the original troubadours. It cuts to the heart, *coupe au coeur*, tells you what's going on. The songs are about friendship, sorrow, and happiness. *L'amitié, la douleur et le bonheur*," Kai said as he touched his chest.

Valentina looked at Kai. "I think I'll listen to them differently now."

They were quiet for a few minutes. Valentina asked, "What other music do you like?"

"Besides Cajun and Zydeco? Almost anything."

"Do you ever go to Jazz Fest?"

"When it doesn't conflict with harvesting crawfish or *Festival International de Louisiane*."

"Kai, you mentioned your mom and aunts before. Do you have a big family?"

"*J'ai une grande famille*," Kai grinned. "Huge. In my immediate family, it's just my parents and a younger sister. *Petite* by Prejean standards. Each of my parents has four siblings, so that makes 16 aunts and uncles and 21 first cousins. Holidays are wild."

"That sounds like a lot of fun. Do you go back and forth from southwest Louisiana every week?"

"Most weekends I do, especially at this time of year. Crawfish harvesting is pretty labor intensive. It's a good thing there're so many of us. For now, until those cousins get older, I go when I can. I have an apartment here with a couple of roommates and stay with my folks when I'm at the farm."

Kai found parking a block from Tipitina's on Napoleon Avenue. They walked under the streetlights that scattered a soft glow through the oak trees. Homes more than a century old lined the block and a group of palm trees centered the median.

"During Carnival, the floats and marching bands organize on Napoleon and Tchoupitoulas," Valentina said. "It's a great place to hang out with family and friends, like a block party on the neutral ground. People bring out their grills and their lawn chairs—and naturally—the kids' ladders to see the parades. I especially like the costumes. Sometimes a whole family wears the same thing, and you'll see ten pink flamingos—all sizes—walking down the street. The best kind of craziness. Have you been to Mardi Gras?"

"I've been, and had a wild time in the French Quarter. A little too wild for me. *Trop fou!* What you're talking about around here sounds nice."

"St. Charles Avenue is like that, too. Lots of families, friends, a pretty relaxed atmosphere.

"Besides school, and of course the French Quarter on Mardi Gras, have you spent much time in New Orleans?" Valentina asked.

"Not really."

"I've lived here all my life. I haven't traveled much, but it's got to be one of the best cities in the world. I know a ton of things you should see."

They walked into the two-story yellow frame building, past the iconic peeled banana sign and the bust of Professor Longhair. After paying the cover fees, they continued farther into the bar, crowded with fans. Kai asked, "Do you want something to drink, or would you rather dance?"

"Dance," Valentina said definitively.

"*Bien sûr.*"

The first set had started, and the band was in the middle of playing "La Terre De Mon Grand-père." Kai led an easy two-step. From there, the band transitioned to a Zydeco number, with Valentina and Kai moving easily to the syncopated beat.

Doucet then announced, "We're going to slow it down a little now with 'Recherche D'Acadie.'"

Kai looked at Valentina. "*J'peux?*"

When Valentina nodded, he gathered her close with his right hand at Valentina's back, extending his left arm to hold her right hand in a classic waltz position. Valentina put her left hand on Kai's right shoulder.

"I've been looking forward to this all day." He moved gracefully in a three-step rhythm, weaving among the other dancers.

Valentina lost herself in the old dance. She loved the haunting, wistful melody about searching for Acadia, the homeland of the French in Nova Scotia, and finding new Acadia in Louisiana. When the song ended, Kai held onto her for a moment longer as the next song began.

"Would you like something to drink?" Kai asked.

"Sure."

As they were getting their drinks, a familiar voice called, "Valentina! Kai! Over here."

Valentina laughed. That voice was impossible to miss. "Hey Gemma! They threaded their way through the crowd toward Gemma, who was with another woman about her same age.

"Hey, you two. This is my partner, Lisa. Lisa, these are my bioethics classmates, Valentina and Kai."

"Good to meet you."

"Hi, Lisa. You look familiar," Valentina said.

"You do too. Are you a teacher?" Lisa asked.

"No, I work at Winslow Park. What do you do?"

"I teach math at McLarin Urban Prep ..."

"Oh, I bet that's where we've seen each other. McLarin is one of our partner schools. I did a presentation there recently. We're starting a new interactive seed bank for the kids."

"That's right. The science teachers are pumped about your new program. They've asked me to work with them on designing the assessment measures."

"It's exciting for us too. After getting the refrigeration equipment, we put together a drying space for the seeds. We'll be ready to start pretty soon."

"If you don't mind, I'll get your contact information from Gemma. It would be nice to communicate directly if I have questions."

"Perfect," said Valentina.

"New Orleans is such a small town," Gemma said. "Instead of six degrees of separation, there's three."

"I know. Next thing you know, we'll find out Gemma and I are related. *Nous sommes cousines.*" Kai said.

"Are you enjoying the music?" Lisa asked.

"I love this band," Valentina said.

"How do you feel about another dance?" Gemma asked Lisa.

"Sure."

Valentina looked over at Kai. "Ready for another two-step?"

"*Mais ya.*"

They spent the next few hours dancing, talking, and laughing. Valentina considered dancing one of life's essential activities, although she was starting to get hungry. The band finished their last set, and Kai asked, "Do you want to get something to eat?"

"You must have read my mind. I'm starved."

"*Moi aussi, j'ai faim.*"

They walked further down Tchoupitoulas Street to Barracuda, a small restaurant that sold tacos. Picnic tables, some covered with colorful umbrellas, were scattered across an outdoor patio. Valentina decided it was one of the best dates she's had in a while. Wait a minute, it was the only date she'd had in a while.

When they reached her apartment, Kai jumped out and opened her car door. At her small porch, Kai pulled her to him gently.

"I don't want to scare you away, but I've been thinking about being close to you ever since we spent a little time together at the food court."

"That got my attention too," Valentina said softly. They kissed. She felt Kai's excitement as he deepened the kiss and pulled Valentina closer. "May I come in?"

"I guess that's not for coffee?" she asked.

"We've had a great evening. *Je veux être prôche de toi.* I'd like to get to know you better." Kai said while trailing kisses beneath her ear and chin.

"Wait a minute, Kai. I'm not ready for that. This is our first date."

"I understand. I'll give you a call soon."

"I'd like that."

Kai waited until she opened the door then waved as he walked back to his car. Inside her apartment, Valentina leaned against the front door, confused about what she was feeling.

CHAPTER 28

Will rolled over to find Susan's side of the bed empty. He checked the time. It was almost 4:00 in the morning. It was an old pattern that recently re-emerged. Will padded downstairs and found her watching television.

"Couldn't sleep?"

"No." Susan yawned, moving over to give Will room on the sofa.

"Anything on TV?"

"I'm watching an old DVD that Mia gave us—*Moonstruck.*"

"That's her favorite movie."

"I see why."

"Can you get back to sleep?"

Susan only looked at Will.

"I'll go make coffee."

"Thanks. I need to be at my desk by five."

"Hey, why don't I grab my laptop and a TV tray? I'll sit with you while I check the farm report."

A little while later, Will settled next to Susan on the sofa. "There's nothing like the first cup of coffee of the day."

Susan shushed him. "This is really a good movie."

"Okay, okay."

After powering up his computer, Will went straight to the Nebraska agribusiness site. The headline screamed: *Record Number of Farms Struck by Wheat Virus.*

"Oh, man," Will moaned.

"Sshh."

"Susan, pause the movie for a minute?"

Recognizing his serious tone, Susan asked, "What is it, honey?"

"It's unbelievable. Almost 20,000 farms across the country have been hit by the virus. Not only wheat and sweet corn like us, it's affecting barley, oats and rye. Thousands of farms in the U.S. grow these crops. Susan, a lot of them have been wiped out."

"This is like watching a train wreck. How could this happen?"

"I don't know," Will said. "But it's not normal. There's never been anything like this."

"Let's see if there's anything on the national news," Susan said, grabbing the TV remote.

"It's too early."

"There's a station that rebroadcasts the news on a continuous cycle. It keeps looping until the next one comes out. We'll probably catch the broadcast from last night." Susan flipped through a few stations. "Look, here we go. See, they're finishing up with the weather. It'll just be a minute."

"Okay."

"Want more coffee?"

"Sure."

Susan drifted to the counter and poured them both another cup. "Why is she so perky?"

"You mean the weather person? She gets paid to be perky."

"Even so. That's excessively perky."

"You're trying to distract me. She's never bothered you before."

"Guilty."

Will and Susan waited as the commercials advised them to buy a better detergent, get a new car, and join a different cellular network, any of which would improve their lives beyond recognition.

"Have you talked to Mitch lately?" Susan asked.

"Yeah, we spoke yesterday about the alfalfa. He's fine. Mitch and Erin have been real smart about not getting into too much debt.

They owe money on the extra acreage they bought a few years ago and the mortgage, of course, but that's about it."

"I talked with Erin for a minute. She's worried but is feeling more secure. At first, we both expected a loan shark with a baseball bat at the door any minute, looking to break legs." Susan laughed, and Will managed to chuckle a little.

Finally, the television anchor began the top story of the day.

"Our nation's farmers are reporting devastating losses for most of the small grain crops, including winter wheat, barley, oats, rye and sweet corn. From Texas to the Canadian border, across the plains and east of the Mississippi River, a deadly disease known as the wheat streak mosaic virus complex is causing widespread devastation. Estimates suggest at least 35,000 farms have experienced 90 - 100% crop loss.

Will sat back in his chair. "That's over a third of the farms in the US. People aren't going to have enough to eat."

"Shh, wait, let's listen."

"The source of the virus is unknown. However, the wheat curl mite, which cannot be seen with the naked eye, transmits the disease."

Behind the announcer, a screen displayed a large photograph of a microscopic mite. It looked like a large white sweet potato with horizontal stripes on a charcoal gray background. Four small legs extended on one end, with small hairs protruding from its body. The announcer continued, pointing to the display:

"When they feed, the mites use these stylets to pierce the leaves of the plant, which spreads the virus. The mites reproduce rapidly, and can decimate a field within days."

Susan said, "That thing is hideous!"

"No effective pesticide exists to combat the mites, which have run rampant across the country. Farm experts indicate this is a particularly bad year for the wheat curl mite and advise complete eradication of all crops damaged by the virus. They stress that living plants infected with the virus spread it to healthy crops. Many farmers rely on limited tilling to avoid disrupting the soil, as that increases erosion. Under current conditions, advisers with the U. S. Department of Agriculture strongly recommend against this practice as all plant material must be destroyed. Plowing is necessary to turn the soil over completely to destroy the contaminated plants, killing the mites and mosaic virus.

"Louis Gibbens, Secretary of the U.S. Department of Agriculture, met with the president earlier today to discuss emergency relief for farmers. Grain futures have spiked. There is some discussion among congressional leaders regarding modifying the law regulating the Strategic Grain Reserve, also known as the Bill Emerson Humanitarian Trust, to allow assistance to domestic growers. The reserve was designed to respond to international food crises only. Currently, the trust is solely a cash reserve, and does not contain grain commodities. As America is a leading exporter of grains, food shortages are anticipated worldwide as well as here at home. This will affect people and livestock.

"First Lady Katherine Linden has asked all Americans to plant Unity Gardens. Citizens across the country can help by growing their own gardens to combat hunger and alleviate shortages. Community groups are encouraged to participate. For those of us new to horticulture, instructional videos are available at www.garden4unity.org. On a historical note, home gardens or Victory Gardens during World War II produced eight million tons of food through an estimated 20 million home gardens. This was almost 75% of what all farms in the United States produced back then. The First Lady urges each of us to get involved with our own gardens.

"Landever Industries, one of the world's largest agricultural companies, has announced successful production of a wheat strain that is resistant to the virus. This cultivar has been in development for years. Due to the farming crisis, Landever will offer seeds at no cost to farmers for this year on condition of future contractual commitment.

"In other news, ..."

Will clicked the TV remote. They sat in the quiet room, looking out the large windows into the darkness of the early morning.

Susan turned to Will. "This is a lot bigger than us and our friends."

"It's a lot bigger than Lancaster County, Nebraska. Susan, I don't think this is a 'particularly bad year,' or divine intervention, or a weird confluence of events that prompted the mites to spread through most of North America."

"What are you saying, Will?"

"I don't know what's happening, but it isn't natural."

Susan shook her head, almost in denial. "I've got to get ready for work. Are you hungry?"

"No, I don't want anything. You go ahead."

Will sat for a few more minutes, listening to the familiar noises of Susan starting her workday upstairs. He opened his laptop again and went to his Facebook account. There were messages from the small group of farmers who found the drone and drone parts. None of them had seen a registration number or markings anywhere. Will sent another message to the group:

What would you think of sharing our contact information and each of us going to our local sheriffs? Or what about the FAA? I'm Will Torino of Lancaster County, Nebraska, and here is my contact information...

Almost immediately, the farmer who found the drone wrote back. *Will, I'm Roger Mundine and I live in Douglas County, Kansas. I agree, something's not right. The timing is too coincidental. Should we go to the FBI? I'm not sure our sheriff would know what to do any more than we do. I thought about the FAA too. Although if this was deliberate, then it's domestic terrorism, right?*

Will replied, *I wish we had met under better circumstances, Roger. If it's domestic terrorism, maybe it would be Homeland Security? I'll start making calls today and let you know what I find out.*

Sounds good, buddy. Signing off now, Roger.

As he was about to close his computer, another message appeared. *Brad Livingston here. I'm in. Contact me at ...*

Will compared notes with Brad and after a few minutes, shut down his laptop to start his workday. Later that morning, he called Mitch.

"Hey, what's up?" Mitch answered.

"How about 'Farmers' financial ruin caused by zombie drones'?"

"A little far-fetched, but it's got a nice ring to it." Mitch paused. "Will, are you letting all this get to you?"

"Of course I am. But seven other farmers found drone parts. One of them found an intact drone."

"That's too crazy, like a sci-fi show or something."

"I know. I may contact the sheriff."

"What about Homeland Security?"

"I'll probably get laughed out of the country. Let me start local."

"Sounds like the right move. Everyone around here already knows you're crazy."

"Thank you, Mitch."

"Did you hear about Landever's offer?"

"Who hasn't?"

"It's the talk of the town."

"What do you think?"

"You know Norris does my thinking for me."

Will guffawed.

"I ran into him at the hardware store. Norris is so cool. He said, 'Sounds pretty patriotic, huh? Take a closer look, young man.' He has a breakdown of the seed costs by company over the last ten years. Hands down, Landever has been the most expensive," Mitch said.

"Norris? What, like a spreadsheet?"

"Nah. he's kept track in a notebook. Even if we got the seed free for a year or two, we'd still be in the hole."

"Figures. Is anyone going for the deal?"

"James probably will. Bill is thinking about it, just to aggravate Norris."

"Susan and I may expand the vegetable garden or try organics."

"I've heard the certification process is pretty complicated."

"Something to look at while we sit out the grain market."

"Erin and I are looking at cattle, goats, or alpacas. You saw the USDA has a new disaster assistance program?"

"Yeah, we're going to apply."

"Us too. Okay, buddy. We'll get through this."

"We will. Talk to you later, Mitch."

Will decided he'd make the rest of his calls when he went in for lunch. In the meantime, he had fields to plow and alfalfa to plant.

CHAPTER 29

In Indianapolis, Landever's chief entomologist Stephen Angus turned off the morning news, not waiting for the football club results or weather report. He had watched an interview with one of his former entomology classmates, Skip Millington. Skip, not a bad bloke, provided a brief tutorial on the life cycle of mites and then gave his expert opinion about why they were decimating wheat fields across America. Not just any mites. Skip said they were the same strain as Angus's mites: *Aceria tosichella*.

Angus leaned back in his desk chair. Things bothered him, starting with that dobber Stillman. He thought about their interactions. Stillman—hot and cold about the research. In retrospect, he believed Stillman was blowing smoke up his arse during the whole executive dining experience. He'd had an inkling at the time, but Angus didn't care because he wanted more funding for his research. He felt ridiculous, knowing the man had played him. He thought about the bonus Stillman arranged, fattening up his bank account. And now he couldn't come up with the money for a new freezer? It was preposterous. Angus looked around the small, comfortable room he used as an office and den, the upholstered chairs a little frayed around the edges. He had thought of getting a new leather recliner or a better outdoor grill, but Angus was hesitant to use the money. He was glad he didn't spend any of that odd, gratuitous bonus.

Angus remembered Stillman's son, who worked a few summers at the lab. Nice kid, checked in with him every once in a while. Too bad he had an arse for a father.

After the lab power failure, Stillman turned off the funding. That in particular didn't make sense. The reasons for his research hadn't changed. Angus hoped to investigate new methods of controlling the mites through his research. Identifying the conditions under which they could survive—such as extreme cold—was only the first step in a long process. The next step would be to find their vulnerabilities. Why cut off funding now, when the need was so critical?

The explanation of the power failure was lame—the cleaning crew did it. Angus recalled late-night conversations with Tomas and Maria, who took care of the entomology section. Both worked two jobs, saving money for their kids' education. Always responsible, careful. That's not something they would have done. And now they were, what, reassigned? He hoped they still had jobs.

Throwing out the freezer containers before an investigation? No one considered he might have wanted to examine the remaining tissue samples? When Angus asked around, he didn't get satisfactory answers. Vague responses pointed to a head office decision to clear the lab. He knew the executive wing never got involved in things like that.

The trip to India wasn't necessary. Angus thought back to his Mumbai visit. The head of research, Anand Darsh, had things well in hand. Good bloke. Angus enjoyed the time he spent with Darsh, talking about their research over the best curry dishes he'd ever eaten. Angus left India as mystified about what he was supposed to do there as when he arrived. Other than taking him out of the office for over a week, there was no point.

To allow for the spread of wheat streak mosaic virus carried by *Aceria tosichella.* Of course. But how did it get across America and Canada so quickly? Agricultural scientists across the world were trying to figure that out.

The real clincher that chilled him to the bone—Landever's offer of free seed to farmers. Right in time, Landever announced a breakthrough development of a wheat cultivar resistant to the virus. No cost to the farmer, but only if the poor fellow signed a multi-year contract.

What an effing coincidence. Jack Stillman. The problem was, it was all circumstantial. He didn't have proof. And how in the world could Stillman have spread the mites across all those crops? Disgusted, Angus pushed back his worn desk chair. Step away, he told himself. He had a football match—no—they called it soccer here, a little later. He'd call his mate Barry and grab a late breakfast.

CHAPTER 30

After her date with Kai, Valentina slept in. She stirred once during the night, thinking about how things could have gone differently. Was she relieved or disappointed they didn't go further? Mostly relieved. There would be time for that. It was too easy to start something physical without having a sound foundation, or really knowing the other person. She found a lot to like about Kai, but it was too early to tell. At peace with her decision, Valentina fell back to sleep.

At nine, Valentina woke up with a start. *Oh my goodness,* she thought. *I promised Mia a flourless chocolate cake and a fruit coulis sauce. What was I thinking? Well, my family has to love me no matter what.* She had the ingredients. She'd just never baked it before. Valentina pulled out her stash of exceedingly important ingredients, which mainly consisted of different types of chocolate—beautiful dark chocolate, luscious raspberries and fresh eggs from the farmer's market. She even had time to make her own whipped cream.

About two hours later, Valentina had a slightly lopsided cake with a fruit sauce ready to go. At least being under pressure, she couldn't moon about Kai, or the mess in her kitchen. Valentina left through a cloud of powdered sugar and arrived at her grandparent's home with minutes to spare.

"Valentina!" A thin, older Italian man wearing dark sunglasses and a soft linen shirt was sitting on the front porch. He was a stylish, perfectly groomed version of her grandfather.

"Uncle Tony! I'm surprised to see you."

"I got in town Friday for a meeting."

"How long are you staying?"

"I have an early flight tomorrow morning back to Houston, but I had to stop by and check on my little brother. And I couldn't miss a chance to see you, doll. What have you got here?"

"Dessert."

"Looks fancy."

Dean stepped onto the porch and smiled broadly at Valentina. "What did you find out here, Tony?" He hugged Valentina. "How are you sweetheart?"

"I'm fine. It's good to see you."

"You too. Yum, you smell like chocolate."

"It's our dessert."

"Boy, that looks delicious. Why don't you go say hello to your grandmother," Dean said. "We'll watch the cake."

"Not a chance."

Dean joined Tony in the glider rocker and took the cigar Tony offered him. Valentina shook her head and turned toward the kitchen to find Mia. Dean called after her, "You know we won't smoke them until after dinner."

"We might chew on them a little," Tony said.

"I don't want to know."

Wonderful smells filled the house. Mia stirred a pot of red gravy on the stove. She was making a pork roast, and a green salad was waiting to be dressed. She gave Valentina a hug. "You beautiful thing!"

"Mia, you look wonderful." Wearing a casual spring dress, Mia's stray brown and silver curls escaped from a loose bun at the nape of her neck, and her light green eyes twinkled. She looked like home. Then Mia's gaze narrowed.

"Tell me about your date," her grandmother said, waving her wooden spoon.

"Boy, that was fast," Valentina said.

"Come on, before your grandpa comes back."

"Well…. It was good."

"And?" Mia looked at Valentina more closely.

"We'll have to see." Valentina shrugged.

Mia turned down the burner and tugged Valentina over to the table. "Sit with me for a minute and tell me about this young man."

Nothing like the Inquisition on an empty stomach. "He's at school with me in my ethics class.

"Yes?"

"He's getting a graduate degree in Plant Physiology."

"Sounds smart."

"He is smart, and attractive. He gets along with everybody."

"What's his name again?"

"Kai Prejean."

Mia waved her spoon encouragingly. "So your future holds a second date with this young man?"

"Probably so."

Mia nodded with satisfaction and got up to stir the gravy. "Why don't you call Dean and Tony? We're eating in the dining room today."

Mia and Valentina filled plates and carried them to the table. Dean and Tony came inside, the screen door swinging shut behind them.

"Tony, you're the old man here," Dean looked down at his lap piously, "you say the blessing."

Tony winked at Valentina, "My little brother has been a pain since the day he was born. Remind me to tell you about that day sometime."

Mia, Valentina, Dean and Tony held hands, and Tony said, "Bless our family near and far. Thank you for this wonderful food. More importantly, thank you for this company."

For a moment, no one said a thing as everyone took their first bite.

"Mia, this is incredible. I follow your recipe but it doesn't taste like this." Valentina said.

"We'll do it together next time. Better yet, I'll sit and watch."

"That would drive you crazy."

"That depends on how you do, Valentina," Mia said. Everyone laughed. The Sorelli Sunday dinner continued loudly and with much teasing. Valentina's cake was a hit, despite its slight tilt.

Toward the end, Tony looked serious. "Don't you have a young relative who farms? Has that wheat virus affected him? A lot of farmers are hurting right now."

"That's right, Will, our grandnephew," Dean said. "From what he's told us, it's all over the country and parts of Canada."

"I talked with him yesterday," Valentina said. "Grandpa, remember how you thought those plastic bits looked like parts of a model airplane?"

"Oh well, yeah, but they might have been anything."

"No, you were right. A couple guys in my class worked in aviation, and they think the pieces are part of a busted-up drone. After Will posted the images on Facebook, a few other farmers posted their own pictures. One guy found an entire drone. It's wild."

"Wait, what is this?" Tony asked.

"Will and a friend were walking in a field to inspect the crop damage. They discovered a drone part literally by stepping on it. They found several more pieces and sent us pictures." Valentina recalled that her great uncle had some connection to law enforcement. "My classmates should know what they're talking about. Xavier was a drone pilot in the military and Ellis was an engineer with a helicopter manufacturer. They said it had to be an expensive drone because the material, some kind of composite, is really expensive. Will is going to talk with the other farmers about going to the FAA."

Tony looked at Mia and Dean. "You don't mind if I talk to Will about this, do you? This is the first I've heard about drones."

"Not at all," Dean said. "I'll share his contact information after dinner. You think this could be a coordinated attack?"

"I don't know, but it's worth checking into. Valentina, you said one of the farmers found an entire drone?"

"Yeah, but there wasn't a registration number, or anything to identify it."

"Okay," Tony said, "Valentina, tell me about your classmates who looked at the pictures for you."

"Well, Xavier Richard is a few years older than me, early to mid-30's. He was a UAV pilot in the Marines and did patrols along the border of Saudi Arabia and Kuwait. He's going to NOU on the GI bill. Ellis Morrison retired from Bell Technology where he developed helicopter propellers."

"Interesting," Tony said. "So they might have known what they were looking at. I'll touch base with your grandnephew and see what he has to say. It's probably a coincidence." Tony changed the subject. "How are the Saints looking this year?"

"Since we lost Drew? It's been hit or miss on quarterbacks," said Mia. Everyone continued discussing the travails of the football team that had broken their hearts too many times to count.

As they cleaned up the kitchen together, Valentina said, "I've got to go. Finals are this week. There's a study group this afternoon at school. Let's schedule my red gravy session after that." She hugged everyone.

As she was leaving, Tony said, "If you talk to Will, tell him I'll be giving him a call. I think the last time I saw him he was a kid."

"Will do, Uncle Tony. I forget you work in law enforcement. "What agency—FBI?"

Tony nodded.

"I should have suggested it myself."

"Look, he took pictures and hung on to the plastic bits. No harm done."

"Have a safe trip back," Valentina said.

"Good luck with your exams."

"Thanks."

*   *   *

When Special Agent Anthony Joseph Sorelli returned to his hotel room that evening, he looked at the time. Too late to call Mia's grandnephew. He could still check some things out. Tony opened his laptop to start the three-part verification process to log on. First his password then his credentials for the VPN that would link him to the government server. As usual, this took forever as his request to connect passed through layers upon layers of security levels. At least he was able to use his computer in the hotel. That wasn't possible five years ago. As the Supervisory Special Agent of the Houston Violent Crimes and Domestic Terrorism Squad, Tony had been around long enough to remember when things were a lot more cumbersome.

Finally, Tony inserted his PIV card to verify it really was him. Using a masked identity, he checked out the online chatter on Facebook. He found Will's initial post, as well as the discussion of possible drone components. After a few minutes, Tony went to Diaspora, Vero, Path, Nextdoor and a few other social networking sites. He flagged a couple of other comments. Tony sent a note to another agent to arrange a thorough sweep—*One more thing, can you run these names for me: Xavier Richard and Ellis Morrison. Thanks, Freddy.*

CHAPTER 31

Barry Carlson was waiting when Angus walked into Sweeney's, a bustling cafe on the outskirts of downtown Indianapolis. The game was on the television over the bar that operated from the time they opened until Sweeney threw out the last patron at midnight.

Barry was in his early 70s, still working and enjoying his careful, detailed studies. Much of their research at Landever was proprietary, but Barry had made a practice of nurturing young melittologists, or bee scientists, and giving them a nudge in the right direction. More than one academic had recognized Barry's influence in his work. He wasn't in the best of health and needed a cane to get around. Angus thought he hung the moon.

"I didn't see you this morning," Barry said. Angus and Barry were both in the habit of working one weekend morning, at least once a month, to catch up on their notes, emails, and the minutiae of their work as researchers at Landever. Afterwards, they would catch a late breakfast or lunch at Sweeney's.

"What's the point, Barry? I've got to start over. What's the rush?" asked Angus bitterly.

The waitress walked over carrying a coffee pot. "Coffee?"

"Please." Barry said.

Angus shrugged.

"What else would you gentlemen like today? We have some lunch specials. Or Todd will make you breakfast."

"Breakfast would be lovely, Frances," Barry said.

He ordered a full breakfast, and Angus said, "I'll have the same. And do you have Macallan? For my coffee, please."

"Nope."

"Lagavulin?"

"You should know better, Mr. Angus," Frances said. "Johnny Walker?"

"That'll do."

"Make that two."

Angus looked at Barry in surprise. "What will your wife say?"

Barry held his gaze for a moment. "What are friends for?" Looking more closely at Angus, he said, "Bring us a pint, love, for medicinal purposes only." As Frances turned back to the bar, Barry nodded at Angus. "We haven't talked much lately."

Angus was silent, gathering his thoughts. Frances returned and opened the Johnny Walker.

After fortifying his coffee, Angus said, "It doesn't make sense."

"You've lost everything?"

"Well, not the data or my notes. Several strains of mites, yes."

"If you've got the data, what is your concern? They reproduce quickly. You could start things up pretty quickly, couldn't you?"

"It's the equipment, Barry."

"That's right. Your space age freezers."

"My space age freezers. Stillman won't replace them."

"How did you fall so quickly, Angus? You were the golden boy last year and now you're the poor cousin."

"At best." Angus looked at his empty coffee cup, and Barry filled it with whiskey.

"What else is it?" Barry asked. "I thought you'd moved on."

"I thought I had too, until I heard the news this morning. Tell me this, Barry, how did my wee mites fly across the country?"

"Are you sure they're your mites?"

"Am I sure, no. But if you're a betting man, Barry, I'd bet you 90 to 1 they are."

Barry sat quietly and sipped his coffee. "Did you hear about Kiefer's breakthrough?" he asked conversationally.

"Kiefer, he's the bloke in crop development? I haven't heard anything. What's he done?"

"New wheat strain. You heard about the company's offer to farmers?"

"I heard it on the telly this morning," Angus paused, then said, "Bloody hell! Stillman planned this whole thing. I am such an arse."

"It's a lot of supposition, Angus. We don't really know anything."

"I know, I know. But I can't stand the idea of Stillman getting away with it." Angus paused. "I guess I could contact the USDA, but what would I say? And an anonymous tip? If I were on the other end of the phone with me, I'd think it ridiculous."

"Let's give it more thought, Angus. The damage is done. We may see a way through."

CHAPTER 32

Martha Jane Bruning, Supervisory Plant Physiologist at the National Center for Genetic Resources Preservation in Fort Collins, Colorado, pulled off her insulated gloves and left the cryopreservation seed storage area. Her assistant, Louis, continued removing tubes of samples from the large, round freezers. Over the years, Martha Jane's team had preserved the existence of hundreds of thousands of seeds and plant material. Messianic in her work, Martha Jane knew their collections of genetic material sustained agricultural biodiversity and bolstered food security.

With the grain crisis, the USDA's Agricultural Research Service had asked every private seed producer for genetic samples of any grains not already in storage. They were expecting a new batch from Landever today. One of Landever's executive staff insisted he would bring the samples himself. Martha Jane didn't get it. That's what UPS or FedEx were for.

There was protocol. The donor filled out a Plant Variety Protection Seed Voucher Deposit Form, attached it to an email, and sent a printed copy with the sample consisting of 3,000 untreated seeds. If it was a hybrid plant, there would be 9,000 seeds, consisting of 3,000 from each parent and the offspring. Landever's request was highly irregular. Martha Jane didn't like deviation from protocol. Her success was based on adherence to established procedures, established for a reason.

Upon arrival, the properly labeled seeds began an exacting journey. The samples were verified within the database, assigned a serial number, and only then carefully unpacked. The seeds dried for a few weeks in an equilibrium room, reducing their moisture content. Martha Jane's analysts removed contaminants—such as seeds of weeds or inert material—using sifters, blowers or rubbing boards. Her staff planted some of the pure seeds on germination blotters to test their viability. From there, many of those seeds, all now properly labeled and recorded in the database, were carefully stored in heat-sealed, moisture-proof, foil-laminated bags in the cold storage vault at a uniform temperature of minus -18 ° C. The rest were transferred to clear plastic tubes and crimped closed, before being placed in metal boxes, and stored in cryogenic tanks that maintained temperatures of -195 ° C through liquid nitrogen. In the vault, seeds would last 100 years. In cryogenic storage, they could last a thousand. The center preserved wild crop relatives, such as einkorn, emmer, spelt and Khorasan wheat, the ancient ancestors of modern-day wheat. Martha Jane hoped one of her charges contained the genetic material to resist the wheat streak mosaic virus that was decimating the country's farmlands. Since this crisis began, the nation's seed companies had given Fort Collins complete access to all their plant genetic resources. Everyone wanted to find a way to beat the wheat virus. Well, almost every company. Landever would give the center their seeds for preservation, but not for research purposes. Martha Jane didn't get that either. Didn't Landever executives understand how serious the situation was? The other companies did.

Protocol. Meticulous adherence to protocol meant the USDA's seed collection was backed up both in Fort Collins and at the Global Seed Vault in Svalbard, Norway. Martha Jane worked with over 80 different organizations, from botanic gardens, universities, NGOs, national and international gene banks in other countries, and indigenous groups. The Fort Collins seed bank was like a library, except no plant germplasm was ever released without sufficient redundancy and documentation through an electronic database. Martha Jane found it ironic that the database, formally called the Germplasm Resources Information Network, was known as GRIN. There was nothing funny about it. Global food security hinged on the interdependency of the seed banks and their duplicative reliability.

Martha Jane met the Landever representative in the lobby of the large, tan-colored building.

"Hello, I'm Jack Stillman of Landever."

"Yes, Mr. Stillman. I am Martha Jane Bruning. The ARS appreciates Landever's willingness to provide additional samples to preserve during this crisis."

"Please, call me Jack. And anything we can do to help."

Martha Jane paused and looked at Jack. "The samples?"

"Yes, of course. You'll see that the seeds are patented."

"I am aware of that, Mr. Stillman," Martha Jane said with acerbity. "Landever's rights will be protected."

"Then here they are."

"Thank you, Mr. Stillman. Now, if that is all, I will wish you a good day." Martha Jane turned to go.

"I hoped that I could tour the facility?" Jack said quickly.

"Mr. Stillman, this is highly irregular. You could have requested a tour through our normal channels."

"I thought while I was here ..." Jack smiled at Martha Jane.

Reminding herself that Landever had possibly the only wheat cultivars resistant to the wheat mosaic virus, Martha Jane steeled herself to continue the unpleasant distraction.

"Of course. Please follow me," said Martha Jane with resignation. Recognizing that it could be an opportunity, she asked, "Perhaps Landever would consider joining the agricultural consortium?"

"I'm sorry, could you tell me more about this, this consortium?" Jack said.

Martha Jane knew that Landever had been asked and refused to participate in a cooperative research effort in partnership with the government. "I'm surprised someone in your position would not be aware of this effort, Mr. Stillman. The other large agricultural companies, Foranda, BSYN and Zynagrain, are working in tandem with our researchers, the Department of Agriculture, as well as many smaller producers to expedite our development of mite resistant wheat cultivars. Surely your office informed you?"

"Ah yes, I may have heard something about that. I'm sure you understand that we have been busy with the roll-out of our own resistant strain," Jack said.

Martha Jane gritted her teeth. *What a pompous ass.* Over the next half hour, compressing the typical forty-five minute tour, Martha Jane brought Jack through the storage rooms and the labs, explaining what materials were being stored, the purpose and processes of the seed storage and their research. Thanking her profusely, Jack left.

Shaking her head, Martha Jane took the stairs to the second floor. Mr. Stillman wasn't interested in helping their research efforts. He paid more attention to their protection systems than study protocols. Maybe Landever had a security issue, she thought.

CHAPTER 33

Valentina pulled into the student lot at NOU. At 3:00, the entire bioethics class was meeting to prep for the final. She was early, so she decided to call Will.

Will answered and Valentina heard an engine cut off in the background.

"Have I caught you in the field?"

"No problem, Valentina. What's up? Oh wait, how was the big date?"

"BeauSoleil was terrific."

"I bet they were. But that wasn't my question. What's your impression of the guy now that you've spent more time with him?"

"Good."

"You don't sound that enthusiastic."

"It was okay. Enough okay that I'll give it another try. Anyway, that's not why I called. I wanted to give you a heads up. Do you remember Uncle Tony, Dean's brother?"

"Vaguely. I met him years ago."

"You probably were never around Mia's at the same time when you were older. He works for the FBI and never talks about what he does. Anyway, he's in town and stopped in to visit. We all had Sunday dinner together today. He'd like to talk to you about the drone parts and plans to call you."

"That would be good. Maybe he can point me in the right direction. It's not like I'm routinely in touch with any government agency. Well, just the county Extension service, and frankly, this seems a little above their pay grade. Mine too. I did think about contacting the sheriff."

"How could you know what to do? This is outside your normal experience. Anyone's. Listen, I'm going to have to go. Finals are this week, and I'm heading to a study group."

"Okay, thanks for the heads up."

"Love you."

"You too."

Valentina walked to the food court, stopping at PJ's for an iced coffee. Sam and Tala sat at a small table off to the side. Valentina started to call hello and then hesitated. Sam looked animated and Tala's face glowed. They both broke out laughing. *Three might be a crowd.* Then she sensed someone close to her and looked up to return Kai's smile.

"Hey."

"Hi. I had a good time last night," she said.

"I'm glad. Me too."

"Ready to head to the library?"

"Let me get something to drink. You need anything?" Kai asked.

Valentina shook her head.

"I'll be right back."

Unnoticed, Ellis arrived and stood across from Valentina. As Kai left, he said, "That looked cozy. What's up with you guys? I'm picking up a few sparks."

"I don't know if I'd go that far."

"Oh?"

"We had a date, that's all." Valentina and Ellis continued talking as they waited for Kai. She always felt comfortable with Ellis. All rumply, a little overweight, he wasn't exactly a father figure but something close.

"How are you, Ellis?"

"Good. I've decided to apply for a teaching position in the fall. It's a better fit than the other things I was thinking about. There are a few openings for math instructors. Most schools will help with getting certified."

"That sounds great. Had you thought of teaching before you went into engineering?"

"I did, but frankly, it didn't pay enough to support a family. I always enjoyed math, so engineering came easily for me. But yeah, I'm pretty excited. It leaves things open, too. I wasn't ready to invest in a business or commit to something long term. This way, I step into it and see how it goes."

"Fantastic. I know a few teachers through Winslow's connection with a couple of local schools. Oh wait, Gemma's partner is a teacher. She teaches math at McLarin Urban Prep."

"I will definitely talk to Gemma," Ellis said.

Valentina and Ellis didn't notice Gemma had come through the door.

"Talk to me about what?" she asked as she approached.

Valentina sometimes thought that Gemma should be an announcer or social director instead of applying to medical school. She was impossible to miss.

"I'm applying to be a math teacher," Ellis said.

"You have to meet Lisa!" said Gemma.

"That's what I understand."

Gemma's eyes widened with excitement as she told Ellis about Lisa and her work.

Leaving them to their discussion, Valentina and Kai walked over to the library where they had reserved a study room. The rest of the class arrived soon after. Leo lingered at the entrance, watching as Kai bent his head to whisper something to Valentina. A faint blush began at Valentina's collarbone and swept across her face. Looking toward the doorway, Kai caught Leo's eye across the room, and Kai smiled. Leo shoulders sagged.

Ellis saw him and called, "Come on, Aquatics Man, we have an ethical dilemma to solve."

Leo laughed and said, "Yeah, I guess so." He sat down as far as he could from Kai and Valentina.

"Hey, before we get started, let's talk about the beach trip," Sam said. "I have the all clear to use the house."

"You talked to your dad?" Valentina asked.

"No, we're avoiding each other. I arranged things through his secretary and the property management company."

"This coming Friday afternoon, right? After exams?" Gemma asked.

"Mm hmm," said Sam. "I'll need to get back no later than Monday evening."

"We have a friend who invited us to his condo in Destin for the next week. If we could get a ride to your house with someone, Lisa and I would love to go."

"Annie and I would be glad to give you a ride," said Ellis. "It will give me a chance to grill Lisa about her teaching experiences."

"Sounds like a plan!" Gemma said.

"May I get a ride with someone?" Tala asked.

"We could give you a ride there," Xavier said. "But Bailey and I are driving to St. Augustine after that."

"Tala, you could ride back to New Orleans with us," Ellis said. "Since Gemma and Lisa plan to stay with their friend in Destin, we'll have room for you on the way back."

"That would be appreciated," Tala said.

"I'll have to get back to work by Tuesday, but a beach weekend would be transformative," Valentina said.

"The weather is supposed to be great—no rain in the forecast," Kai said.

"We can caravan over to the coast. Why don't we meet in the parking lot right here?" said Xavier.

"It's a plan," Gemma said. "What about if each of us takes responsibility for a different meal? That should get us through the weekend. Lisa and I can make quesadillas. Ellis, what about you?"

"Annie and I will take one of the lunches. We'll fix a salad—buffet style—everyone can grab what they want whenever. Here, I'm going to write down the meals for Gemma and me and pass this around. But we need to start studying. No beach trip until we get through the coming week."

"You'll be a good teacher, Ellis, keeping all of us on track," Valentina said.

Everyone pulled out their notes to start their review.

"Dr. Chen said we needed to choose an ethical dilemma to present, to demonstrate our understanding of the ethical decision-making process. I like that he gave us the option of doing a group presentation," Ellis said.

"What about the consequences of government intervention in agriculture, both good and bad," Xavier said.

"Well, in class we considered more than agriculture," Tala said.

"True," Gemma said. "We've looked at several medical topics, like allocation of care and our obligations to individuals at the end of life."

"Don't you think medicine has been done enough already?" Sam said. "End of life, assisted dying, that's all such old news."

Gemma sputtered then said, "I get that I'm outnumbered here. Your interests are plant physiology, phytochemistry, marine biology, biotechnology ... yada yada yada. I'm good. When I'm a famous physician, remember how kind I was to you."

"We, the little people, admire your benevolence," Valentina said with a mock bow.

"Not to be confused with beneficence," Ellis said. "Speaking of which..."

"You are going to keep us on track here, aren't you?" Xavier said.

Tala spoke in her calm, soft manner. "There are many instances where ethical questions arise, for example, depletion of natural resources, water rights, and perhaps most significantly, how national interests have caused disparities across cultures."

"Those issues don't seem exclusive," Kai said.

"What do you mean?" Ellis asked.

"If you look at all those things in a broad sense, large megabusinesses have consolidated, creating monopolies. Smaller players, everyone from individual consumers to small or medium size farmers, are locked out. Look what happens with 'just in time' inventory systems. You get supply chain issues and empty supermarket shelves. Large corporations control both their suppliers and consumers."

"That's overly simplistic," Sam said. "You're making big business the villain. Lots of times large conglomerates are more socially conscious than small operations."

Kai started over. "I think it's reasonable to look closer at agritech's business model and the consequences. About 50 or 60 years ago, my grandparents farmed rice on a couple hundred acres. You can't make a living doing that anymore because of the high costs of farming and the international grain markets. You have to be really big, have thousands of acres to make a living farming rice now. Independent rice farmers turned to crawfish. Luckily, there's enough demand for domestic seafood. But that's a niche. The same thing is happening with small grain farmers of wheat, corn, soybeans and oats. They can't compete."

"I know what's happening with my cousin and, to some extent, farmers in the Midwest," Valentina said. "Their livelihoods are in jeopardy. You're saying this ties into the global markets?"

Tala leaned forward. "Consider this, Valentina. There used to be hundreds of smaller seed companies. After mergers and acquisitions, basically only nine exist now worldwide."

"Take a step back for a minute," said Kai. "Large agricultural companies control everything: the seed, the fertilizer and the pesticide or herbicide. They create customers for their entire line of products by requiring the purchase of seed every year. The seeds can't be saved or used for the next crop. The seeds need specialized fertilizers and herbicides to create optimum growing conditions.

Mass marketing leads to mass monoculture. Even the way the farmer plants his crops is designed to accommodate huge tractors and machinery. A farmer has to go big or go home."

"So what's our ethical dilemma?" Gemma asked. "It's true that the price of grain is skyrocketing. But from what I've seen in the news, the grain companies have nothing to sell because of the wheat virus."

"Except Landever. Sorry, Sam," Leo said.

"My dad and I don't always get along, but he has always been one of the smartest people I know. He started research into virus resistant wheat strains years ago. It's only in the last year or so that they've had a breakthrough."

"Yes, but Landever is capitalizing on a disaster," Xavier said.

"Does it matter if Landever earns a little money from years and years of research?" Sam looked around at everyone. "Think about what the company has invested in the cultivars that may save the wheat crop."

"Let's narrow down our ethical dilemma," Ellis said.

"What about GMO foods?" Gemma said.

"A lot of scientific groups support genetic-modification, but the question seems to be how GMOs affect surrounding vegetation. The problem is we don't know and likely won't for years to come," Leo said.

"What about climate change?" Gemma asked.

"That's narrowing it down?" Xavier laughed.

As the discussion continued, Valentina looked over at Leo. She had felt him watching her silently for most of the study session. "Let's talk after?" Valentina mouthed silently.

Leo nodded.

After another hour, the class had an outline of their presentation, assigned tasks, and set a time before class to put it all together. As everyone got up to leave, Valentina remained at the table, as did Leo. They sat quietly, while the class said their goodbyes.

Kai paused and turned. He looked at Valentina and asked, "Call you later?"

"Sure," said Valentina.

For what seemed like forever but was less than a minute, Valentina and Leo sat without saying anything.

Leo looked down at his notes, as though he would find the answer to a difficult equation there. "What makes this hard is that I like Kai, or thought I did. I was waiting for the end of the semester to ask you out. I don't have a lot of free time right now, and I wanted it to be special when we got together."

"We can still see each other. You're a great guy. Just because Kai and I had a date—"

"Don't do that." He stared at Valentina. "It's obvious how you feel about him."

"You seem to know more about that than I do."

Leo got up to leave then hesitated. "If I had asked you out first, would things be different?"

"I'm not sure how things are with me and Kai. Don't do this, Leo."

"Fair enough. See you later."

"Okay." Valentina sat in the quiet of the study room, thinking about how she was happier when she was only anticipating a date with either Kai or Leo.

CHAPTER 34

Will's cell phone buzzed. He didn't recognize the number and almost let it go to voicemail. "Will Torino."

"Will, this is Tony Sorelli. Your cousin Valentina gave me your number."

"She mentioned you might call, Mr. Sorelli."

"Call me Tony. We're sorta related by marriage, huh?"

"I guess so."

"Valentina said you'd found something unusual in your field. Why don't you tell me about that?"

Will went through everything, how they found the debris when he and Mitch were inspecting the field, and Valentina's idea about drone parts. He couldn't believe it when he heard from other farmers. Tony listened carefully, asking pointed questions, getting a timeline of events and contact information for the other farmers in the Facebook group.

"Are there any farms in your area that aren't affected by the virus?"

"Maybe the dry bean and sugar beet growers. Even the cattle ranchers are hurting because the cost of feed has gone up."

"Has anyone offered to buy your farm? Or approached your neighbors about their land?"

"You mean like a land speculator or an investment group?" Will stifled a laugh. "No, nothing like that. I bet a few folks would jump at the chance to sell."

"I appreciate your taking the time to talk with me. Someone will come by real soon to pick up the evidence."

"Mr. Sorelli, um Tony, I think this was deliberate."

"I'm coming around to that way of thinking myself."

"But who would do this?"

"We've seen a few cases of agroterrorism. Sometimes fanatics go that route, trying to make a point."

"Unbelievable."

"We'll know more once we evaluate the types of drones used. We'll have someplace to start looking."

"I hope you figure it out. Neighbors around here are in trouble."

"We're going to find out, Will. We're going to find out."

CHAPTER 35

In a small building on the outskirts of Denver, a slim woman in her early forties left the bathroom after throwing up her lunch. Evie had met friends at a sports bar where five televisions blared. All the coverage was about people not having enough to eat, farms failing, social agencies overwhelmed. Then, a fragment of the broadcast hit her like a gut punch. " ... on social media ... unconfirmed ..." She kept repeating the commentator's announcement: "Drones may be implicated in the largest crop failure in the history of the United States." She made excuses and hurried back to her office.

Evie found the email correspondence between E-AeroSystems and Richard Arlington, representative for Wisk Recreation. After she got full payment, she had no further contact with Arlington. Evie found his phone number and called. The number was disconnected. *Okay, it's been a while. Numbers change.* Evie took a big gulp of water. She sent an email, and it immediately bounced back. Evie looked on the Secretary of State's website and couldn't find Wisk Recreation. There was an Arlington Landscaping business, and Richard Arlington Tech Support, but nothing associated with retail businesses, hobbyists, or recreation. She checked other states, retail associations, and business registries. No Wisk Recreation.

Evie, you were such a chump. She exhaled heavily into the stillness of her small office and swallowed more water. She went online and found the confidential hotline established by the FBI for the grain crisis. Carefully blocking her phone number, she made the call.

"Parker Livingston speaking. How can we help you?"

"I may have information about the drone parts found near the destroyed crops."

"Can you tell me more about that?"

"This has to be confidential."

"Absolutely. No one will know you've called unless you wish to reveal your identity."

"Okay."

Evie took a deep breath, then another. "There was a man, a year ago he approached a drone manufacturer. I understand his name is Richard Arlington, and he said he represented Wisk Recreation. He ordered a large number of drones."

As Evie hesitated, Parker alerted her supervisor to monitor the automatic transcript being made of the call. An immediate response popped up on her screen: *Keep her talking. Get her to trust you.*

"So, this drone manufacturer received a big order?" Parker asked.

"Yes," Evie said.

"Was there anything special about this order?

"Yes." Evie hesitated again.

"It's okay, take your time. Can you tell me what made it exceptional?"

"The drone company is small, and they had never had such a big order."

"Other than being a large purchase, what else was different about it?"

"There were inconsistencies. He said the drones were for recreational use."

"You mean this man, what was his name? Richard Arlington, he said that?"

"Yes, but I don't think he exists. It must have been a fake name."

"What makes you think that?"

"His phone number and email address don't work anymore, and his company isn't registered anywhere."

"That does sound strange," Parker said in a sympathetic voice. "Tell me about the inconsistencies in the order itself."

"Like I said, the drones were supposed to be for recreational use."

"So, what were you concerned about?"

"Mr. Arlington wanted the drones constructed of a carbon fiber composite. That's too expensive for recreational use."

"I'm not sure I understand. Can you tell me more about that? Why do you think he wanted to use a composite instead of plastic or something cheaper?"

"Composites are much lighter and stronger—capable of flying farther. Only commercial or military drones are made of carbon fiber composite."

"So this man, Richard Arlington, gave the company a big order for drones fabricated of materials that usually are for commercial and military purposes."

"Yes, and he said hobbyists with a lot of money would buy them. He had a special market for them. But now I don't think that's realistic."

"Was there anything else strange about the order?"

"He asked a lot of questions about remote ID. Wanted to know if it was necessary. After I told him it was an FAA requirement, he backed off."

"What else?"

"These drones were more efficient than other carbon fiber composite drones," Evie said, with a hint of pride creeping into her voice. "They could be activated from greater distances once charged up. They could operate autonomously, without operators or observers."

"Sounds pretty advanced." When Evie didn't respond, Parker pushed a little. "It sounds like you really know a lot about drones."

Evie took a shaky breath. "I designed them. They could fly farther than other drones on the market. And they were automated. He could have set the whole thing in motion from a thousand miles away. I should have asked more questions, been more careful. I have a small company, a startup. When Mr. Arlington approached me, it was bigger than anything we had ever done. I jumped at the chance. I should have looked at the deal more carefully." Her voice broke. "My work may have been instrumental in the crop disaster."

"I know this is hard."

"It really is. During my meeting with Mr. Arlington, I kept suggesting ways to reduce the cost for hobbyists, and he wasn't worried about the expense. It didn't make sense until now."

"Do you mind telling me your name?" Parker asked.

"My career is probably over, why not? I'm Evelyn Lariott, Evie. The name of my company is E-AeroSystems."

"Do you have any information that can help us locate Arlington?"

"I can send you copies of the contract and the contact information I had for him."

"You've done a heroic thing, Evie, by coming forward. If you want to reach me again, my name is Parker Livingston. If you remember anything else, or just want to talk, let me give you my direct line. Do you mind giving me your contact information?"

"Okay."

•   •   •

After Evie hung up, Parker walked over to her supervisor's office. "Evelyn Lariott sounds legit. It's our first break."

Every branch of government was scrambling to address the crisis.

CHAPTER 36

Ellis steered the car on to Santa Rosa, smiling at Annie. "Hey gang, we're almost there. You want to wake up Gemma?"

"It's been so quiet while she's been asleep." Annie said.

Lisa guffawed. "She is hard to ignore."

"Her future patients will certainly know what she thinks." Ellis snorted.

"I'm not sure the school system is ever Gemma's first choice for conversation. Hey, Gemma." Lisa shook her partner who woke with a start.

"Lisa, I really appreciate your giving me the ins and outs of teaching," Ellis said.

"Anytime. A day in the life of a school teacher is a lot more dramatic than you would expect, particularly in Orleans Parish."

"I see that now. Some of your experiences have been wild."

Annie looked up from her notes. "Hey, we're here."

"Look at that house!" Gemma said. "All that sand, and the water."

Ellis eased the car under the deck overhang.

"Thanks again for driving." Lisa said. "The other challenge that goes with the life of a school teacher is the paycheck. Our car is fine in town, but we don't trust it on long trips."

"Fair trade, Lisa."

"There's Sam's jeep," Ellis said. "Let's unload and go up."

Everyone grabbed bags and coolers and started up the stairs. Sam stepped onto the deck with a big smile. "Welcome!"

"Sam, this is great," Annie said.

"Your home is beautiful," Tala said softly, coming out of the house and joining Sam.

Sam beamed, looking relaxed. "I love being here. It's nice to share."

Leo appeared on the deck. "We've got a pitcher of pina coladas ready to go."

"Leo!" Gemma exclaimed. "We didn't see your car."

"I got a ride with Sam!" Leo said, mirroring Gemma's exuberant tone and volume. Everyone laughed, and Leo added in his normal voice, "My car wasn't up for the trip."

Gemma and Lisa walked up the stairs, carrying backpacks and an ice chest. Gemma said as she passed, "Ours wasn't either, Leo. Join the impoverished teacher club. Graduate students are honorary members."

"Let me show you where to put your stuff." Sam went ahead, leading them into the house. He brought Gemma and Lisa into a vast room on the top floor that had a large window overlooking the Gulf. Bunk beds lined each of the other walls.

"The bathroom is right next door."

"What a great space," Lisa said.

"Watch out, Sam. I think I'm going to move in," warned Gemma.

"Don't worry. We have a friend who is going to pick us up on Sunday afternoon, and we'll stay with him next week," Lisa assured him.

"There should be room for Valentina and Tala up here too," Sam said.

•   •   •

Pulling up on Santa Rosa, Kai parked his truck next to the driveway. Valentina opened the passenger door, standing to stretch. "Hey Leo," she called.

"Hey," he smiled at Valentina. "Y'all want help?"

"Sure," Valentina said, "maybe with the ice chest or—"

Kai interrupted, "We got this." No longer smiling, Leo turned and went inside.

•   •   •

Less than thirty minutes later, everyone relaxed in beach chairs, watching the waves. The sky, sand, and water blended into an iridescent glow. Valentina wanted to freeze the moment, being with new friends on such a beautiful beach. It was all so mellow. For a while, everyone sat and talked as they sipped their pina coladas.

Gemma jumped up. "I can't sit still. It's beautiful!"

As the class laughed, Lisa said, "Why am I not surprised?"

Gemma ran back toward the shoreline. Suddenly, she crumpled with a pained yell. "Ow, that hurts!"

Lisa ran to Gemma, followed closely by Annie. "What happened? Did you sprain your ankle?"

"No, it's my foot," Gemma said shakily.

"Gemma, let me see." Annie knelt down beside her. The rest of the class rushed over and watched as Annie pulled a sharp piece of glass from Gemma's foot.

"Someone must have taken a glass bottle to the beach," Lisa said. "Stupid."

"When was the last time you had a tetanus shot, Gemma?" Annie asked.

Wincing, Gemma said in a subdued voice, "About four months ago."

"Sam, do you have a first aid kit?" Annie asked.

"Yeah, I know there's one around," he said then turned and ran toward the house.

"I'll help look." Valentina ran after Sam.

Annie carefully examined the cut. "I don't think you'll need stitches, Gemma. If Sam has decent supplies, I can take care of this.

Since you just had a tetanus, we should be able to avoid an ER visit. What do you think?"

"That would be a relief. I don't want to spend half the night in an ER."

"I'll be able to wrap it so you can have some beach time, but you'll have to stay out of the water," Annie cautioned.

"Bummer," Lisa said

"That doesn't mean you can't go in the Gulf," Gemma said. "I will sit in splendor on the beach."

Lisa hugged Gemma, who grimaced as she jostled her foot.

After carefully checking for more glass, Annie took her scarf and wrapped it around Gemma's foot. "Hey guys, let's get Gemma to the house so we can get this cleaned up."

Leo and Xavier carried Gemma up from the beach. Kai looked up as they passed. "Need help?"

"Nah, we got this," Xavier said. "You guys stay. We should be back soon."

In the house, Sam and Valentina checked the bathrooms for a first aid kit. "Nothing." "We may have to take Gemma to a clinic," Valentina said.

"I know a couple more places we can check. Let's go to the utility room."

Sam and Valentina hurried back to the first floor, a large open area with ceramic tile walls.

"Ready for the next storm?" Valentina asked.

"After a hurricane, we just wash down the floors and walls. We don't keep anything of value down here except the laundry equipment. Speaking of which, let's check those cabinets above the washer," Sam said.

As Sam grabbed a stepstool to access the cupboards, Valentina noticed sheets of wrinkled paper sitting on top of the washing machine.

"What's this?" she asked.

"Grab those, Valentina. Do you mind taking those upstairs? My dad has a habit of leaving notes in his pocket that he occasionally wants to keep. The cleaning crew always checks his pockets before throwing things in the wash." Reaching above, Sam said, "Look, here's the kit. I'll meet you outside."

While Sam left the basement through a door that opened to the beach, Valentina ran up the stairs to the main floor, where she left the notes on the coffee table. She joined Sam, watching Gemma being carried up the path. "Bring her to the outdoor shower," he called. "It's off to the left."

A little later, they were back on the beach, enjoying the sunset. Gemma sat, the cut on her foot washed, disinfected, and sealed with butterfly stitches. A large plastic bag covered the bottom of her leg, taped securely to protect it from sand and sea spray. As the sky became dark, Ellis and Annie gathered their hats and flip-flops. "We're going to head in. Sam, this is fabulous."

"We are too," said Xavier. "Gemma, do you want us to bring you back to the house?"

Holding her palm against her forehead, Gemma said, "Please, my footmen."

As everyone began picking up to leave the beach, Kai tugged on Valentina's hand and said, *"Mon amour, assieds-toi ici avec moi sur cette belle plage.* Let's wait for a bit. It's beautiful, and we haven't had a chance to talk."

Valentina sat back in her beach chair and looked out at the horizon.

CHAPTER 37

The next morning, Valentina woke up to the sound of the waves and the aroma of coffee. It was Bailey's and Xavier's turn to make breakfast. Xavier announced they would do a typical Marine Corps breakfast: eggs to order, bacon, hash browns, pancakes and toast. Bailey offered fruit and yogurt for the non-combatants.

"Help yourself to coffee," Xavier called from the kitchen.

"Thanks. 'Morning." Valentina settled on the sofa with a large mug. She thought about what didn't happen last night. She and Kai sat on the beach long after the others had gone in, talking, then not. Valentina enjoyed the silence between them and the sound of the tide rolling onto the beach. They cuddled on one of the recliners together. Kai brought a bottle of wine, and Valentina felt pleasantly buzzed. Kisses, soft at first, then more insistent. When Valentina knew it was time to stop, Kai wouldn't quit. He poured more wine into her mostly full glass and another for himself.

"Cherie, t'es si belle." He kissed Valentina's neck and pressed his hand below her waist. Valentina pushed his hand away and tried to sit up. Kai kissed her again and then reached for the clasp on her top. *"Je veux t'voir au clair de lune."*

"You can see everything I want you to see just fine in the moonlight. Kai, I told you, I'm not ready for that." He didn't listen and kept trying to convince her. Kai pushed himself on top of Valentina, grinding against her. She finally said, "Get off me!" and stomped away.

She saw Kai on the deck talking with Tala and decided she'd stay inside for a while. Xavier and Bailey were pretty busy and didn't want help or conversation to distract them. Valentina looked out at the Gulf of Mexico, stormy that morning. Glancing down, she saw the papers she found in the utility room. They were covered with drawings and scrawled notes. Valentina sounded out the scribbles: "stasis .... 48 hours without a host ...." Sam walked down the stairs, got a cup of coffee and sat across from Valentina.

"Oh, are those the notes you found yesterday?" Sam asked.

"Yeah. I was trying to figure them out. It's like part of a graphic novel."

"Let's see. Yep, my dad's handwriting. Look, here's something I can make out: 'Angus.'"

"What is this part? Is that 'A. tasidella?'"

"I bet it's *tosichella.* Angus works in entomology research at Landever. My dad was probably on a work call. A lot of times he takes notes to help him stay focused."

Valentina and Sam continued looking at the notes together.

"Look at these pictures," Valentina laughed. "Your dad's a pretty good artist. This is better than a comic strip."

Sam laughed with her. "That looks like a wheat field with an army of bugs coming."

"This one has little flying saucers over the field."

Ellis walked up to them and glanced down at the paper. "I think they're drones. See, here are the propellers," he pointed, "and the wings. With really weird looking bugs hanging out of them."

Sam laughed again but Valentina picked up the drawing and felt herself grow cold. "Sam, when was your dad here last?"

"It's been at least six months. I haven't spoken to my dad in ages. The property manager said he griped about not being able to get here in such a long time. Why?"

"Sam," Valentina said, the paper in her hand shaking. "My cousin Will is a farmer. His wheat and sweet corn have been decimated like most of the growers in the Midwest."

"Oh, wow, Valentina. I'm sorry. I didn't know. Why don't I talk to my father about getting your cousin Landever's new seeds …"

"I think your father may have done enough, Sam."

"What?"

"Will and several other farmers found drone parts in their fields. One guy found an entire drone."

Staring at Valentina, Sam asked, "What are you saying?"

"It seems strange to me that months before the virus outbreak, your dad is talking to one of his evil lab rats about bugs in drones flying over farmer's fields."

"Wait a minute. You don't know Angus. He's the reason I'm going into research. I met him the first summer I worked at Landever. He's one of the most ethical people l know. He would never do anything like that."

"You don't think this is a little coincidental?" Valentina said, her voice rising as he gestured to the notes.

"We need to get more information," said Ellis. "Second step in resolving an ethical dilemma. Could you get in touch with him?"

"My dad? I'm not sure that would help. We're not on the best of terms."

"He let you use the beach house," Ellis reminded him.

"I'm not sure he remembers we're here. His secretary told me he's out of the country. There's a standing order with the management company that I can use it if it's not occupied."

"What about Mr. Angus?" Valentina asked.

"I can reach Angus," Sam said quietly. "I talked with him before choosing my graduate program. He's a great guy."

"What would he say if he were involved in this?" Valentina asked.

"Involved in what, Valentina?" Sam said with some heat. "You're implying that my father—my father—Valentina, and one of the best, most honorable scientists I've ever met are involved in a plot to decimate the agricultural industry. That doesn't make sense."

"What's the value of Landever's stock price today compared to six months ago?" she asked.

"Landever has been researching the mites and that virus for years. Like every other agricultural corporation. They aren't supposed to recoup their investment?"

"Look, we can't be certain of anything yet," interjected Ellis. "Sam, do you know this Angus well enough that you could call him? It is the weekend."

"Yeah, I have his cell. We've stayed in touch. What do you want me to ask him—hey, did you collude with my father to get control of the grain market in the United States?"

Valentina looked at him, eyebrows raised.

"Why not call and talk about your classes, then ..." Ellis said.

Bailey walked over from the kitchen. "Hey, breakfast is ready. Our cook is taking orders for eggs however you want them. Come on, folks, this looks like way too serious a conversation before breakfast."

"Valentina ..." Sam stopped, apparently unsure what to say.

"I'm sorry, Sam. Maybe this is coincidental, but my cousin may lose his farm because of the mites."

"We'll get some answers. Why don't we eat now," said Ellis.

Everyone gathered at the large counter, joking with Xavier as he finished up the eggs. With plates loaded, they went outside to the big table on the deck. Lisa and Annie carried out the serving platters. Valentina managed to slip in between Tala and Gemma, avoiding Kai for the time being. Xavier and Bailey walked out, followed by Leo wearing dark glasses.

Sam, remembering his role as host, asked, "What did you guys want to do today? We have a small sailboat, and jet skis are available for rent down the way."

"For me," Tala said, "I would like to walk along the beach."

"That sounds about my speed," Leo said.

The others continued discussing their plans for the day and agreed to regroup before dinner. Valentina, Sam, and Ellis helped everyone pick up then settled into the large sofa and chairs in the great room.

Kai approached Valentina. "We need to talk," he said, insistent.

"Yes, we do." Valentina nodded. "Can I catch up with you later? There's something else I've got to deal with first."

"With him?" Kai flipped his hand at Sam, narrowing his eyes.

"Yes, with Sam."

"I'll be on the beach."

After Kai left, Sam pulled out his phone and found his contact for Angus. He looked at Valentina then tapped the small icon to connect. He put the call on speaker so that Valentina and Ellis could hear.

"Hullo."

"Angus, this is Sam Stillman."

There was a pause, then Angus said, "How's it going, Sam?"

"Going okay. I started that graduate program we talked about."

"Well done! What are your classes?"

"Genetics, biochemistry, statistics and bioethics."

"With labs, that sounds like a pretty big load."

"I'm actually calling about the ethics class."

"Sam, I'm not sure I can help you with that. When I was in school, no one thought you needed a class to learn how to be ethical."

"Bear with me for a minute?"

"Sure, Sam. What's on your mind?"

"Are you still researching *Aceria tosichella*?"

The line went silent. When Angus spoke again, his voice had an edge to it. "Yes, but we've had a few setbacks. Several months ago, we managed to achieve stasis with the mites at below freezing temperatures. When revived, more than eighty percent were viable and able to reproduce. You may remember we were looking to develop a large enough population to identify measures to control them. Then there was a lab accident late last year. We lost everything. I haven't been able to get funding to replicate our efforts."

"Did you talk to my father about this?"

Angus paused then asked, "What is this all about?"

"I'm in Florida at my family's beach house. We found some notes that may have been from a conversation you had with my dad."

"Who's 'we,' Sam?"

"Two students from my bioethics class. We're here celebrating the end of the semester. We saw papers that may have been from a phone call with you."

"What makes you think that?"

"They were doodles really, notes about the mites and your name. The funny part is the drawings look like mites flying on drones over grain fields."

"Bassa," Angus muttered.

"Excuse me?"

"Sam..."Angus stopped.

"You think my dad is involved in wiping out the crops." Sam sat up straight, his hands clenching.

"Your father asked me to go to India immediately before the electrical failure in the lab. When I got back, I learned my lab was the only one affected, and I was told we lost all the mites. They threw everything out. And the funding spigot was shut off straightway. A month before, Sam, I could have asked for the moon and gotten it."

Sam became completely still and didn't respond. Valentina and Ellis watched as his face paled.

Angus continued, "Sam, I'm sorry. These events are strange by themselves, but taken together ...."

When Sam said nothing, Ellis spoke up. "Mr. Angus, this is Ellis Morrison, one of Sam's classmates. One of our other classmates, Valentina, is here with us. Her cousin is a wheat farmer in Nebraska. He found debris that, to me, looks like parts of a drone. An expensive drone, not one a kid would have. Let me ask you something, would it have been possible for your mites to survive in their frozen state, then reproduce once they landed in the wheat?"

"It's very likely, Mr. Morrison." Angus stopped, and a heavy silence enveloped the room. Then Angus said, "Sam, you can't let him get away with this."

"We don't know that he caused the crop failure," Sam said.

"You're right," said Ellis. "How can we get more information?"

"There may be some residue on the drones. If I could get access to any organic matter, I should be able to identify whether they are mites, and if their lineage is the same as the ones from my lab."

"Mr. Angus," Valentina said, "my great uncle works with a federal agency that's involved in the investigation. Would you be willing to talk with him?"

"Let me have his contact information. I'll try to reach him this weekend. I'd rather not talk with him at my office."

Sam said very little during the rest of the conversation. After a few more minutes, they ended the call.

"Sam, do you want to talk about it?" asked Ellis.

"Not now."

CHAPTER 38

Valentina walked slowly toward the beach, carrying water, snacks, and a book she knew she wouldn't read. She saw Tala and Leo in the distance, bending toward the sand and talking animatedly. Kai, Xavier, and Bailey had rented jet skis, and Xavier was holding onto Bailey from behind while she guided the ski gracefully across the horizon, spray flying into the air in their wake. Kai was driving erratically, and kept trying to splash them and other skiers.

Valentina saw Bailey turn and speed away from Kai.

From under her beach umbrella, Annie motioned her over. "Come sit with me, Valentina."

"Oh, Annie."

"Want to talk about it?"

Valentina twisted her hair with nervous fingers and looked down at the sand.

"I mean about Kai." Annie motioned toward the jet skiers in the surf.

"He's not who I thought he was."

"The north end of a south-bound horse?" Annie asked.

Valentina laughed. A shadow fell across her book—Sam.

He stood next to their beach chairs. Looking down at Valentina, he asked, "How about a walk?"

"Okay."

As Valentina got up, Ellis settled next to Annie, saying, "Sam, remember who you are. Separate and distinct from your father or anyone else."

"I don't know who I am anymore. This is a nightmare."

Valentina said nothing but nodded in agreement.

Sam looked out at the horizon. He and Valentina walked along the edge of the beach, getting wet as the waves swept past their ankles. The sea oats stood above the white sand along the dunes, bending slightly in the breeze.

"There could be another explanation," Valentina said.

"I keep trying to tell myself that." Sam spoke quietly. "In the last few years, my father changed. He and my mom always competed with each other. Conversations could be like a fencing match, but it was fun. They had incredible chemistry but with a sharp edge. Then, after my grandmother died, the dynamic shifted. My mom inherited a pile of money and started acting like she could call all the shots... I think I'm part of this too. When I didn't want to go to medical school, that was the last straw for my dad. It was like a personal betrayal. He used to be in control—that's gone."

"Does your dad have that much invested in Landever? Sure, he gets a bonus or something since they have the only virus-resistant wheat, but that wouldn't be megabucks? Would it?"

"Knowing my dad, he's probably leveraged his bets. He trades futures. Risky, but he's had some big wins. He paid outright for our house in New Orleans after one of his deals."

"Impressive," Valentina said.

"From what I've gathered, he's taken a few hits, but mostly he's done well. In this case, how could he lose?" Sam asked rhetorically. "If he expected the shortages."

They continued walking on the beach as the morning wind blew against them.

"What do you want to do?"

Sam sighed. "Like Ellis said, let's find out. We can check in with your great uncle once Angus gives him the data. Who is he with, anyway?"

"Uncle Tony is with the FBI." She shrugged. "He never says much about the specifics of his job. I do know that he's connected enough to get the information to the right people."

"What happens then, Valentina? My father gets arrested?"

"I think they'll talk to your dad and ..."

Sam shook his head and walked away, back toward the house.

As Valentina stood on the beach, she heard someone call her name. She looked up and saw Tala and Leo.

Valentina tried to smile, but the effort was clear. "Hey Tala. Leo. Beautiful day."

"We're going to walk up to the point," Leo said. "Want to come?"

Nodding, Valentina joined them as they continued walking along the beach. "I came here a few times with my grandparents," Valentina said. "One summer we had a Sorelli/Torino clan gathering and rented a townhouse. My cousin, Will and his parents came. It was the best."

"That sounds nice. My family also used to gather at the seashore," Tala said.

"You must miss them," Valentina said.

Tala looked sad and simply said, "Yes." Changing the subject, she asked, "What does that green flag mean?"

"It's a flag warning system," Leo said. "Green means there's very low danger from the surf or sharks. Yellow means there's danger of high surf or an undertow, and red is the most serious."

"Isn't blue or purple for sharks?" asked Valentina.

"Right," said Leo.

They walked along the shoreline, waves lapping against their legs. Valentina started to relax, soothed by the cadence of Tala's comments and Leo's quiet responses. When they returned to the house an hour or so later, Tala went inside to shower. Valentina and Leo stayed on the deck enjoying the sunset. Funny how comfortable she was with Leo. There was no hidden agenda. She was attracted to him, and knew he liked her too. But she didn't feel any pressure. She was about to tell him about Jack Stillman's notes when Kai walked up from the beach.

"Really Valentina? Do you remember who you came with?"

As Kai brushed past them, Valentina said, "Hard to forget, Kai."

CHAPTER 39

After hanging up the phone with Sam, Angus sat back in his desk chair, the leather cracked and worn. *What the bleedin' hell*, he thought. He felt sorry for Sam. Angus remembered the first time he met the kid. He initially thought: *Here was another one of the anointed ones.* Blond, slim, and tall for his age, perfect grin achieved through careful breeding and expensive orthodontics. To Angus's surprise, Sam was different from the other entitled children of upper management and board members. He was earnest and polite. He listened, asked questions, and had thoughtful answers half the time himself. He would get curious about something, and off he'd go. It had been a kick. Sam had a fine, logical mind to go with that enthusiasm. Angus encouraged his interest in research. When Sam called every once in a while, he enjoyed their conversations.

But Angus hated the conversation he just had with Sam. He actually insinuated Sam's father was a criminal. *Do I really believe that? Well ... yes. Was it necessary to say it in front of his mates?*

Angus thought about his research. Could he have done the work with a university? He knew getting funding was tricky and came with its own set of problems in the public sector. He took the corporate route, enjoying easier access to equipment and the immense freedom from the publishing game. Now it seemed like a heavy compromise. Too late. Generally, Landever was supportive in a distant sort of way. He got most of what he asked for, even before

Stillman poked his nose into his lab. The company seemed to be on the right track until this.

The nerve of that bawbag, using his research, for what—money, ego, control? When it broke, would the company survive? *Could Stillman get away with it?* Angus looked around his warm, comfortable home office. He loved his cozy house on the outskirts of downtown. Angus heard the clear soft voice of Sam's friend talking about her cousin. There were thousands of farmers who lost their crops and might lose their homes. He said to himself, *Absolutely not!* He looked down at Anthony Sorelli's contact. The only way out of this was forward, for him, Sam and Landever. He hoped they all survived. Picking up his cell phone, he tapped Tony's contact.

•   •   •

Tony was relaxing in his den after a long week when his cell phone rang. Not recognizing the number, Tony answered, "Sorelli."

"This is Stephen Angus ..." followed by a paused.

"How did you get this number?"

"I got it from your niece."

"How do you know my niece? And to which one of my lovely nieces do you refer? I happen to have a few."

"Valentina."

"Valentina, how in the world ..." Tony muttered to himself.

"What's that? Valentina," Angus repeated.

"Yes, of course," Tony said. "And what may I help you with today, Mr. Angus?"

"I have information regarding the distribution of the wheat streak mosaic virus."

Tony sat up a little straighter, clutching his cell phone a little tighter. "What gives you that idea, Mr. Angus?"

"Because it's my mites the bastard used!"

"Could we slow down a little, Mr. Angus?"

"It's just Angus, Mr. Sorelli. Mr. Angus was my father."

"Then call me Tony, Angus. How did you run across Valentina? And you mentioned mites?"

"She's friends with a young man I took under my wing several years ago. Sam Stillman. Sam is the son of Jack Stillman, head of new product development at Landever, where I work, at least for now."

"You work at Landever?

"Didn't I just say that, man? We're not going to get anywhere if you repeat everything I tell you."

"You're absolutely right, Angus. Could you please continue?"

"I received a call from Sam a little while ago. Apparently, he was with friends from school at his family beach house. They found some notes, likely written by Sam's father during a conversation we had together. The notes included labeled drawings of my mites in aircraft flying over wheat fields."

"Your mites?" Tony asked.

"Shortly before an incident at my lab, I had an early morning call with Jack Stillman, while he was at that same beach house in Florida. I had a breakthrough in my research. My field is arthropods, specifically *Aceria tosichella*. I was able to freeze them and wake them up again, if you will. Although there is a strain of mites, Red Velvet, that is freeze tolerant, it's quite rare. Mites generally are freeze-avoidant or chill susceptible. Not Red Velvet mites, which are quite the exception. One purpose of my research was to determine the freeze tolerance of *Aceria tosichella*. Could we achieve stasis and then reawaken the mite?" Angus paused for a moment. "It worked." Angus continued with a touch of pride in his voice. "This is only the second incidence of freeze tolerance in a micro-arthropod." With the regret softening and slowing his voice, he said, "I had hoped this would lead to better understanding and control of the mite, as well as of the wheat viruses."

"Keep going, Angus."

"After that call, Stillman basically ordered me to our research facility in India. Completely random and uncharacteristic. Invented some story about how the Mumbai office needed me. I knew it was bollocks. The bloody arse took my mites."

"Angus, could we get together and talk more about this?"

"You mean come down to your office? You must be daft, man."

"Would you meet me for a drink?"

"Look, the only way I'll be able to tell you anything for certain is to get a DNA sample from the drones. Have you acquired the drones yet?"

"What do you know about the drones?"

"Very little."

"Well ..."

"Look, are you daft? Sam, your niece, and their friend told me about the drawing with the mites on drones. The only way to tell if my mites were used is by doing a comparative DNA analysis. Get the drones, and we'll see if it's my strain of *Aceria tosichella*. Call me back, Mr. Sorelli, when you have the drones or you've done the analysis. We can have that drink when you get the samples." With that, Angus ended the call.

As he listened to the silence, Tony mused at how one young woman, his niece in New Orleans, Louisiana, could be at the intersection of a national agricultural crisis. He would talk to Valentina later.

Tony called Freddy Ackerman, part of his Violent Crimes Squad and his go-to person at the Houston field office of the FBI. "Do we have the drone parts yet?"

Accustomed to hearing from Tony at any hour of the day or night, Freddy appeared nonplussed by getting a call on Saturday morning. "We picked all of them up late last week. They're at the lab."

"Can you light a fire under them, Freddy? I have a guy who may be able to identify the source of the mites."

"You bet, boss."

CHAPTER 40

Angus tried to remember how he acted when he was going to the lab on a Sunday. Definitely not pissed off. *Casual,* he thought. *Put in a few hours, act like I'm going to meet my mate, Barry, afterwards.* He liked the work, and it wasn't unusual for him to go in on the weekend, particularly when he was immersed in a project. Tony Sorelli had called back. It surprised Angus they processed the residue on the drone parts so quickly, especially over the weekend. Angus wished he still had the actual mite samples, but he had plenty of data that would allow a comparison of his *Aceria tosichella* with what Tony found. After the phone call, Angus rushed to the mall to purchase a portable hard drive before he headed to Landever's campus.

Arriving at the security gate on Sunday, Angus realized that the vehicle a few cars ahead was a large black limo. There were only three executives who used a limousine, and Stillman was one of them. Too late to turn around. That would be too obvious. And it might not be Stillman, although he often worked weekends. The limo passed through the gate, stopped for a moment as Angus passed, then turned toward the executive offices. Relieved, Angus drove to the low red brick building where entomology and the other duller departments were housed.

Angus bypassed the elevator, taking the stairs that opened on the third floor at the rear of the building near his lab. A few of the other research staff came in on the weekend if they had a project underway, or to make a dent in the endless administrative busywork. His mate, Barry, whose office was near the elevator on their floor, was in. He'd see if Barry had time for lunch another day. Barry had been at Landever longer than anyone else he knew. He didn't want to involve him in this mess any more than he already had.

Angus walked down the long hallway, only the emergency lights glowing in the semi-darkness. Unlocking the door to his lab, he was still jarred by the missing freezers. He usually loved the quiet times on weekends here. Every sound was magnified—the clicking of the wall clock, the hum of the equipment, the printouts he planned to review again before tossing, the paper rustling slightly as the air conditioner cycled on.

Angus sat down in front of his computer and removed the new hard drive from his leather case. He pulled up the first of the *Aceria tosichella* folders and began backing up his data. If he could copy enough of his files, and if Sorelli could retrieve sufficient organic material from the drone parts, they'd perform a morphometric analysis with DNA barcoding. Copying his files would take a while. He had a large capacity hard drive, so there would be plenty of room. Angus began reviewing interoffice mail and reading the latest scientific articles in his email, stopping frequently to select another folder to copy onto the hard drive. Images flashed quickly on his computer screen. Skimming through his journals, he became engrossed in an older edition with an article about honeybees. Angus lost track of time. *Snodgrassella alvi* protected bees from pathogens. Ah yes. He'd like to see what Barry thought about it. Then the back of his neck tingled. Angus listened. Nothing ... but he heard or sensed something. He closed the file he was copying and clicked "remove device." As his hand closed over the drive, a tall figure appeared in the doorway. Angus turned in his chair and slid the hard drive under a pile of printouts.

"Working on the weekend, Angus?" Jack asked quietly.

Angus's thoughts scrambled at the sound of Stillman's oily voice. He had copied only half his data, but it would have to be enough. "Yes, yes sir, starting to put together a research proposal on honeybees, rather, a pathogen, *Snodgrassella* ..."

"Really?" Jack asked.

"Fascinating really, so important to agriculture ..."

"Honeybees are a little outside your lane, aren't they, Angus?" Jack asked.

Angus didn't answer.

"How naïve do you think I am? What are you really doing here today?"

"Catching up on paperwork. It's hard keeping up with the professional literature and one's research at the same time."

"Bullshit, Angus. Your research is in the toilet. You're not working on anything."

Pushing away from his desk, Angus rose to his feet. The Scotsman wasn't as tall as Stillman, but he was more stockily built. He rocked on the balls of his feet, ready for anything. They looked at each other for a long moment.

"Give me that hard drive."

"I don't know what you're talking about. Which one do you want? I probably have a dozen."

"The one you just pulled out of your computer," Jack hissed. He lunged for Angus, grappling for the drive.

Angus grabbed the storage device, scattering the printouts. He stepped back and to the side. Jack's momentum carried him forward. Unable to stop, he slammed into the wall behind the desk. Pushing off the wall, Jack swung wildly. With his longer reach, his fist connected above Angus's right eye.

Angus bellowed, "You bloody bastard!" He gripped Jack's shirt, pulling him closer. He smelled the acrid odor of Stillman's sweat, overwhelming his expensive cologne. "Stay the hell away from me, you hear?" he roared. He shook Jack, almost lifting him off the floor, then threw him back against the wall. His head struck the wall hard.

Stunned, Jack shook his head and lunged toward Angus. Angus punched him hard below his ribs, and Jack sank to the floor. Looking down at Jack, Angus was tempted to beat him into a pulp. He could.

"I'll call security," Jack said, seething.

Angus stared down at Jack, breathing hard for what seemed like forever, but was probably only seconds. If he hit him again, Angus didn't know if he'd be able to stop.

From his position on the floor, Jack looked back at Angus, fury clear in his scarlet face. Then, visibly recalibrating, Jack said, "Angus, let's forget about this incident. I won't press charges. Just give me the hard drive."

"Yeah?"

"I bear you no malice, Angus," Jack said smoothly from the tiled floor as he got control of himself.

Ridiculous. "That's it, huh? Bygones be bygones?"

"Absolutely. We can talk about better equipment, more funding," offered Jack.

"That sounds quite interesting," Angus managed to say through the tightness in his throat, his heart beating wildly.

Relaxing for a moment, Jack pulled himself up and carefully sat on the edge of the desk. "We could build on your success at freezing *Aceria tos* ..."

Angus dove for his briefcase, still holding tightly to the drive. He rushed toward the door. Stillman started to follow him and slipped on the printouts that had fallen to the floor. Angus ran down the corridor leading to the front hallway. After a pause, he heard footsteps pounding behind him.

Barry poked his head out of his office. "Angus? What's going on?"

"Barry, take this." Angus thrust the hard drive at Barry. "Go back in your office and shut the door. Quick!" Angus wheezed. He slapped the lift button, then ran past the elevator toward the front stairwell. Angus sensed rather than heard Barry's door close softly behind him. Relieved, he stopped in an alcove before the stairs, waiting for Stillman to pass him. Stillman flew by, racing down the stairs. Angus quietly hurried back the way he came and caught the elevator down to the first floor. Angus stood, breathing heavily, as the lift descended. He calmed with each exhale.

Stillman confronted him as the doors opened. "I've alerted security."

Angus looked at Stillman with disgust and turned to leave the building.

Two security guards ran up behind Stillman.

"Search this man. He is attempting to abscond with company property."

Angus stood quietly as the guards patted him down. They opened his briefcase, Stillman watching silently as they rifled through the contents: a mobile phone, its charger, hand sanitizer, a small umbrella, a journal, and the last novel by Kazuo Ishiguro.

"Sir?" The security guard looked between Angus and Stillman. Already a deep pink, the skin around Angus's eye was starting to swell. Stillman's expensive shirt was rumpled, his usually well-groomed hair disheveled.

Jack bit out the words, "You're fired."

"For what? Working on the weekend?"

"Don't think I'm joking." Jack spit out. "We'll have your final check for you tomorrow."

"You have no grounds," Angus said evenly.

Stillman turned to the two guards. "Call whomever else is on duty. I want this building searched from top to bottom."

As Angus turned to go, he brazenly said, "My lawyer will be in touch."

•　　•　　•

Unnoticed, Barry watched from his third-floor window. While Angus was being searched, Barry took a faded insulated lunch bag from his desk. He hadn't expected to see Angus that day, so he brought his lunch. He carefully wiped away the mayonnaise on his sandwich and took out the chicken. Wrapping the hard drive in a piece of plastic, he placed it carefully inside the sandwich. With shaking hands, Barry rearranged the lettuce and left a bit of mayo exploding from the packaging. Then he returned the sandwich to his bag. After riding the elevator to the ground floor, Barry walked slowly down the hallway to the front of the building. The clicks of his cane punctuated the silence. As he exited the building, Barry limped toward the group surrounding Angus. "Gentlemen, is anything the matter?"

Angus looked down at his feet. Stillman motioned to the second guard. "Check his case," he ordered.

"What's this all about?" Barry asked.

The guard went through Barry's case, finding folders, a pack of Kleenex, and his lunch bag. He opened it quickly, saw the wrapped sandwich, and asked, "Not hungry today?"

"Not as much energy as I used to," Barry said. "I had planned to work longer."

Stillman strode over to the guard and Barry and grabbed the lunch bag. He looked down at the sandwich with the mayonnaise oozing beneath the lettuce. Disgusted, Jack said, "Let them go."

As they walked slowly across the parking lot, Barry asked Angus, "Mind telling me what this is all about?"

"I will, Barry. But what did you do with the drive? Stillman will find it if you left it in the building."

"Relax, Angus, it's safe." Barry said as he limped slowly toward his car. "Did we commit espionage or prevent Stillman from the same?"

"Have time for a drink, mate?"

"I should say so, Angus."

CHAPTER 41

Late Sunday evening, Sam drove west on old Highway 90, abandoning the interstate for a slower paced ride back to New Orleans. Valentina watched the play of light on the waves from the back window of the Jeep. Leo offered her the front seat, but Valentina wanted to brood. Sam seemed too upset to talk. Leo appeared to recognize the mood of the trip had changed.

After mutual avoidance for the rest of the weekend, Valentina had approached Kai Sunday afternoon. "Are we going to talk about this?"

"Valentina, I thought we had a connection. You can't tell me you don't feel it too. And you left me hanging."

"It takes me a little more time."

"You either feel it or you don't."

"Can't we take a step back?" asked Valentina.

"Yeah. Sure," agreed Kai as he literally stepped back and turned toward the house.

Valentina wondered how she could have misread things so completely. Or she was way too old-fashioned. She didn't expect to be—well—married, but she needed at least a mutual understanding that having sex was a serious step. What a bust, she thought. Valentina cringed, remembering her younger dating, something she thought of as her girl-gone-wild phase. Who knew what she was looking for back then. It never felt good past the initial excitement, and she got tired of the confusion. Valentina saw a counselor for a while who suggested it had to do with her parents leaving her so young. From that point, she committed to taking better care of herself. And that meant asking Sam if she could ride back to New Orleans with him.

As they approached Ocean Springs, Leo said, "I like this town. It's artsy, a little old-fashioned, not as developed as Biloxi with all the casinos."

"I've never stopped except to get gas," Sam said.

"It's the home of a visual artist, Walter Anderson. Actually, he was crazy, so he lived here when he wasn't tying himself to a tree during a hurricane, or rowing out into the Gulf for miles and miles by himself. One of his brothers started Shearwater Pottery. There's a museum too. I wish we had time see it."

When neither Valentina nor Sam responded, Leo said, "Okay, what's going on? Something's upsetting you both."

Valentina watched from the back seat as Sam's neck and ears turned red. Looking at her in the rearview mirror, Sam slowed down. "You want to stop?"

Leo waited.

"Sure," Valentina said.

"It's early for dinner, but why don't we get coffee?" Sam suggested. "Maybe they have biscotti."

Valentina laughed and Leo looked confused.

They got their coffee and found a table on the outdoor patio. After sitting in silence, both Valentina and Sam began talking at the same time.

"Leo, ..." Sam started.

"We think that ... Sam, you go first."

Starting over, Sam said, "We think there may be a connection between my father and the farms being hit across the continent by the wheat virus."

Stunned, Leo looked at Sam then Valentina. "Run that by me again?"

"You know about the virus that struck all the crops?" Valentina asked.

"Of course. It's a disaster. How could your father possibly be involved? Doesn't he work with Landever? They developed a resistant strain of wheat."

"That's the point, Leo," said Valentina. "It's beginning to look like Sam's father orchestrated the spread of the virus on purpose."

"No one would do that."

"I keep trying to tell myself that," Sam said. "But I also know my dad."

"People don't have enough to eat," Leo said.

"My cousin Will," said Valentina, "who happens to be a Nebraska wheat farmer, lost all his crops to the virus. It's spread by a mite."

"I read that. *Aceria tosichella*, isn't it?"

"Two points to Leo," Sam said bitterly.

"Will was walking in his friend's field," Valentina said. "They discovered parts of a drone. Seven other farmers found drone parts. One of them found an entire drone."

"That doesn't make sense," Leo said. "I read up on that specific mite. You're saying the mites flew across the U.S. from Landever in drones? The mites wouldn't survive without food."

"We called an entomologist Stephen Angus who figured out how to freeze and then revive the mites after several days with over an 80% survival rate." Sam said.

Staggered, Leo whispered, "If the mites were frozen then transported on drones, they would revive in the fields."

"Two more points to Leo," Sam said.

"The researcher, Mr. Angus," Valentina said, "told us Sam's father sent him out of the country. When he got back, his mites were gone. Sam's dad told him there had been an accident with the cooling equipment, but he didn't believe that."

Valentina, Sam, and Leo continued talking on the outdoor patio, not noticing when another car pulled in next to Sam's in the parking lot.

•　　•　　•

Outside the coffee shop, Ellis told Annie, "It's really not any of our business."

"We're just going to stop and get coffee."

Tala looked at them both. "I don't understand. We've been following Sam's vehicle for several miles. We saw Sam pull into this coffee shop. His Jeep is right here. Why don't we go say hello and get you your coffee?"

Annie looked at Ellis, "Yes, why don't we?"

"Because it's none of our damn business, that's why."

"Your friends are hurting, Ellis."

"I am afraid I do not understand," Tala said softly.

Annie waited, and finally Ellis nodded. He held the door open, and Annie walked in, followed closely by Tala. After getting their coffees, Annie pretended to just notice the group sitting by themselves on the outdoor patio. "Hey," Annie said. "We love this coffeeshop."

Valentina, Leo, and Sam looked up in surprise.

"Wait, Annie, it looks as though we're interrupting a very serious conversation," Ellis said.

"That's okay. Here, sit down, why don't you join us?" offered Sam as he pulled chairs over from a nearby table. "We were helping Leo catch up."

"I'm having trouble getting my head around this," said Leo.

"Tell me about it," Sam said.

"You all seem very concerned. What is it, Sam?" asked Tala.

Sam looked stricken and said, "My father may be a criminal."

Ellis, Leo, and Valentina all began talking at once.

"Please, talk more slowly," Tala asked. "I do not understand."

Ellis summarized the recent events and their suspicions.

"How can we help?" Annie asked.

"Do you want to get back in touch with Mr. Angus?" Valentina said. "He's probably contacted my Uncle Tony by now."

"It stops me short when you say Mr. Angus, Valentina. He always asked me to call him Angus. And contacting him isn't a bad idea."

"Wait, what does your uncle have to do with this?" Leo asked Valentina.

"Please, I still do not understand," Tala said.

Valentina explained quickly, while Leo and Tala listened in disbelief as she filled in the gaps.

"What are our options?" Ellis asked.

"It's not up to us, Ellis," Leo pointed out. "Sam and Valentina have the most on the line."

"If it's true about my dad," Sam said, "there's no coming back from this. I ... couldn't allow him to get away with it."

"Sam, although it looks very bad for your father, we cannot be sure of his involvement," Tala said.

"You're right, Tala," said Valentina. "As bad as it looks, we don't know."

Sam seemed paralyzed. Then squaring his shoulders resolutely, he found Angus's contact in his phone and made the call.

CHAPTER 42

After leaving Landever, Angus and Barry drove separately to Sweeney's. Before leaving his car, Barry carefully retrieved the hard drive from his lunch bag, wiped the mayo off the plastic, and placed it in his jacket pocket. Once inside the restaurant, he unwrapped one of the silverware bundles and slipped the drive under the cloth napkin. Casually pushing it toward Angus, Barry reached for another swathed set of the silverware. Angus absentmindedly pulled the napkin toward him and felt the drive.

Angus let out a soft exclamation and a breath he didn't realize he'd been holding. "I don't ken how you managed this, mate, but it's pure dead brilliant."

"Now you owe me a story, my friend."

"Yes, I do."

Frances appeared and told them about the specials.

"I think I'll do the full breakfast, love," said Angus.

"Same here." Barry pushed away the menu. "And we'll have one of those fine Johnny Walker's, Frances."

"Two glasses?" she asked.

"Make it a pint."

"You gentlemen seem to be making this a habit," Frances said in a questioning voice.

Angus waited for Frances to bring the whiskey before beginning. He told Barry about Sam's call from Florida and the additional evidence, albeit circumstantial, of Jack Stillman's involvement in the grain crisis.

"Why were you copying your files?" Barry asked.

"One of these kids has a contact with the FBI. They're going to do an analysis of the drone residue and compare it with my data." Angus recounted the feeling of being watched in his office as he copied his *Aceria tosichella* files. Finishing up with the fight and his dismissal, Angus sat back and poured them both more whiskey.

Barry listened closely, shaking his head from time to time. "Stillman's in it up to his neck."

"Past that," Angus agreed.

Frances brought their breakfast, and without a word, they ate ravenously and drank some of the scotch. At first, Frances joked about their new Johnny Walker habit. When neither Angus nor Barry returned her good-natured jibes, she left them alone with their uncharacteristic drink order. She glanced their way from time to time. Barry caught her eye once when she started over with the check, shaking his head. Instead, she returned with a large coffee decanter and a pitcher of ice water.

Angus vaguely realized that his phone was ringing. Fumbling it out of his pocket, he looked at the display. "Oh, this isnae real. It's Stillman's lad. What the hell am I going to say?"

"Do you have to tell him?" Barry motioned for Angus to hand over the phone. "Let me answer it. Take a minute."

"Hello?"

A few moments of silence was followed with, "Er, this is Sam Stillman calling for Stephen Angus. Is he available?"

"He'll be with you in just a moment. Sam Stillman, you may not remember me. I'm Barry Carlson and work at Landever with Angus. We met a few summers ago. How are you, my boy?"

"Oh, fine, sir. You worked on bees, didn't you?"

"That's right, Sam. And you did a little of everything, as I recall. Ah, that may be Angus coming now."

Angus nodded, as ready as he would ever be. "Sam? How are you?"

"I've been better. Did you try to reach Mr. Sorelli, Valentina's uncle?"

"We spoke yesterday, Sam. They've found organic residue on the drones. The mites transmit the virus through their salivary glands. I agreed to give him my data so we can do a comparative analysis of the DNA."

"Do you use mass spectrometry or a fluorescent microscope?" Sam asked, apparently curious about the science despite the circumstances.

"They will need to sequence the genes. I'm not sure how they plan to do it, and I doubt the feds will let me do the analysis myself," Angus said.

"Got it. Well, do you think my dad's involved?"

"Um..." Angus thought about telling tell Sam what happened at the office, then hesitated. Simple was best. "I don't know for sure, Sam, but I believe so. Your dad was at the office earlier today when I was there. He seemed extraordinarily interested in the files I was copying. I'll turn those over to your friend's uncle in the morning. I'll get back in touch when I know something for certain."

"Okay, thanks."

After signing off, Angus looked at Barry and said, "What a clusterbuach."

"That sounds like cluster—"

"Yeah, well, you have a better description?" Angus said. "We'd better let them have this table for the dinner crowd."

Leaving a generous tip for Frances, they made their way slowly out to the parking lot.

Before getting in his car, Barry stopped. "Do you need anything to tide you over for a bit? Until you find another position?"

"I'll be all right, mate," Angus said. "I've got some savings and a bit in the 401K. Thanks, Barry, for everything."

"I'm glad to help. Whatever you need."

Angus drove home carefully, constantly looking in his rearview mirror. Pulling into his driveway, he sighed with relief. It wasn't fancy, but he loved his old Craftsman cottage. He couldn't wait to get inside. He'd copy the files and get them to Sorelli tomorrow. Angus sent a text to the agent, letting him know he had the files. Tony said he would have someone pick up the hard drive late Monday morning.

CHAPTER 43

After a fruitless search of the entire building, Jack finally allowed the security officers to leave late Sunday evening. He insisted on a painstaking inspection of individual offices, laboratories, as well as the basement. They checked the HVAC system. They looked for loose ceiling and flooring tiles, inside trash bins and plumbing boxes. Bewildered and tired, the captain of the security force called Jack at close to 9 pm.

"Sir, we have searched every inch of this building. You have all the external hard drives we've seized. If it's not with those, I don't think we're going to find it. We've got to let the crew go."

Jack begrudgingly agreed. He had gone through the collected drives and found nothing. "Let them go, Captain. I appreciate your effort and that of your staff. Naturally, everyone will be paid overtime." After disconnecting the call, Jack threw one of the boxes of computer files across the room.

•   •   •

Early Monday morning, Angus was directed to the human resources department, where he received his final check and officially lodged a protest to his termination. Apparently, he was being dismissed for insubordination and attempted theft of proprietary information. Escorted by two security representatives, Angus picked up the personal gear from his office. On his way to the elevator, he passed

Barry, who smiled in support. A few of the other researchers came out of their offices with puzzled looks and questions about what was going on. Angus shrugged. The guards searched his box of books, photos and other belongings before he left the building. Stillman was nowhere to be seen. As he pulled up to the security gate checkpoint, the attendant asked Angus to step out of his car.

"We were instructed to inspect your vehicle, Mr. Angus."

Angus didn't say a word as they opened the trunk and glove compartment. He had thought of keeping the drive with him but was afraid something like this might happen. The drive was safe at home in a locked drawer in his desk. Finished with the inspection, Angus nodded at the guard and started home. He never expected his career with Landever to end like this. He had hoped to be another Barry, plodding away in his lab as he doddered into retirement. He needed to decide what came next—after putting that arsehole behind bars.

Passing the community college, Angus heard sirens and pulled over to allow the fire engine to pass. He continued north and realized he was following the path of the emergency vehicle. They seemed awfully close to his neighborhood.

"What the ..." Angus said out loud, as the fire engine he was following, quickly joined by another, turned down his street. Realizing they were continuing toward his house, Angus sped across the familiar roads. He pulled up down the block, staying clear of the fire fighters hustling back and forth between the trucks and his home. A cherry picker rose from the truck, a man in protective gear holding on to a hose on a small platform at the top. A gush of water struck the roof.

Jogging toward his house, Angus saw smoke and flames at the back near the kitchen. He had to get into his office. The hard drive was locked in his desk. Angus started toward the back door. A fireman stopped him. "Sir, you can't go in there."

"That's my house. I have to go inside."

"Sorry, sir. You'll have to wait out here until it's safe."

"What set it off?"

"We don't know for sure yet. It looks like it started in the kitchen. Usually someone leaves a burner on the stove. Starts a grease fire."

"Bollocks!"

As the firefighter hurried away, Angus turned and ran through his neighbor's yard a few houses down from his own. From there, he saw the arbor supporting his trumpet honeysuckle vine, smoke billowing out the back door. "Shite." Angus hopped his neighbor's fence and climbed over the rock border of the next bungalow. He bent down, waiting for one of the firefighters to pass. Angus then ran in through his backdoor. Heat seared his face and chest as he tried to reach his office. Thick black smoke made it difficult to measure distances. It was so dark Angus couldn't see anything. He crouched to the floor where there was less smoke and he could draw a breath. Crawling along the tiled back entrance, Angus felt along the wall and the baseboard, finding the doorway to his office. Finally, his desk. "Shite." He had left the keys in his car. He reached for the small shovel near the fireplace and dropped it. It was effing hot. Angus quickly pulled down the mantle covering and heard knick-knacks crash to the floor. A piece of glass, probably from his mother's vase, stabbed his cheek. He wrapped the fabric around his hand and arm and grabbed the shovel. Fitting it between the drawer and the front desk panel, he forced the drawer open and found the hard drive. Angus started toward the back door. He couldn't breathe. Getting halfway down the hallway, the Scotsman collapsed on the tiles, unnoticed by the fire fighters. But not by everyone.

●　　　●　　　●

A nondescript man, wearing a baseball cap pulled down low, watched Angus run from the side toward the back of the house. He waited, prepared to accost him when he exited. When no one left the house after several minutes, he ran to the back door and pulled on a mask and head lamp. He saw Angus's large frame sprawled across the tiles. Richard Jurgenson, as he was calling himself now, tried to reach Angus. Pushed back by the smoke, he made a hasty retreat then watched as the roof collapsed and the flames shot out of control. As he turned to walk away, Richard pulled off his headgear and stuffed it into a small backpack. A few blocks later, he climbed into a rented black SUV with tinted windows. Using a prepaid cell phone, he made a phone call. "You won't have to worry about anything."

"Any problems?" Jack asked.

"No."

"Did you get it?"

"It's gone."

"What do you mean?"

"Let's just say your concerns have gone up in smoke," Richard snorted. "Melted away."

Jack said. "I'll make the same arrangements."

"Very good, sir." Ending the call, Richard calmly steered the SUV out of the neighborhood then dumped the phone in one of the trash cans at the strip mall. He drove a while on surface streets, before catching an entrance to the interstate.

•   •   •

Anthony Sorelli had put surveillance on Angus ever since their first phone call. He received notification of the fire from his team as they watched the fire department arrive. When Angus ran into the burning house, one of the agents followed a short distance away and waited beneath a shadowed overhang. At the back entryway, special agent Luis Gonzalez radioed his partner, Jenn Livingston, when Richard followed Angus. "Unidentified male entering the back of the premises."

"Not Stephen Angus?"

"Following Angus."

Richard stepped outside and pulled off his mask and head lamp. Gonzalez was ready with a small long-range camera, snapping pictures as he waited for Angus to emerge from the burning structure. When Angus didn't appear, Gonzalez spoke urgently into his radio. "Jenn, follow him. I'm going in after Angus."

•　　•　　•

At first, Richard didn't notice the unassuming gray sedan following him, several cars back. Nor did he hear Jenn make the request for a local cop to check the trash can at the small shopping mall. On the beltway, he figured out he had picked up a tail. A gray sedan, looked like a Honda. He needed to disappear for a while.

CHAPTER 44

On Monday morning, Valentina waited for Amy at the front of Audubon Park. They hadn't been able to run for a couple of weeks because of Valentina's finals and Amy's work schedule. They exchanged brief texts, and agreed to catch up once they got together in person. Valentina arrived early, and started stretching. She looked across St. Charles Avenue, where a few students wandered near the front entrances of Tulane University and Loyola, next-door neighbors for more than a hundred years. The Gothic spires of Holy Name of Jesus Church soared into the sky between them. A streetcar clanged past, heading downtown. Leaning in to her tight muscles, Valentina didn't notice Amy until she was next to her, bending into a hamstring stretch.

"Hey, long time no see."

"Girl, do we have a lot to talk about," Amy said.

"We sure do. Do you have time for PJ's after our run?" Valentina asked. The local coffee chain had a small kiosk on Tulane's campus.

"Sure," Amy said. "I've put in so many hours lately my office will do fine without me for a bit."

"Great, I've got the day off."

"Nice."

They started a slow jog around the park, picking up speed as they ran beneath the oak limbs that stretched overhead.

"So?" asked Amy.

"Where should I start? You go first. How was your date with Mike?"

"Amazing."

Valentina waited as they continued running past the dark, reflective lagoon on their left. When Amy said nothing else, Valentina let out an exacerbated, "And ..."

"And we've gotten together almost every day since then." Amy blushed.

"Wow."

"I know, huh? He's ... we have such a good time together. With the end of the school year, we've both been working crazy hours. But we've met for late dinners, a quick lunch near my office ..."

"What do you like about Mike?"

"Besides being really hot?" Amy fanned herself. "He's got a quirky sense of humor. I think we have the same values. He works hard. He puts a lot into his work with the kids and their parents. We've run into some of his friends when we've been out. It's obvious he's liked and well thought of. Plus, it was easy to check out his reputation. There's enough overlap in our professional lives that I know people who know him or know of his work. He treats me with respect. It's early, but the more I find out, the more I like."

"What does he do for fun?"

"He plays soccer with a bunch of guys he's known since college. Mike has a big family in Miami, and he stays in touch with them. His mom and two of his brothers will visit in another week."

"Are you planning to meet them?"

"That's the plan."

"Holy cow."

"I know. I'm excited and terrified. Okay, enough about me. What's going on with you? Your text said you enjoyed your date with Kai. How was the weekend in Florida? Was it awkward with Leo?"

"Oh, Amy."

"Uh oh. What happened?"

"What didn't?"

"Just take me through it."

Valentina told Amy about how Kai had become aggressive at the beach. "Maybe it's because he had a couple of drinks, heck—we all did—but he didn't respect my boundaries. I totally misjudged him. At first, Friday night was loads of fun, and then things changed."

"I'm sorry. You thought he had potential. Better to find out now, though."

"Yep."

"How was the rest of the weekend?"

"Okay, here's where things got a little strange."

Amy's head swiveled to look at Valentina. "Then they got strange?"

"You can't tell anybody about this, Amy."

"Okay."

Valentina described how she found the notes made by Sam's father and what they suspected. She went through the later events, explaining about the entomologist and how she put him in touch with her Uncle Tony.

"I remember your talking about your Uncle Tony. He works in some capacity with the government, right?"

"FBI. Angus said he would call Sam once they compared the data on the mites. We should hear in the next week or so."

"It's hard to believe Sam's dad could be involved in something like this. Valentina, the grain crisis could put the country into a depression. People are hurting. This is surreal."

"Tell me about it."

Valentina and Amy finished their run through the park. After getting coffee, they continued talking as they walked back toward their cars.

"I know you've got a lot more important things to worry about," Amy said, "but sometimes a crisis crystallizes how we feel. So ... what about Sam and Leo?"

"Sam is as sweet as can be and brilliant. At first, he felt like a little brother to me."

"Now you're not sure?"

"Now I'm not sure."

"And Leo?"

"Amy, it's hard to think about that now. He pulled me aside when we were leaving the coffee shop." Valentina paused. "He said, 'This isn't the right time. There's too much going on to think about getting together. But if you need anything, I'm here for you. Let's have that dinner once things settle down.'"

"Oh boy."

"It was exactly the right thing to say." Valentina's phone chimed. "Amy, let me take this. It's Uncle Tony. I'll catch up with you later."

Amy mouthed, "Talk soon," while miming a phone to her ear. Valentina nodded as she answered Tony's call.

"Hey, Uncle Tony."

"Valentina, we need to talk," Tony said in a serious voice.

"Gee, I hope you didn't mind my giving your number to Stephen Angus."

"No, no, not at all. Valentina, can you get in touch with your classmate, Sam?"

"Sure, what's up?"

"The researcher, Stephen Angus, is badly injured. He may not make it. I want to let him know, but I'd rather you be there. He may need a friend."

"Oh no! What happened?"

"There was a fire at his home."

"Is he in the hospital?"

"They've taken him to Eskenazi Health. They have the best burn unit in Indiana."

"I've got to ask, Uncle Tony. Did you get his data on the mites?"

"He has it on a hard drive, but it was damaged in the fire. We should be able to recover what's on it, but it's going to take time. Shoot me a text when you get hold of Sam, and I'll call him."

"Do you need his number?"

"No, sweetie. We have that."

Shaken, Valentina reminded herself to take deep breaths before she called Sam. Better yet, she would text, see where he was and go to him.

•　•　•

After Tony got off the phone with Valentina, he walked over to Freddy's office. "I only have a second. Can you get in touch with Indianapolis? Brad Icorn is still in charge of Violent Crimes last time I checked. We need a tail on Stillman."

"Stillman isn't going to get his hands dirty."

"That's only 'cause he's up to his eyeballs in horse manure and he's waving them over his head."

Freddy laughed. "Sure, boss."

CHAPTER 45

Sam looked around to find his phone when he heard it chime. He was sitting in his bedroom upstairs at his parents' house on State Street, looking into the trees that shaded the backyard. Where was his phone? There, on the dresser. The text was from Valentina.

Where are u?

Home alone lol. U?

Can I come over?

Yes

Be there in 15

Valentina ran the rest of the way back to her car. She drove quickly to Sam's address, a few blocks from the streetcar line. The house was a beautiful creamy white, set back from the wide street. She parked on the side street, where a line of black bamboo was restrained in a tall, elegant brick planter. Thirty feet high, the bamboo created a privacy screen that ran along the side of the house. Oak trees graced the front, and Valentina saw more at the back of the house. Before getting out of her car, she texted her uncle. Valentina climbed the beautiful, silky gray wooden steps and rang the bell. Sam answered the door quickly, and she impulsively hugged him.

Sam hung on to her briefly then said, "Come on in. It's good to see you." He took Valentina through the foyer, past an ornate stairway that led to the second floor. "We live in the back." They walked into a large kitchen that opened into an expansive living area, filled with light from large windows on three sides. "Let me get you something to drink."

"Just water, please."

"Are you sure? We could have iced coffee. I have CoolBrew, mocha flavored."

"You talked me into it."

Sam scooped ice from the ice maker and opened the custom refrigerator. "Milk?"

"Sure."

Sam got their drinks together, and they sat on a large sofa that looked out on the patio and landscaped yard. The bougainvillea and mandevilla blooms were a blaze of color in the sunny corners of the patio.

"Do you want to talk about things?" Valentina asked.

"What do you have in mind? We were going to wait to hear from Angus."

"I know."

"We don't know anything. Maybe the note we found was a coincidence. It could be a different strain of mites."

"Hmm ..." Valentina started to respond, then Sam's phone rang.

Sam looked down at his phone. "Probably spam. I don't recognize the number. Houston area code, I think."

Valentina shrugged. "You never can tell."

Sam decided to answer. "Hello."

"Is this Sam Stillman?"

"Yes. To whom am I speaking?"

"This is Anthony Sorelli, Valentina's uncle. I've been working with Stephen Angus."

Startled, Sam looked at Valentina. "Yes, sir."

"Sam, your friend Angus was injured."

"Oh, no. He's going to be okay, isn't he?"

"We hope so, but he's in bad shape."

"Where is he? Can we see him?"

"Not yet. It's touch and go."

"What happened?"

"There was a fire at his home in Indianapolis."

"What can I do?"

"Nothing at the moment. We wanted you to know ..."

"What are his injuries?"

"He has severe burns and lung damage. We understand he's on a ventilator."

Sam gasped. "He called you? I mean, before the fire."

"Yes, we were planning to meet this morning."

"Yesterday, he told me he was going to give you his data."

"We have the hard drive, but it was damaged in the fire."

"How badly?"

"We don't know yet. Our engineering team is still running diagnostics. It depends on how hot it got, whether it got wet. It's going to take time."

"Were you able to retrieve organic residue from the drones?"

"You're asking for pretty confidential information, young man." Tony's voice bristled.

"Well, did you? I involved a friend in this mess and look where it's gotten him!"

Tony paused. "Yeah, we have enough to analyze the DNA if we can recover Angus's files."

"What are you going to do?" Sam asked.

"We're evaluating our options. Look, I just wanted to tell you about Angus."

"Okay, I appreciate your calling."

As Sam ended the call, Valentina thought he looked sick to his stomach. "Tell me."

"Angus is hurt. He may not survive," Sam choked out. "Valentina, were you aware of this?"

"Uncle Tony called me about thirty minutes ago. He told me that Angus was at the burn unit in Indiana and I might want to be with my friend."

Sam didn't say anything for a full minute. "Things are so messed up. If I find out that my father had anything to do with this, it's all over for me."

"We still don't know," Valentina said, emphasizing the last word.

"I need to find out."

"Could you talk to your dad?"

"Are you kidding?" Sam asked. "We haven't had an actual conversation since I told him I wasn't going to medical school."

After 45 minutes of thrashing about for a solution, Valentina knew they had to stop.

"Sam, we're getting nowhere. And I've had so much iced coffee I can't sit still."

"We can't leave it like this. Angus is hospitalized and may not make it."

Valentina stopped her pacing suddenly. "I know what we need to do."

Sam looked at Valentina, his jaw dropping. "You do?"

"Yeah, let's go see my grandmother."

CHAPTER 46

Will walked quietly downstairs, looking for Susan. He heard the murmuring of the television in the family room.

"There you are," he whispered.

It was dark outside, and the soft glow of the lamp lit the seating area. Wearing Will's robe, Susan was stretched out on the sofa, fast asleep. Her light brown hair fell across her shoulders. Her tea cup, half-full, was on the coffee table with a copy of their application to become an organic farm. Will lowered himself into the armchair across from her, pushing a pillow out of the way. Since they refinanced, Susan was sleeping better. She had a bad night once in a while, and this must be one of them. They were both anxious about their inspection by a Farm Service Agency representative on Wednesday. The FSA would review their application for organic certification. Will mulled over all the steps they'd taken. It was critical to show no pesticide use for three years on their fields where they would plant vegetables. Luckily, the previous owner, Mr. Jennings, used the land around the kitchen garden for an embryonic Christmas-tree operation for a while. It didn't work out, and the land laid fallow after that. The results of the micronutrient soil testing were good, and Will signed up for one of the educational programs on production and marketing practices. He and Susan decided they would start with five acres. They would have a buffer between the organic crops and the rest of the farm. Will pulled together records of fertilizers and anything he had used on the farm and where. It would have been harder if they had been farming longer than a few years. He was fairly optimistic they would get the certification. He talked with Mitch, who, of course, insisted he consult Norris. Both considered going organic at different times and had useful suggestions.

An early news show was on. Behind the announcer was a graphic of a mite and fields. He grabbed the television remote and adjusted the volume for the announcement: "... a breakthrough in our fight against the wheat streak mosaic virus. The National Center for Genetic Resources Preservation in Fort Collins, Colorado announced the development of a wheat cultivar resistant to the virus. Let's go now to Fort Collins, where our reporter, Casey Rogers, is there with Dr. Martha Jane Bruning. Casey?"

On camera, Casey Rogers turned to Martha Jane and said, "As reported previously, many of the largest agricultural companies, with limited exceptions, are collaborating with the Department of Agriculture during the grain crisis by allowing complete access to their plant genetic resources. Dr. Bruning will give us some exciting news. Dr. Bruning?"

In her deliberate way, Martha Jane spoke to the camera. "The nation's scientists are working nonstop to develop crops protected against the wheat virus that is carried by the mites. We announce today this collaborative effort is paying off. We now have a resistant wheat cultivar that can withstand the onslaught of the wheat virus. Our research center is speed-breeding the wheat under LED lighting 22 hours a day. Soon we will be able to distribute seeds to the consortium of the agricultural corporations. They will partner to reproduce the mite-resistant seeds and provide them at no cost to farmers across the world. This collaborative effort has been led by Foranda, BYSN, and Zynagrain Corporations. Although the consortium cannot project exactly when the new wheat plant will be widely available, at least some supplies should be in the pipeline by next planting season."

"Thank you Dr. Bruning," Casey said. "Back to you, Chip."

The news anchor, Chip Jergens, faced the camera. "Up to this point, there has been only one grain seed resistant to the virus, produced by Landever. As previously announced, Landever has offered the seeds for free the first year, provided that buyers commit to a multi-year contract. For the new wheat plant developed in cooperation with the agricultural consortium, farmers will receive a limited amount of seeds at no cost for two years and be able to save their seeds, allowing them to recover a portion of their losses. After this period, copyright protections will be in effect. In other news ..."

Will sat back in his chair. *Wow. Things were looking up.*

"Did I hear that correctly? They've got a resistant wheat plant?" Susan asked from the sofa.

"Sounded like that to me. And one without contract obligations."

Susan yawned. "Fantastic."

"Oh, hey, I hope I didn't wake you up."

"I need to get up." Susan looked at Will and smiled. "What a relief."

"Do you want to rethink our application for organic certification?" Will asked. "This is going to be a lot of work."

"No, we've gone this far. It makes me a little more relaxed about the inspection."

"That's what I prefer too. We'll be a little more diversified," Will said. "We might be able to get back to grain as early as next year, at least on a limited basis."

"And we'll still have my job. With the organic produce, we should be okay."

Will weighed what to say. He wanted to tell Susan that she never had to worry again, that he would always keep them safe. It bothered him they needed to depend on her working.

"I can read your mind, honey," Susan said. "Look, that's why there are two of us. Partners, right?"

"Always," Will agreed. "Let me go make coffee, partner."

•   •   •

About seven hundred miles away, Jack Stillman stirred in the early morning hours. Inside his lavish condominium in downtown Indianapolis, well insulated from the street noise, a voice intruded. It was female. He turned over in his expensive sheets, enjoying the thin, perfectly tailored, smooth subtleness of the sateen. As usual, unless he had company, Jack went to sleep with one of the news channels playing. He started to slip back into the oblivion of sleep.

Wait a minute, he recognized that voice. The dry, superior tone. *Was it really that woman, what's her name, from the Fort Collins research center? What was she saying?* Resistant wheat cultivar ... next year ... no cost. *What?* Jack jumped up, fully awake. He grabbed his phone and checked his news app. Foranda, BYSN and Zynagrain. *Really? How could they? How could they make money on that deal? Free seeds for two years with no long-term contract? The government was backing them up. Socialist economic policy, that's what this was. This was a disaster.* He checked grain futures. Lower, lower ... If that trend continued, he would be in a lot of trouble. As it was, his financial gains were starting to disappear. He probably shouldn't have put as much into commodities. He needed to think. He had to do something. Good grief, he needed caffeine.

Jack paced in front of the floor to ceiling windows as he waited on his fully automatic imported coffee maker. A few moments later, he threw back a cup of espresso. As the caffeine triggered the release of adrenaline, he looked out across the lights of downtown Indianapolis dimming as the sun rose. He could fix this.

CHAPTER 47

When the doorbell rang, Mia opened the door and saw Valentina. "Oh, you beautiful thing! What a wonderful surprise. And this is your young man?"

Silently willing Mia to stop talking, Valentina said, "Mia, this is Sam Stillman. Sam, this is my grandmother, Mia Sorelli."

Sam looked confused. "It's nice to meet you, Mrs. Sorelli."

Mia glanced sharply at Valentina then said quickly, "And you as well, Sam. Come in, come in." Leading the way into the kitchen, Mia asked, "How about some coffee?"

Both Valentina and Sam looked aghast. "No thanks, we've had our quota," Valentina said.

"Well, you're just in time for lunch. You both seem a little peaked. I have some red gravy I cooked over the weekend. Valentina, you set the table. I'll be right back. I need a bottle of olive oil from the pantry."

Valentina took silverware from the drawer. "It's okay, Sam. This is what she does. We both need some carbs and a little time with Mia." Valentina continued setting the table then filled a pot with water for pasta. "Besides, it makes us both happy when she feeds me." She found the red sauce and meatballs in the refrigerator, and put them in another pot to heat.

Mia came back with the oil to make a simple salad dressing. Valentina didn't understand why it always tasted so good. She tried making it at home, and it wasn't the same. She washed and dried the iceberg lettuce then watched her grandmother rub a garlic clove around the sides of the bowl and mix fresh olive oil, vinegar and a little salt and pepper. Since Mia never measured anything, Valentina kept trying different proportions of the ingredients. She got close.

"Where's Dean?" Valentina asked.

"He has to meet a roofer at the house on Carondelet. He'll be home later. He'll probably stop at Domilise's for a po'boy." She turned to Sam. "We have some rental properties. Valentina's grandfather does most of the work himself, except for the roofing."

A few minutes later they sat together at the table in the kitchen.

"This is life-changing, Mrs. Sorelli. Way better than Irene's."

"Thank you, Sam. Home cooking tastes better sometimes just because you're home. Now tell me how you know my Valentina."

"We were in class together, bioethics."

Mia went to get the pitcher of tea, giving Valentina a searching look outside of Sam's line of sight. "Hmm, from everything Valentina told me, it seems like it was such an interesting class." Valentina got the message. The first second they were alone, Mia wanted to know what happened to Kai and who the heck was this Sam.

"I'm surprised at how applicable the material is to the real world." Sam made a face at Valentina. "At first, I thought Dr. Chen was being fussy about terminology that didn't matter. But the more we delved into ethical questions, I understood that the way we discuss the issues, the language we use, makes a difference in framing the dilemma and what actions are possible." They continued talking about the class, with Sam doing a flawless imitation of Dr. Chen.

The easy conversation transitioned to other topics and updates on family members. One of Valentina's cousins got engaged and was nervous about meeting her soon to be in-laws. Sitting in the sunny kitchen, Valentina relaxed for the first time since the beach trip. Sam looked better, not as overwhelmed.

As they were picking up from lunch, Valentina asked Mia, "Would you mind if we hung out here for a while and worked on a project?"

"I thought the semester was over."

"Oh, it's something we're thinking about for next semester."

"Yeah, a dilemma," Sam said.

"You have a dilemma? You're joking." Mia stopped because both Valentina and Sam suddenly were more serious and seemed tired, the way they looked when they first arrived. Instead, she asked, "Do you mind finishing up the kitchen? I have a ton of bookkeeping I've been putting off and need to spend a little time in my office."

"Sure. Thanks, Mia."

"Mrs. Sorelli, thank you for lunch. You're an amazing cook."

"It's nice to meet you, Sam. You take care now."

Mia hugged Valentina and whispered in her ear, "You have things to tell me."

Valentina nodded.

After Mia left the room, Sam turned to Valentina, "Your grandmother is great."

"Isn't she? She's been there for me my whole life. I grew up in this house."

"Really?"

"It's home." Valentina paused for a moment. "Sam, I have an idea."

"That's a relief. I got nothing except a belly full of really good meatballs and spaghetti."

"Our dilemma is that we're afraid that your father is involved in this whole mess, and we don't have enough information. Angus's data may determine that, but the hard drive is damaged."

"From what your Uncle Tony said, they'll be able to recover it, but it could take weeks."

"Get ready, this is a crazy idea. What if we said that we were engaged and asked your parents to have dinner with us? We could get your dad talking."

"Valentina, my family is not like your family. If my mother was there, it might get real, way too fast. Before we knew it, there would be notifications in the Times-Picayune, the Denver Post, and we'd be planning a wedding. I mean, not that I'd mind, but ..."

"Okay, forget that idea."

"No, the dinner idea is good. I would know if my dad is lying."

"When do you ..."

"Wait a minute. I have to figure out how to approach my father. We haven't been in touch since I started NOU. What about if I tell him I'm getting serious about you and want you to get to know each other. With some groveling, of course."

"Remember, I met him at the park gala."

"Yeah, but this would be different," Sam said. "I'll tell him I want his opinion of you before things go further."

"Sam, are you sure about this?"

"No, I'm not. But I don't have any other ideas, and it could work. I can't imagine that my father would pass up the chance to choose my fiancée."

"How do we set it up?"

"I'll call my dad and text the cook."

"Your family has a cook?"

Sam blushed. "Just part time. She's not half as good as Mia—well with Italian dishes anyway. Her empanadas are amazing."

"We could ask your dad about Angus, too. I bet he would have more information." Valentina paused. "Wait, on second thought, better not. Your dad would question how we knew about Angus."

"You're right. I'll call the hospital tonight."

CHAPTER 48

After five shots of espresso, Jack prowled his living room like a caged animal. He couldn't get through to Richard. No response—to any of their pre-arranged methods of communication. Day or night, Richard was always available. *Where the hell was he?* He looked at the time. Almost seven in the morning. He was going to be late. He'd try again this afternoon. Jack told himself it would be weeks, maybe months, before Fort Collins had enough seeds to distribute to the agricultural consortium. Landever had time to redefine its marketing approach, and get out in front of it. Enough time to stop the distribution of the Fort Collins cultivar.

That afternoon, Jack sat back in his executive chair, pleased with himself. His product development team had developed a new campaign for their mite resistant wheat, emphasizing Landever's research breakthroughs, dependability and world leadership. They'd work with their ad agency and develop something snazzy. He would make this happen.

Next, Jack started working on a plan to stop the consortium's development of competitive seeds. Late that afternoon, he finally heard from Richard, who explained he'd picked up a tail leaving Stephen Angus's house. They agreed he should lie low for a little while. Richard suggested Jack might want to watch his step too.

Okay, I'm on my own. Using his personal tablet, Jack looked for the security measures surrounding the Fort Collins research facility. *Easy pickings, considering how much information was available on the*

Internet. That information, plus what he'd picked up on his tour, and he was in good shape. Aerial photographs revealed no security gates and open access to the campus building on the eastern edge of Colorado State University. Nearby, the Mason Trail was a north/south hardscape that ran almost five miles parallel to US highway 287. Permitted parking was readily available next to the building, with nearby street parking too. He'd fake the permit. Thinking back to his tour, he remembered the closed circuit TV monitors, but Jack didn't intend to do anything that would raise an alarm until it was too late. With the disguise he had in mind, he'd be unrecognizable on camera. He would use a fake ID to rent the vehicle, leave it in the parking lot, and set off the bomb remotely.

The explosive would be easy. Working at Landever introduced him to ammonium nitrate, a nitrogen fertilizer. Mixed with fuel oil, it would act as the oxidizer to make ammonium nitrate-fuel oil, or ANFO, the main ingredient in improvised explosive devices. Farmers had used ANFO to blow out tree stumps in their fields for years. Although newer fertilizers were made with ammonium sulfate, a little of the older stuff was still around. He'd have to secure it before the protective coating was added that made it less combustible. He didn't need that much, either. Jack didn't want to take down the entire building, only disrupt the power supply. In the Oklahoma City bombing, thirteen barrels of fertilizer were used to take down a nine-story building. For the seed bank, one barrel in the back of an SUV should do it. Jack learned online that he didn't need much more than a cell phone connected to an electrical firing circuit for the rest of the bomb. He'd get another throwaway phone that couldn't be traced. It would be almost too easy, resolved in a couple of weeks. While he was in Colorado, he would ask Elizabeth to meet him for dinner in Denver. In a much better mood than when he arrived at the office, Jack started working on one of his other projects.

A little while later, his cell phone buzzed. Looking at the display, he saw that it was Sam. They hadn't spoken in ages.

"Yes, Sam?"

"Hi Dad. Am I catching you at a bad time?"

"No, not at all."

"I know it's been a while."

"I'm a little surprised to hear from you, Sam. You disappeared."

"Sorry, I didn't mean to ghost you. It's … you were pretty upset last time we talked."

Jack debated with himself about bringing up medical school then decided to wait to see what Sam had to say.

"It's been too long, son."

"That's why I'm calling. I was hoping we could get together. Are you going to be in town soon?"

"I don't have anything scheduled. Work is keeping me pretty busy. Why, what's up?"

"Um, I met a girl."

"That sounds serious."

"Maybe it is."

"Well, well, well. Who is the lucky lady?" Jack asked.

"You met her not that long ago, Valentina Sorelli."

"I'm not sure I recall her, Sam."

"She works at Winslow Park. You talked with her at their gala."

"Oh, sure."

"Dad, I'm crazy about her." Sam's voice shook slightly with sincerity. "I wonder if you could take time to meet her. Before this goes further, I'd like to see what you think. Could we have dinner together at the house?"

"Have you mentioned this to your mother?"

"No, I'd rather wait on that, Dad. This would be between us."

Flattered, Jack said, "Of course. I could catch a flight on Friday afternoon. How about dinner that evening?"

"That would be perfect. I'll call Merida and ask her to put something together."

"Are you sure you don't want to go out? We could go to Commander's, Gautreau's, do something special?"

"I'd like it to be more casual, more relaxed."

"Sure, Sam."

"Really appreciate it, Dad."

"Thanks for calling. I'll be there by seven on Friday."

As he hung up the phone, Jack tried to recall the young woman who had captivated his son. Oh yeah, she was planning a seed bank for kids at the park. A "do-gooder"—well, there were worse things. Jack laughed. What a kick that evening was. He remembered the auction when he got the humidor. He liked the humidor, but he liked beating that old coot, Ferris Jefferson, more. Ferris hadn't seemed too amused.

CHAPTER 49

Valentina dressed carefully, asking herself what she would wear if she were having dinner with her boyfriend's father and wanted to make a good impression. After trying on several outfits, she settled on a simple linen dress, flats, and understated jewelry—her mother's gold bracelet and earrings. She managed to tame her unruly hair in a curly chignon.

Once she left her apartment, Valentina drove down Carrollton Avenue toward St. Charles Avenue. It rained earlier, and fog slipped in from the river. Valentina felt as though she was driving into a long tunnel, with the branches of the oak trees meeting overhead and the wet streets below glistening silver, green, and red as the street lights changed. She reviewed the last few days. Sam insisted they prepare for the evening with the same intensity he approached his academic training. They created an entire storyline of their fictional dates and relationship. Valentina now knew Sam's favorite foods, the name of his first pet, and his success as a high school track star. He won the state championship for the 400-meter in his junior year. Sam knew Will was like a brother, Amy her bestie, and Mia was her heart.

When she stepped up to the porch, Valentina saw Sam through the leaded glass of the front door. He walked from the small sitting room off the foyer and opened the door. "I'm glad to see you."

Valentina hugged Sam. "Are you ready for this?"

"The empanadas are almost ready, and my dad should be here any minute."

"That wasn't what I was asking."

Sam shrugged and stared back at Valentina.

She waited then smiled. "Merida's famous empanadas."

"A Stillman family favorite."

"Let me see if I can help." Valentina walked to the kitchen.

A middle-aged woman with dark brown hair and eyes stood at the counter, her hands flying as she placed the empanadas on a baking sheet then brushed them with egg wash. Valentina introduced herself as a friend of Sam's and offered to help.

"No, no, gracias."

Sam came in while they were talking and side-hugged Merida. "Now two of my favorite people have met." There was a soft light in Sam's eyes as he looked at Valentina.

"I have known this one," Merida said as she side-hugged Sam back, "since he was a little boy."

In the distance, the front door opened.

"That must be Dad." Sam said. "I'll let him know where we are."

"*Ese*," that one, Merida said derisively under her breath after Sam left the kitchen.

Startled, Valentina realized Merida was referring to Jack. She couldn't say anything to that. Instead, she said, "It has been a pleasure to talk with you."

As she turned to follow Sam, Merida murmured quietly to herself as much as to Valentina. "*Mi Samuel te tiene cariño. Sé gentil con su corazón.*" My Samuel is fond of you. Be gentle with his heart.

Valentina heard the serious undertone in Merida's voice and responded in Spanish, "*Lo guardare con cuidado.*" I will treat it with care.

Merida looked back at Valentina, her eyes luminous.

When Valentina entered the foyer, Sam and Jack were talking quietly. She was struck by their resemblance—both tall, slim, and blond—yet there was a brittleness to Jack's posture, his movements, and mannerisms. Hearing her footsteps, Sam said, "Here she is."

"Hi, Mr. Stillman. It's nice to see you again."

"You too, Valentina. Please call me Jack."

"How was your flight?" Valentina asked.

"Not bad. And the new airport is okay. I could use a glass of wine, though. Why don't we go sit down?" They went into the large family room where Merida had set out salsa, guacamole and charred peppers. "Although since we're having empanadas, we should have margaritas."

"Merida has it covered, Dad." Sam walked over to the small bar in the corner, picked up a cocktail mixer and shook it briskly. "Salt?"

"Margaritas—that's one thing those beaners got right," Jack said.

Valentina gasped, then covered her reaction with a cough.

Sam ignored Jack's comment. Valentina raised her eyebrows but wasn't surprised. Sam had shared with her that when he was younger, he used to laugh along with his father when he said something insensitive or racist. Later, he was mortified. Nothing he said or did had any effect on Jack's behavior, so Sam had given up. He knew his father could be respectful and culturally aware, but he also seemed to enjoy being offensive. He turned it on and off like a switch. And as Sam had indicated, Jack was immediately solicitous of Valentina, asking questions about her family, her job and her plans after graduation.

Merida came to the doorway and said, "I am going."

Sprawled across the sofa, Jack asked, "Do you need anything for groceries next month?"

"Yes, Mr. Stillman. The price of flour is ten times higher than it was."

Jack pulled out his wallet. "Here," tossing some bills on the coffee table.

Sam got to his feet and took the money to Merida. "Here, let me walk you to your car."

Merida squeezed his arm. "No need, Samuel. It is very close. Everything is in the warming oven, and the sauces are on the counter."

Valentina stood and said, "Thank you for going to so much trouble."

Merida looked back at Valentina, held her hand over her heart, then turned away.

After she left, Sam and Valentina brought the serving dishes to the table. Jack opened a bottle of wine and poured generous glasses. Valentina had taken only a few sips of her margarita before dinner, and Sam had done the same. She looked around the graceful room, with the outdoor lights giving a soft glow to the exquisite patio and garden. Valentina was cold in the air conditioning and cavernous space. It felt different from her earlier daytime visit. Sam continued their carefully planned small talk, allowing Jack time to finish his second drink. Jack asked if Sam was rethinking medical school.

Sam said, "I think about it some," and reached for the wine decanter. He poured Jack another glass of wine and topped off theirs, nodding at Valentina. She steeled herself as Jack continued talking about medical school.

During a pause in Jack's soliloquy, Valentina jumped in. "Researchers are the new heroes since the wheat virus struck. It must be rewarding to lead the company with a solution to the crisis."

"Our research has put us out in front of our competitors," Jack said.

"What a visionary approach to have cultivated wheat plants resistant to the mites," Valentina said.

"We started that years ago." Jack preened. "It was only a matter of time before something like this was going to happen. With a little foresight, it was easy to prepare for crop vulnerability. The tough part was getting the plants out of the Middle East."

"How did that work out?" Valentina asked.

"Oh, well, if you know the right people...," Jack said smoothly.

Valentina thought about Tala and expected this was another situation where a developing country wasn't reimbursed for its natural resources.

Sam quickly changed the subject "Didn't something like this happen to bananas a long time ago?"

"It was in the 1950s," Jack said. "A soil fungus caused banana wilt and wiped out most of the world's banana crop. What a business opportunity."

"I guess if you plan strategically, you anticipate things like that happening," said Valentina. "You must have expected a danger to wheat from the virus and the mites."

"Exactly." Jack said.

"Dad, didn't Landever have a researcher who was studying mites?"

"Um, yes, Scottish fellow. He left Landever a while back. What was his name, Simmons? Alton, Angus Simmons, something like that." There was a pause as Jack's face reddened. "Could you pass the Chimichurri sauce? Didn't Merida do a nice job with the empanadas?"

"Yes, the best I've ever had," Valentina said.

"Merida doesn't do as well with the usual American fare, but we give her some latitude because she's worked for us a long time."

"That's very nice of you." Valentina tried not to grit her teeth.

Sam brought the conversation back. "I'm surprised Angus left. I worked in his lab one summer. He seemed really into his research."

"Sam, he left under a cloud. From what I recall, there was some question about his research."

"Was any of his work helpful?" Sam asked.

"Not really. I hadn't had contact with him for months and months, more than a year. We got feedback that his work wasn't on the up and up, so we came to a mutual agreement about his leaving. I heard he was heading back to the UK."

Sam nodded and seemed to close in on himself. Valentina redirected the conversation to less dangerous topics, telling Jack how much the class enjoyed the beach house. She got him to talk about Santa Rosa and how much it had changed since they first started visiting there. Sam was very quiet as Valentina concentrated on being charming and discussing innocuous subjects. After dinner, she and Sam picked up the dishes, as Jack sipped a glass of port. Once they were done, Valentina said, "Jack, this has been such an interesting evening."

"It sure has, Valentina. I'm glad I could get to know you more," he said, winking and slurring his words slightly.

"I'll be back in a minute." Sam said to his father.

Valentina and Sam walked to the front porch. "I'm right there," Valentina said, pointing to her car.

"Let's go together," Sam said. They walked silently to the ten-year-old Toyota. "I can't talk about this yet."

"You don't have to." Valentina hugged Sam as hard as she could. "Try to get some sleep."

"Promise me you won't call your uncle yet."

"I promise. Let's get together tomorrow. We'll figure out what to do."

•　　•　　•

Sam stood in the thick night air as he watched Valentina drive away. He couldn't go inside yet. Pulling out his cell phone, Sam found the number for the burn center where Angus was hospitalized. When the switchboard answered, he said, "I'm calling regarding a patient, Stephen Angus."

"Mr. Angus is in critical condition."

"Can you tell me anything else?"

"We can only report that Mr. Stephen's condition is critical."

Sam stood, oblivious to the rain beginning to fall through the oak branches. A few minutes later, he realized he was getting wet and went inside. Sam paused in the doorway to the den and saw Jack sprawled across the couch. It wasn't like his father to drink that much. Then again, what did he know? He didn't think it was like him to lie, either.

"Sam?"

Sam walked a little closer. "Yeah?"

"She's a lovely girl."

"She is."

"Sexy too," Jack muttered.

Sam looked at Jack, trying to decide if he was pissed off or just sad.

CHAPTER 50

Valentina was glad to leave the chilly elegance of the Stillman house. She drove home slowly through the humid summer night. It was raining again, and the streets were slick. She wanted to get home and slip into her pajamas. As Valentina pulled in front of her apartment, she saw a familiar pickup truck parked across the street. Kai was waiting in front of her door with a small bouquet of flowers. She couldn't believe it. Not tonight.

"Valentina, I want to apologize. *Tout n'était qu'un malentendu.* It was all a misunderstanding. May I come in?"

"It's been a long night, Kai. Another time."

"Come on, Valentina. It's raining."

"Not tonight, Kai."

"Let's go in and talk about this."

"I'm going in. You are not."

"Wait, that's it? I've been waiting here for two hours."

"That was your choice, Kai. I need to get inside."

"Talk to me for a minute. *Une minute, c'est tout.*"

"Look, it's been a long night and ..."

"Were you with Leo?"

Valentina didn't respond.

"Well?"

Valentina told herself not to let her temper get the best of her. "How I choose to spend my evening is none of your business. Please leave."

"We never talked about what happened. I want you to understand."

"I understand things pretty well, Kai."

"What was I supposed to think? You sent out some pretty strong signals about what you wanted."

Furious, Valentina started to justify in her mind how she felt that night on the beach. Then, she stopped herself. "I don't owe you an explanation. I don't owe you anything. This discussion is over. In about thirty seconds, I'm going to set off my car alarm. My next-door neighbor is with NOPD. He will not like being woken up." Valentina started counting backwards from thirty. "Thirty, twenty-nine, twenty-eight, twenty-"

"You know what they call women like you," Kai muttered something under his breath.

"- seven, twenty-six, twenty-five ..."

"The heck with it. The heck with you," Kai spit out. He stormed off the small porch, throwing the flowers down on the pavement.

With hands shaking, Valentina got her key in the lock. Once inside, she leaned against the door and asked herself what would have happened if Kai called her bluff. Her ten-year-old car didn't have a car alarm—well, not one that worked—and her neighbor, Mr. Devereaux, retired from the police department at least twenty years ago.

A little while later, Valentina cocooned in her bed, surrounded by pillows and blankets. *What a ridiculous end to the night. Kai showing up on my doorstep was the last straw. Dumb-ass. No, what was that term Amy used? Pissant, that's better.*

She considered the dinner. Well, it worked. Not that they had real proof. But as soon as Mr. Stillman said he hadn't talked to Angus in over a year, she and Sam both knew he was lying. Poor Sam. Her father would never have gotten an award for his parenting, but he never tried to cause world famine, let alone profit from it.

CHAPTER 51

Jack was frustrated. It had seemed so simple. His plans to disrupt the Fort Collins power supply hit not one but two snags. First, he learned that more than 90% of the power lines in Fort Collins were underground. Colorado State University, the research center and seed bank were no exceptions. Jack regrouped and decided that with a larger explosive device, he could dismantle part of the building. This would serve the same purpose as disrupting the power supply. He was pretty confident that would take care of the resistant wheat cultivar developed by the Agricultural Consortium. Fort Collins was only an hour and a half drive from Denver. For a handy alibi, he would take his estranged wife to dinner at a fancy Denver restaurant—Safta or LeRoux. That would add a nice symmetry to his planning.

A homemade explosive device was basically an initiator, switch, main charge, power source, and a container. Pretty simple. Then Jack researched sources of the ammonium nitrate. Conveniently, there was a plant in Indiana with several supply stores for the farming community along the way. From another throwaway mobile phone, he called one store. Plenty of ammonium nitrate was available. As he was getting ready to end the call, the sales rep asked Jack for his permit number, since the fertilizer was now regulated by Homeland Security. Jack quickly said he didn't have it handy and would call back. He ended the call. What would have happened if he had shown up without the permit? Infernal government interference. He was going to need Richard.

A few hours later, Jack explained his quandary.

"You only want to take out the power supply?" Richard asked.

"Yeah. Can you hack into their system?"

"Probably not but not necessary. A HERF gun would do the job."

"A what? Wait a minute, I don't want unnecessary violence."

Richard chuckled. "A HERF is a high-energy radio frequency pulse emitter. It works by blasting high-intensity radio waves at electronics, disrupting their operation. If it's aimed properly, it can take out the circuitry for the refrigeration system. It's like a microwave gun. It directs an electromagnetic pulse, an EMP, which is a burst of energy. The military has had these for years. North Korea probably has one aimed at us right now."

"Interesting."

"By overloading the circuitry, it should blow out any electric equipment, damage generators, back-up batteries, controls, computers, and temperature sensors used in the refrigeration equipment. Collateral damage would only occur if someone is physically touching a live electrical conductor at the time."

"How long will it stay out?"

"Should be fried for good. It's like a lightning strike. You'd short out their communications systems, microphones, circuitry. Cell phones, radios, or walkies in the blast radius are screwed. To sound an alarm, they would have to walk to another building."

"I'm liking this. Okay then. How do we go about it?"

"It's pretty simple, really. We need a generator, capacitors, transformers, magnetrons, a wave guide, and a trigger mechanism. All the equipment is readily available, and it's not regulated. We still have a few weeks' rental on an old building in the Nebraska Panhandle. We could set up there. Fort Collins is four hours away by road, and the capacitors could charge off the vehicle alternators the whole way. The trickiest part will be the wave guide to direct the EMP."

"Why is that?"

"Metal acts as a shield," Richard said. "So, if it was in a truck bed, that might prevent the electromagnetic blast from hitting its target.

"Then the HERF gun would have to be in a place open to the air, with no metal in the way?"

"Yeah, open to the air, or near large windows."

"What about using a panel van or utility truck and opening the back doors or replacing the metal sides with canvas?"

"Not bad." Richard laughed, "You're getting into this, huh?"

Jack didn't laugh. Things were too serious. If he didn't eliminate the other wheat cultivar, he was screwed. "What's the range?"

"For something that you could transport in a truck or van, 50 meters, give or take."

"About 160 feet. That works," Jack said. "There's parking right next to the building. Let's get this done."

"I can put this together for you. Give me a week to get the equipment and construct the HERF. But you're going to have to do it yourself. I need to lie low. I'm sure the cops followed me after I left Angus."

"But you lost them."

"I did. But they were close. And it's going to cost you," Richard added.

"Your usual fee is pretty costly," Jack said. "And none of the equipment you mentioned is that expensive,"

"Consider this my IRA. Get it? I'm retiring."

"What kind of fee are you talking about?"

"A cool mil."

"You must be nuts," Jack sputtered. "I don't have that kind of money."

"Sure you do, Mr. Stillman."

Jack felt himself grow cold. He had never used his actual name in their interactions. He covered his face the only time he'd seen Richard in person.

"How stupid do you think I am?" Richard asked. "Whatever the drones carried, it wiped out the wheat fields. Landever's got the only resistant wheat." When Jack didn't respond, Richard said, "I bet the feds might like to talk with me."

"You rotten son of a ..."

"I guess it takes one to know one, wouldn't you say, Mr. Stillman?"

"All right. When can I pick up the HERF?"

"We'll have a different kind of transaction this time, Mr. Stillman. I want the money in cold hard cash, small bills."

Jack started to argue then said, "Okay."

"I'll be in touch in a week."

Jack held the phone, listening to the sound of his heart pounding. It was blackmail. He couldn't—no—wouldn't let it happen.

CHAPTER 52

On the fourth floor of Eskenazi Health in the Richard M. Fairbanks Burn Center, Stephen Angus's eyes opened. A hoarse croak escaped his throat, where a tube was removed. After 72 hours under sedation with high-frequency percussive ventilation, his pulmonary specialist was allowing him to wake up gradually.

A voice murmured, "Hang on, my friend. I'll get a nurse."

"Barry?" Angus's raspy whisper was barely audible.

"I'm here."

"The drive?"

"Sorelli is pretty sure they can recover your data."

Relief was better than a drug, and Angus allowed himself to slip back under.

A few hours later when he awoke again, Angus learned he was recovering from smoke inhalation and partial thickness thermal burns on his back, legs, neck, left arm and hand, as well as on the left side of his face. A bandage about the size of a credit card was on each of his thighs, where small skin samples were taken to create spray-on skin cells. His own skin was mixed with an enzyme to make what the burn specialist called RECELL, an autologous skin cell suspension. Basically, they sprayed this solution of his live cells across the burned areas. It was likely he wouldn't need skin grafts or have excessive scarring. He would probably lose part of the index finger on his left hand, but he could live with that. He would live.

In between sessions of respiratory therapy and something called "aggressive ambulation," Angus discovered that he owed his life to Luis Gonzalez. The federal agent pulled him out of the fire and was also being treated for burns. Barry was going to send the federal agent a bottle of Glenlivet. Angus's sister, still in Scotland, had given Barry authorization to make essential or critical decisions. Angus considered the bottle of scotch essential.

Over the next several days, Angus recovered. Pulmonary complications and infection were still risks. With 30% of his body affected, Angus learned he would be at the Burn Center a few more weeks. Barry visited almost every day.

One evening, Tony Sorelli called to see how he was doing. "Feeling better?"

"Aye, except for the itching. It's driving me aff my heid."

"I bet. I've heard it can be pretty bad."

Disregarding Tony's attempt at pleasantries, Angus demanded, "Have you been able to analyze the drone residue yet?"

"We're working on it. Your drive has a lot of damage, but it's going to happen. And thank you for that. It will definitely help."

Angus made a self-deprecating noise. "As long as you get him."

"We will. And on a more personal level, you won't be able to return home for a little while. The roof is gone, and there's water damage. The kitchen is ..."

"I needed an upgrade there anyway."

"You could definitely use new cabinets. And if you want to expand into the storeroom, the wall won't be a problem."

This forced a laugh out of Angus. Then, in a serious tone, he said, "I don't know how that fire started. There was nothing on the stove."

"We're pretty certain it was arson."

"That bastard had someone else do his dirty work."

Tony didn't respond to that. "I've had your house boarded up, Angus. We mounted a tarp on the roof."

"Thanks for that."

"We think it might be a smart idea for you to avoid your house until this is over," Tony said.

"Hasn't it just begun?" Angus said.

Tony didn't answer directly. "We have a place you can stay for a while. It's close to the hospital. You'll probably need burn therapy for a while yet. Agent Gonzalez will take you there when you're ready to be discharged."

Angus was quiet for a moment. "I want to check on my house, figure out what needs to be done to start the repairs."

"Well ...."

"I'd appreciate it if you'd also let me know when you've finished the analysis on the organic material."

"Will do." Tony said. "Think about laying low. And try to concentrate on getting better."

After Angus ended the call, Barry chimed in. "Angus, be realistic."

"What?"

Barry appeared to have no qualms about eavesdropping. "You're not going to be able to fix your house yourself. You can't tolerate the heat or the sun for a while. Were you asleep when the doctor said you needed to avoid high temperatures and stay in a clean environment?"

"Come on, Barry."

"You bang up your skin, and you're going to set yourself back. You could scar, get infected. Why take chances?"

"I wasn't that pretty to begin with, Bar. I'm going crazy in here."

"Look at your progress."

"Pfff."

"Let's take a walk, my friend. I got permission to show you something."

Angus was silent as he slowly pushed himself to the edge of the bed. "I need to take a piss."

"Like I was saying, progress. You were peeing in a tube not too long ago."

A short while later, Barry pushed Angus in a wheelchair toward the elevator bank. Although still busy, the hospital common areas were empty of most visitors. Barry greeted the nurse at the charge desk, who nodded back, then looked back at her computer screen. Barry pushed Angus through the pedestrian walkway to the outpatient center. From there, they took one of the green elevators to the seventh floor. Angus hadn't traveled this far since being admitted to Eskenazi. Sitting in the elevator, Angus realized how trapped he was feeling.

"It's not the burns, Barry. It's all the people walking in and out, checking on me constantly. The constant beeping. I just want to be left alone."

"Let's see what we can do about that."

As the elevator door opened, Angus was surprised to find they were outdoors. The lift opened onto the roof and a wide expanse of rows upon rows of vegetables and flowers. Beyond the planting beds, the skyline of Indianapolis brightened the deepening sky.

"This is incredible," Angus said. He rose slowly from the wheelchair and walked into the garden.

"A five thousand square foot oasis. They call it the Sky Farm."

"Look at that view of downtown."

"It's 360 degrees."

More lights flickered across the night sky. "Thanks, Barry. That room was closing in on me."

"No reason you can't visit this when it cools off in the evenings or early mornings." They continued walking in the cool night air.

"Want to know the best part? They have honeybees, Angus. Can you believe that? Seven stories in the air."

Angus smiled but didn't say anything.

"You must be getting tired. Let's head back, okay? You can explore more tomorrow."

"This makes my day, mate."

CHAPTER 53

Valentina was at her desk early. She and Sam talked over the weekend and hadn't figured out anything. On one level, Sam knew his father was responsible for the grain crisis. But emotionally, he couldn't get a handle on it. Whenever they tried to come up with a response, he froze. To his credit, he wasn't making excuses for Jack. He had called the burn unit again to check on Angus and told Valentina he was doing better. That was one bright spot.

Valentina was glad to go to work to think about something else. One of Winslow's school partners asked if Winslow would consider expanding their enrichment program later in the summer. A lot of the McLarin students were at loose ends during the day since most parents had jobs. The seed bank was continuing through the summer with volunteers, and the kids loved it. Every day, a different group of children rotated through the varied responsibilities each week. Although the project started late in the school year, the teachers had seen an improvement in student behavior and more interest in school. Renny Plaisance, Winslow's director of maintenance, was the program's biggest fan. He checked in at the seed bank daily, connecting with each group of kids. Valentina wanted Renny's thoughts before she talked with the teachers.

Renny answered his cell phone after a few rings. "Hey, Valentina."

"Got a few minutes?"

"Sure, but I'm a little tied up at the moment. Can it wait until this afternoon? Or why don't you come to me? Gabby and I are out by the back fountain."

In her office, Valentina smiled. "Gabby's here today?"

"Just for the morning. Her mama had an appointment, and all her aunties are busy, so Miss Gabrielle is helping me until lunchtime."

Valentina heard a high-pitched announcement in the background, "Then we'll have a picnic!"

"Then we'll have a picnic," Renny agreed.

"I'll come to you. It will be great to see Gabby. Give me a couple of minutes."

Since the back fountain was near the pavilion at the other end of the park, Valentina took her car. She parked and saw Renny using a hose to clean the fountain pump, hand tools and wire brushes lay nearby. A few feet away, Renny's six-year-old daughter, Gabrielle Emmeline Plaisance, was drawing hearts with chalk on the pavement.

"No school today?"

"It's summer, Miss Valentina!"

Valentina hit her forehead with her hand. "You're right, Miss Gabrielle."

"Hey, Renny."

"Thanks for coming to me, Valentina."

"I'm glad to get out of the office. And it's not too warm yet. Let me ask you something. One of our partner schools asked us to expand the enrichment program later in the summer."

"Let me guess, it was McLarin?"

"Yep. The parents at Perrier Elementary are doing fine without us. McLarin's a different story."

"What did you have in mind, Valentina?"

"I've read about programs that offer a garden-to-table experience. Why not do that with our kids? Plant a big garden and use the produce to teach the kids how to cook meals? Broaden the scope. The kids could learn about nutrition, restaurant management, and marketing. Hands-on activities work the best. The teachers at McLarin like that idea and are working on an outline. We would start small, a half-day a week. What do you think?"

"Valentina, it sounds terrific, but my staff is maxed out as it is."

"I hear you."

"Can you talk Dee into letting me hire another staff member?" Renny shook his head. "We're so busy right now. You know New Orleans in the summer. We're just trying to keep up with the mowing."

"It was a long shot. Maybe I can put something together with volunteers. I might drive over to NOU later today and see if the faculty advisors are receptive."

"I'm sorry, Valentina. I wish we had more staff. I love what we're doing for those kids."

"I'm not giving up. It's worth asking Jamison, too."

"The group that gave us the grant?"

"Yeah. Let me see what kind of reception I get. And at NOU, I'll try the education department and hospitality, or what the school calls Hotel, Restaurant, Tourism." Watching Gabby color the sidewalk, Valentina said, "Maybe I'll go to the art school and marketing as a segue into advertising. It can't hurt."

"Those are good ideas. If I figure out a way to squeeze some time for you, I will."

"I know. Thanks, Renny."

That afternoon, Valentina drove to NOU. Cicely Ambrose, assistant chair at the education department, agreed to meet with her during a short break she had between appointments.

"Hello, Ms. Sorelli. How can I help you?"

"Please call me Valentina. Thank you for seeing me, Dr. Ambrose. I'm here on behalf of Winslow Park and one of our partner schools, McLarin Preparatory. We developed a student enrichment program ..."

"Valentina, let me stop you right there. One of our graduate students teaches at McLarin. Although she isn't involved in Winslow's seed bank, she knows about it from the other teachers and has mentioned it here. You're running a good program. What can we do for you?"

Valentina laughed. "I've lived here all my life and reminded almost every day that New Orleans is a big small town. Someone always knows somebody who knows somebody."

"No kidding. I got here three years ago, and that happens to me all the time. Please, call me CeCe."

"We're interested in expanding the program to offer more learning opportunities to the students. One possibility we've considered is a garden-to-table program to build communication and organizational skills. From there, we could offer training in financial management and leadership, initially one day a week, more or less. McLarin's staff will support the project, but the park's resources are tapped out. Would it be possible for your department to help?"

"So, you're looking for volunteers to facilitate the interaction with the kids?"

"Exactly."

"As part of their program requirements, all our students are required to have community involvement. I can see if anyone is interested, but they may all have commitments by now. Being the summer, I'm not sure we have anyone available, but it's worth a try. We'll have better luck in the fall."

"CeCe, that would be wonderful! I'm planning to talk to the Hotel, Restaurant and Tourism Department, as well as the marketing and art departments."

"So, an interdepartmental project?"

"Exactly. Would that work for you?"

"I'd be interested in the specifics, Valentina. It sounds quite interesting."

"We should have a program outline done in the next week or so. I'll send it your way as soon as it's finalized."

"Let me see what I can do. This kind of community outreach is consistent with the goals of the education department. But right now, I need to leave for my next meeting."

"Of course. Thank you for seeing me without an appointment."

"We'll be in touch."

Encouraged, Valentina called on the other departments. Faculty members were receptive and said there might be one or two students who would be available during the summer. For fall, they were all in. One teacher in the hospitality program suggested including guest coaches from the local community. Valentina loved the idea. She found her advisor in the marketing department, and they brainstormed about different restaurant chefs and business leaders she could ask. It was late when she arrived at the art school, and no one was there.

On the way back to her car, Valentina stopped at PJ's before heading home. If her life was normal, today would be a win. They might not be able to extend the enrichment program until the fall, but it would happen. She had always wanted to make a difference, make things better. If she didn't consider the broader context of the agricultural disaster, it had been a stellar day. Now that she wasn't focused on her job, thoughts of Sam's dad and the wheat crisis came flooding back. Valentina took her iced coffee to a table outside. It was hot, but the worst heat of the day had passed.

The last time she spoke to Will, he was optimistic about the new wheat strain developed by the partnership with the seed bank. Some farmers had signed on with Landever, but Will thought the multi-year contract was too risky and would wait for the new cultivar from Fort Collins. Based on her experience with Jack Stillman, Valentina was confident Will had made a wise decision. Heaven knew what Landever would do in the future. How could Sam, good to the bones, come from that evil man? Jack Stillman had to be stopped. Her conversations with the hospitality instructor and her advisor gave her an idea. A pretty wild idea, to be sure. She sent Sam a text, but he didn't respond. Deep in thought, Valentina didn't notice when someone approached her table.

"Hey, stranger."

"Leo!"

"You're here pretty late. Looks serious, too. Want to talk about it?"

"Where do I start? That's not a rhetorical question."

"When I last saw you, you were suspicious that Sam's father was instrumental in the wheat crisis. How about there?"

"We're sure of it. That man is guilty as the day is long."

"How is Sam doing?"

"Coping. The problem is we know his father is responsible, except there's no proof. But I have an idea about how to get it."

"I'm all ears."

"Winslow is going to be extending the enrichment program ..." she began.

"Outstanding."

Valentina waved his comment aside. "I plan to pull in guest coaches and speakers from the community. I'll ask Jack Stillman to do the inaugural speech. Since he's the most egotistical person I've ever met, I think he'll do it. After the talk, I'll confront him about his role in the wheat virus and make a recording of him admitting to it."

"Whoa, wait a minute, Valentina. Let's back up. One thing at a time. First, how did you meet Jack Stillman?"

"I met him for the first time at the Winslow Gala this past spring. Landever is one of our corporate sponsors. Believe me when I tell you he was obnoxious. That's a story for another day. The second time was when Sam asked his dad to have dinner with us so that he could get his opinion about whether Sam should ask me to marry him."

Leo blinked. "Run that by me again?"

"It was a ruse, Leo. Sam pretended we're dating seriously so his dad could weigh in on whether I'm suitable. Our idea was that we would ask him about Angus and the mites, and see if he would lie. Well, it worked. Big time. Sam thought he'd be able to tell if his dad was lying, and it was obvious. The man turned purple. He made up a story about how he hadn't spoken to Angus in over a year and Angus was no longer with Landever because his work wasn't satisfactory. What really happened is that Jack found out that Angus was copying his data and Jack confronted him. Angus got the hard drive out of the building, and then was badly injured in a house fire. Arson. This all took place only a few days before our dinner conversation, and Angus's last day at Landever was the same morning as the fire. Jack is lying, but we can't prove it."

"How are you going to get him on tape?"

"Ellis is pretty tech-savvy. I bet he'll help me."

"Valentina, I'm pretty tech-savvy and could set up a hidden recorder. But how will you get him to admit that he's responsible for potential famine in multiple countries?"

"I haven't figured that part out yet. But flattery is at the top of my list."

"Do you want to talk about this more?"

"That might not be a bad idea. Why don't we call Sam and meet at my apartment later?"

"I've got another hour or two here at the lab before I can leave. Do you want me to pick up pizza or anything?"

"That would be great. Eight o'clock?"

"See you then."

CHAPTER 54

Jack's head pounded in time to the car wheels hitting the pavement. He was driving slightly over the speed limit. Fast enough to reach Lincoln in about three hours, but not so fast as to attract attention. Empty fields, others with cover crops of alfalfa or clover, stretched past the windows. He could be passing the same terrain over and over, with the same dilapidated barns, the rows of cedars planted for a windbreak, solitary farmhouses and their outbuildings. The Midwest was boring. There was a reason it was called flyover country. This was interminable. No one was working in the fields. Oh yeah, he chuckled, there wasn't anything to harvest.

Jack decided not to visit Elizabeth in Denver. Too close for comfort. He shouldn't be identified anywhere near Colorado. Since Richard told him he was being followed, Jack speculated whether someone was watching him, too. He needed to cover his tracks.

Instead, Jack signed up for a large convention in Kansas City, one that didn't monitor attendance too closely. He told himself he'd be able to handle things in Fort Collins and be back before anyone realized he was gone. At the hotel in Kansas City, Jack approached the registration desk. A tall, athletic-looking man sat in the lobby, looking toward the window. Was he at the airport? Outside Starbucks, and later, standing by the newsstand? I can't let him see me leaving the conference, Jack thought. He checked in and walked to the bank of elevators, being careful not to glance at his pursuer.

His room was on the third floor, so he rode the elevator up to the fifth, then walked down the stairs hauling his luggage. He could lose that guy.

On the first day of the conference, Jack visited the exhibit hall and attended professional sessions throughout the morning. He flirted with a few different women, making a point of being seen. On the second day, Jack left his hotel room early, dressed in an expensive jacket and custom-made shirt. Taking the stairs to the fifth floor then the elevator to the basement, he found the head of housekeeping, tipped her extravagantly, and made sure she noticed his wedding ring. He explained he had a friend visiting him and didn't want to be disturbed for at least 24 hours. With so many guests staying for the convention, she was delighted to scratch one room off her list. A philandering husband would give her hard-working crew a break. He stopped for coffee at a lower-level kiosk then got back on the elevator in the company of an attractive woman. Again, he got off at the fifth floor, strolled leisurely down the hallway, then ran down the stairs to the third floor back to his room.

About 20 minutes later, Jack put a do-not-disturb sign on the door as he left his room, his transformation complete. An overweight Hoosier stepped from the elevator wearing polyester slacks, a tight-fitting polo shirt, Skechers, wig, and pilot frames. For a little insurance, in his room he had hours of porn on a loop playing on his portable media player that was slightly audible in the hallway. He wouldn't take any chances. Careful not to make eye contact, he spotted the federal agent sitting in the lobby. He timed his exit from the hotel with the mid-morning break and left in the middle of a group of conference attendees.

At a busy Kansas City car rental service, Jack used a fake ID to get a vehicle for the drive to Nebraska. He would meet Richard outside of Lincoln at a small warehouse to pick up the equipment.

Jack had a little surprise for Richard in his backpack. He hadn't worked out the details yet. But he'd be damned if he gave the man a fraction of what he'd worked so hard for. Jack couldn't believe that someone who was basically his employee had the audacity to challenge him like that. He didn't allow that at the office or in his personal life. It was unacceptable. One thing for sure, he wasn't bringing a million dollars in cash to their meeting. He contacted Richard and told him he could do a transfer, but it would be impossible to get that much cash without setting off alarms. Richard agreed to those terms, if Jack would send earnest money ahead of their meeting. Jack agreed to $250,000, which was more than Richard's expenses for the purchase and modifications of the cargo van, his transportation from Fort Collins and most importantly, the HERF gun. Jack thought that was a reasonable investment. Another $750,000? Not on his life. Well, Richard's.

After searching online and through an anonymous transaction, Jack acquired a ghost gun. He carefully packed and mailed the gun components to his hotel. The shipment was waiting for him at the front desk when he arrived. Untraceable, none of the parts had serial numbers. He assembled and disassembled the gun until he could do it in his sleep. Richard's attempt at blackmail soon would be irrelevant.

As he drove, Jack reviewed his plans. Just to be safe, he'd get rid of the firearm at Lake McConaughy in Ogallala, conveniently on the way to Fort Collins. Lake Mac was the deepest reservoir in Nebraska. Over a hundred feet deep at the dam, despite the drought. From there, it was less than four hours to the seed bank. He'd disable the refrigeration units, then head back to Kansas City. It would be a lot of driving, but he had Provigil to take. He could stay awake 40 hours on the stuff. The wonders of pharmacology. Maybe he'd consider drug companies for future investment.

Jack was working through in his mind where he needed to set up the HERF gun. When he visited the seed bank, he didn't notice how close he could get to the research building from Mason Street without entering the parking lot. There was something called the Mason Trail, running parallel to the lab, with a lot of parking available. When he reviewed the Google Earth photographs, he couldn't tell if there was a barrier between the trail and the building. Courtesy of Wikipedia, Jack knew the HERF could be used discreetly, would not generate sound, and the energy pulse wouldn't be visible. Gravity or wind wouldn't affect the beam. A thunderstorm would be problematic, but no rain was forecast. He hoped to park the panel truck along the trail and aim it at the building without needing to get closer. At his direction, Richard stashed a motorbike nearby. After the blast, he'd grab it and slip away on the interstate. Then he'd haul ass back to Kansas City, ditch the bike, and return to the conference.

Jack's GPS chirped an update, startling him. Right, first things first. He pulled off the interstate, taking a minute to pocket the gun. Richard told him to wear brown clothing with gold trim if possible. Weird. Per Richard's request, Jack had changed again at a rest stop. He now had a baggy shirt and a pair of loose pants with ample pockets. Underneath, he wore a close-fitting shirt and shorts. It would be easy to change his appearance after the blast. He had a backpack full of other things: two wigs, eyeglasses, hats, and assorted clothing. Jack was wearing gloves, and had put them on before he got in the rental car. He wouldn't leave a print anywhere.

Jack planned to get Richard to show him how to operate the HERF then take care of his little problem. It really was a shame he wouldn't be able to use the man any longer. He was impressed with how resourceful Richard was in finding the original launch sites for the drones. The current meeting place was in the middle of nowhere. And the idea for the HERF gun, just brilliant. And how he'd handled Stephen Angus. Jack wasn't sure what Richard did, but the last time he checked, the Scotsman wasn't doing well. Jack took care of the data on Angus's computer personally.

Unfortunately, Richard was a little too ambitious. Trying to blackmail Jack Stillman? He crossed a line. He would fix his Richard problem soon. If Jack was honest with himself, he felt a tingle of excitement ahead of the meeting.

He took the exit and followed the rural road for a few miles. Just as Richard said, a medium-sized metallic building sat back from the road. The paint had faded a long time ago, and large dents were visible on one side from its industrial past. Jack parked and left his rental vehicle. He stepped around the pigweed growing through cracks in the broken concrete.

Walking from of the storage building, Richard nodded to Jack.

"Anyone follow you here?" Jack asked.

"I lost them. Changed vehicles a few times before picking up the van.

"Show me what you got."

"Do you have the money, Mr. Stillman?"

"Of course I have the money," Jack snapped. "We talked about this. It'll be a transfer. I couldn't put my hands on that much cash. Where's the gun?"

"It's more accurate to call it an EMP generator." Richard led him into the metal building. A brown cargo van with a rich gold trim was parked inside.

"Where'd you get the van?" Jack asked.

"Well, I didn't buy it. Don't worry, no one can trace it."

"It looks like a UPS truck."

"That's the idea."

"That's the reason for the brown clothes."

"Yep. All the drivers wear brown uniforms. I tried to get one of their decommissioned cargo vans, but they never let those go. This just looks like one."

"Nice."

"Come see." Richard opened the cargo door. Inside, what looked like the horn of a huge gramophone gaped open. It was covered in tightly wound copper wire. Instead of the turntable and crank, the end of the horn attached to what looked like part of a rifle, the handle and forestock.

"Is that copper?"

"Yeah."

"It must weigh a ton."

"Not quite, between a quarter and half ton. I had to build the generator inside the van because of the Faraday cage."

"That's the part that looks like an antique Victrola?"

"Right. It will direct the blast."

"How does the rest of this work?"

"You've got a series of batteries that work together." Richard gestured at the device. "Here's the resistor that prevents their discharge. You've got two switches. To fire the electromagnetic pulse, turn the battery switch off. It's hooked up to the capacitor, where the energy is stored. Only when you're aimed and ready to fire, you'll flip the second switch. This bypasses the resistor and the battery, and the capacitor will discharge. Understand?"

Jack repeated the instructions, fumbling a little.

"Let's go over it again."

Jack recited the procedure again.

"Better. While you're driving, it'll charge. Are you sure you understand what to do?"

"I got this."

"Okay." Changing the subject, Richard said, "I checked out the campus and the seed bank. Security is a joke. You can park right next to the building."

"No, it's permit parking only. They have closed circuit cameras."

"Pfft," Richard laughed. "None of the vehicles in the lot had permits. You can park in front or behind the building. No one's watching anything. Even if someone is, they'll think you're a delivery driver until it's too late. And there's a transit lane in back of the building with more parking. It'll be like shooting ducks in a video game."

"You make it sound easy." He wished Richard hadn't used that analogy. It reminded him about what was coming next. "Let's talk about transportation once I'm done."

Richard reached into the van. "Here's your helmet."

"Where did you stash the motorbike?"

"Once you leave the research center, walk toward East Elizabeth. I parked it on Remington behind the Best Western between College and East Elizabeth. Remington runs parallel to South College."

"What's the model?"

"It's an older Yamaha FJR 1300, pretty quiet. Here's the key."

"Also stolen?"

"You didn't want anything that could be traced."

"Exactly." For the first time since he heard the television broadcast about the new wheat strain, Jack took a deep breath. *This guy is useful,* he thought. *Maybe I can keep him on a leash.* He would be hard to replace. Jack stood, pretending to inspect the generator, going through the set up. He asked a few more questions to buy time.

"Okay, Mr. Stillman. We're done. Make the transfer."

"Look, Richard, I had trouble coming up with the money. I need a little more time."

"You scumbag."

"Just a couple more weeks. My investments aren't as liquid after the agricultural group went public with their new cultivar."

"Not my problem, dude."

"Oh, come on, I'm good for it."

"Nope," Richard said.

"I don't have it."

"I figured you'd pull something like this." Frowning, Richard said, "Okay, another week. Transfer half right now, and the rest in seven days. And if you want me to stay quiet about this, it's going to cost another quarter mil."

Jack's fists clenched. "That's blackmail," he managed to get past the constriction in his throat. "No way."

"Yeah, well. Your choice." Richard paused then shrugged. "I guess I'll keep the keys for the van." He looked at Jack. When Jack didn't respond, Richard turned to go. He walked around to the driver's side door. "See you around, Mr. Stillman."

"Okay, okay. You'll get the money. Half a million now. On my cell phone, I'll have to do it in two transfers."

Richard turned and waited.

Jack reached into his pocket and pulled out the gun. His hand shook.

"You don't have the guts, pansy-ass."

Furious, at first Jack didn't respond. A long moment passed. "Want to bet?"

"You bastard!" Richard ran toward him, scraping Jack's face and grabbing his arm.

Jack shook him off and pulled the trigger. The noise was deafening in the metal building. The shot hit Richard in the chest.

CHAPTER 55

Jack stood in shock as Richard fell to the ground. There was so much blood. His arms twitched then were still. His chest rose and fell, rose and fell, slower and slower. Then stopped.

Jack felt detached, as though he wasn't part of his own body. Nothing seemed real. He couldn't remember what he was supposed to do next. He turned away, not able to look at Richard any longer.

Jack realized he was looking at the EMP generator. Right. Fort Collins. The first step was to get rid of the gun. He walked to the rental car. Okay, the backpack. He put the gun inside. What was next? He needed to make it to that lake... what was it called? He couldn't think. That was it, Lake McConaughy, near Ogallala. As though from another life, he remembered reading that Lake Mac connected to the Platte River and stretched into Colorado. Jack grabbed a towel and wiped down everything on the van and the rental car, inside and out. He looked around the storage building, searching for anything that might give him away. Nothing. He put the towel on top of the gun in his knapsack. He checked the rental car one more time.

Jack edged around the pool of blood on the ground. Reaching across Richard, he picked up the keys to the van. Closing the cargo doors, he walked to the driver's seat. He got in, turned the ignition, and eased out of the building. He watched his hand shift the gear lever to park. Jack stopped got out, and closed the doors to the building. He couldn't catch his breath.

The van moved sluggishly. He would have to be careful accelerating and braking. Jack followed the access road to Interstate 80. After he reached the highway, he checked the rearview mirror and saw a sheriff's car waiting to turn onto the access road. Had someone heard the shot? No, the place was deserted. No one would put the van together with that shed. He maneuvered the van into the right-hand lane and used his turn signal to merge into the next lane. He put the vehicle on cruise control. From outside himself, he knew he was driving. He couldn't think—he had to plan.

In Ogallala, Jack followed the signs to the lake. Adrenaline kept him going until he arrived at the reservoir. He bought a day pass with cash. A few people were out, enjoying the beach. He found a place to park near Kingsley Dam. His hands shaking, Jack pulled the gun from his backpack and put it in his pocket. He walked about a mile until he was alone. In the distance, an angler sat on a small skiff, his back to Jack. No one else was around. He heaved the gun with all his might, low across the water. It splashed then sunk. He stared at the horizon, then looked down at his feet. This would finish it.

Jack got back in the van, driving south. He noticed a fast-food restaurant with a drive through and stopped because it was time to be hungry. The hamburger tasted like cardboard, inedible. The Coke had a metallic taste.

Less than twenty miles later, Jack took the exit for I-76. He drove 60 miles and exited. He spotted the state highway, CO-14, and continued for another 75 miles. He turned on West Pitkin Street into the campus, watching students walking between buildings in the summer sun. They all looked like hicks. That was one thing he always hated about working for Landever. It was a bunch of farm rubes who thought they knew something about management. After this, he'd move on. With his track record, he could land a CEO position with a pharmaceutical company or a medical equipment manufacturer. A step up, for sure. He'd be recognized for his vision.

But, first—the National Laboratory for Genetic Resource Preservation. What a pretentious name for such an unassuming building. Inside, there was a seed cultivar that could destroy him and his plans for the future.

Jack found parking on Mason Street at the back of the building. Across the trailway, kids were practicing on the track. Other vehicles were parked in between. They shouldn't be able to see anything except the top of the van. From his angled parking space, Jack thought the EMP blast would reach most of the building.

It was quiet. Taking in his surroundings, Jack wondered if the blast would get through all that concrete. Not willing to risk it, he circled back and parked at the front of the lab, with the cargo doors facing the windows. More exposure but worth it. No one was around. Jack got out of the vehicle wearing a black wig, horn-rimmed glasses, and brown clothing. He opened the cargo doors and reached in, flipping the battery switch. With his hand shaking, Jack hit the second switch. Was it working? It seemed anticlimactic.

Leaving the back doors open, Jack walked around to the passenger side door and grabbed the backpack. He started down Mason Street toward University Avenue, crossing over Mason Trail. Past the closed-circuit cameras, he bent down and pulled off the wig, glasses and outer shirt and stashed them in the backpack. He turned onto College Avenue, past the Best Western, and entered a coffee shop. In the restroom, he put on a pair of motorcycle pants and leather boots. When he left the shop, Jack's new wig was light brown with purple streaks, and his jacket was dark blue. He headed toward Remington and saw the bike. Pulling on the helmet, he settled dark glasses over his eyes. Time to head back to Kansas City.

CHAPTER 56

Sam heard his phone ring across the room. FaceTime call from Valentina. No way, he must look terrible. He hadn't slept or shaved and had gorged on junk food since the dinner with his father. He felt like death warmed over. Instead, he sent a text—*Let me call you in a min.* As he did, Sam realized he had missed five texts from Valentina over the last few hours. Tala and Ellis had also tried to reach him. He splashed water on his face and reached for his cellphone.

Sam had felt frozen ever since the dinner with his father. Jack left the house for Indianapolis early the next morning, so Sam didn't have to interact with him. Which was good. What would he say? Hey Dad, did you let loose a virus that is decimating grain crops across North America? And what about Angus? What happened to his mites? Did you try to burn his house down?

Sam touched Valentina's name on his phone screen.

She answered a second later. "Are you okay? I've been trying to reach you."

"Sorry, I just saw your texts.

"I have an idea."

"Valentina, I'm not sure I've recovered from your last idea."

"Sam ..."

"It's okay." Sam took a deep breath, noticing his unwashed clothes. Whew, he smelled bad. He rubbed his chin with its three-day stubble. "I'm getting my head around it."

"Let me ask you something, and it's okay, whatever you decide. I know we're coming at this from different places."

"No kidding."

"Could we meet up this evening and talk about my idea? I think there's a way to confirm whether or not your father's involved and document it."

"Umm..." Sam hesitated.

"I understand if you'd rather not. Leo offered to help. I ran into him late this afternoon before I left NOU. We could handle it on our own."

"No, it's okay," Sam said. "I've got to deal with this sometime. I've been in a fog. Tala and Ellis both tried to reach me. Let's pull them in."

"Meet at my place at eight."

•   •   •

Later that evening, Sam parked a few houses down from Valentina's small porch. Warm gold light spilled from the windows into the street. He saw Valentina moving around in the kitchen and heard the soft sound of laughter. He yearned to be inside. But going in meant he had to deal with whatever his father had done. His chest tightened and his nose burned with the effort to stay in control. Sam felt sick, but he didn't have a choice. He rang the bell. He had showered, shaved, and picked up a salad and a bottle of wine.

Leo answered the door. "You look like hell."

"Why thank you, Leo."

Leo pulled Sam in the door and into a hug. "Come on in, my friend."

"We have pizza," Ellis called. "Beer and sodas too."

Ellis, Annie, and Tala crowded around an old pine table. Valentina was getting glasses from a cabinet. "Hey, thanks for the salad and wine. Pull up a chair."

Annie smiled at Sam. "We're glad you're here."

As they filled up paper plates and poured wine, Sam wanted to pretend that the last several weeks hadn't happened. The evening reminded him of Valentina's party, before he knew about the grain crisis. Valentina looked at him across the table, and he knew she understood. For several minutes, everyone talked about food and plans for the next semester. It was the reprieve Sam needed. Finally, he said, "Let's bring that elephant out of the corner. We need to figure this out. What's your idea, Valentina?"

"I think I can get your father to admit what he's done. I want to ask your father to be the keynote speaker at a new Winslow Park initiative. You've all heard about the outreach program we're doing with a couple of local schools. One of them asked us to expand the program. Building on the seed bank, we're going to start a farm-to-table program. We'll connect the school kids with chefs and business leaders to help them develop new skills. Your dad is the perfect person to kick it off. I can get press coverage, and I think he'd love that. After his talk, I think I can flatter him into admitting what he did."

"This sounds like a stretch, Valentina. And even if he does, he could deny it later," Sam said.

"I plan to wear a wire."

"Is that legal?" asked Sam.

"There's something called one-party consent in Louisiana. As long as one person knows and is part of the conversation," Valentina said, "then it's legal."

Ellis spoke up. "It's not really a wire, per se. I can set that up, but how can you possibly get Mr. Stillman to admit anything?"

Not looking at Sam, Valentina said, "I didn't want to say anything before, but he came on to me at the Winslow fundraiser. If I tell him how much I admire what he's doing and suggest he's the mastermind cornering the grain market, I think he might talk. It's more like letting him know that I know, and I think it's fine. Like, it wasn't wrong, it's brilliant. Then we turn him over to the feds."

Leo looked at Valentina, his eyes burning into hers. "Valentina, are you sure about this?"

"I'm not sure about anything."

CHAPTER 57

Martha Jane Bruning was about to leave the research center to meet her sister Nora for lunch. Since she was running late, she picked up her cell phone to text her. It was dead. She couldn't remember if she charged it overnight. Better leave now. She called out to her colleague, Rhonda.

"I'm leaving for lun ..." Martha Jane stopped. Her coworker, Rhonda Williams, was leaning against the wall with her eyes closed. In the dark—*wait a minute, the lights were off.* Sample bags were lying on the floor nearby. "Rhonda, what's wrong?"

Rhonda shook her head slightly. "I'm a little dizzy."

"When did this start?"

"I was feeling fine until a few minutes ago. Strange."

"Let me get Kenny. Didn't he work his way through school as an EMT?"

"I don't remember."

Martha Jane gently squeezed Rhonda's arm and hurried down the darkened hallway. Martha Jane returned minutes later with a slender young man. Rhonda had sunk to the floor, and Kenny sat down next to her.

"Hey, Rhonda, remember me?" He took her wrist to find her pulse.

"Oh, Kenny. Don't you usually work in the livestock sector?"

"That's right, I do." Following the second hand on his watch, he counted for fifteen seconds. Then he said to Rhonda, "Tell me how you're feeling."

"I was getting something from the shelf. Funny, I can't remember what I was trying to reach. Then I got short of breath."

"Have you ever had treatment for your heart?"

"Uh huh. Used to have trouble until I got my pacemaker. Not since then. Funny, this is a little like that."

"I bet. Rhonda, your heart rate is pretty slow, 36 beats per minute instead of 60-90. We should get you checked out, see how that pacemaker is doing. Okay?" Kenny looked up at Martha Jane and said softly, "We should probably call for an ambulance. We must have had a power outage. It's going to get pretty warm in here soon."

"Where's your phone, Rhonda?" asked Martha Jane. "Mine's not working."

"Here, in my pocket."

Martha Jane carefully reached around Rhonda to extricate her phone. "Sit up a second? Got it. Funny, yours is dead, too. Kenny, do you have your phone?"

"Sure." Grabbing it from his back pocket, he stared at the blank screen. When he tried to turn it on, nothing happened. "Let's not waste more time, Martha Jane. Help me get Rhonda to my car, and I'll drive her to the hospital. I'm parked behind the building."

Martha Jane and Kenny helped Rhonda down the stairs and through the back entrance to the parking area.

"Right over there, that black Jeep." Kenny clicked to unlock the car, and nothing happened.

"Martha Jane, where's your car?

"In front."

They moved toward the front of the building, Rhonda walking unsteadily between them. Martha Jane's faded blue Subaru sat in one of the spaces reserved for federal employees. She opened the door. "I never lock it. It's so old, it's not worth stealing." She hastily inserted the key, but the Outback wouldn't turn over. Martha Jane kept trying to start her car.

Kenny looked serious. "Let's go to the next building and check if their phones are working."

As they walked toward the General Services Building, they spotted a campus maintenance worker. Kenny called to him. "Sir, could you help us over here?"

The workman rushed over. "What do you guys need?"

"Can you call 911?"

"Sure." The man quickly called emergency services and handed the phone to Kenny.

"We need immediate hospitalization for a woman, late 50s, likely experiencing bradycardia. Has a pacemaker. I suspect it's not working." Kenny talked for a few minutes then hung up. "Can you help me get Ms. Williams inside while we wait for the ambulance?"

The maintenance man nodded. "Come on."

Martha Jane looked at Kenny. "I better go see what's happening inside the center."

"I'm gonna get someone to call campus security," Kenny said.

Martha Jane hurried back across the street. She passed an unattended brown van—cargo doors wide open—in the parking lot. Martha Jane went in through the front entrance. The overhead lights were out, but windows illuminated the first floor. Martha Jane, who hiked every weekend on the trails around Fort Collins, flew up the stairs. On the second floor, she found everyone milling about, trying to get their phones and computers to work.

"Has anyone checked the cryotanks or the generator?" Martha Jane asked.

"Pat is back there now. We think they've lost power."

"The generators too?" she asked in disbelief.

"Out." A short, overweight man ran in. "What the heck happened?"

Turning to a small athletic intern, Martha Jane asked, "Lynn, can you run over to Facilities Management and ask them to send over an electrician?"

"Where are they?" Lynn asked.

"Head toward Pitkin. They're past the observatory on the left."

Lynn took off at a run.

"We need to keep all the refrigeration units closed. Try to maintain the temperature until we get the power back." Martha Jane said. "Kenny was going to get someone to call campus security. George, why don't you see if you can speed them up."

"Where's Rhonda?" someone asked.

"She's at the General Services Building, waiting for an ambulance. Kenny is with her. He thinks her pacemaker may need to be looked at," Martha Jane said.

Just then, they heard a voice calling from the stairwell. "Is anyone there? Martha Jane? Are you all right?"

"Oh my," Martha Jane said. "That's Nora, my sister. Nora, we're upstairs."

"Martha Jane, you could have called to say you couldn't meet me. I was worried sick." Panting, Nora walked in, found an empty chair and began a rapid monologue. "You know I've got to pick up Cheryl Ann and Patrick William at 2:45. Those are my grandchildren," Nora said to the lab staff with a self-satisfied smile. "Martha Jane doesn't have any, so she sometimes forgets. What's going on? It is hot as blazes in here. Martha Jane, why didn't you answer your phone? I know you don't have a receptionist any more, but couldn't someone have answered the lab phone? Why, hello, Louis. I haven't seen you since the holiday party. You know, there's a crowd of security officers in the parking lot around a brown van. It looks like a UPS truck, with the gold trim, but it doesn't have the insignia. Now what's that about? Did you lose your electricity? The lights are out. It's a good thing you have those windows."

"Nora, wait here." Martha Jane tossed those words over her shoulder as she took off for the stairs. When she got to the front parking lot, Kenny, George, and two campus police officers were standing at the back of the cargo van she passed earlier.

"Rhonda?" Martha Jane asked Kenny.

"On her way to the hospital. Her husband is going to meet her there. She should be okay."

"Ma'am." One officer nodded.

"What's this about?" Martha Jane asked. When no one answered, Martha Jane stepped around another security officer to peer inside the van. "What the heck is that?"

"Officer Riley, whose hobby is reading science fiction," Kenny said, "thinks it's an electromagnetic generator." As Riley looked about fifteen, he did not inspire Martha Jane's confidence.

"It probably zapped all your electronics with something like a high-powered microwave," Officer Riley said.

Turning to Kenny, Martha Jane said, "Come on, this isn't a Batman movie."

Before Kenny could respond, Officer Riley asked, "Is anything with circuitry working in the lab?"

"Well, no. How long will it be out?"

"How long will it take to replace everything?"

Martha Jane doubled over as though struck by a blow. Fist on her mouth, she whispered, "Think, think." She straightened and swallowed hard. "We need as many portable generators as you can find. Freezers, refrigeration equipment, cell phones, computers, a campus radio system. It's no exaggeration to say that we have the fate of North America's food supply in that building. We have to alert Homeland Security."

CHAPTER 58

After a long day, Will sat outside on the patio nursing a beer. Susan had just come downstairs from her home office.

"A glass of wine, sweetheart?" Will asked.

"Love one. I'd like to forget the world of medical coding for a little while."

"Tonight we have a fine vintage from Hy-Vee Grocery, madam." Will poured Susan a glass. "From one of the lower shelves, ahem, I mean the lower valleys."

Laughing, Susan said, "The very finest."

Will loved this time of day, when everything they were going to do or could finish was done, and he and Susan could relax. A light breeze cooled the evening as they sat talking quietly.

Once their application for organic certification was approved, Will got ready to plant. He prepared the beds and let them sit for a week or two. He soaked the seeds before planting beans, squash, and cucumber. Later in the summer, he would add lettuce and radishes, probably beets. Will had applied to become a vendor at a Lincoln farmer's market and expected approval any day. Susan was looking forward to helping him, although he suspected she wanted to check out the other vendors. Will thought he would have organic produce from early July until mid-October. They were going to install a high tunnel system or hoop house to extend their growing season, so they could grow lettuce most of the year. To help matters, they qualified for financial assistance through the USDA's Environmental

Quality Incentive Program or EQIP. It wasn't what he had planned to do with the farm, but it wasn't bad. It would work until they got the seeds for the new wheat cultivar.

"Norris has an old refrigerated truck I'll be able to use," Will told Susan. "I spent some time on it today. The engine's good, but I found a leak. I changed two of the belts and a hose. It's been sitting up for a while, but it should be okay now. Norris was glad to swap the repairs for my using it on Saturdays."

"Sounds like a fair trade to me," Susan said, as she sipped her wine.

"I'm going to go get another beer. Need anything?"

Susan started to answer when Will's phone beeped with a text.

"It's from Mitch. He says to turn on the news."

Susan sighed. "Is there anything we really have to know? But I guess we should go inside anyway and get dinner started."

•　　•　　•

As Will started upstairs to wash up, Susan turned on the television. The running headline at the bottom of the screen said, "Terrorist attack on Fort Collins Seed Bank, The National Center for Genetic Resources Preservation. New wheat cultivar in jeopardy."

Susan sank to a chair, downing the rest of her wine in one gulp. "Will! Come see this."

When the station cut to commercials, Susan switched channels. Casey Roberts, a local TV reporter, stood outside a two-story beige building.

"Earlier today, an act of terrorism struck the National Center for Genetic Resources Preservation, the nation's repository for genetic material for plants and animals. Person or persons unknown disrupted the power supply and all electrical and electronic equipment in the building. Authorities believe the attacker used a homemade device that generated a massive pulse of electromagnetic energy at the building. A brown cargo van contained the device, which Homeland Security is calling an Electromagnetic Pulse or EMP generator."

Will sat down beside Susan.

"Did you catch all that?" she asked.

He nodded. "Unbelievable. Who would do such a thing?"

Casey Roberts continued, "The federal government built the Fort Collins vault, or seed bank, in 1953. The purpose of the vault is to collect and preserve thousands of seeds to protect the biodiversity of our food supply. Many of the seeds are preserved in stainless steel cooling tanks that contain liquid nitrogen, or in refrigerator units set to -18 ° C. Most of the world's crops are based on less than ten plant species. For this reason, the United States maintains genetic samples of hundreds of thousands of other plants to ensure the viability of crops in the future. Inside the Fort Collins vault, scientists research older and more diverse plants to develop ways to address changing climatic conditions.

"The vault has thick concrete walls designed to withstand flooding or other natural disasters, for example, if the Horsetooth Reservoir were to fail. We understand there are backup generators, but the EMP attack damaged these too. The two-story vault contains a collection of plant and animal genetic material that ensures our food supply. Most significantly, it contains the new wheat cultivar that is resistant to the wheat streak mosaic virus. Normally, the staff spends much of their time continually testing the seeds and plants in their care to ensure that they are alive. In a moment, we hope to talk to personnel at the seed bank to learn the status of their collection and its most important specimen, the new wheat cultivar.

"Luckily, most of the 40 employees at the Fort Collins vault are safe. One injury occurred when the EMP stopped a vital pacemaker worn by one scientist. The employee is hospitalized at this time. Her condition is described as serious. Back to you, Michelle."

The camera cut away from Casey Roberts, the reporter on site at the seed bank. The station news anchor, Michelle Haley, then spoke to the camera. "We will check back with Casey in a little while. In the meantime, Dr. Lyle Abramson, an expert in terrorism from the Pennison Institute, will discuss what could be behind this unprecedented attack. Dr. Abramson, welcome to KBRR. We appreciate your joining us today. What can you tell us about what happened in Fort Collins?"

"Michelle, first, we need to understand that terrorism is a tactic. Groups who use terrorist activities do so to cultivate affiliation and support through the notoriety of their actions. We suspect that part of the motivation for the Fort Collins attack is to demonstrate the unreliability of the government in providing food security for its citizens. Thus far, no terrorist organization has claimed responsibility. Considering that the grain crisis is limited to North America, there is some suspicion that foreign players are involved."

Michelle Haley broke in, "Dr. Abramson, I'll come back to you in just a moment. We have an updated report from our onsite correspondent, Casey Roberts. Casey?"

"Thank you, Michelle. What we have learned is that the vault's staff is working furiously to salvage their extensive collection. Approximately 30 organizations worldwide exist to ensure global food security. Fort Collins scientists have sent out a plea to all seed banks across the world for help in temporarily storing the vault's collection. We understand that at least one plane will arrive shortly to take portions of the collection to the Svalbard Global Seed Vault, which protects over a million seed samples from more than 6000 separate plant species. It's unclear if the new wheat cultivar survived the attack. Back to you, Michelle."

"Thank you, Casey. In other news, a body was discovered in a storage facility near Lincoln, Nebraska. The man was likely killed by a gunshot wound, although police described recent burns on his hands and arms. No identification has been made at this time. ..."

Will and Susan sat frozen before the television.

•　　•　　•

Jack leaned into the turn as the air whipped across his helmet. The motorcycle vibrated through him, an extension of his body. It was the most fun he'd had in years. Elizabeth insisted he sell his old Honda after Sam was born. Maybe he would get another. A bike and a gun. Jack flashed back to the floor stain in the metal storage building. Richard had it coming—he was disrespectful. He didn't understand who was in control. He would order another gun when he got back to the hotel.

The Yamaha ate up the miles. He would reach Kansas City in a couple of hours.

CHAPTER 59

Fuming, Angus clicked off the news and started to throw the TV remote across the room. Remembering that he didn't want another visit from the social worker, he put it down carefully on his bed in the burn unit. *Foreign players, my arse.* He didn't know how, but somehow Jack Stillman was involved in the Fort Collins attack. So far, the bugger was getting away with everything. Angus called the feds almost every day to get an update on their efforts to restore his hard drive. It was taking too long.

The walls were closing in. He needed to get out of that room. Angus made the transfer to his wheelchair. Although he could walk, he wasn't up to the long trek to the hospital's Sky Farm, the beautiful garden high above the city. He had explored every inch of those 5,000 square feet of paradise. He was a frequent visitor in the evening when it was cooler and he could watch the clouds change colors across the horizon.

Angus sat near the tall white stems of the leeks, their flat green leaves reaching over a foot. The pungent smell of the earth reminded him of the gardens he had as a kid, more tangible and inviting than the antiseptic corridors of the hospital. *Maybe I should give up and go home,* he thought. He had kept up with a few colleagues at the University of Edinburgh. Calmer, Angus leaned back and considered Scotland. He could teach, garden. Find a good Scottish woman. He remembered Kathleen. They dated before he left for the States. Strong, independent, with beautiful, flame-colored hair.

He'd thought about asking her to come with him but somehow didn't. He hadn't planned to stay in America, believed she'd wait for him. They lost touch over the years. Last time he checked, she wasn't married. The buzz of his mobile phone interrupted his musings. He sighed. It was Sam Stillman. He would need to keep it light. It wasn't his job to convince the kid his father was a bastard.

"Hullo, Sam. How are you?"

"Doing okay. How's rehab?"

"A bloody torture chamber, but it seems to help. I have a lot more mobility."

"How much longer before you're released?"

"Another couple of weeks."

"Your friend, Barry Carlson, still visits?"

"Almost every day. I've told him to bug off, but he keeps coming back."

Sam laughed then paused. "Angus, my father did it."

"What exactly did he do, Sam?"

"You were right. He set off this whole grain crisis."

Angus didn't respond at first. Then, "What makes you think that?"

"Valentina and I set him up at dinner. He lied about the last time he saw you. He implied that your research wasn't ethical. That he hadn't had contact with you in months, and you'd left under suspicion and returned to the UK." There was a pause then Sam asked, "What's that noise?"

Angus found himself thumping a small shovel on the side of the leek bed. "Oh, someone in the hallway," he said and dropped the shovel. He straightened, wincing as his back pressed against the wheelchair. "Sam, that's not true."

"I know."

"I'm sorry, lad. What do you plan to do?"

"We're going to set a trap." Sam told him how Jack would be speaking at an event at the park where Valentina worked. "She'll get him to admit what he's done."

"Just like that? How does your friend plan to do that, Sam?"

"Angus, my parents have been living separately for a while. My dad finds Valentina attractive ..." Sam sounded embarrassed. "She's .... going to come on to him, tell him she admires what he's done and wants to be part of it, maybe marketing the wheat cultivar for Landever."

"Okay, I get the picture. Where is this park?"

"Winslow Park, in New Orleans."

"Then what?"

"The man you spoke to at the beach house, Ellis, is good with electronics. Valentina will wear a wire, and they'll record it. Then we'll take it to Homeland Security or the FBI."

"Sam, this could be risky for your friend. If your father suspects something or, or feels cornered ...."

"What are you saying?" Sam asked, anger in his voice.

"When someone is threatened, they sometimes react unpredictably. I'm not sure this is a good idea."

"It's my dad. He's done some awful things for financial gain, but he wouldn't hurt anyone deliberately."

Angus paused. Why did it keep coming back to that? *It's not my place to tell this boy, this man,* he corrected himself, *that his father is a monster.* "None of us know what we're capable of," he paused again, "if our back is against the wall."

Sam said, "Look, if he suspects what Valentina is doing, he'll do the right thing. She'll suggest he turn himself in, make reparations by distributing the Landever cultivar for free with no limits or obligation."

"But, Sam..."

Sam cut him off. "Look, I just called to see how you were doing."

"Wait, when do you plan to do this?"

"Tuesday."

"That's two days away!"

"Yeah, my dad is flying in tomorrow evening. It's going to be fine, Angus. We have to make him realize what he's doing. And we'll have the recording to take to the feds."

"Sam…"

"It's more important than ever, since the terrorist attack on the Fort Collins seed vault."

"Sam…"

"Look, I've got to go. I didn't mean to get into all that. I'm glad that you're doing better," Sam said politely and ended the conversation.

Angus sat holding his phone, his evening shattered. He tried to reach Tony Sorelli.

Freddy Ackerman answered. "Violent Crimes Division."

Angus recognized her voice as Sorelli's partner or assistant. "This is Stephen Angus. I must speak with Tony Sorelli."

"I'm sorry, Mr. Angus. Inspector Sorelli is unavailable to take your call right now." Freddy delivered the message in a soothing monotone, as though speaking to someone who might explode if not handled carefully.

"It's very important that I speak with him," said Angus.

"If this is about the hard drive, I can tell you we're working on restoring it. There's nothing definitive to report."

"That's not why I called. I have information about the attack in Fort Collins."

"Can you be more specific? I'll be happy to pass it on to Inspector Sorelli."

"I know that Jack Stillman is responsible."

"What makes you believe that?" Freddy asked.

"It could only have been him," Angus began.

"Yes, Mr. Angus, but where is your evidence?"

"It's as plain as the nose on your face, Freddy. And what's more important, I'm very concerned with this plot Tony's niece and Stillman's son have cooked up."

"What plot?" Freddy asked.

"They plan to talk with Stillman and get him to admit that he's guilty," Angus said in an exasperated tone. "They're going to secretly record his confession."

"Hmm, yes," was Freddy's jaded response. "I certainly will pass that information on to Inspector Sorelli when I hear from him. Is that all?"

"Och... yes, that's all." Angus ended the call, carefully putting the phone down before he was tempted to throw it off the roof. *What the hell can I do?* He couldn't blame Freddy. *I wouldn't waste time on my nonsense, either.*

· · ·

When Tony got back from lunch, he asks, "Anything new?"

"Stephen Angus called. He knows Stillman is responsible."

"So do we. Proving it is a different story."

"He's been talking to Stillman's son, too." Freddy said. "He said something about a scheme to get Stillman to confess."

"Freddy, give Sam a call later and tell him to stand down, okay? The last thing we need are civilians mucking things up."

"Sure, boss."

· · ·

After tossing and turning all night, Angus was bleary-eyed and in no mood for the practiced cheerfulness of the food service worker.

"Hello, Mr. Angus! How are we this lovely morning?"

"WE are bloody well tired and not interested in your blather," Angus muttered to himself.

"How about some breakfast?"

Angus said nothing as the attendant set out his breakfast tray, pulling the bedside table closer and continuing to chatter. He felt helpless. As Angus picked at his tray, Barry walked in.

"Oh look, here's your friend," the attendant said. "He'll cheer you up," and left the room hurriedly without a backward glance.

"Hullo."

Angus didn't say anything.

After a long pause, Barry asked, "It can't be that bad, can it?"

"Oh, mate, it's worse."

"Are you in pain?"

"Physical? The usual itching. That's the least of it."

"What's up?"

"You've got to get me out of here."

"Angus, you only have another couple of weeks. You're doing well."

"No, you don't understand. Stillman's kid is about to do something crazy. I've got to stop him." Angus started out quietly, but his voice rose exponentially as he thought of Sam's young friend, Valentina, trying to reason, let alone actually reason, with Jack Stillman.

"Barry, you heard about Fort Collins?"

"Of course."

"You know that right bastard did it."

"Or had someone do it for him," said Barry.

"And so far, he's getting away with it. What's worse, young Sam and his mates are going to confront Stillman to try to make him admit what he's done," Angus said in an exasperated voice.

"What?"

"They have some daft idea that the girl, Valentina, will use her feminine wiles on Stillman and get him to confess that he caused the whole wheat crisis."

"What?" Barry almost laughed.

"No, I'm serious."

"Sam doesn't realize how dangerous his father is. Stillman was ready to kill you that last day at the office."

Angus blew out a breath. "He almost did."

"I guess trying to burn your house down qualifies."

"They're going to pull this stunt tomorrow afternoon, Barry. I've got to do something."

"Have you tried reaching the feds?"

"I spoke to Sorelli's assistant, who thinks I'm an eejit. ... I've got to get to New Orleans. Last time I checked, I still had my motor. Be a mate, help me find my clothes. I think they're in that cupboard."

"Angus, are you crazy? You can't drive to New Orleans." But as he spoke, Barry found himself handing Angus the clothes from the cabinet.

Pulling on his pants, Angus said, "Those kids don't know what they're getting into, poking at a junkyard dog." He winced.

"Your burns aren't healed, Angus. You can't just leave the hospital."

"How many more people will Stillman hurt, Barry?" Angus finished getting dressed. "That's really the question, isn't it? We've missed how many grain shipments to other countries because of that greedy bastard? This won't be the end of it. Without the new wheat cultivar from the other companies, Landever has a monopoly. And Stillman isn't sharing."

"But... it's over 800 miles to New Orleans."

Angus looked up from pulling on his shoes.

"What will he do next, Barry? I can't let him get away with it."

Having decided, Angus seemed much calmer and walked resolutely toward the nursing station. Shaking his head, Barry gathered up the medical supplies in the hospital room.

"I'm checking out of this fine facility this morning," Angus said to the charge nurse.

"Mr. Angus, you've been a little frustrated. Let me call your doctor so we can discuss this."

"No, thank you. I just wanted to let you know."

"Mr. Angus, you would be leaving against medical advice. Please, I ask you to reconsider. There is still the chance of infection, scarring."

"I'm afraid I must."

"There's paperwork you must sign."

"There's no time," Angus said politely as he turned toward the elevators.

As the elevator doors opened, Angus stepped in, followed by Barry. "Could you give me a lift? The feds have my car at a garage a few blocks away."

"Sure, Angus."

They walked together to the hospital parking area. Barry waited until he was sure Angus was comfortable, and drove out of the garage.

"The fed's garage is the other way, Barry."

"I-70 is this way. I've always wanted to see New Orleans.

•　　•　　•

At the FBI office, Tony Sorelli's second in command leaned back in her chair as she ended a call. "Hey boss," she called.

"What's up, Freddy?"

"They've ID'd the body. Richard Miller."

"The one near Lincoln?"

"Yeah. Get this—he's the one that set the fire at Angus's house."

"Really? The one our guys were tailing?"

"Yeah, one and the same. He shook his tail early on, and the agents hadn't been able to pick it up again. So, now, who killed him?"

"Hmm. Any prints from the storage building or the rental car?"

"No. Whoever shot Miller was pretty careful," Freddy said.

Tony nodded. Forensics were effective when they had something to work with.

"No prints," Freddy said, "but they're soaking the fingernails to try to obtain exogenous DNA. And we're tracing Miller's movements. He's been careful the last few years, but we found some older images. We also have a few partials of his face from the fire at

Stephen Angus's house. The local cops are going to show them around."

"What about that drone lady?"

Freddy looked carefully at Tony. She had no idea what Tony was talking about. They had both been working long hours since the wheat crisis started. So had most of their department. Her boss looked tired. "Um, drone lady?"

"Come on, Freddy," Tony said impatiently. "The woman who called the hotline. She manufactured the drones. What was her name? Evie ... Evie something. Has anyone shown the dead guy's pictures to her?"

"Right, let me check," Freddy said. "We'll make it happen if she hasn't seen them. By the way, I can't reach Stillman's son, Sam."

"Well, keep trying, Freddy. He needs to let us do our job and stay out of the way."

Freddy picked up her phone again and rang Sam's cell. It went straight to voicemail.

CHAPTER 60

Valentina opened the door for Leo and said, "Good morning."

"Hey." Leo leaned forward and kissed her on the cheek. "Nice outfit. Stillman's going to love that."

Valentina glanced down at her baggy shirt, pencil skirt and bare feet. "Gets them every time."

"It's got me."

"Yeah?"

"Yeah." Leo continued looking at Valentina with an intensity that made her blush. After half a second, Valentina shook her head. They had work to do. Leo seemed to come to the same conclusion and pulled a tiny electronic device from his pocket.

"That's it?" Valentina asked.

"Yep."

"Come on in and show me what to do."

Leo stepped through the doorway before she backed away. They were inches apart, and Valentina felt her face become warm. Catching her breath, she asked, "If I put this under my clothes, you'll still be able to hear?"

"We can try it out."

"We could do that." Valentina reminded herself they needed to focus. Stepping away, she asked, "How do you know it works?"

"Ellis and I tested it yesterday. I'm going to put it inside this little sleeve. That will reduce interference."

"Okay."

"And we'll test it again once you're wearing it."

"Okay. How do I turn it on?"

"It's voice activated, so you won't need to worry about that."

"So it can last a long time?"

"It's got," Leo paused, "great stamina."

"Good to know." Giving Leo a smirk, Valentina said, "Excuse me while I get things situated."

Leo grinned, and Valentina turned back toward her dressing area. She called over her shoulder, "Help yourself to some coffee."

"Thanks." Leo poured himself a cup and wandered around the large airy room that was Valentina's apartment. "This is a neat place. I didn't really notice it the other night."

Behind the vintage screen that created a small dressing area, Valentina pulled off her shirt and struggled with the lace and clasps of a tight bustier.

"Thanks. I fell in love with the oak trees on the patio. The apartment itself is pretty basic."

"You've got great windows."

"A little drafty, but the light is awesome."

Hands in his pockets, Leo walked around the big open room. "Valentina," he began, then stopped.

When Leo didn't say anything else, she looked over the top of the dressing area. "Yeah?"

"Are you okay about confronting Stillman?"

"I'm hoping that he'll take the bait and I won't have to confront him at all."

"But you're the bait."

"We can't catch a fish without bait," Valentina teased. When Leo didn't laugh, she asked, "Do you have any other ideas?"

Leo didn't answer.

Now serious, Valentina said, "I don't like this either. But what am I supposed to do?"

"This could be dangerous."

"So? We're probably the only people in North America who actually know what happened to our grain crops. I take that back. There's at least one other person and he's in a burn unit in Indiana."

"Exactly!" Leo almost shouted. "Do we really know what Stillman is capable of?"

Angry, Valentina said, "I know he's capable of bringing half the farmers in America, like my cousin Will, this close to bankruptcy." Valentina gestured with her fingers. "People are starving, Leo." Storming out of her dressing area, she exclaimed, "Have you looked at what's happening in other countries because they don't have our grain? Look at Nigeria, heck, look at Mexico. Besides worldwide hunger, our economy is tanking because no one can afford to buy anything except food. And who do you think took down the Fort Collins seed bank? He didn't jeopardize only grain crops. He's put agricultural diversity, heck, let's say every plant species in the U.S., on the line." Face flushed, Valentina took a breath. "We can prove that he's responsible. If we don't, what do you think he'll do next?" Hands outstretched, Valentina paused. "Let me ask you again, Leo, what do you expect me to do?"

Walking slowly toward Valentina, Leo shook his head. Shadows passed across his face. "Exactly what you're doing." He leaned down and touched his lips lightly to hers.

The kiss began softly. Valentina's arms reached for Leo's shoulders, almost of their own volition. He pulled her closer and deepened the kiss. Her lips parted as Leo lightly touched his tongue to hers. She was overwhelmed as a rush of warmth raced through her. She could stay like that forever. Leo pressed himself against her, so she could feel his fit, lean frame and the racing of his heart. More than excitement, she felt a sense of rightness, a sense that she was home. Finally, Leo pulled back, and held her lightly against him.

"This isn't the right time …," he said, resting his forehead on hers.

Slightly out of breath, Valentina agreed, "Not yet."

"As much as I want to, I won't try to talk you out of this scheme you've planned. Selfishly, all I want is to keep you safe, preferably alone with me for … for a long time." He looked down at Valentina. "Can I forget about the rest of the world and what Stillman has done?" Leo shook his head. "Still, when I think of you being near that maniac, it drives me crazy."

"Me too. But it's just long enough to get him on tape."

Leo nodded. They held each other for another moment, then Leo looked down, smiling at the undone clasp at the top of her bustier. "Did we do that?" he asked.

Laughing, she said, "No, I was having trouble getting it closed. My best friend Amy told me to start from the bottom and work my way to the top, but maybe she had that backwards."

"Let me see if I can help." Leo carefully pulled the lace ends of the bustier and fastened it closed. He asked, "You're going to wear that to the presentation?"

"Underneath a jacket." Valentina grinned. "Don't worry, it will be very professional."

Leo laughed. "Tell me again where you're going to put the moves on Stillman?"

"There's a grassy walkway that leads back to the administrative building from the stage area. It goes through a kind of swampy area with lots of trees and vegetation. Very private. You can reach the admin offices by a more direct route, but Stillman won't realize that. You go straight from the parking lot and turn past a small gazebo. I'll head that way if I have to run. The path I'm going to use is more secluded and takes longer."

"Valentina, secluded means isolated."

"It really isn't, Leo. It's just a one-minute walk from the parking area if you go the more direct route. You think you're in the middle of nowhere, and then the path opens up to the back of our office. To get to it from the parking lot, you turn right at the gazebo."

"I'm with you on this, but I don't have to like it."

Valentina touched her lips to Leo's. "Thanks."

CHAPTER 61

As he sipped his cappuccino, Jack turned the pages of the *Wall Street Journal*. Although he followed the financial markets online, there was something familiar and reassuring about the actual newspaper. That, and the drop of Bourbon he added to his coffee was smoothing out the edges. He didn't really need it that sunny New Orleans morning. Landever stock had gone through the roof since the HERF gun attack at Fort Collins. He was making a fortune in the commodities market. He'd received notes of congratulations from colleagues, and requests for interviews from the press. Jack didn't pick up the undercurrent of scorn beneath the surface because of Landever's refusal to participate in the agricultural consortium.

What a wild few days, he laughed to himself. Pumped on adrenaline and Provigil, he was euphoric on the ride back to Kansas City. He felt like he was flying on the motorbike, and hated to leave it at the shopping mall. He loved the control. Still in disguise, Jack walked into one of the ubiquitous men's stores at Independence Center and left with new casual business attire off the rack, paying cash. His clothing never needed to be altered. He was a perfect size 38. He changed in the mall restroom and ditched the extra gear at a dumpster. Within 12 hours of leaving Fort Collins, he was back at the conference.

Strange, Jack hadn't seen his son since he got to New Orleans. His flight was late the day before, and the house was dark when he arrived. Inside, he found the package he ordered on his desk. He spent a little while assembling his new gun. Although he wouldn't need to use it, he would carry it to Winslow today. Jack liked the idea of having it with him. He liked touching it in his pocket.

When Sam asked him to give a presentation for his little girlfriend, he thought, why not? Winslow Park held an affectionate place in the heart of New Orleans aristocrats, the kind that were members of the best social organizations. A favor for Winslow now would give him a quid pro quo opportunity later. He threw a little money to the park too. Landever had the latitude to push a little funding to select nonprofits. Besides, the girlfriend was pretty in an ethnic sort of way.

Where was the boy? Probably spent the night with his hoochie mama. He wouldn't mind giving her a tumble himself.

"Sam," he called out. "Where are you?" When he didn't get an answer, Jack sent a text to his son's cellphone. *Are you home? With your chica? Call me.*

•   •   •

Sam sat on a bench at the 'Fly, the grassy part of Audubon Park next to the Mississippi River. It was a place he loved. As a kid, he played baseball and soccer on the nearby fields. Years ago, he went with his parents to watch the sunset over the river. Now, fog was rising from the muddy water in the early morning light. He left the house at 5 am. Winded from his run, Sam was sweating freely in the 80-degree morning. His phone buzzed. Of course, it was his dad.

Avoidance seemed to be the only option. Sam was tempted to confront his father. He couldn't risk it. What would his father's denial be worth? The whole thing made him feel like he was going insane. Grabbing his phone, he typed: *Out for a run. See you at the park.* Later, he'd go to Winslow for his father's presentation, when there would be no chance of a private conversation.

Sam turned his phone on silent. He noticed a few calls from a Houston number he didn't recognize.

Valentina's plan was crazy, but it was the best they had. He wasn't surprised that his father agreed to give the talk. It hit all the right buttons—public adulation, an opportunity to pontificate, and the attention and gratitude of a pretty woman. When had his father become so shallow? To kill time, he'd grab breakfast before heading home.

•   •   •

On a quiet stretch of the interstate, Angus glanced over at Barry, who was leaning back in the passenger seat, snoring softly. What a mate, he thought with affection. They stopped overnight in Tuscaloosa, Alabama because neither of them was up to sitting in a car almost 13 hours straight. Barbeque for dinner, and grits with their eggs this morning, simply delicious. No comparison to the hospital food of the last few weeks, although he probably made up for all the weight he'd lost in those two meals.

Barry had to be in his early 70s, Angus thought. He continued working because he loved his bees. And now he was making a difficult, likely career-derailing trip for a friend. He would do his best to keep Barry out of the fracas with Stillman.

An exit sign for Slidell seemed to fly past the window. They were passing over marshlands, with cypress trees on both sides of the highway. Traffic started to slow, with morning commuters making the trip into downtown New Orleans. Based on GPS guidance, they would reach Winslow Park in another hour or so. He wasn't sure what would happen, but Angus planned to watch Stillman's talk and be ready to intervene.

•   •   •

Evie Lariott of E-Aero Systems left the federal building in Centennial, Colorado. The Denver field office of the FBI called to see if she could identify the man who had bought her drones. She agreed to go in. Yes, that was Richard Arlington. He was the man who ordered the drones. Relieved, Evie believed she could begin to make amends for her part in the wheat crisis. She would be glad to see him in jail. Then she learned he was dead. He was found shot in an old warehouse near Lincoln, Nebraska. As she suspected, Arlington wasn't his real name. It was Richard Miller. She held it together until she got in her car. Angry tears ran down her face. Who killed him? Were they aware her company manufactured the drones?

·　　·　　·

A few hours later, Valentina stood on a temporary dais in New Orleans, smiling widely at the assembled crowd. Showtime. Her tailored linen jacket was carefully buttoned over the bustier. She felt like a stuffed turkey, but Leo's reaction was reassuring. After Jack's talk, she'd remove the jacket when she walked with him through a more secluded area of the park. The listening device was fastened below the waistband of her skirt, and Leo and Ellis were standing by.

CHAPTER 62

"Welcome! I'm Valentina Sorelli with Winslow Park. We are thrilled you could join us to celebrate our new partnership, WINS Urban Farm and Community. A short time ago, one of Winslow's school partners, McLarin Urban Preparatory, suggested we expand our enrichment program currently managed through the Educational Seed Bank. The seed bank began earlier this year through a grant from the Jamison Botanical Foundation. This program has created hands-on experience for children in our community to learn about horticulture, environmental stewardship and, just as important, responsible work behavior. It's an opportunity for self-discovery and for them to develop self-confidence.

"McLarin Urban wanted to build on the seed bank and suggested a farm-to-table experience, where their students could develop communication and organizational skills. We thought that was a great idea and took it to New Orleans University. NOU helped us to think big. With the guidance of NOU's more senior students, our kids will learn about marketing, hospitality and management to better prepare them for the future. We are excited to announce our community partners, McLarin and NOU, will be joined by representatives from Gulf States Regional Bank. Gulf State staff will lend their expertise as coaches for our kids. And finally, we are thrilled to have the support of Landever Corporation, our most significant underwriter. Here to talk about Landever's contribution to WINS is Jack Stillman, Director of Product Development at

Landever. Mr. Stillman made a special trip from Indianapolis to introduce our program. Please join me in welcoming Mr. Stillman!"

An enthusiastic round of applause erupted as Valentina finished talking. Jack approached the podium, waving at everyone and smiling complacently as though the applause was his due. Two members of the *Times* Picayune were there to record the event. Jack preened for the photographer. "Thank you, Ms. Sorelli, Landever's goal is to provide an opportunity for young people in New Orleans to gain practical experience in the world of work. Through their participation in WINS, we hope these students become excited about their future careers ...."

·   ·   ·

In a small van parked nearby, Leo and Ellis listened to the speeches, carefully recording everything being projected by Valentina's audio bug. Ellis looked over at Leo. "She did great."

"Yeah, she did." Leo looked down at his laptop, fiddling with the keyboard. "But ..." He began, then stopped.

"Why so glum, my friend?" Ellis asked with concern. "Things seem to be looking up between you and Valentina."

Leo started to agree, then said, "What?"

"Um, Leo, the recorder picked up your earlier conversation with Valentina. She's a beautiful young woman, both inside and out."

Realizing what Ellis must have heard, Leo flushed deeply.

"Hey, don't worry, I started a new recording once we got out here," Ellis assured him.

Embarrassed, Leo didn't say anything for a minute. "I think I've got a chance now."

"I would think so. Let's go back to my original question, why so glum?"

"I'm worried, Ellis."

"Leo, what's the worst that could happen? He embarrasses Valentina?"

"I don't think that's the worst. If she's right, things may get ugly. Sam, his own kid, suspects him. By the way, where is Sam?" Leo asked.

"In the audience, trying to act like everything's normal."

"Tough job," grunted Leo.

"I bet he's had plenty of practice listening to his father. It's hard to imagine how Sam turned out normal."

"Sam may be a little naïve, but he's doing the right thing."

"An ethical dilemma," Ellis said. "It's funny how Dr. Chen's class has so many applications in real life."

"I know. Valentina wants to help Sam pick up the pieces when this is all over."

"Annie and I were talking about that," Ellis said. "We hope he'll spend some time with us before the next semester. He probably shouldn't be by himself."

"Agreed. Let's listen for a minute. Stillman may be winding down."

"I hate to break it to you, pal, but it sounds like he's just warming up."

•　　•　　•

As Jack pontificated, two men looked on from a clump of small trees. "Sounds like a worthy program," Barry said with approval. They were sitting on a concrete bench that was almost hidden by the lush vegetation.

"It's hard to accept that cheap bastard is giving away money," Angus murmured.

"Landever has a long tradition of supporting things like this, Angus," Barry said. "We haven't seen too much of it since Stillman came into power. He likes to funnel money to causes where he's going to get some attention. I'm sure our fearless leader is interested in the fancy pants in the audience."

Angus looked at the audience. A few women wore expensive summer linens and tasteful bling and sat next to men wearing seersucker. Casually dressed younger attendees with earnest faces had staked out the front seats. He pegged them for teachers. "Spot on, Barry."

"This is a beautiful park. Everything is so lush in New Orleans."

"Effing hot."

"Burns giving you trouble?"

"Aye," Angus said flatly.

"Nothing likely will happen for a bit. Do you want to run back to the car for more of that ointment?"

"Later. Let's not take any chances, mate."

"Right. We've driven a long way."

●　　●　　●

Finally, the presentation wound down. Jack bussed the cheek and shook the hand of each socially connected member of the audience and followed with a brief interview with the press. Valentina made sure to say hello to everyone, including the NOU staff and university students who would work in the program. She stopped to talk to one parent who came, recognizing her girls from an earlier visit to the park.

"Could this be Maya and Keisha?" Valentina asked.

"It is, Ms. Valentina!"

"Will you be with us in July?"

"Yes!"

Keisha's mother, dressed in a hospital uniform, smiled at Valentina. "Ms. Sorelli, I'm Savannah Jones."

"Please, call me Valentina. Nice to meet you."

"It's a pleasure to meet you, Valentina. The girls were excited about the new program. I had the morning off and wanted to learn more about it. Now I'm excited too."

"When Maya and Keisha visited here on their field trip, they gave me the idea for the seed bank. Your girls are wonderful."

"They're cousins, and Maya spends a lot of time with us as she lives with her grandmother. They're better together than alone. And busy! I'm glad they'll have an enrichment program for the late summer."

"I'll be sure to visit to see how you're doing," Valentina told them. She turned, feeling as though she was being watched. "Oh, Mrs. Benfield! I haven't seen you since the soiree. It's nice to see you."

"I wouldn't have missed it. What an auspicious program, Valentina."

Savannah waved goodbye to Valentina as she shepherded Maya and Keisha toward the parking lot.

"We're excited about how it's all come together so quickly."

"As you should be," Sophie Benfield said.

"How have you been?"

Sophie looked up as an older gentleman approached. "Very well, Valentina. Do you remember Ferris Jefferson? We met the night of your soiree?"

"Of course I remember Mr. Jefferson! Should I be jealous? We shared a lovely waltz together."

Ferris Jefferson's eyes twinkled as Sophie said, "We are enjoying each other's company, Valentina."

Jack Stillman appeared beside Valentina, ready as always to enhance his social connections. "Hello, Sophie. Ferris."

"Hello, Jack," Sophie said politely.

Ferris Jefferson nodded.

"I haven't seen you since the last time we were all at Winslow. That was some auction, wasn't it? Quite the contest for that humidor," Jack said.

Valentina found Jack's self-congratulatory tone annoying at best. "We appreciate everyone's participation at the auction, and the dancing was lots of fun."

"Yes, dear." Sophie turned to Ferris. "We should be going," and rested her hand on his arm.

"It's always nice to see you two," Valentina said.

Mr. Jefferson carefully bent his arm for Sophie. He gave Valentina a quick kiss on the cheek and nodded slightly to Jack as they turned away.

Deciding that it was now or never, Valentina smiled coquettishly at Jack. "Jack," she purred, "I was hoping to get your advice. Would you mind walking me back to my office?"

"Of course, Valentina." Jack was obviously flattered, loving all the attention. "What can I do for you?"

"Let's talk about it as we walk, okay?" Valentina looked up demurely as she took Jack's arm. "I asked Sam to run an errand for me after the presentation, so we'll have a little while to chat."

Intrigued, Jack followed Valentina down the path to the administrative offices. As they walked away from the small arena, Angus and Barry followed, staying close to the edge of the trees.

CHAPTER 63

Valentina walked slowly ahead of Jack, adding a slight sway to her hips. The secluded path wound through a marshy area with bald cypress trees. Soft, feathery needles brushed against her on the elevated wooden boardwalk. She passed under one of the oldest cypress trees, Spanish moss dripping from its branches, the wide folds of its trunk standing steady in the dark water. Valentina was ambivalent about her plan, wondering if it would really work and slightly embarrassed by it. Well, no one else had come up with anything better. Valentina shook her head. Okay, showtime.

As she approached a bench, Valentina wobbled on her four-inch heels. Jack, a gentleman of opportunity, rushed to steady her balance. She eased onto the bench saying, "Oh, thanks. It's so hot today." As she unbuttoned her jacket, Valentina felt Jack's gaze on her low-cut top. "Take a break for a second? You saved me from a twisted ankle."

"I'm glad that I could be of assistance," Jack said, watching Valentina as she slowly slipped off her linen jacket and fanned herself with the notes she carried.

"Your talk went well," Valentina said. "Everyone is impressed with Landever's support for the kids. Jack, we're grateful you could be here for the presentation. I know how busy you are. Your secretary was so helpful."

Jack basked in the compliment, saying, "I'm glad Marta could make it work. She had to juggle a few things."

"Winslow and all of New Orleans are lucky to get the attention of a national company like Landever and a leader such as yourself."

"You are too kind."

"Landever," Valentina began as she took a handkerchief and patted the moisture above her lip and the top of her breast, "is so far ahead of the other agricultural companies." In a breathy tone, Valentina recalled developments referenced in the most recent annual report. "The soil and water sensor systems, the mini-chromosomes for plant genetic modifiers, why, that's remarkable. You're taking farming into the future."

"I am pleased with our progress. Besides my operational duties, I've directed the research in emerging technologies, things like new applications for mass spectrometry-based protein discovery analysis. Our research is the answer. Genetically-modified DNA is the future. Those biodiversity nuts can say what they like, but the world needs large scale scientific approaches that only companies our size can offer. With high yielding plant varieties, we're on the path to solving problems on a macro level ..." Valentina focused her gaze on Jack, pretending to listen with rapt interest. Fanning her neck and bare shoulders, Valentina got up from the bench and pulled her shoulders back. Jack's attention shifted.

•　　•　　•

More than 20 feet behind, Angus and Barry watched from a dense grove of azaleas, too far away to hear their conversation. They were standing on the last bit of solid ground in the marshy area. They wouldn't be able to reach Valentina and Stillman without using the boardwalk, where they would be exposed.

"Shite," Angus whispered. Marsh birds called back and forth, their soft songs mocking his tension.

* * *

As Jack's litany of self-glorifying remarks slowed, Valentina realized she wouldn't have a better chance.

"Jack," she said, leaning forward and putting her hand on the bench near his shoulder, "It's almost as though you had a crystal ball to predict this grain crisis."

Stillman smiled in a self-congratulatory way.

"Landever's research didn't happen overnight. You must have foreseen something like this happening. Having a mite-resistant wheat ready and available, why, that's genius."

"The right planning is critical," Jack agreed as he stood up and moved closer.

"I would love to be involved with a company, and work for an executive who was so ... visionary." As she said this, Valentina looked up at Jack and put her hand on his arm. "I'm getting an MBA with an emphasis in botany. And I've been handling the marketing for Winslow for a while. I know I could make a difference in Landever's public relations department, with the right...," Valentina paused for effect, then softly said, "guidance," as she moved closer.

"Someone working in public relations would need to be at the corporate office to be available," Jack said, "to the product development director."

"I would do anything to have such an important role," Valentina murmured, as she ran her fingers down Jack's chest. "I can be so creative."

"But aren't you interested in staying in New Orleans with Sam?"

"Oh, Sam knows we're just seeing each other casually. He would never stand in my way. It would be exciting to explore another city like Indianapolis. You would have a lot to show me."

"Hmm," Jack said, seeming to shrug off any concern for his son. "Would you like to discuss an arrangement?"

"Oh, yes. I could be ... helpful."

"You could be helpful this evening," said Jack.

"Dinner?" Valentina asked coyly. "To lay out our plans?"

"Among other things." He skimmed his fingers down her bare arm, tightening them around her wrist.

"Where should I meet you?"

"Let me make arrangements. I'd like to talk to you privately," he said, emphasizing the last word as he pressed his lips to her neck.

"Of course," Valentina said, trying not to flinch. She had no intention of meeting Jack but had to let this play out.

"Give me your number, and I'll text you later," Jack said.

"Why don't we head to my office, Jack, and I'll give you a business card. After I got dressed this morning, I realized I didn't have a pocket or anyplace to keep them." Valentina ran her hands over her skirt. It was skin tight, one she never wore except with a long jacket or top.

Jack followed her hands with his gaze. Moving closer, he reached for Valentina and pinched her bottom. "I want my hands on your ass."

Stepping back, Valentina said, "This isn't quite the setting I imagined for us, Jack. Let's walk together, shall we?"

Jack watched Valentina as she walked ahead. They came to the end of the boardwalk and Valentina decided to push things a little farther. She continued down the tree-lined path with a slight swing of her hips.

•   •   •

From the thick bushes, Angus and Barry could see Valentina and Jack on the other side of the boardwalk. When Jack grabbed Valentina, Angus started forward. Barry took his arm. "Wait, Angus.

You'd be too exposed. Look, she's gotten him back in line. We can cross after they go a little farther.

•   •   •

"What other ideas do you have for market, um, dominance?" Valentina turned to look at Jack as she stressed the last word.

"I've been pretty focused on rolling out the new wheat cultivar."

"It was brilliant," Valentina gushed. "To project that the wheat virus could happen, to have a mite resistant wheat in development, it's almost as though you planned it."

Jack looked at Valentina carefully.

"Taking control," turning her head to smile at Jack, "of the market, of course, was so clever. So creative."

Mollified, but a little wary, Jack said, "All the pieces came together."

Deciding that it was time, Valentina faced Jack and pulled him forward by his silk tie, steeling herself as she kissed his jaw. "It was brilliant. They're Landever's mites, aren't they?"

"What makes you say that? A corporation that would do that..."

"Would be ingenious," Valentina finished.

"You feel that way?" Jack groped her breast and pinched her nipple.

Pretending to enjoy the assault, Valentina said softly, "I would love being part of that, next to a powerful man who makes things happen."

"You would, huh?"

"Tell me, did you think of it yourself?" Valentina looked up at Jack, her eyes wide with admiration.

"I might have."

She knew it was close but not enough. "You must have put in years of effort." She licked her upper lip. "The creativity." Valentina tossed her hair back as she looked at Jack with half-closed eyes. "I bet you're the kind of person to handle everything yourself."

"As a matter of fact, yes," Jack said smugly. "When you know what you want, you need to go after it." He lightly bit Valentina on the neck. "It took years to get everything in place, especially the virus and the mites. I now control the entire grains market. Impressed?"

"You're amazing! I bet you have all sorts of hidden talents." Valentina slowly ran her hand down the side of her skirt. "Maybe I'll uncover some of them later." She turned back to the walkway and tried not to rub her neck.

"Definitely," Jack said, as he tugged on the back of her skirt and squeezed her butt again.

Valentina rolled her eyes as she kept walking. She decided to push things a little further. "Were you involved in the Fort Collins seed bank, too?"

Something snapped in Jack. For a split second, all he could see was Richard, lying on the concrete floor, covered in blood. In a flash, his left hand gripped Valentina's upper arm like a vise, twisting her around, while his right yanked her hair, pulling her head back. Furious with himself, with Valentina, he demanded, "How naïve do you think I am, you stupid little fool?"

"Whhaat ...?" Valentina stammered.

"You had me going for a bit." Before she could blink, Jack had Valentina's arm behind her back and was marching her forward. "You're about to discover what happens when you mess with the wrong person."

●　　●　　●

In the van, Leo tore off his headphones. As he ran out the door, he shouted to Ellis, "Don't stop the recording!"

Stunned, Ellis sat in the van, listening. He grabbed his cell phone and shot off a text to Annie.

Call the police. Advise to go to administrative offices at Winslow. Hurry!

• • •

As Leo sprinted for the parking area, Sam arrived at the van. He and Valentina had agreed on the errand excuse so she could get his dad alone. Leo's panicked run was like a kick in the gut. "Leo!" he shouted. Leo kept running, and Sam took off after him. In moments, he pulled even with Leo, driven by his fear and years as a championship runner.

CHAPTER 64

Angus thundered across the wooden bridge, a surge of adrenalin propelling him faster than he'd moved in weeks. He didn't notice when the newly healed skin on his leg broke, or when it opened on his lower back. Before he could reach Valentina, a gun appeared in Stillman's right hand. Jack tightened the hold on Valentina's arm that he had twisted behind her back and pointed the gun at her head. Seeing Angus, Jack Stillman said bitterly. "You're supposed to be dead."

Time stopped. "I realize it's inconvenient," Angus said calmly.

"Step away, Angus, very slowly, or I am going to shoot this beautiful but trashy young woman in the head."

"If you do, Stillman, how will you get away?"

"I will shoot you immediately afterwards."

Barry Carlson walked forward, carefully positioning his cane on the wooden planks of the boardwalk. "And me as well?"

"I knew you were involved!" Jack spit out. "But I bet I shoot faster than you move, old man."

"Even if you manage to kill all three of us, you think you won't get caught? Everyone noticed you left with Valentina," Angus said.

"Precisely. You gentlemen attacked me and caught this poor young woman in the crossfire. I did my best to get the gun away from you. Unfortunately, I won't be successful. Poor Ms. Sorelli. In the struggle that followed, all of you met your demise."

"That's absurd. What possible motive would we have?"

"Ah, that's interesting. Your lackluster employment with Landever ended involuntarily when we discovered you had dispatched your mites to wreak havoc across the country and ruin my fine corporation. You took in your gullible friend Mr. Carlson, with your claims of mistreatment by Landever. Unfortunately, he was collateral damage."

Angus was desperate. Anything he tried could backfire badly. Barry, Valentina, any of them might die before he caught Stillman.

In the trees behind Valentina and Jack came the sound of pounding feet. The noise distracted Stillman for less than a second. Before Jack could turn around, Valentina pushed his arm down then stomped ferociously on his instep with her four-inch heel.

"Witch!"

Valentina swung around, her arm flying. The back of her hand connected with his nose.

Angus ran forward and struggled with Stillman for the gun. Valentina was close enough that she kicked Jack between his legs. He dropped the gun, and Angus pushed him to the ground, putting one foot on his back. Barry, wielding his cane, walked slowly to Jack and held it over his head. "Give me a reason, Stillman."

At that moment, Sam ran out of the trees. "What the hell is going on? Angus? Mr. Carlson? What are you doing here?"

Angus looked up to see Sam skidding to a stop. Directly behind him another young man reached for Sam, who twisted away to run toward his father.

"Dad, Valentina? What's happening?"

Valentina stepped back, as did Barry, who kept a firm handle on his cane. Valentina looked at Sam, pity in her eyes.

From his position on the grass, Jack closed his eyes, and his face paled.

Angus imagined that Stillman never intended to involve Sam. Judging that he wouldn't shoot anyone with his son standing there, Angus eased his foot off his back. Jack slowly pushed away from the ground then lunged for the weapon. Before Angus could reach him, Jack grabbed the pistol and pointed it at Angus.

"Step back, Angus. All of you, step back."

"Dad, what are you doing?"

"Sam, Mr. Angus and Mr. Carlson created the wheat crisis. I've been trying to stop them."

"Sam, he admitted he did it," Valentina said, her voice breaking.

"Your girlfriend's confused, Sam. Why don't you and Valentina go call the police and wait for them at the office."

The young man standing behind Sam looked as though he was about to speak. Angus shook his head almost imperceptibly. He doubted Jack knew the bloke was there—could be an advantage. When Sam erupted from the trees, the fellow had hung back, waiting.

Angus was all for clearing Sam out of the way while he figured out a way to smash Stillman's face in. He could see no downside to getting Sam and Valentina to safety. "That's not a bad idea, Sam. The police can straighten this out."

Valentina put her arm around Sam. She turned him gently and started walking past Leo toward the administrative offices. As she did Valentina reached below her waistband and tore off some kind of device, tossing it behind her. Aha, a recording device—smart girl, at least in some regards. It must still be recording.

Angus watched as she walked past the newcomer, whose eyes widened and followed Valentina. He tensed then nodded at Angus. Slowly, imperceptibly, Leo edged forward, closer to Jack.

Valentina and Sam walked away, swallowed by the dense trees and the rising sounds of birds and insects.

Jack's attention shifted back to Angus and Barry. Holding the gun, he said in a low voice, "You morons, who are the police going to believe, a couple of disgruntled ex-employees, or a top executive of a multi-million dollar company? You don't have proof."

Seeing Leo inching forward, Angus worked to keep Jack's attention focused on himself. "You sent me to India on a bogus trip. That's when you stole my mites and destroyed my lab equipment."

"And it worked beautifully, Angus. Who will credit what you say?"

"Don't you think the bobbies are investigating the fire at my house?" Angus said.

Jack laughed. "The bobbies?"

"The police, you blighter."

"You got nothing, Angus," Jack said. "If the police recover the mite data, it will prove it came from your lab—from you! Your professional record shows what happens when a corporation misplaces its trust in an unqualified and unscrupulous so-called scientist."

"What about all my reviews? They've been stellar."

"Oh? Landever's records tell a different story of Stephen Angus."

"You think the feds are only interested in the mites?" Angus said. "They know you did it, Stillman."

"We'll have to see what they say, won't we? Of course, you won't be around to offer much insight." Jack smiled. "I like my original plan better." Jack cocked the gun, aiming it at Angus. "Ms. Sorelli may be a temporary problem but nothing that I can't fix later."

Angus met Leo's gaze and nodded. He was only a few feet behind Jack. In a sudden burst, Leo hurdled across the grass and tackled Jack while Angus dove under the gun. He slid on the path and grabbed for Jack's legs. Barry limped quickly forward, as Jack, Leo, and Angus struggled for the gun. Leo and Jack grappled on the ground, fighting for control. Jack's outstretched arm trembled as he pointed the gun at Angus. Barry swung his cane, missing Jack and striking a glancing blow on Leo's shoulder. Leo's grip loosened, and Jack threw him off.

The four men scrambled in the grass and mud. Barry swung his cane again and again, striking Angus and Leo as much as Jack. Stillman changed his aim and pointed the gun at Barry. He pulled the trigger. Barry dropped his cane, clutching his arm as he sank to the ground. Leo pushed Jack's arm high as another bullet snapped out, but Leo fell back when Jack whipped the gun across Leo's face.

Angus felt a red-hot rage flash through him. His throat closed, choking on the curses he needed to spit at Stillman. He grabbed Stillman by the arm and tried to punch him at the same time. Angus was able to wrest the gun lower.

Struggling to get loose, Jack shot the gun, and a bullet grazed Angus's leg. The gun flared again, this time in the direction of the walkway. Angus dove on top of Stillman, his leg and back bleeding. Blood dripped into his eyes from the burns on his face. Angus's hand was slick with blood and he couldn't get a good hold on the gun and felt Stillman aiming it at him. With a great bellow, Angus pushed the gun down as Stillman pulled the trigger.

Stillman stopped fighting. Angus eased back slightly, and felt warm liquid pulsing between them. When he was sure Stillman wasn't moving, Angus crawled to Barry who lay on his side.

CHAPTER 65

As Valentina and Sam got to the admin parking lot, they heard a popping sound, a slight pause, then two more. Sam stiffened and turned to go back. Valentina grabbed his arm. "Sam, we can't. Let's call the police."

"Valentina, someone could be hurt."

"Yes," she whispered, "you're right. That's why we have to call the police."

"But ..." As Sam started to object, they saw two parked police cars, lights flashing. Then Annie swerved into a parking space and leapt from her car.

"Annie? What are you doing here?" Valentina asked.

"Ellis sent me a text and said to call the police."

"Ma'am, sir. Tell us what's going on," one officer demanded.

"We heard gunshots. Our friends .... Sam's father ... Back through the trees." Valentina frantically pointed, realizing she wasn't making sense.

"Call for backup," the officer directed his partner. Turning back to Valentina, he asked, "What's past the trees?"

"It's an open area with a boardwalk."

"Is there another way to the area?"

Valentina quickly explained how to approach it from the presentation area. As they talked, Dee, Valentina's boss and Winslow's Executive Director came from her office. "Officers, I'm Dee Claiborne. How can I help you?" Then Dee noticed Valentina's appearance and gasped, "Valentina, what's going on? Why are you dressed like that?"

The senior police officer stepped forward. "We're going to secure the area where the gunshots were reported. In the meantime, we need you all to wait separately." The officer directed Valentina, Sam, and Annie to wait in individual offices off the main entrance. "Ms. Claiborne, we have to ask you to return to your office. You'll be able to talk to the young lady in a little while." Another police officer arrived and stood guard in the hallway. A little while later, they heard the stark wail of an ambulance.

From a small window, Valentina could see only a portion of the parking area. Two EMTs, carrying a stretcher, ran toward the pathway. Several minutes later, the same medical professionals walked more slowly toward the ambulance, weighed down by the gurney they carried between them. The flashing lights illuminated the small office. Horrified, Valentina rushed from the room, running past the guard.

"Ma'am, ma'am. Stop! You can't leave the building."

"I have to see," Valentina cried. "Someone's hurt. Let me leave."

"Ma'am, for your own safety, you have to stay here."

Sam burst forth from the adjacent office. He went to Valentina, pushing past the officer where she stood with her eyes streaming. Putting his arms around her, Sam held her tight. "I keep asking myself, what else could we have done? Valentina, the answer is nothing. We didn't have a choice. This was too important to keep quiet. Whatever it means. Even if I have to testify against my father."

"Sam, someone's hurt, maybe dead." Valentina said, determined to stop crying. "The paramedics carried someone away on a stretcher."

Sam closed his eyes tight. "We don't know anything yet."

The police officer came closer. "Ma'am, sir. Please, you have to wait separately."

As the officer brought her back to the cubbyhole of an office, Valentina called to Sam, "Was that Angus who ran across the boardwalk?"

"Yes. I told him about our plan," Sam said, shaking his head. "I didn't expect him to leave the burn unit."

"From Indiana?"

"Yes."

The first, obviously more senior police officer, walked into the entrance of the administrative building and looked angrily at his junior officer. "I told you to keep them separate, Pell."

Embarrassed, Pell explained, "Sir, the young lady became upset when she saw the paramedics. It's been less than a minute. They didn't talk much. I remember what they said."

"I have to ask you again to stay in your independent rooms," the senior police officer said. "We're going to talk to each of you individually. We'll get to you soon. Please wait where we asked," and he motioned to Sam to follow him.

•   •   •

A few miles away at the WPRY news desk, Robin Theriot tried not to fall asleep at her computer. It was late May in New Orleans—slow, hot and humid. Robin was one of the reporters hired to support the station's social media presence. No leads, nothing was happening. Then, shortly before noon, there was a post: *Wassup at Winslow?* with a brief video of two police cars, lights flashing, racing into the park.

"Finally!" Dropping everything, Robin rushed to her car to be first on the scene.

•   •   •

Valentina stepped outside the administrative offices, wearing an old smock that she kept in her office for the occasional messy tasks that came with working in a botanical garden. She left her jacket behind during her interaction with Jack, and now it was part of the crime scene. That was fine. She never wanted to see it again. Or the tight skirt that her gardening shirt barely covered. She waited forever to be interviewed by the officers and saw the doubt in the detective's face as he questioned her. He revisited the same points over and over, asking the same questions. Why hadn't they called the police earlier? What made them suspect Sam's father? A drawing of bugs flying on drones? She came up with this scheme? As she heard herself try to explain, Valentina felt like she was going insane. It sounded pretty lame, even to her. She told him about the recording device, and he wouldn't tell her if they found it. She didn't know what happened. An undercurrent of terror swept through her. It was as though she was five years old again, knowing something awful happened and being told only to wait.

After her interview, she stood in the parking lot, getting her bearings. Valentina saw a figure slumped on a bench near the entrance and her heart leapt when she recognized Leo. The worst hadn't happened. She raced to his side and said softly, "Leo."

Leo startled awake, then closed his arms around Valentina for a hard hug. "Hey, stranger."

"Oh ..." Valentina had to stop talking and try hard to catch her breath. "I'm so glad you're here. What happened to your face? We heard gunshots, and then the police arrived. They wouldn't tell me anything."

"I'm okay. How are you?"

Valentina paused, "I'm not sure. What happened after Sam and I left?"

"We struggled for the gun." Leo stopped, closing his eyes. "Time seemed to slow down, but I couldn't move fast enough. Sam's father ..." Leo couldn't go on.

"Tell me, Leo. What happened?"

"Stillman's dead."

"No, Leo, no." Valentina felt as though she was falling through the pavement. This was because of her stupid idea.

Leo paused, staring at his hands. White-faced, he reached for Valentina and she held on tight. Gradually, he told her what happened.

After describing the struggle, he said, "Valentina, I froze. It was like everything stopped. Angus got off Stillman and stared at him. I guess he wanted to make sure he wasn't going to hurt anybody else. Then he went over to Carlson. I couldn't hear anything. It was like being inside a bubble. Everything seemed to be in slow motion."

"Is Mr. Carlson okay?"

"He was bleeding a lot. Angus ripped up your jacket to bandage his arm. One ambulance arrived a few minutes later, and they took Mr. Carlson away. A police officer rode with him. They wanted to take Angus to the hospital, but he wouldn't go."

"I could see a little from the window," Valentina said. "The paramedics brought out a stretcher, but I couldn't tell who it was or anything."

"How can Stillman be dead?" Leo shook his head.

"It's horrible. How is Sam?"

"I'd been waiting for a while, so I saw him come out. He didn't stop when I called. The police must have told him about his dad. He looked bad."

"We should go find him."

"He walked over to wait for Angus. Ellis and Annie left a little while ago. They're pretty upset."

"When they were questioning me, I realized they didn't accept anything I was saying. Did they separate you?" Valentina asked.

Leo nodded. "Once they finished with me, I came over here. They were still talking with Angus. They seemed pretty suspicious of both of us."

"What about the recording?"

"I saw you drop the bug, so I told them about it. They found it. It was close enough that it should have picked up Stillman's threats. That should help. They talked with Ellis too and took his audio file."

"Leo, what have I done?"

"We," he emphasized, "did the right thing. You know that."

Valentina felt as though she stepped into an abyss. "Someone died because of things I put in place."

"No, Valentina. Stillman died because of what he did."

When Valentina didn't respond, Leo said, "Why don't you let me take you home?"

"Not my apartment. Mia's."

"Okay, Mia's."

CHAPTER 66

WPRY news reporter Robin Theriot was flush with her success. She was first on the scene at Winslow with Cal Bordelon, a young cameraman. They caught a young couple as they left the parking lot of the administration building. The man's curt "No comment" and bloody shirt, coupled with the woman's tear-stained face, would be a poignant image for their viewers. Robin just had to find out who they were and what happened. She saw lights through the trees. "Cal, let's head through there." They hit pay dirt. Not only were the police cars still there, there was an ambulance and the coroner's van. Best of all, no other news stations had arrived yet. Robin overheard mention of a gun. A little while later, Robin learned that an unidentified white male died under "suspicious circumstances."

WPRY interrupted their regular programming to air footage of Valentina and Leo leaving the administration building, both obviously upset and Leo wearing bloodstained clothing. "There was a shooting at Winslow Park earlier today. An unidentified male died of a gunshot wound, and at least one other person was injured. Stay tuned to WPRY for further updates on this breaking story."

·   ·   ·

Working at her computer, Mia had a home renovation show on in the background as she entered expenses for one of their rental properties. She looked up when the Special Report notification flashed across the television screen. Noticing the sign for Winslow Park in the background, Mia grabbed the television control and increased the volume. When she heard about a shooting incident, Mia called, "Dean, come quick!" Dean ran in just in time to see Valentina and a disheveled young man on camera, and hear his, "No comment." Shaken beyond words, they stared at the screen as the broadcast switched back to the renovation show.

•　　•　　•

Robin spent the next few hours trying to get more information. By checking Winslow's website, she identified the young woman who left the park as Valentina Sorelli, a Winslow employee. She called the number listed and a friendly voice mail announced, "Hello! This is Valentina Sorelli, marketing director at Winslow Park. I'm sorry to miss your call. Please leave your name, number and a brief message and I'll get back to you at the earliest opportunity. I look forward to speaking with you soon."

Next, she tracked down Winslow's executive director, Dee Claiborne, who provided a statement: "Our hearts are heavy tonight. Our beautiful park is a haven for so many in New Orleans. We who work at Winslow Park are devastated by this tragedy. Winslow is a partner to our law enforcement agencies and schools to create a positive, safe environment for the public. We condemn the violence and offer our support to those involved in the investigation."

Before Dee turned away, Robin hurriedly asked, "Ms. Claiborne, isn't it true that one of your employees, Valentina Sorelli, was involved in the shooting?"

Dee pulled herself to her full height and answered cooly, "As with all our park employees, Ms. Sorelli was working on site in the performance of her duties. Each day, Ms. Sorelli helps to create a fun, nurturing public space for the people of New Orleans and our visitors. We are grateful she is unharmed."

•   •   •

When Valentina rang the bell, the door burst open and Mia pulled her close.

"We saw the news. Oh baby."

Valentina hugged Mia tight.

"Come in, come in." At first, Mia didn't notice Leo standing on the porch behind Valentina.

"Wait." Valentina turned back and reached for his hand. "This is Leo."

Mia looked carefully at Leo, assessing. He was older than the other boy, Sam, that Valentina brought some weeks back. Sam had been expensively dressed and looked young. Like he hadn't found his feet yet. This Leo looked like hell. Tired, disheveled, and the reddish-brown stain on his shirt might be blood. But he stood like a rock and looked her in the eye. Resolute. There was substance to this one.

"Both of you, let's get you inside. I bet you haven't eaten,"

Valentina started to laugh and then began to cry. "Mia..."

"Shh, shh." Mia pulled Valentina into the living room, where Dean waited to hug her. "Let's talk after we get you two something to eat."

They sat around the table, the tablecloth reflecting Mia's mood. It had a black background with wisps of lightning throughout. Valentina and Leo ate ravenously. No one talked for a few minutes. Leo finished first, and Mia loaded his plate with more linguini and red sauce.

"You were right about your grandmother's cooking."

Valentina looked at him quizzically, and Leo said, "You told me she was a great Sicilian cook."

Valentina reminded Mia about that visit weeks ago when Leo brought her iris bulbs. Leo explained that once he saw her garden, he knew Valentina needed the iris. Mia laughed, enjoying the comfortable teasing between them. The front doorbell rang.

"Who could that be?" Dean mused as he walked to the living room. Two police officers stood on the front porch.

As Dean opened the door, one officer said loudly, "We are looking for Valentina Sorelli. We understand that you may know her whereabouts."

Valentina walked slowly to the front door, closely followed by Leo.

"Valentina Sorelli?" the officer asked.

"Yes?"

"You are under arrest as an accessory to murder. You have the right to remain silent. Anything you say can and will be used against you in a court of law. You have the right to an attorney. If you cannot afford an attorney, one will be provided for you. Do you understand the rights I have just read to you? With these rights in mind, do you wish to speak to me?"

"Um ..."

"No, she has nothing to say," Leo said.

"And you are?" the second policeman asked.

"Leo Danekin."

"Two for one." The first officer smiled grimly. "Leo Danekin, you are under arrest for murder. You have the right to remain silent. Anything you say can and will be used against you in a court of law. You have the right to an attorney. If you cannot afford an attorney, one will be provided for you. Do you understand the rights I have just read to you? With these rights in mind, do you wish to speak to me?"

"No."

"Please come with me, both of you."

Valentina ran to Mia, who hugged her fiercely. Dean said, "Go head, Valentina. We'll get this straightened out. You don't need to say a thing. I'm going to call your Uncle Tony and Molly, our attorney."

The first police officer looked at Leo. "Are you going to come quietly?"

"Would it make any difference if I didn't?" Leo asked.

"Not really."

•　　　•　　　•

The following day at the FBI Office in Houston, Tony Sorelli received unofficial notification that Jack Stillman would be identified as the man killed in New Orleans. When Tony heard it happened at Winslow Park, he pulled up everything he could find on the incident. Learning that Angus was in custody and Valentina arrested as an accessory to the crime, he yelled for Freddy. Stuffing papers into his briefcase, Tony called out into the hallway, "Ackerman!" Freddy hurried in to see what Tony needed. "Can you take care of my afternoon appointments? I've got to be on the next flight to New Orleans, Freddy."

"Let me see what I can do, boss."

About 15 minutes later, Freddy stood in Tony's doorway. "Cheryl scheduled your flight. Your boarding pass is in your email so you can download it into your wallet. But you can't leave until late this afternoon. You have a two o'clock meeting with the Western Regional Director about the Strickland case, and I can't take that one for you."

"Oh, man. I forgot all about it. Let me find my notes."

Freddy handed Tony a folder. "Here."

"You're the best."

"That's right," Freddy said. "I have something else for you," handing Tony a hard drive.

At first, Tony looked quizzical. "Angus's data? Finally! They managed to restore it?"

"Yep."

"And?"

"It supports everything Angus said. There's a definitive match to the organic residue on the drones. He was researching the same type of mite that caused the virus, and the timing coincides with his trip to India and the electrical failure in his lab."

"Bingo," Tony said.

"Bingo."

"Has the DNA analysis come back on Richard Miller?" Tony asked hopefully.

"Too soon, boss, you're getting greedy."

Tony laughed.

"I have one more thing for you."

"This is like Christmas, Freddy. What else have you got?"

"Evie Lariott, the CEO of E-Aero Systems, identified Richard Miller as the buyer of her drones."

"Yes!" Tony shouted.

Freddy smiled and turned to leave. "We both have to get back to work."

"Wait a minute." Tony leaned back in his chair and looked directly at Freddy. "We need to talk about something else."

"What's that?"

"My potential conflict of interest."

"Valentina?"

"Not only my niece. Will Torino too. He's the farmer who found the drone parts in his friend's wheat field, and happens to be my brother's grandnephew. If you followed that, and not to mix metaphors, a defense attorney would make a good bit of hay out of that."

"Tony, we wouldn't be where we are right now without their information."

"Doesn't matter, Freddy."

They were both quiet, Tony drumming his fingers on the desk while Freddy leaned on the arm of Tony's visitor chair.

"You want me to get Ed Lawson? He did a lot of the background investigation."

"That abrasive S.O.B.?"

Freddy shrugged. "He knows the case."

Tony thought about Ed Lawson. Federal/local territorial disputes could get ugly, and Lawson had a knack for rubbing people the wrong way. "Anybody else?"

"Richardson?"

"Nah."

"How about Connor?"

Tony shook his head. "Got any other ideas?"

"Not really."

"Hmm. I do."

"Enlighten me."

"You."

"It's been a while, boss."

"Come on, Frederica. You've got to take over the investigation."

"It's been almost three years since I've been in the field, boss."

"You know this case better than I do, Freddy. Better than anyone."

For a moment, Freddy didn't answer then nodded.

CHAPTER 67

Valentina shuddered and stared at the cement block wall. From a distance, she heard someone protesting, "Stop. Stop. Don't do that. You're hurting me." No voice answered, and the woman sounded weaker as her cries continued. From a different direction, another woman yelled, "Leave her alone! She don't mean no harm."

Like any native New Orleanian, Valentina heard horror stories about Orleans Parish Prison or OPP for as long as she can remember. It didn't matter that there was a new jailhouse. The violence from the street continued inside. The sheriff took Valentina to Central Lockup on Perdido Street for processing, and transferred her to OPP, where they gave her an orange T-shirt, maroon sweatshirt and pants with OPSO, the abbreviation for the Orleans Parish Sheriff Office, printed in sickly pink letters. She looked around the small beige room. The door, with a glass window, was bluish gray. A light gray metal bunk stood along one wall. A metal sink, shelf and toilet and one chair furnished the rest of the room. Everything except the chair was attached to the walls. She kept telling herself that her family was helping on the outside. Echoing up from the toilet bowl, she heard a disembodied voice saying, "Hey, new girl." Valentina didn't answer. She hoped she wouldn't be here long enough to make friends.

Much later, Valentina heard her name called. A deputy brought her to a small room where she sat on one side of a glass partition. An older woman with white hair and a warm smile sat on the other.

Valentina recognized Molly Fontenot, the attorney who handled her grandparents' legal transactions. She had known Molly since she was a little girl.

"How are you, sweetheart?"

"I've been better, Molly."

"We're working as quickly as we can. My representation is temporary until we're able to retain someone more specialized."

"I'm relieved to see a familiar face. How is Leo? Was Angus arrested too? And how is Mr. Carlson?"

"Your friend, Mr. Danekin, is incarcerated not too far from here. Other than a few bruises, he's fine. Stephen Angus is being treated for his injuries and complications from earlier burns, which apparently became infected. They may transfer him to a burn center. Unfortunately, Mr. Barry Carlson was shot in the arm and then suffered a mild heart attack—"

"Oh no! This is all my fault."

"I doubt that, Valentina, but I need you to tell me what happened. And Mr. Carlson is doing well and should make a full recovery."

"This all started when my cousin Will found the drone parts in his friend's field."

"Excuse me?"

"I guess it didn't really start then. Sam's father, Mr. Stillman, set things in motion a long time ago. He's responsible for the wheat crisis."

"That's a pretty serious accusation, Valentina."

"Mr. Stillman admitted it too. We have a recording of him saying that."

"Tell me about this recording."

Speaking softly and with determination, Valentina started from the beginning. Will's crop loss, finding the drone parts, the reports of other farmers on Facebook, finding Jack's notes at the beach house, calling Angus to learn about his research, the dinner with Sam and his dad, then her awful, terrible idea to get Jack to admit what he had done. "I had to do something to stop him. Molly, it just went horribly wrong."

After clarifying several points, Molly shook her head. "Valentina, I'm not going to sugarcoat this. We should be able to get you bail, but you'll probably have to stand trial. I've contacted Leon Bergeron, an old law school buddy who practices criminal law. We'll meet this evening, and he's planning to come see you tomorrow."

"Molly, when ...."

"We're working as quickly as we can. Hang in there. Don't rock the boat. Stay to yourself. Don't give any statements. Do whatever the corrections staff tell you."

CHAPTER 68

As Tony's plane made its descent, gold and crimson lines of the sunset crossed the sky above the Rigolets. Dean and Mia were expecting him. Valentina's defense attorney would be there to fill him in, although she wasn't really a criminal lawyer. *I need to understand the situation better,* Tony thought. Will Torino, Mia's grandson, was catching a plane in Omaha and would arrive a little later. *I haven't seen him since he was a kid. We'll need to assess what kind of witness he'll make in the case against Landever, if or when it comes to that.* What a mess. He thought about Freddy Ackerman, one of the best field investigators on the Violent Crimes Squad. He'd let her coast in the office too long. Time to get the rust out.

• • •

Special Agent Frederica Millicent Ackerman, known to her friends and coworkers as Freddy, waited patiently in a small office at the headquarters of the New Orleans Police Department. Sitting next to her was Hank Webster, another investigator with the FBI. She and Hank worked other assignments in the past together, but Freddy hadn't done fieldwork or traveled for the FBI since a work accident. After her injury, she spent six weeks at Mount Sinai in New York, then several more weeks in outpatient rehab at TIRR, the premier rehabilitation program in Houston, learning how to use her prosthetic leg. She still worked out at their gym. The therapy staff liked to point out Freddy as a success story. She kept her job with the FBI. The fact she no longer worked as a field operative, well, that was an example of successful job modification. Yeah, right. She couldn't decide if Tony was throwing her a bone or if he actually thought she could do field work again.

The door opened, and a tall, no-nonsense, dark-skinned man walked into the room, which suddenly felt crowded. Wearing a crisp uniform and captain's bars, he reached out a hand to Agent Webster. "Vernon Simoneaux."

Hank Webster looked bemused and shook hands. "This is lead investigator, Agent Fredericka Ackerman, and I'm Hank Webster, assisting her today." He handed Captain Simoneaux his card, then sat down with his notepad.

With a disarming smile, Freddy stood and offered her hand. "Captain."

Simoneaux shook Freddy's fingertips carefully, apparently from the Southern belief that he might cause injury if he actually gave her a handshake. "I am a little confused, Agent. This is a murder case." He looked down at the agents' business cards and jerked his head in disbelief. "What possible interest does the FBI have in this matter?"

"Jack Stillman has been under investigation for several weeks regarding his role in the wheat virus contamination, a biological weapon that is causing widespread crop loss across the country." Freddy said, "We would like to talk to the individuals present during the altercation yesterday."

"With all due respect, Agent, I don't think I'm the only one confused here. Jack Stillman was a prominent, quite successful businessman. I wouldn't have called him a philanthropist, but Landever has been very supportive of New Orleans."

Freddy disregarded Simoneaux's comment about Jack. "I recognize that we're late to your table, Captain. We'd like to interview the suspects and witnesses."

"They've lawyered up. Or they're in the hospital. You won't get much out of them."

"Captain?"

"This is how we see it," Simoneaux said. "We got a call from an Annie Morrison yesterday around midday, concerned about an incident underway at Winslow. We sent officers and found a man later identified as Jackson Stillman dead and several individuals present. The girl, Valentina Sorelli, pretended to befriend the victim's son, Samuel Stillman. She used him to get an introduction to his father. Ms. Sorelli was trying to seduce the father then blackmail him. She pulled in one of her fellow students, Leo Danekin. Probably promised him sexual favors for a job with Landever. Who knows?" Simoneaux shrugged.

"I see," Freddy said as Webster made notes. "And the other two gentlemen?"

"Yes, Stephen Angus and Barry Carlson." Simoneaux nodded. "It went down like this. Valentina Sorelli," he said, drawing the name out, "met them through the son, Sam Stillman. We're not sure what arrangements she made with them, but we believe they were also blackmailing Jack Stillman. Stillman recognized what was going down and tried to fight them off."

"We hear that both Stephen Angus and Barry Carlson are well known in their respective fields," Webster said.

Captain Simoneaux shook his head. "Washed up. We contacted Landever's personnel office. Angus was fired recently, and Carlson was about to retire."

Freddy nodded. Then, taking a chance, she said, "We understand there is a recording of the altercation?"

"How do you know that?" Captain Simoneaux blustered. "We've kept that under wraps."

Freddy thought back to her conversation last week with Angus about Sam and Valentina's plans to record Stillman admitting his involvement in the wheat crisis. It sounded so far-fetched they didn't take it seriously. She had tried to reach Sam, and she should have kept trying. Another lesson learned, she told herself. "We would like the recording."

"I'm not sure that we can release that, Agent."

"Captain Simoneaux, I am sure you recognize the primacy of the federal government in this case," Freddy said with a touch of steel underneath the velvet in her husky voice. "And let me suggest an alternative theory of what actually happened before you face a lawsuit for wrongful arrest and false imprisonment.

"What I am telling you is to be kept confidential. I'll have to trust you in that regard," she said with an edge in her voice. "Stephen Angus was working closely with the FBI when he was badly injured in a fire. The subject of his research is a small organism, *Aceria tosichella*, a microscopic mite. This same mite carried a virus which could decimate crops across the country. Coincidentally, right before the virus began spreading across the country, Dr. Angus was sent out of the country, and his lab was compromised. We believe that Jack Stillman was responsible. We would appreciate your cooperation, Captain."

Captain Simoneaux sat back in his chair. "I've seen the news. And the price of flour. A man can't get a po-boy. It's hard to believe someone like Jack Stillman could be involved."

"Then you understand why it's important that we talk with the witnesses to make sure we understand what happened. Your local knowledge will be of tremendous importance in determining if our information is incorrect about Mr. Stillman. We would appreciate any help you can offer." Freddy smiled, hiding her annoyance with the captain.

Simoneaux pushed up from his chair. "I have a lot of concerns about this," Simoneaux said. "But hey, it's your funeral. I'll set you up in the conference room."

"Thanks, Captain."

"Excuse me while I get things organized. We're a little short of space so give me a little time."

• • •

After their meeting with Captain Simoneaux, Freddy and Hank drove to the Medical Center of Louisiana, the new public hospital in Mid-City. They talked briefly with Barry Carlson, who had a gunshot wound to his left upper arm. The medical staff was able to stabilize his heart and he would undergo surgical repair to his arm in a few days. Barry told them about getting the hard drive out of the Landever offices and the altercation with Jack Stillman, confirming what they knew from earlier interviews with Stephen Angus. He further explained how Sam called Angus and their fear the students would get hurt. Then he filled in some of the gaps from the fight. Not surprisingly, he was confused about what happened after he got shot.

Learning that Angus was transferred to the regional burn center at Baton Rouge General, they headed west on I-10. At the burn unit, they found Angus in the process of getting new spray-on skin cells. The first treatment in Indiana wasn't in place long enough to survive the fight. Once again, the doctors took small, two-inch by two-inch squares of healthy skin and mixed it with a solution to create a spray mist of Angus's own skin cells. Freddy and Hank waited outside the treatment room until cleared to walk in.

"Hello Mr. Angus. I'm Freddy …"

Angus was laying on his belly and turned his head toward the door. "You bloody well show up now? This whole fiasco could have been avoided if you'd listened to me!" Angus yelled.

"You couldn't tell me anything! You had nothing specific." Freddy countered. "And I tried to reach Sam Stillman. He wouldn't answer my calls."

"Mr. Angus…" Hank said.

"It's just Angus!" he bellowed.

"Yes, that's right. Angus, we'd like to talk with you about what happened."

About an hour later, Freddy and Hank were back on the road. "Two down, at least five, or 10 more to go," Freddy said.

"Who do you want to take next? Danekin, Sorelli or Sam Stillman? Or the Morrisons?"

"Let's do Danekin then figure it out from there. Our friendly captain should have things arranged by now."

•   •   •

Several hours later, Hank looked at his watch. "Freddy, we need to give this a rest. It's after ten."

Freddy stretched in her chair, her leg swelling above the prosthesis. During a normal day, it was easy to elevate her leg, or add or remove padding at the site of her residual limb. But it was not a normal day. She needed to lie down. However, having avoided Tony's calls all evening, she knew he wouldn't let the day end without an update. "Hank, what's your take on what happened?"

"All the reports are consistent. Jack Stillman tried to kill Angus and threatened Carlson, Danekin and Sorelli. As broken up as Sam Stillman is, even he believes his father instigated the wheat crisis. Ellis Morrison corroborates they were setting a trap for Jack Stillman, and the recording confirms everything. Another tidbit— the DNA evidence just came in. Richard Miller had Jack Stillman's skin under his fingernails. And, for good measure, Jack had a big scratch across his face." Hank looked up from his notes. "We're done."

"You're right. Let's head to the hotel."

"I'll catch up the notes," Hank offered.

"You're my hero. I'm beat."

"Not a bad first day back in the field, Freddy."

"No, not bad."

•   •   •

The next afternoon, Valentina heard her name called. A silent guard escorted her to one of the antiseptic visitor rooms, with the off-white cement block walls and metal table. Expecting Molly or her new attorney, Valentina was stunned when she saw her visitor.

She picked up the telephone and stared through the window in the gray wall. "Uncle Tony!"

"Hey, doll. I can't say I like your new outfit."

"Not my colors." Valentina forced a laugh past the tears that wanted to fall.

Tony shook his head. "No, it isn't you." He paused, looked down, trying to find words. "We should have stepped in before ..."

"This is all my fault," Valentina said.

"No, sweetheart. Sam talked to Angus, and when Angus called, we should have realized you were serious."

"Sam told Angus what we were planning. That's why he and Mr. Carlson showed up."

"He was worried about you kids. With reason, I might add."

"Don't say it, Uncle Tony. It was irresponsible."

"It sure brought things to a head."

"Yeah, and someone died." Valentina's voice broke.

"Would Jack Stillman have tolerated being in prison for the rest of his life? Or worse?" Tony asked.

Valentina didn't answer. They sat quietly for a few minutes. "We accomplished nothing. No one believes us."

"Actually, they do." Tony looked at her steadily.

"They act like I'm a femme fatale!"

Tony laughed on the other side of the glass partition and leaned back in his chair. "I think we've cleared that up."

"Really?"

"We've got the recording. Our agents have interviewed everyone, including the Morrisons. And we found Jack's DNA at a related crime scene, Valentina. It's only a matter of time before you're released."

"When?"

"Soon, I hope. You'll probably have to testify."

Valentina couldn't speak for a minute and looked away, shutting her eyes tight.

"Are you okay?"

"I don't know what I am, Uncle Tony. Someone, not a nice person but a human being, is dead. Two other people are injured."

"Those two people are recovering. Don't be so hard on yourself."

Valentina sighed and her shoulders sagged with relief.

• • •

Mia and Dean waited outside the metal fence, watching the doors of the Orleans Parish Prison. Rain poured onto the concrete. When Tony called, they raced to Perdido Street. Will stood next to them, holding a large umbrella over their heads. They started toward the gate several times as the door opened, thinking it might be Valentina. Each time they were disappointed as the person exiting the building scanned the sidewalk, then hurried toward someone else standing sentinel in the summer rain.

Hours later, a slender figure stepped outside the door. They rushed as one to hug Valentina as she walked slowly toward them.

EPILOGUE

The stillness of the fall morning was broken by a familiar ring tone. Half awake, Valentina reached for her cell phone. Next to her, Leo opened one quizzical eye. She mouthed, "Sam." Leo waved a sleepy hello and turned into his pillow.

"Hey there."

"Hi, Valentina. You sound sleepy. Did I wake you up?"

"Not really."

"I forget about the time difference," Sam said apologetically.

"That's okay. How's school? Well, first, how's Edinburgh?"

"Interesting. Different from the States."

"Duh. Tell me something I don't know. Were you able to get an apartment?"

"Yes, in Abbeyhill. Very old, it's a flat in one of the colony houses. It's about a 30-minute walk to the city center and close to the rail line, so I won't need a car."

"All good. What about school?"

"I was accepted in the doctoral program in molecular plant sciences. Great professors and terrific research program. I'll be able to pick up my Masters along the way. They do a lot of research in connection with the Royal Botanical Gardens."

"That sounds wonderful, Sam. What about Angus?"

"He's a rock star. After the police cleared him, the Entomology Department offered him a position as an honorary professor. Since the feds were able to recover his data, that helped too. The university gave him a lab to continue his research in counteracting the mites. There's a waiting list a mile long to get in his classes. He'll be able to transition to a permanent position easily. We get together for dinner about once a week. And get this—he reconnected with his old girlfriend, Kathleen, so he's a little busier than he was."

"It's hard to believe things turned out this well."

"It looked pretty bleak for a while, didn't it?" Sam said.

"Like when Angus, Leo and I were arrested?" Valentina laughed. "I'd rather not visit Central Lockup or OPP again in my lifetime. Thank you very much. Since he helped spring us, Uncle Tony now refers to me as 'Jailbird.' I'm lucky I still have a job. Dee, my boss, was not amused."

"I expect that being on the WPRY evening broadcast didn't help."

"There's that." They were both quiet for a moment. "Did you hear they opened up the Strategic Grain Reserve to domestic famers?" Valentina asked.

"Yeah. And with both new wheat cultivars, it's got to make a difference. The additional funding for bankrupt farmers will help. It's not going to be easy, but we can come back from this."

"The news reports sound a little more optimistic." After a pause, Valentina asked, "Sam, how are you really?"

"I don't know. Better since Landever agreed to make reparations."

"They've committed a significant amount of their revenue for the next ten years, with an emphasis on biodiversity. If this hadn't happened, they would never have agreed to developing more variety in their plant stock."

"I know, Valentina. They're also working with the Fort Collins consortium for rapid production of both resistant wheat cultivars. Along with the corporate funding, we arranged to donate my dad's pension and stock. It's not enough. I'll spend the rest of my life trying to make amends."

"Sam…"

"Let's not go down that road anymore. I can't."

Her heart aching, Valentina asked, "What's going on with your mom?"

"She moved to Denver permanently, went back to her maiden name, and is doing a decent job of pretending my father never existed," Sam said matter-of-factly. "Maybe me too."

"Wow."

"Meanwhile, Angus has stepped in as a surrogate parent, though I reached the age of maturity, chronologically at least, years ago."

"He's a pretty amazing guy. He probably saved my life." Valentina thought back to that hot summer day in the park. Changing the subject, she asked, "You remember my cousin, Will?"

"Yeah, I do, despite the chaos. Seems like a stand-up guy."

"Part of the Valentina Sorelli legal defense support group. It's funny, after everything that happened, he may not go back to grains."

"That's right, he started some organic crops, didn't he?"

"Yes, and built a small greenhouse. It's going well, particularly the lettuce. He would never have tried for organic certification if not for this. He has a few contracts with some Omaha restaurants."

"I'm glad there's a silver lining," Sam said. "Infinitesimally small but there."

After a beat, Valentina said, "Mia wants to know if you're coming for Thanksgiving."

"Not this one. Maybe next year. Why don't you and Leo visit next summer? Tala plans to come then."

"Sam, we might just do that. Neither of us have been to the U.K."

"Think about it."

"I'll talk to Leo," Valentina said. "Let's talk again soon?"

"Definitely."

After she ended the call, Leo pulled Valentina to him. "Talk to me about what, Valentina Sorelli?" as he placed light kisses along her collarbone.

Valentina was having a difficult time answering Leo as a soft warmth started in her belly. Returning his kisses, and pulling herself closer, she finally managed, "Scotland next summer?"

"Talk about that later ..."

"Hmm...."

READERS GUIDE FOR BOOK CLUBS AND QUESTIONS FOR DISCUSSION

How can my community protect itself from monoculture?

What is the origin of the foods in your grocery? With so many products to choose from, how can there be a lack of food diversity?

What would you do if you saw a drone flying in an unexpected place?

What are the potential consequences of the use of drones?

Did the students have any other alternatives for confronting Jack?

How can I help preserve the diversity of seeds and protect them?

Did Valentina's relationships with Sam, Kai and Leo affect the outcome of the story?

How does Sam's character evolve?

How does Tala's background affect her world view? Does she influence her classmates during the course of the semester?

Each of the students had a different reason to be in the Bioethics class. What did each of them realize from the experience?

ACKNOWLEDGEMENTS

My deepest thanks to my husband, Mark Winter, for his unfailing patience, creativity and support. He was always willing to listen and offer ideas.

I am grateful to my children, Camille Seyler Brookman and Sable Seyler, whose suggestions helped me through many stumbling blocks.

Rebecca Asante was my first beta reader and offered stellar recommendations. Cindy Harris was another early reader and enthusiastic supporter. Thank you both for your friendship.

I appreciate the encouragement of my nephew, Michael Casey. You lived every day like someone who had just been rescued from the moon.

Lori Hobkirk helped me understand the logistics of the publishing world.

Sarah Warner provided editing and helpful advice, in particular an introduction to the work of Bernard Werber.

My thanks to Juliette Kuylen, whose linguistic expertise allowed Kai to speak Cajun French.

My gratitude to my later beta readers—Sherry Alexander, Clark Gantzer, Kristin Homer, Jane Ross and Cam Torrens—each had a unique perspective and powerful insight that improved this work immeasurably.

The Central Colorado Writers' critique group read portions of this work and helped me believe I could be a writer. Their support and guidance were instrumental in learning how to recognize my characters' voices.

My appreciation to Wendell Berry, who allowed me to use *A Place Unmade* as the title of this book, and his poem, "I go from the woods into the cleared field" from This Day: Collected and New Sabbath Poems 1979-2012. Copyright © 1979 by Wendell Berry. Reprinted with the permission of The Permissions Company, LLC on behalf of Counterpoint Press, counterpointpress.com.

This novel would not have been possible without the support, advice and expertise of my publisher, Black Rose Writing—Reagan, David and the rest of the staff as well as the BRW community of authors.

The idea for this book came from an article written by Dan Barber and published in the New York Times, *Save Our Food. Free the Seed*. Several other materials helped me understand this topic and gave me a glimpse of the challenges in the world of agriculture. A list of significant resources can be found on my website, www.carlaseyler.net. It was necessary to take some liberties regarding the trajectory of the wheat virus infection for the narrative drama. All errors in this work are my own.

ABOUT THE AUTHOR

Carla Seyler worked for years as a vocational rehabilitation counselor, when sometimes the truth was stranger than fiction. This is Carla's first novel, an imaginary disaster story that easily could be true. She is a native of New Orleans, a place that has been unmade by disasters both natural and engineered, but one that offers a master class in grace, patience, resilience, and joy. Carla lives in New Orleans with her husband and has two independent daughters.

NOTE FROM CARLA SEYLER

Word-of-mouth is crucial for any author to succeed. If you enjoyed *A Place Unmade*, please leave a review online—anywhere you are able. Even if it's just a sentence or two. It would make all the difference and would be very much appreciated.

Thanks!
Carla Seyler

We hope you enjoyed reading this title from:

www.blackrosewriting.com

Subscribe to our mailing list – *The Rosevine* – and receive **FREE** books, daily deals, and stay current with news about upcoming
releases and our hottest authors.
Scan the QR code below to sign up.

Already a subscriber? Please accept a sincere thank you for being a fan of Black Rose Writing authors.

View other Black Rose Writing titles at
www.blackrosewriting.com/books and use promo code
PRINT to receive a **20% discount** when purchasing.